Praise for Lorraine Kelly

'Warm and wise . . . a Scottish Maeve Binchy'
Veronica Henry

'A gorgeous novel'
Marian Keyes

'It's a winner!'
Ian Rankin

'A delightful debut novel about the importance of honesty and community'
Platinum

'Like getting a warm hug on a freezing cold day'
Jane Fallon

'So warm and engaging. A total treat'
Beth O'Leary

'Suffused with her love for the Orkney islands'
My Weekly

'A compelling and complex story written with wit, compassion and warmth. I devoured it'
Santa Montefiore

Lorraine Kelly CBE has worked in breakfast TV for forty years, joining TV-am as Scottish correspondent in 1984 and now presents *Lorraine* on ITV.

She is married to cameraman Steve and they have one daughter, Rosie, a journalist and broadcaster.

Lorraine is a Dundee United fan and gets her best ideas when out for a walk with her beloved border terrier Angus.

She first visited Orkney in 1985 and goes back every year.

Also by Lorraine Kelly

The Island Swimmer

Lorraine Kelly

THE ISLAND SECRET

ORION

First published in Great Britain in 2026 by Orion Fiction,
an imprint of The Orion Publishing Group Ltd.
Carmelite House, 50 Victoria Embankment
London EC4Y 0DZ

An Hachette UK Company

The authorised representative in the EEA is Hachette Ireland, 8 Castlecourt Centre,
Dublin 15, D15 XTP3, Ireland (email: info@hbgi.ie)

1 3 5 7 9 10 8 6 4 2

A CIP catalogue record for this book is
available from the British Library.

ISBN (Hardback) 978 1 3987 1450 2
ISBN (Export Trade Paperback) 978 1 3987 1451 9
ISBN (Ebook) 978 1 3987 1453 3
ISBN (Audio) 978 1 3987 1454 0

Typeset by Born Group
Printed and bound in Great Britain by Clays Ltd, Elcograf S.p.A.

MIX
Paper | Supporting
responsible forestry
FSC® C104740

www.orionbooks.co.uk

To my dad, John, who taught me to always be curious.
We all miss you Dad xxx

THE ORKNEY ISLANDS
NORTH RONALDSAY
PAPA WESTRAY
WESTRAY
SANDAY
EDAY
ROUSAY
STRONSAY
Marwick Head
SHAPINSAY
SKARA BRAE
Yesnaby Cliffs
Ring of Brodgar
STROMNESS
MAINLAND
KIRKWALL
ORKNEY
Old Man of Hoy
Italian Chapel
SCAPA FLOW
HOY
FLOTTA
BURRAY
NOT TO SCALE
Hand-drawn map by Peter Gander
N
W
E
S
SOUTH RONALDSAY
LONGHOPE
STROMA
John o' Groats
SCOTLAND
(The island of 'Hrossay' remains a work of fiction)

Chapter One

Orkney, February 2026

Evie Muir was engrossed working on a new painting all day, so didn't check her phone until late that night. It was winter and the long days of the Orkney Summer Dim when it was light until almost midnight were long gone.

Evie's bright green eyes narrowed as she squinted at the dramatic seascape she'd created. Her blonde hair had been hastily tied back in a messy bun and there were smudges of blue and green paint on her nose and forehead.

She was a striking-looking woman, and the fine lines at the corners of her eyes and mouth crinkled with laughter these days rather than the distress and trauma of the past. She'd returned to Orkney only two years ago, after a long time away, and her Island home had worked its magic and almost healed her.

The painting was so nearly complete, and although she was sorely tempted to finish, Evie reluctantly put her paintbrushes aside for the night. She'd take a fresh look in the morning.

As was her usual habit, she had put off checking her texts and emails. For all of her twenties and most of her thirties, Evie had been scrupulously careful to be offline, terrified of being discovered if she posted so much as a photo. She still avoided her phone as much as possible.

She logged onto her work inbox and saw an email that read

URGENT. PLEASE READ. She clicked to open it.

Dear Miss Muir,

Please forgive me for getting in touch with you out of the blue like this. I will get straight to the point.

I think we might be related. I live in Seattle and my father was James McLean. He died in 1989 and going through his personal belongings, I found two letters from a woman named Sheila who lived in Hrossay. It looks like she and my father were the parents of a little girl called Cara.

They never married and as far as I know he never saw Sheila again. In fact, my father never met his daughter, but I know he sent her money until she turned sixteen.

I've been doing a bit of digging online recently and discovered Sheila passed away but that Cara married a man called Duncan Muir and had two daughters, Olivia and Evie.

I couldn't find out much about Olivia, but I did discover your website for your paintings which had this email address. I have to say your artwork is really good.

Anyway, I think you might be the Evie I am looking for and if Cara turns out to be my half-sister, I might be your sort of half-aunt, I guess?

I guess I finally feel ready to come to Orkney to find out more about this side of my family. Would you be willing to meet with me?

I know it's a lot to ask but it is very important to me to find blood relatives as I have no one over here since my dad passed. My mom died giving birth to me and she was an only child.

I can explain everything in much more detail when we meet.

Yours in hope,
Amelia McLean

*

Evie sat down, in shock. If she'd been tired before, there was no way she was going to be able to get to sleep now. She was buzzing with adrenaline and found it difficult to take all this in. She forced herself to get up and make herself a cup of tea, though what she really wanted was a stiff whisky.

She made herself re-read the email several times. It really did seem as though this woman could be her relative. The names and dates seemed right. Evie's mother and father were indeed called Cara and Duncan, and how else would she know about Sheila?

Of course, her dad was dead – it was his death that had triggered her returning to Orkney in 2024 after so many years away – and her mum was in a nursing home living with dementia. She was well looked after but existed in her own twilight world. Evie went to see her as often as she could but if she was honest, it was more out of duty than love. There was no way she could talk to Cara about this email. She would be confused and upset.

Evie was torn. Coming back to Orkney, she had finally achieved a sense of peace, and she wanted to protect that new life. But how could she deny this woman's longing to know more about where she came from?

As always when she had a problem or needed advice she would turn to Freya, the real mother figure in her life. Evie shut down her laptop and got into bed, resolving to message Freya first thing. She slept fitfully and got up earlier than usual. After two strong cups of coffee, Evie called Freya, knowing she would be up. If she slept longer than 6am she would joke that the day was almost half over.

Freya bustled over right away, driving the short distance from her cottage to Evie's house overlooking Scapa Flow. Freya had lived in Orkney most of her life but never took the view of the mountains of Hoy, the ever-changing blue hues of the sea and emerald-green fields dotted with candy floss sheep for granted.

She was almost eighty years old now and had grown even more pleasantly plump. She was wearing one of her usual multi-coloured, cheerfully flamboyant outfits. Today, in her blue silk caftan, loose yellow cotton trousers, straining a bit at the belly, and her dainty red silk slippers, she was like a glorious vision from *The Arabian Nights*. She'd recently taken to wearing all sorts of jewels in her hair kept in place with Kirby grips, and she gleamed like a disco ball. Evie made them both a cup of strong builder's tea, and they sat down at Evie's kitchen table.

"Well, all the way from America, this really is a turn up for the books," said Freya after reading the email. She took her glasses off and turned to Evie.

"You know your mother and I didn't get on, but I do remember once when we were very young, she told me that her real dad had gone to California and become rich and famous, and would soon be coming to take her back to live in a big house in Hollywood."

Freya shook her head and added, "My sister, Anne Marie, and I felt sorry for her. She was always making up stories like that, and then she met your dad at the high school, and they got married so young. I know she hoped her long-lost father would turn up at her wedding, and there would be a big emotional reunion, which of course wasn't to be, but after that I don't remember her talking about him ever again."

"Did granny Sheila ever say anything about him?" asked Evie.

"Not to me, but I vaguely remember someone once saying he worked on the fishing boats during the war and from what I could gather it was a one-night stand and he didn't want anything to do with the baby. But I know he sent money to your granny. So, he wasn't a total arsehole I suppose."

Evie sighed. "My poor mum, growing up without ever knowing her father. I wonder if that was part of the reason she was so unhappy. I know it broke my dad's heart that he felt he wasn't enough for her, and I always thought it was my fault she was so on edge all the time."

"You and your dad tried your best," said Freya, "and you should never feel guilty. Your mum pushed happiness away all her life. I could never understand it."

She squeezed Evie's hand lightly. "Don't you ever forget your dad adored the bones of your mum and that fine man almost killed himself trying to please her. But he never could.

It wasn't easy for him, but you made up for it. You were the light of his life. You were his 'Teenie'."

Evie's eyes filled with tears. She whispered, "And I didn't get the chance to stay goodbye."

The memories were still so painful.

After a tragic accident, Evie had fled Orkney aged eighteen, cutting all ties with her friends and family, and only rarely keeping in touch with Freya. It had taken all her courage to come back when Freya had contacted her to say her father was gravely ill – but she hadn't arrived in time. The guilt still haunted her, as well as the sorrow of all the time they'd missed together.

"Oh, Evie love. You must stop beating yourself up. The past is the past and we can't change it, but you can remember the happy times with your dad when you were young. How many times do I have to tell you to hold on to that?"

"I know. I do try. Honest I do. But look, what do you think I should do about this Amelia woman. If she's my grandfather's daughter, won't she be ancient?"

"Well thanks a bunch," said Freya, pretending to be outraged. Evie laughed and said, "You are timeless and ageless as well you know. I just meant this woman might need to find out about her family before it's too late."

Freya nodded. "Maybe. People do get to a certain age and decide they want to find out more about their past."

"And he'd have been my granddad," said Evie thoughtfully. "This James McLean." She picked nervously at her fingernails, and Freya put a hand on her arm to steady her nerves.

"What do you think, Evie? It's your decision. You need to ask yourself if this is really a box you want to open and peer inside?"

Chapter Two

Alaska, 1965

James McLean sat in the almost deserted bar in Fairbanks nursing a pint in his giant paw and, for the first time in his life, realised he was pondering his future. James had come to this frozen land twenty years ago after a one-night stand with a barmaid in Stromness had given him a hell of a shock.

Orkney's Stromness may have been a dry town in 1945 but – due to the vital naval base at Scapa Flow – it was filled with thousands of sailors and soldiers looking for a good time. Underground drinking parlours popped up in every military hotel and outpost. It was the perfect spot for a drunken stag do of fishermen looking to escape their naval reserve duties for the night. In one of these hidden speakeasys, Sheila had given James the glad eye and had become more attractive to him with every beer he sank.

When the customers were finally turfed out, the two of them went to her freezing flat down the road and tore the clothes off each other.

James had gone back to his home in the bombed-out town of Fraserburgh the following morning with a desperate hangover. The deep scratches on his back and arse reduced the rest of the stag do to howls of belly laughter and led to him henceforth being renamed 'Casanova'.

The nickname stuck but James didn't give Sheila a second thought. He was too busy freezing, throwing up and working like a dog on the fishing trawlers in some of the worst seas in the world. The arrival of the war when he was just nineteen meant fishermen were expected to support the navy: clearing mines, dropping nets and protecting the coast from deadly German U-boats.

James was horrified when, on his next night out in Stromness, Sheila hunted him down and told him she was pregnant. James was not a man who wanted to get married, and children had never figured in his plans. He had been dragged up in Aberdeen by a feckless drunken father and a worn-out mother who seemed to be forever pregnant. (She died giving birth to her eighth child, a tiny scrap who didn't even have the strength to take a gasp of air and left the world at the same time as his mother, never uttering so much as a whimper.)

Sheila had thought James might feel shamed into proposing but was secretly relieved when he didn't grudgingly say they might as well get married. She'd seen too many of her friends settle for loveless marriages and they had regretted it ever since; Sheila didn't want to grow bitter and sour like them. She found herself looking forward to being a mother without having a virtual stranger of a man under her feet, demanding meals and attention and getting in the way whenever he was back home from the sea. So, when James said he wanted nothing to do with the baby, but would send her money every month, she nodded curtly and said that would do very well.

She wasn't going to refuse his offer of cash. She reckoned he made a good enough wage and anyway she shouldn't have to be the one to bear all the responsibility on her own while surviving on rations. She might not want him, but she'd take his money to give her child a proper start in life.

Sheila continued to work in the pop-up drinking dens serving the thirsty sailors until her swollen belly prevented her from reaching the beer pumps. A fortnight later she gave birth to her daughter in the cottage hospital in Kirkwall and named her Cara.

As soon as she was able, the pair took the ferry to the island of Hrossey where Sheila was enfolded into the embrace of her large extended family of fierce red-headed women. They stared down any of the old biddies tut-tutting that Sheila 'was no better than she should be' and helped her with baby clothes and cots handed down from their own mothers and grandmothers.

By this time, James was long gone to the other side of the world, with no idea that his child had been born and was a baby girl. A fisherman in Fraserburgh had told him they were looking for experienced hands to join the whaling fleet in Alaska. James saw it as an escape route and applied immediately. He quickly jumped on a ship sailing across the cold Atlantic, followed by a long sea voyage to Juneau in Alaska. He fitted in easily with the horny-handed, tight-mouthed whalers, but it was a brutally tough life, even for a man used to the rough grey North Sea.

On his first voyage one man disappeared overboard and another was trapped by the harpoon ropes on the side of the boat and crippled forever. Worn down by the conditions and increasingly sickened by the smell of slaughter and the blood-red waters, James saw the writing on the wall for the whole whaling industry and tried his hand at working in the oil industry in the Alaskan north slope.

It was still a brutal environment but nowhere near as dangerous, and his pay packet weighed double what he earned as a whaler. He was used to hard work and was the first to volunteer for overtime at the weekends. He fell into bed at night exhausted and was happy with his own company, not one to make friends easily.

He sent regular cheques to Sheila – the postmark told Sheila where he was and after the baby was born, she sent him a two-line letter care of the town's post office: "We've had a daughter and she's called Cara – we're living with my family in Hrossey. We expect nothing from you but the money."

The name neither pleased nor offended James. He rarely thought of them both. He wasn't a man who did much soul-searching and apart from booze-fuelled benders on his weeks off, he had little to spend his cash on.

Sixteen years later in 1961, Sheila wrote him another curt letter telling him that Cara was engaged to a young man called Duncan and they were moving to the Orkney mainland to Duncan's family farm just outside Kirkwall, and that he should now consider his debt fully paid. Sheila didn't give him an address for his daughter and he didn't ask for one.

He supposed he should have sent them a wedding gift, but all contact had been effectively severed. He rarely gave his daughter a thought, only occasionally wondering if he should try and find out what she had made of her life, but he never actually got round to doing anything about it.

James had no idea where the years had gone, but here he was in a dingy bar with a sticky floor, reeking of stale beer and neglect and a worn-out forty-one. In a rare moment of reflection, he asked himself what he had to show for his nearly half-century. Although still in good shape, with only a slight softness to his belly, James had grown weary. His dark hair was shot with grey and his rough hands scarred from working so long in sub-zero conditions.

His eyes had become narrowed from all those years squinting at steely waves on the lookout for whales breaching the surface and now jet-black oil was engrained into every deep line of his face. James found it increasing difficult to keep up with the younger men on the pipeline and was finding the work utterly exhausting, but he didn't think he was educated enough to apply for a supervisor's job.

At heart, he was still a working-class poverty-stricken teenager who didn't believe he was good enough for a promotion. Anyway, James regarded the white-collar workers as little more than a bunch of pen pushers, looked down upon by the 'real' workers. They sat on their fat arses in comfy offices with decent tea and biscuits and a massive salary.

He sat in the gloomy bar nursing his drink, sighed and decided to venture into the cold to clear his head of troublesome thoughts and wondering what would become of him. Just then the door opened letting in the freezing night air. James looked up to see a woman shivering and stamping her feet to get rid of the snow on her boots.

Marge Svenson was thirty-two and had come to Alaska with the sole purpose of finding herself a husband. With one woman to every ten men, she had been repeatedly told the odds were good, but as she had swiftly discovered, the goods were mostly odd.

She had given herself a year working in one of the few stores in town, before giving up and returning home to Minnesota. Her time was almost up and she hadn't met one single man she would be willing to settle down with. She never thought for a second she'd meet someone she could love. That was never a factor in her plan. She just wanted respectability and a bit of companionship, with enough money to live on without scrimping and saving.

Her wage from the store was more than she would earn back home, but here it was barely enough to live on. Everything was so ridiculously expensive in Alaska that by the time she had paid the rent, heating bills and bought food, there was barely enough left over to bother her piggy bank. The only thing that stopped her from packing up her few belongings and leaving after a few miserable weeks, was the thought of giving her mother the satisfaction of saying "I told you so."

It began to snow heavily on the way back to her cheerless lodgings, so for the first time since she arrived, Marge stopped outside the one bar in town that served hot food and decided to treat herself and blow the budget with a meal she wouldn't have to make herself.

Shaking off the snowflakes from her coat and boots and squinting into the half-darkness, she saw a large man sitting at the bar looking as though he had the weight of the world on his shoulders.

He wasn't conventionally handsome, but Marge thought he had kind eyes and, surprising herself, she asked him, "Can a person get a bite to eat in here?"

He merely shrugged, but something about him made Marge bold. This would be her last throw of the dice, so she decided to persevere. She had nothing to lose so she added, "Mind if I sit here?"

He looked up at her briefly and his first thought was that she had a warm smile, and it had been a long time since someone had looked at him with interest. He turned back into the bar.

"Please yourself," he growled, but he took up his seat again and pushed another bar stool towards her. She smiled.

"Let me buy you a drink big fella and you can tell me your sad story."

Without looking up he replied, "How do you know my story is sad?"

"Well," she answered. "You're here all by yourself with a face like a cat's ass caught out in the rain." She gave him a slow smile.

Despite himself, he burst out laughing and held out his big rough hand.

"I'm James. Pleased to meet you."

"Marge. Good to meet you too. You are definitely not from around these parts with a cute accent like that."

"I'm from Scotland. Aberdeen to be exact. You?"

"I moved up here from Minnesota. At least I'm used to the cold. Been working at the hardware store but I'm thinking of calling it a day."

James looked at her properly and found he liked the look of Marge. She wasn't beautiful but she had a pleasant, strong face. Her faded fair hair was cut short in a sensible side-parting and curled around her ears. She had rather small eyes, a large nose and wide mouth, and was dressed in layers of warm, practical clothes.

James found himself saying, "Well, we're both far from home so maybe we should get to know each other better. Let me buy you a drink."

Marge didn't mention that she had planned to spend most of tomorrow packing up and making arrangements to return home.

She simply nodded and asked if they had any pop. James looked bemused.

"Pop," she replied. "You know. Coca-Cola or Seven Up. That's what we call soda back home."

"Have a proper drink with me, Margie," said James with a grin. He found he wanted her to stay, sitting beside him at the bar. So, she accepted an overpriced bottle of imported beer. And decided to stay.

Chapter Three

Evie's Studio

Evie had woken up early again and was finishing her painting of the view from her light-filled studio in her cottage overlooking Scapa Flow. She needed to distract herself from the strange email she'd received from Amelia McLean a few days ago.

Evie sighed in frustration. She still hadn't decided what she was going to do.

She kept thinking about this poor woman so far away in America, checking her emails and eagerly waiting for her reply.

Evie felt terribly guilty, but she wasn't even sure how, or even if, she was going to answer. She'd begun tentatively drafting replies, but none of them felt right. Maybe she should pretend she'd never got the email in the first place.

Today the wind rattled the windowpanes, and the sea was so rough she suspected Freya would be in touch soon cancelling their wild water swim. They were both part of a group known as the Selkies after the mythical Orcadian sea creatures that were half-woman, half-seal. The Selkies plunged into the water every Saturday morning almost without fail.

She loved this view from her window. The ever-changing sky and sea meant she never grew tired of looking out at the same horizon and the tourists couldn't get enough of her paintings of sun-kissed green fields and sparkling waves. They declared they could almost smell the salt in the air and feel the wind on their faces. Back home, they hung up her work in their living rooms and remembered holidays filled with sunlight and rain.

Although they sold less, Evie preferred to paint the same view in winter when the waves crashed ominously on the grey shore and the sky was a hundred different shades of purplish black. Perhaps people could sense the sorrow and longing in every one of her brush strokes.

Evie found creating these paintings often reduced her to tears as it made her remember back long ago to when her first love, Brodie, had drowned in those very same waters. It was his death that had caused her to flee the island.

He was her first and only real love. Evie had just turned eighteen and Brodie, the son of an old family friend, was nineteen. She could barely recall those feelings of nerve-jangling joy at the sight of him, and the long summer nights talking and then kissing for hours.

Walking home together with bruised lips and a tingling inside that led to them eventually making hesitant, fumbling love. It was nothing like the movies, but raw and real and full of meaning. They had such a short time together before a chain of events unfolded that led to tragedy, unleashing her sister Liv's terrible jealousy.

After she ran away to London, Evie has been plagued by nightmares of Brodie diving into the freezing sea. She'd wake up shaking, sweating and heaving with sobs for hours on end, wishing she could turn the clock back. She lived a drab and unhappy life, trapped in a toxic relationship she only managed to escape when she returned to Orkney.

Six months ago, around the anniversary of his death, Freya had gently asked her if it wasn't too sore to be looking out on that view every day, even though the tragedy had been over twenty years before.

Evie told her that she'd made her peace with the past and that now she could remember Brodie with fondness, although tinged with regret and grief.

Evie put down her brush, narrowed her eyes and gave her painting a long, hard stare, looking for flaws and ways to improve her work. She needed more subtle tones of grey in the sea and more of a threat of a dark storm to come. She went into the kitchen to make herself yet another pot of coffee, and noticed she had a text from Sophia, the only real friend she had made during those years of exile in London.

I'm coming to Orkney this weekend. I had yet another row with Finn but we've patched things up over a long phone sex session, so things are back on track. See you soon!

Evie laughed out loud, her mood instantly lifting. This was typical Sophia. She'd met Finn, a handsome Irishman who worked for the RSPB in Orkney when she had visited Evie.

Sophia had not just fallen in love with the beautiful islands, but also with Finn, a scruffy outdoorsy charmer.

On paper he was hardly Sophia's type. She normally went for a metrosexual, groomed, cologne-scented professional man with a flashy job and a healthy bank balance. All of the things Finn was mostly definitely not.

Evie was extremely fond of Finn, but not at all convinced this long-distance relationship could work. Sophia would never be able to leave her busy life in London and settle in Orkney, even if – as she gleefully reported to Evie – sex over the phone with Finn was better than most couples enjoyed in bed.

Finn desperately wanted her to move up north to be with him, and his dream was for them to live in a cottage in Rackwick

Bay on the island of Hoy where he monitored Sea Eagles. It sounded idyllic, but Sophia was clear-eyed enough to realise she would eventually become bored and resentful and miss her life in London.

So, they had limped along for the past year and a half, with Sophia spending long weekends in Orkney, often arriving exhausted and fractious after delays with the London flights. The two of them circled each other warily for a couple of days, only really settling into a routine when it was almost time for Sophia to return. Finn had looked so appalled when she asked if he would come down to London for a change one weekend that she didn't bring it up again.

She had poured her heart out to Evie on her last visit and told her that she couldn't go on like this much longer. Evie was careful not to try to sway Sophia one way or the other, but it was hard when she had *never* regretted her decision to come back home, even in mid-winter when the fierce gales threatened to blow you over, and the persistent freezing rain worked its way past the nape of your neck, trickling down your back and then into every crevice.

Sometimes Evie wished she could experience the high drama of Sophia and Finn's intense relationship. She missed that tingling feeling of falling in love. Evie only ever had that with Brodie and after he died, she had never felt she deserved to be loved and shut down her feelings.

Admittedly, she had felt a spark with the shy and ridiculously handsome craftsman, Ross, who made beautiful Orkney chairs, but she wasn't ready to find out if he felt the same. The scars of her past were too raw. On the rare occasion they were in the same room together, both were acutely aware there was electricity between them but neither knew how to make the first move.

Evie's phone screen lit up again, but this time it was Freya.

Far too rough out there today. Tea and cakes at mine in half an hour, don't be late. X

Evie smiled. As much as she enjoyed the wild water swimming with the Selkies, she also loved these stormy mornings when the women *didn't* swim, and instead sat in front of a roaring fire, lounging on Freya's comfy sofas with hand-knitted blankets over their knees. She would look across the room at Freya, whose round, almost wrinkle-free face shone with happiness at having her house filled with her friends and think how lucky she was to be a part of it all.

She quickly texted Sophia and Freya back, cleaned her brushes, whipped off her painted stained apron and headed out into the storm from the quiet of her studio. Every time she stepped outside in Orkney it took her breath away – but particularly on a day like today. There really wasn't a place more beautiful on earth. And yet she was denying the healing power of Orkney to Amelia McLean. She knew she would have no peace of mind until she answered her email, but the longer she left it, the more difficult it would be to write a reply.

Evie was torn. Although she wanted to help this stranger, their shared family history was dark and complicated. Evie thought it would be safer to leave well alone, but she was still riddled with guilt and doubts.

Chapter Four

Freya's House

Arriving in Freya's living room was like stepping into a rainbow. Freya loved colour, the brighter the better. From the painted walls and colourful throws and rugs over the sofa to the collection of works from local artists (including Evie's, of course), Freya's home was as cheerful, charismatic and welcoming as its owner.

Evie smiled as she looked around the room at the different women who, along with Freya, had become her closest friends: Maureen, Kate, Delima and Patsy.

Maureen was a mature bride of almost eighteen months, sitting upright on a comfy armchair with her hands filled with knitting as usual. She'd had to put down those knitting needles for a while after her mastectomy, but she had healed well and was now busily making yet another baby cardigan in fluffy yellow wool. She was wearing a soft emerald-blue dress and felt hat gifted to her by Freya to keep her head warm.

Her beautiful thick black hair was long lost to chemotherapy. It had slowly grown back, wiry and curly and white as snow but Maureen had grown fond of wearing a hat, and truth be told, she still felt sensitive about her hair.

Her face was unnaturally swollen because of the ongoing cancer treatment. She had just recently finished another round of chemo. But her gentle eyes had the glow of a woman who knows she is much loved. Despite everything that had happened to her, Evie knew that Maureen felt lucky and deeply contented to be married to such a kind and wonderful man; Andrzej had made her so very happy.

Their wedding in the famous Italian Chapel was still talked about, and Maureen loved to show off the photographs and watch videos of that very special day, especially the ones with her beloved Polish husband and her teenage son Rory, whose dad had died young. Maureen, Andrzej and Rory were now a close-knit family and had found real happiness in challenging times.

Evie couldn't help being worried about Maureen, but the signs were hopeful, and the treatment seemed to be working. If only you could bottle contentment and use it as a cure-all, then Maureen would sail safely through these stormy waters. In the early days after Maureen told everyone she had breast cancer, Evie had often felt at a loss as to what to say to her. Everything seemed trivial compared to the overwhelming reality of the ever-present disease.

Freya had gently told the other Selkies shortly after Maureen started her treatment, "Just treat her the same as we all used to do before she got sick. Of course, you can ask her how she's doing, but she just really wants to talk about her boy, Rory, and boast to you about how clever he is, and how Andrzej treats her like a princess. She also wants to hear your news. Just normal stuff. You know what she's like; she doesn't want a fuss."

Freya was a wise woman. There weren't many left who remembered she had once played on the beach on the island of Hrossey as a little boy called Magnus. That was several lifetimes ago and the fact she happened to be a trans woman was the least interesting thing about her.

She was just Freya. Everyone's friend and supporter, always there if you needed to pour your heart out and be given sound advice or could do with a quick chat to make you feel better about yourself. She seemed to have an endless supply of coffee, cake and whisky and a deep well of wisdom.

Evie was sitting beside Kate and thought again how relieved she was to have mended fences with her childhood friend, who'd been so hurt when Evie had fled the island aged eighteen and cut all contact for years. The two of them were now as close as they had been at school, making up for lost time.

Evie loved babysitting Kate's two hilarious little girls who sometimes made her run into the kitchen and muffle her laughter into a tea towel. One day last week, when Evie had been looking after them after school, six-year-old Claire had solemnly told her big sister, Louise, that Siobhan at school had said daddies and mammies made babies just like cats and dogs and sheep and cows. They had both asked Evie if that was really true.

"Did someone have to throw water over mammy and daddy like Mrs Finnegan did when that big black dog was stuck to her peedie poodle," Claire piped up, all wide-eyed innocence, with Louise looking to Evie for clarification.

Evie managed to keep it together to say she didn't think that had happened to Kate and Edwyn before she had to flee from the room, hiccupping with laughter. It was moments like these, and just being with her friends today, that made her so glad she'd moved back to Orkney.

That afternoon, everyone's attention was on Delima and her precocious-yet-adorable daughter Ola, and new baby Hari, a fat contented bundle with big brown eyes and a shock of blond hair. Delima was recounting how appalled Ola had been to witness his first nappy change.

"She asked me to send him back and get a clean one," Delima said, taking a sip of tea. "I explained to her that daddy was changing Hari's nappy for a new one. And that's when she explained – no, she wanted a new baby! She even said, 'This one smells bad.'"

Evie and the other women collapsed in giggles and Ola looked at all of them, smiling. She was a beautiful child and the image of her mother with shiny straight black hair and nut-brown eyes. She was as bright as a button and chatted constantly. Baby Hari had just turned two months old, forever smiling and fat as Buddha. He'd arrived into the world a fortnight overdue and no one could quite understand how such a stoater of a bairn had come out of such a peedie thing as his mum.

Delima had a tough time but had been dead set on a natural birth like she'd had with Ola. Even her husband, Jack, couldn't talk her out of it. After twenty-eight hours of labour in Balfour Hospital, anxious midwifes had wanted her to have a C-section, which gave Delima the determination to push out young Hari with the last reserves of her strength.

Evie looked at Delima with affection and deep admiration. She appeared to be a delicate flower but really, she was a steel magnolia, and very much the brains behind the success of the seal sanctuary and animal hospital she ran with her husband. It was by the shore in Hoxa, just over the barriers in South Ronaldsay, and everyone in Orkney knew to call them if they found a stray kitten or a stranded seal pup.

"Isn't it time for me to get a cuddle of that peedie mite?" said Freya, holding out her plump arms and engulfing baby Hari in soft sweet-smelling silk. The baby instantly cooried into Freya and fell into a contented sleep.

Patsy, a raw-boned woman who worked with Maureen's husband, Andrzej, who declared her to be the best carpenter he had ever come across, observed wryly,

"I wouldn't call that baby peedie. You could send him out to work in the fields. He could pick up a coo, put it under his oxter and carry it to market. He's as strong as an ox."

Patsy shook her head and added, "I still don't know how the hell you ever managed to push him out Delima and I can't believe you aren't still walking like John Wayne with rickets."

Delima laughed, "You forget the pain as soon as you have the baby in your arms. Otherwise, no woman would ever give birth again."

"If I'd ever been unfortunate enough to have kids," said Patsy grimly, "it would have been as nature intended, with me lying flat on a hospital bed numb from the neck down."

Freya smiled and rocked Hari in her arms. "Behave yourself Patsy. He's just a bonnie big boy like his daddy." She sighed happily, "It's lovely to have a peedie newborn to fuss over again. Ola has grown up so fast. And it feels like such a long time since your two were bairns, Kate."

Kate smiled, "And they were both so contented to be held in your arms. You were the only one who could stop them crying and wriggling. Mind how our Claire looked like a chimp when she was born with all that hair."

"I remember," said Freya chuckling. "She had sideburns like Elvis and a hairy back."

Although she didn't know it, Freya's words cut deep into Evie's heart. She often realised just how much she'd missed during those years away. Seeing a look of sadness come over Evie's face, Freya came over and placed baby Hari in her arms.

"You're back now," Freya whispered, squeezing Evie's shoulder.

"Now then everybody," Freya said loudly as she'd sat back down clinking her cake fork against her cup of tea. "How is my surprise eightieth birthday party coming along?"

"How the hell did you know about that, Freya?" asked a scandalised Kate.

"Well, I didn't for sure, but I absolutely do now . . ." said Freya laughing. "Come on. There was no way you weren't going to do something special for me, and whenever I come into a room these days, you all look panicked and start talking loudly about the weather."

She added, "Just make sure there's loads of food, tons of booze and lots of fine fellas to dance with me. I will need a steady supply of young men and I fully intend to wear them all out."

"Consider it done," said Evie. "But you have to promise to leave it all to us. No interfering and look suitably surprised in front of everyone else or they will all be mortally disappointed."

"I promise," said Freya. She grinned round at all her friends. "Am I really not to have any idea about what you've planned for my birthday?"

"No," said Kate. "So don't ask again."

Freya got up again from her comfortable chair, "I think I will pour us all a dram if that's OK with you." They all agreed they'd have a drink apart from Delima who was breast-feeding and anyway thought whisky tasted like ashes and smoke steeped in sea water.

A couple of hours passed catching up on gossip and passing sleepy baby Hari around like a plump parcel until they all reluctantly headed home. Jack picked up his wife, daughter and baby son. Andrzej came to collect Maureen and Evie gave Kate and Patsy a lift in Florence the Beetle, her beloved bright yellow car. They all chatted happily on the way home about plans for Freya's eightieth, but Evie had no idea just how much that birthday celebration would change all their lives.

Chapter Five

Alaska, 1965

In no time at all, and very much to his surprise, James found himself in love, spruced up, squeezed into an ill-fitting black suit and swiftly married to Marge. Every day, he marvelled at how this woman had opened up his heart in a way he hadn't thought possible. He'd never allowed himself to have a proper relationship before. It was all one-night stands and no commitment.

He hadn't felt he was missing out and scoffed at the men he worked with who in his opinion threw away their money on ungrateful floozies. His feelings for Marge had crept up on him so quietly he hadn't realised it was happening, but now he knew he couldn't live without her. There were no fireworks, but a kind of peaceful contentment that enriched his life.

Marge had surprised herself by falling hard for this solid, quiet man, too. Every single day she felt like she was discovering something new about James. His love of literature and classical music. The fact that his flat was spotless and filled with books and an eclectic record collection that included Marty Robbins, Frank Sinatra and Maria Callas. And that his most prized possession was a radiogram with a record player which he polished until it shone.

Marge was also introduced to Maggie, a timid black-and-white cat who James had found yowling outside his door when she was just a kitten. Maggie would have frozen to death if he hadn't taken her in, given her some warm milk and made her a bed out of a cardboard box lined with his oldest woollen jumper. Maggie was a house cat who never went outside, despite James trying to coax her out of the front door.

The shy little animal took a liking to Marge right away, which is what finally convinced James that it might be rather pleasant to have a woman around the place. After a few months of gentle courtship, Marge moved in. It seemed silly for them both to be paying high rentals. She brought a sweet softness to his house with cushions and flowers and her own collection of Ella Fitzgerald records.

When James said they may as well make it official, Marge made all the arrangements and they had a quiet wedding in the local courthouse. Two of his workmates acted as witnesses and they had a bottle of champagne in a small overpriced Italian restaurant, which they both declared tasted nasty and smelled like Maggie's litter tray. James was relieved it was so low-key. Neither of them liked a fuss, and Marge's family couldn't come all that way at short notice. It also made it less of an issue that he didn't have anyone to invite. He hadn't told Marge about his daughter, Cara – now that he was no longer sending money for her, it felt like that link had been completely severed.

Many of his fellow fishermen, whalers and oil workers surely had children they'd fathered and didn't know about. James felt he had done more than most in sending money to his daughter, and there was no point upsetting things with Marge for no reason.

A few weeks after the wedding James was dragged to Minnesota to be shown off to his new mother-in-law, an overweight, sour-faced pensioner who had long expected her daughter to remain a spinster.

The old woman had it all planned out. Marge would move in and act as her companion when she was in her dotage and be at her beck and call at all times. It would have been a dull and miserable life for Marge who would have ended up as a thankless workhorse. The old harridan was not best pleased at this turn of events.

James and his formidable mother-in-law eyed each other up like prize fighters in the stuffy uncomfortable parlour where every possible space was filled with dusty bric-a-brac.

Mrs Svenson had a particular fondness for squirrel ornaments and brass horseshoes, but not enough to give them a proper clean, so they were tarnished with neglect. She narrowed her eyes and glared at James and he knew this was a battle he couldn't win.

"This is all very sudden," she snapped. "I wasn't aware that Marjorie even had a boyfriend." She laughed harshly and added, "How stupid it sounds to call you Marjorie's boyfriend. It makes her sound like a young girl instead of an old maid." She leaned forward to James and hissed, "You do realise she's almost forty."

Marge bridled, "Mother, you know full well that I'm thirty-two. You tell me often enough what a struggle it was for you to bring me into the world and that you were in labour for days, so I think you would remember the exact year I was born."

James said mildly, "Well now, Mrs Svenson. Or would you prefer me to call you Gertrude?"

"Indeed, I would not," said the old woman folding her arms with a glare that could strip wallpaper.

James pressed on, " Mrs Svenson, as you well know I am actually Marge's husband and not her boyfriend. We got married up in Alaska two weeks ago. I'm sorry we didn't invite you, but it was all last minute and it was a very small ceremony."

James saw his mother-in-law's mouth purse so tight it resembled his cat Maggie's bum. "I wouldn't have been able to come anyway." Her voice took on a horrible whine, "Not in my state of health. I can hardly walk and I can't keep anything down, not that Marjorie would care."

James looked at her ample figure and thought she could do with losing more than a few pounds. There was clearly nothing wrong with her and she was obviously lying about not being able to eat and, if she couldn't get around, it was because she was bone idle.

'Christ,' he thought. 'Poor Marge dealing with this horrible old bag. Whatever happened to the Minnesota Nice I've always heard so much about? I thought they were all super polite and at least outwardly friendly here, even if they loathed each other.'

He ploughed on regardless, "You see, we didn't want any fuss and Marge said you wouldn't have wanted to travel all that way up there. But we wanted to come down to see you and share the good news in person."

This was a long speech from James, who was a man of few words, but he had seen the hurt and fear in his new wife's eyes, and already he despised this horrible bully who obviously thought of his Marge as her very own long-suffering slave. No wonder she had left home and headed north to Alaska in search of a way out. He felt a rush of tenderness for his new wife.

They had initially planned to set up home with Marge's mother until finding a place of their own nearby, but clearly that would have made them both deeply miserable and killed their marriage. James reckoned Mrs Gertrude Svenson would have taken a grim enjoyment having them living with her, giving her something to whinge and moan about, and she'd get a real kick out of making their lives unbearable. James would never give her the satisfaction.

So instead, James and Marge decided to go back up north to Alaska. James to finally apply for a job as a supervisor on the new oil fields in the very far north, and Marge to put in for a job in the library. They ended up moving to Barrow, the most northerly town in Alaska, with a population of just four thousand people, most of them Inuits. It was an isolated and quiet life and they rubbed along happily enough.

Although she loved James, sex was a duty for Marge and she forced herself to lift her nightie, shut her eyes and bear her husband's clumsy lovemaking once a week.

After James retired, they moved south back to Fairfax into a modest little house on the outskirts of town.

They both found it a bit too noisy and busy after the stark calm and quiet of Barrow, and they missed the awe-inspiring northern lights and sense of isolation, but Marge soon made a circle of friends through her bridge club and volunteering at the local charity shop.

James mostly read his Scottish history books, listened to his new Beethoven collection and watched the PSB channel for historical documentaries. Their lives were uncomplicated and reassuringly dull.

That was until 1978 when Marge hit forty-five and found her periods had petered out and weight had gathered around her belly. She chalked it up to 'the change' but when she went to the doctor with agonising stomach cramps, she was shocked to be told that not only was she pregnant, but the baby was on the way.

"At my age. That can't be possible," she gasped. Their doctor smiled at her, "It's certainly unusual but not impossible. I had a mother and daughter in here last week. Both pregnant. The daughter was twenty-four and the mom a year older than you." Marge looked at him with a mixture of panic, but also a glimmer of hope in her eyes.

She had longed to have a child, and in the early years of marriage had hoped she might conceive, but it wasn't to be.

She had told herself over and over again she would be nothing like her own mother. Marge had gone through the ordeal of a cold and lonely childhood, and she wanted a chance to surround a cherished baby of her own with love and care.

Back then she had knitted some tiny white cardigans and delicate blankets, wrapping them in tissue paper and putting them away in her bottom drawer. As the years passed with every month being a disappointment, she had given up on her dream and passed on the precious tiny clothes to new mothers she hardly knew.

She and James rarely had sex these days, but she remembered that after a bottle of cheap red wine at Thanksgiving, they had a quick fumble before going to bed. Now here was the result. She gave a deep sigh. This was simply overwhelming. She couldn't believe she was in labour and started to panic.

"I've nothing ready for this child. I don't have a crib or any nappies or clothes. I can't be having a baby at my age. You must have made a mistake."

The doctor patted her arm. "Don't worry. You're in good health and everything seems to be perfectly normal. There's still time to get you to the hospital. I've called for an ambulance."

Marge was becoming tearful, "My husband is too old to be a dad. He's almost sixty and he's never wanted children. I don't know how I'm going to tell him."

"Well now, Marge, he's certainly going to find out pretty soon. So dry your eyes and wait here while I give him a call. These things have a way of working out. You'll see."

Once James had recovered from the shock, he surprised himself by being overjoyed to find out he was going to be a dad. As he'd grown older, he'd had pangs of regret about never getting to know his daughter Cara back in Orkney. He had often thought about writing to Sheila to find out how she was doing, but he always put it off, and after a while he felt too much time had gone by. She would be thirty-two now – possibly with her own family.

Maybe he could now tell Marge about Cara when they had their own child.

He drove to the hospital hoping that this wouldn't be too much for his Marge. She'd been complaining about stomach pains and feeling tired these past few months and he hadn't paid enough attention.

'I've taken her for granted,' he thought guiltily. 'But I will make it up to her and I need to let her know our baby will have the best of everything.'

He paced up and down the waiting room, drank endless cups of what could have been either tea or coffee from an old vending machine, and worked himself up into a state.

Once again, he thought of how he had left Sheila to have Cara on her own all those years ago, even if that's what she said she wanted at the time.

'I was a selfish bastard,' he told himself. 'But now I have another chance to be a father and I will not screw it up.' He was allowed into the room once his newborn daughter had been washed and weighed and put into a borrowed white baby gown.

James gazed at the red-faced furious babe in her mother's arms, chuckled, shook his head in wonder and exclaimed, "There's life in the old dog yet. Who would ever have thought it?"

Chapter Six

Inganess Beach, late March

With spring and the better weather finally on the way, the winds were growing softer and the rain more gentle, perfect weather for a swim in the sea. Freya and Evie were sitting by the shore waiting for the other Selkies to arrive so they could go in for their Saturday morning dook.

There was still a bit of a chill in the air, but the two women were wrapped up in their cosy dry robes and wearing bright purple woollen beanie hats with 'Selkies do it all year round' emblazoned on the front. All the girls had been given the hats as a gift by Maureen, who had knitted them during her chemotherapy when she hadn't felt too nauseous or tired. They were practical, cosy and so precious to everyone.

Evie had already been at her gallery in Kirkwall earlier that morning. As she pulled her special Selkie hat down over her ears, she asked Freya "Do you think we should stock these in the gallery shop? I think a lot of people would love them."

Freya looked a bit uncomfortable. "I know they would go down a storm," she said, "but I just feel as though they are too personal and important. I'm not sure I want to see every man and his dog in Orkney wearing our Selkie hats." She frowned, "Oh dear. Is that really selfish of me?"

"Not at all," Evie responded quickly, "I know exactly what you mean. It's our club, isn't it? And we have all been through a lot these past two years."

"That we have," said Freya. "Including you, my love. You have achieved so much. I'm really proud of you. Look how you've managed to overcome your fear of the sea. That was such a massive achievement. You're a fully-fledged Selkie now."

Evie smiled back at her dear friend. She could barely remember herself as that broken, defeated woman who had come home to Orkney. Her fear of the water had been deep and dark. She hadn't even liked *looking* at the sea, let alone plunging into it. Now, she looked forward to a wild water dook, feeling light and tingly each time she resurfaced.

"None of it would have been possible without you, Freya. I don't thank you often enough."

"Och, away with you," said Freya, her face reddening, but she looked mightily pleased.

Evie went on, "Honestly, it's true. And you introduced me to Andrzej who helped renovate my house and turn it into a proper home."

Freya smiled, "Well, we all have to help each other or what's the point of being here?" She paused for a moment, deep in thought, "What's that old saying I've always liked? Oh yes, I remember. A society grows great when old men plant trees whose shade they know they'll never sit under."

She laughed and went on, "That goes for old women too. We don't have many trees here in Orkney, but my garden will bloom and grow long after I'm gone. And you will continue to blossom too, Evie."

"I hope so," Evie replied. "I'm just so happy to have found a sense of peace and purpose. It's taken me a long, long time to feel like this you know."

Her mind flicked guiltily to the email from Amelia. Over a month had gone by and it still lurked unanswered in her inbox. As if she'd read her mind, and Freya had an uncanny knack of seeming able to do that, she leaned in and nudged Evie.

"I've been meaning to ask, did you get a reply from that Amelia?"

Evie chewed on her bottom lip. "I haven't actually answered her yet. I've been putting it off."

Freya looked concerned and squeezed Evie's arm.

"What's worrying you, my lamb? It's not like you to leave things hanging in the wind."

Evie could feel her chest tighten. After everything she had gone through, she just wanted the chance to enjoy the life she had so carefully rebuilt, the friendships mended and the new ones made. For the first time in a very long time, she was living without anxiety and a sense of dread.

She sighed: "I know I'm being daft, but everything is going so well and I'm just worried how it might all change." She looked at Freya and blushed, "I know it's terrible of me, but I've just got a bad feeling about it all."

Freya leaned over to give her a hug. "I know you have your worries, but you might just be overthinking things. I'm sure she just wants to come and visit and get to know more about her dad and her family. Maybe she doesn't have many American relatives. You know we get so many people coming here from all over the world to find out more about their past. It's what comes from us being such fearless explorers and being scattered all over the globe."

She looked at Evie and held her gaze. "You never know, you might end up getting along just fine."

Evie had to admit Freya was probably right. To be fair, she usually was. She gave herself a shake. "Thanks, Freya. I've been thinking the worst and getting myself in a state. I really should reply to her, and I promise I will. It's the right thing to do," she said with a small smile.

"You're stronger than you think, Evie, that's always been true." Freya glanced up. "Look, here they all come. Let's get into that water."

As more of the Selkies arrived on the shore, Evie and Freya were wrapped in hugs from Delima and Kate while Patsy plonked down her backpack filled with flasks of hot chocolate, coffee, tea and some slightly squashed cakes and biscuits. It was Patsy's turn to bring the goodies this week, so there was nothing homemade.

Instead, she had raided the local deli. Patsy didn't do home baking, she preferred to spend her time making beautiful wooden sculptures of mythical animals and sea creatures.

Evie was desperate to persuade Patsy to let her sell them in the gallery, but she always refused, saying no one would want to buy them and it would be a waste of shelf space. Evie thought for the thousandth time that although Patsy gave the appearance of being as tough as an old boot, she was a sensitive soul deep down.

Maureen was dropped off by Andrzej who was picking her up later. She looked a bit pale and frail but her eyes sparkled and her glorious smile showed how glad she was to see all of her friends. Getting up from the sand, Freya hugged Maureen and told her to get stripped off as quickly as possible.

"Right ladies," she yelled. "Get your arses in that sea. Let's see what you're made of." They all quickly took off their clothes and ran into the water shrieking and giggling and gasping at the salty stinging coldness.

By now Evie was a good swimmer and loved to dive headlong into the waves. She had finally made her peace with the sea and no longer feared its power. Being in the water made her feel renewed and energised, and she couldn't imagine life without her regular swimming sessions, and the chance to spend time with these wonderful women.

She floated on her back, looked up at the sky and thought how lucky she was to find such peace and contentment. She realised she had to give this Amelia woman a chance to share in what she herself had found. Amelia could turn out to be a friend, or maybe even the kind of older sister she'd always wanted.

Chapter Seven

Fairfax, 1978

It was really no one's fault that poor Marge died. They didn't notice she was losing so much blood until she went chalk white just a few minutes after James had kissed her cheek and told her she had done good and their daughter was beautiful. She'd whispered to him that she was so happy and wanted to call their daughter Amelia after her grandmother.

Then her eyes fluttered and she lost consciousness.

The doctors did everything they could, but she slipped away quietly as her newborn baby cried and cried for her mother. James was left awkwardly holding his tiny daughter who looked up at him with her face puce and crumpled in distress and her mouth wide open in a powerful unhappy yell.

He thought he had never seen anything more frightening in all his life, but at the same time he was overwhelmed by a rush of love for this tiny screaming, motherless babe. He rocked her in his arms until she grew quiet and started snuffling like a little piglet.

A nurse came over and said she would take her away to be fed. James nodded numbly and handed her over. The next few days were a blur of pain and confusion. The hospital staff looked after Amelia and the local undertakers made all the arrangements for the funeral. Thankfully, James had medical insurance to take care of the massive hospital bill.

He felt as though he was moving underwater. He wasn't taking in anything anyone was saying to him. They sounded muffled, out of sync and so very far away. He found himself thinking a hundred times a day that he'd better ask Marge what to do and then with a sickening sense of loss, realising anew that she was gone. He'd never again look over at her sucking on the end of her pen trying to do the crossword or making him his nightly cup of tea and chocolate biscuits.

Unbeknownst to him, over in Orkney his first-born daughter, Cara, had just given birth to his granddaughter, Liv, after years of devastating miscarriages. He had become a father and a grandfather on the same day.

The hospital kept his baby daughter for a week, but she was now gaining weight and doing well, and they needed to think about her future. James was taken to a side room to meet Beryl, a middle-aged, kindly social worker who asked if he had any friends or family who would be able to help him. He shook his head.

Marge's mother had gone to her grave five years ago, miserable to the last and had left all her money to the startled young carer who had wiped her bum for the last year of her life. Not because she particularly cared for the overworked young woman, but because she knew it would wound her daughter deeply and annoy James intensely.

He sighed wearily, "I don't have any family over here and the two of us pretty much kept ourselves to ourselves. Marge has some cousins in Minnesota, and she mentioned relatives in England. They used to send Christmas cards but that's about it."

Beryl gently asked if James had considered having the baby fostered or even adopted. He got to his feet and yelled, all the grief and rage exploding out of him: "She's my child and I will never, ever give her up. I've done that to one daughter already." His voice broke and he slumped back down in the chair sobbing as though his heart would break.

Beryl patted his arm and waited until he was able to speak.

"I made a solemn promise to Marge I would look after our little girl," he said firmly. "I have the house and some money put by, and I have my pension. I can afford to get a full-time nanny to help."

Beryl looked at him with compassion. "Of course you can. I am so sorry, I didn't mean to upset you, James. I just wanted to let you know of all the options available. But you are right. It's 1978 and there's no reason why a man shouldn't bring up a child on his own these days."

James wiped his eyes and blew his nose on the sparkling white starched handkerchief, washed and ironed by his Marge, who always insisted he kept it in his pocket.

"I'd like to take my daughter home now."

"Of course. And we can help you with some of the basics you'll need right away and give you a list of all the things you should buy as soon as you can. The health visitor will go with you now and come round first thing tomorrow, but I think you should get full-time help as soon as possible."

Beryl stood up to shake his hand. "I'm always here," she said kindly. "Don't hesitate to call me. All we want is what's best for the baby and for you."

James nodded. "Thank you. It's all been such a shock. A week ago, my wife was still alive and we had no idea she was even pregnant. Now the whole world has turned upside down."

The health visitor brought the baby into the room in a Moses basket. She was a tiny little thing with the most enormous blue eyes and a rosebud for a mouth.

James gazed at her, and his eyes filled with tears. "Hello, my little one. I'm your daddy and I will love and protect you until the day I die."

Which he suddenly realised with a rush of fear would be far too soon. He would be well over seventy by the time his daughter was ready to go to high school. He had to make plans to ensure she would be safe in the future.

Chapter Eight
Maureen's House

Andrzej clucked over his adored wife as he helped her out of the car and into their comfortable, messy home. On the drive back from the beach after her swim with the rest of the Selkies, he had regaled Maureen with stories of his morning. He'd been taking a look at the Old Manse in Birsay to give the new owners some help and advice. They had come up from the south, with all sorts of plans to turn it into a family home but the whole place was tumbling around their ears.

Andrzej told her: "He's a good man and has lots of enthusiasm. We had a long chat about the history of the Brough of Birsay and the archaeological dig that was going on there. He was very interested."

Maureen smiled to herself and felt sorry for the poor fella who would have been subjected to the entire ancient history of Birsay in great detail whether he wanted to hear it or not.

Andrzej rattled on, "As soon as they got here last month, they walked from the house across to the island, at low tide of course. He said the children loved seeing the puffins on the cliffs, but he really had no idea of just how important a location it was. So I put him right. He seemed really grateful and said he would tell his wife all about it. She's just got a job in town as a solicitor."

Once inside, he helped Maureen take her coat off, plumped up the cushions and settled her on the sofa. He threw another log on the fire and said happily, "I've a stew on the stove for our tea. It's your favourite, and I made dumplings."

"I'm sorry, love. I'm just not hungry, Freya has filled me up with so much cake." Maureen saw his anxious face and she said quickly, "Maybe a peedie bit later on though." He smiled, and she put her arms out for a hug.

The two of them had adored each other for ten years, but it had taken Maureen's breast cancer diagnosis to make them finally declare their love, with more than a little help from Evie, who persuaded them both they were destined to be more than just good friends.

Rory was upstairs doing his homework but he ran downstairs to greet them. His hair had long grown back, after he had shaved it all off to cheer his mum up when hers fell out from the chemo, and to raise money for the local breast cancer charity.

Maureen had cried at the loss of his curls but had been fiercely proud of her splendid boy who suddenly looked so grown up. He had taken a stretch over the past six months and was all clumsy knees and elbows like a baby giraffe learning to walk.

"What gossip have you got from the witches coven?" he said cheekily.

"Behave yourself. There's no gossip to speak of at all," replied Maureen.

He grinned, "Come off it, mum. You've spent the morning with Freya and all those mad Selkies. You must have a million things to tell us."

Maureen smiled at him and ruffled his spiky hair. "Maybe when you are older."

"You always say that."

"Well, I'm sure you don't really want to hear all the details about Hari's nappies."

"Yuck. I'm about to have my tea. Thanks a lot."

"Actually, we did talk a lot more about Freya's birthday party," said Maureen.

"Was that not supposed to be a surprise?" Andrzej peered out from the kitchen.

"You know what she's like. She managed to winkle it out of us when we were at her house last month, but she has promised to leave it all to us and not to interfere."

"Good luck with that," said Andrzej, going back to his stew, a recipe from his mother in Poland.

"Are you sure you are OK mum?" said Rory. "You look a bit tired. Would you like a cup of tea?"

"I'm fine, and I've had so much tea this afternoon I'm swimming in the stuff."

Both Andrzej and Rory tried very hard not to treat Maureen like a priceless piece of porcelain, but they perched like anxious hawks watching for any sign of pain or tiredness. She was well aware of their scrutiny and always tried to be cheerful and positive around them. Frankly, she was finding it exhausting.

Thank the lord for Freya. She was always just a phone call away and Maureen could cry and pour her heart out, telling her of her fears for herself and for Rory and Andrzej. She didn't have to be brave for Freya and it was such a relief to have her as a friend.

"What on earth would we all do without her?" sighed Maureen. She couldn't bear the thought of ever being without Freya and the mention of her upcoming birthday had made Maureen realise that she really was growing older.

Freya's energy and positivity was extraordinary, and she seemed timeless, but she would soon be eighty years of age and she wouldn't live forever.

Maureen pushed these morbid thoughts from her mind. As she well knew, with her own devastating illness, you never can tell when your time might be up, and the most important thing was to live each day to the fullest.

They'd give Freya the most special party of her life and cherish every single moment.

Chapter Nine

Fairfax, 1978

James had taken his tiny newborn daughter home to a cold and lonely house that echoed with Marge's absence. Moving slowly, he started a fire and boiled a kettle. The health visitor who had come with him had given him a stock of nappies and formula with instructions on how to feed the little baby girl who had barely made a sound since she was born a week before.

Amelia rarely cried and didn't seem all that interested in the bottle, but after a while she managed a small amount of formula and fell asleep, whimpering a little. Feeling increasingly anxious, James placed her in a borrowed cot, also brought along by the brisk, efficient health visitor who informed him she would look in every morning and evening until James had sorted out childcare.

James knew he should be grateful for all the help given, but he felt terrified at the thought of being a father and enraged and in despair at the loss of his wife.

Marge had made his home comfortable in an old-fashioned and slightly fussy way, with lots of heavy, dark wooden furniture and cabinets filled with her collection of cut crystal. The sofas and chairs were well used and sagged a little and were covered in Marge's handmade crotchet blankets and cushions with fringes and tassels. Marge had polished the coffee table until it shone and her kitchen was spotlessly clean with something usually bubbling on the stove or baking in the oven.

She had only been dead a week and already everything looked dusty and neglected. James had been living out of tin cans while his daughter was in hospital. The kitchen smelt of unwashed dish cloths and food gone bad.

Left alone, James had no idea how he was going to do this by himself and felt overwhelmed by the responsibility of taking care of a vulnerable little baby. He was in over his head. He sent up a silent prayer – James had never been one for religion, but in this most stressful moment, he found himself murmuring for help to a god he wasn't even sure he believed in.

He heard a loud knock at the door and glanced up to see if it would waken Amelia. She merely stirred a little in her sleep. He looked at her intently. She was such a tiny scrap of a thing but she had become his whole world.

He didn't recognise the woman at the front door who was holding a delicious-smelling meat and potato pie in a massive Pyrex dish, still warm from the oven. She was around sixty, plain and plump with greyish hair in a bun on top of her head and wearing a floral apron over a red dress straining at the hips.

She smiled hesitantly. "I hope I'm not disturbing you," she said softly. "I wanted to come before but I didn't want to intrude. I live nearby and Marge and I used to say hello and pass the time of day. I heard what happened, and I am so very sorry for your loss. I just wanted to give you this as I'm sure you haven't eaten a decent square meal since, well, since she was taken from you."

James felt tears well up. He coughed and said, "That's mighty kind of you."

"I'm Eloise. Eloise Parker and I'm number 48. You just turn left and there I am. Come round anytime you need help. And try and eat that pie. You need to keep your strength up if you are looking after that little one all by yourself."

James took the dish from her and said he would try and thanked her again. He was about to close the door when the baby began to cry. He looked so panicked that Eloise asked if she could have a look at her.

"I don't want to trouble you after you've been so kind," said James. His daughter's howls grew louder and more insistent.

Eloise smiled at him. "It's no trouble. I'd sure like to meet her if we are going to be neighbours."

Eloise peeked at the furious-looking baby who was screaming at the top of her lungs. She had finally found her voice and it was a piercingly loud one.

"Oh, she's beautiful and so tiny," exclaimed Eloise. "I think she might need her nappy changed and she also could be hungry."

James said humbly, "I've never actually changed a nappy. They showed me in the hospital, but I don't think I took it in."

Eloise tutted, "Well of course you didn't, you poor man. You've had a terrible shock with the loss of your Marge. Look, I've had five kids of my own. All grown up now and I'm going to be a grandma soon. I've changed thousands of nappies. Let me show you."

Eloise expertly cleaned and changed the baby, wrapping her in a clean terry towelling nappy fastened with a pink safety pin. She found a bucket and told James to pop the dirty nappy in boiling water, telling him she would wash it for him and hang it up.

Amelia was wrapped in a shawl and tucked under Eloise's arm while she made up her bottle. She helped James hold it properly to feed his daughter who sucked hungrily.

"They showed me this at the hospital too, but you make it a whole lot easier to follow."

"You are doing fine. It just takes practice that's all. Now James, I'm going to pop that pie in the oven to heat it up a bit more while you sit with your daughter. Then you can get her winded, and I will get her to sleep while you have something to eat."

Eloise bustled into the kitchen and turned on the oven. She nodded with satisfaction at Marge's organised cupboard under the sink and quickly cleaned up the sticky surfaces and gave the whole place a going over.

She glanced back at James who was giving his daughter her bottle with a look of fear and wonder on his face. 'The poor man,' she thought. 'Life has dealt him a hard hand and he needs all the help he can get.'

She showed James how to hold the little baby to burp her and she gently took her and rocked the little one to sleep before popping her into her cot. She brought him a tray with the pie piled high on the plate and told him firmly to eat up.

The baby hadn't settled so she picked her up and sat in Marge's chair opposite James and began singing a lullaby. Feeling calmer with Eloise's help, James found he was starving and scoffed down the homecooked food. It was delicious and he devoured every crumb while Eloise looked on fondly.

Despite being grateful to her, he knew Eloise would have to go back to her own home soon and he just didn't know if he was going to be able to get through this. The whole world had shifted beneath his feet.

James had been looking forward to a quiet life, reading, listening to his records, smoking his pipe, enjoying Marge's cooking and watching TV with her beside him quietly knitting or crocheting.

Then just a week ago, he had found out she was pregnant and the baby had arrived into the world before he had time to properly take in the news. He had been so proud and happy, and then his Marge had died. She had been his strength and stay, and although he never told her how much he loved her, he felt sure she had known. If he was honest, James had always thought he would go first and had never imagined a world where he would have to live without Marge. They didn't even get a chance to say a proper goodbye.

He hadn't wanted to think about her death, but now the memories of that terrible day came rushing back. He had been unceremoniously pushed out of the room while they worked to save her life. He remembered calling her name and then a kind nurse taking the baby from him, vaguely recalled the doctor coming to say how sorry he was, and that they had done all they possibly could and did he want them to call anyone.

He was told they would look after his daughter for now and that he should go home. James had stumbled out into the fresh air, sank to his knees in the snow and sobbed like a child. He felt old, worn out and terrified.

When he got back to his front door, he'd called out to Marge just like he always did and then remembered she couldn't hear him anymore. She would never hear him again.

His usual way of coping with any crisis was to disappear into a bottle of whisky. That night, he had gazed at the half-open bottle on the sideboard, got up, opened it and then threw it down the sink. 'I'm not going down that road,' he thought. 'That little one needs me and I can't let her down.'

He had already abandoned one daughter, but not this time. He would do right by this one. He just needed a plan. He hadn't touched a drop that whole week and intended never to drink again.

Blinking back to the present, James finished his meal, scraped his plate and thanked Eloise for being so kind.

"That's what neighbours do, James. We look out for each other." She hesitated and then said, "Look, I know it's early days and you might have made different plans with your friends or family when it comes to looking after little Amelia, but if you need me I would love to help out."

James mumbled that he didn't have any family, nor did Marge really, so he was pretty much on his lonesome.

"Well," said Eloise. "We might just be able to help each other if you don't mind hearing me out." The baby had fallen into a contented sleep and was snuffling happily.

She looked at this tiny scrap in her arms and smiled. "I married young and my husband left me years ago. I brought up my kids on my own. They have all left home now and are doing well. My daughter is about to have her first baby, but she's in New Zealand." Eloise sighed and said quietly, "She might as well be on the moon."

She went on, "Well darn it, James. I like to take care of people, especially babies and I'm good at it. The truth is I want to be useful, and I really love kids. So why don't I help you?"

James was silent.

"Oh, I'm so sorry, James. It's too soon, isn't it? I've put my big foot in it." She was flustered and embarrassed. "I'd better go."

James stuttered, "No. Eloise, I'm just trying to take in the fact that you have appeared at my door like a fairy godmother and you are the answer to my prayers."

Eloise smiled at him in relief.

James told her that it had to all be done properly. He would hire her as a nanny and pay her a proper wage. When Eloise waved him away, he stood firm. This was the way it had to be or it was a no go. They would work out a proper contract and Eloise would begin first thing tomorrow. She was given a key and a handshake.

In fact, she never did start the next morning. Around 1am she heard the baby wailing from next door and popped in to see James struggling with a dirty nappy. She elbowed him aside and took over.

James gratefully staggered to his bed and fell into the first deep sleep he'd had in seven days, and he thought that maybe, just maybe, it was going to be alright.

Chapter Ten
Evie's House

Later in the day, after her swim with the Selkies, Evie sat down in her kitchen on the beautiful Orkney chair that Freya had gifted to her, restored and crafted by Ross, and made several attempts to reply to Amelia.

She wished that the woman had given her a phone number. It was always so difficult to get the tone right in an email. It either came across as cold and clinical, or over-friendly. And if you tried to be funny it could fall flat. Eventually she had a version she was reasonably happy with.

Dear Amelia,

Thank you for your email.

It was a surprise to hear from you, but from what you have found out it looks highly likely we could be related.

If you are planning a trip to Orkney then of course I would be more than happy to meet you and help in any way I can. I'm afraid our family is very small. Neither my sister Liv or I have had children.

My father died in 2024 and my mum has dementia. She still has some good days but I'm not sure if she would be able to give you much information.

I do have a lot of uncles and aunts and cousins on Hrossay and I know they would also help with any questions you might have.

Let me know if you are coming.

Evie

She read through her words one more time, then took a deep breath and hit send. Writing the email had stirred up painful memories.

When Evie had travelled back to Orkney two years ago, it was because of Freya's desperate attempts to let her know her father was dying. It was only knowing that she needed to say goodbye to him, that she managed to find the courage to travel home. Her friend Sophia helped her, but Evie had been too late.

Her father died before she landed in Orkney and she never had the chance to tell him she was sorry she left him, and that she loved him. She would never again hear him call her 'Teenie', his pet name for her when she was a little girl.

Then there was Liv. She hadn't seen her older sister in months. Evie and her friends had paid for Liv to go into rehab and helped her find a rented flat in Stromness. As far as she knew, her sister was still clean and holding down a job as a waitress.

Evie had sent her a few texts but heard nothing back and had eventually given up. Despite this, Evie had decided from the start to give Liv a founding stake in her gallery, but hadn't worked up the courage to tell her yet. Liv had been so defensive about the money for her rehab, and Evie wasn't sure how her sister would react. But it was important to Evie that there was some fairness between them both. She had been left the house by her father, and so felt giving Liv a stake in her business redressed that balance, but she'd need to let Liv know soon and have all the paperwork drawn up.

Then there was her mother. The last time Evie went to see Cara in the care home, she hadn't recognised her at all, and that had hit hard.

Even if Cara had never been the mother Evie and Liv had needed, there was still the heartache of watching the person who raised you slowly disappear.

Evie wasn't sure what Amelia was expecting, but their family was complicated, and she still wasn't at all sure how much she wanted to let this stranger into her life, even if they were related. Would it bring back those dark feelings from the past when she'd finally found peace in the present?

Her iPad pinged. Amelia had replied right away.

Evie

You have no idea how much this means to me! I am checking flights now and will let you know when I am due to arrive. I don't want to bother you too much and I know you are really busy but it would be so helpful if you could give me some tips on somewhere to stay?

It would be wonderful to talk to someone who knew Sheila and might even have met my dad and I would love to talk to you and your sister Liv about your parents, and to meet all the relatives on Hrossey. Let's keep in touch.

Thank you again. See you soon.

Amelia xx

'Well,' thought Evie, her heart racing. 'There's no going back now.'

She knew nothing about Amelia and hadn't wanted to ask her too many questions in her email, so she scrolled through

Facebook and Instagram trying to find an Amelia McLean. She didn't have much to go on. She didn't even know Amelia's age or even her address or place of work.

There was a long list, but no sign of anyone who might fit the description. She was pretty sure that she wasn't a 29-year-old ski instructor in Utah or a bizarre Kardashian lookalike from Santa Monica. Evie sighed and got up to make herself a coffee. She felt like she was being daft, but just couldn't shake off feelings of dread.

Chapter Eleven

Fairfax, 1979

It was inevitable that James and Eloise would end up getting married. They enjoyed each other's company and Eloise was more like a mother to little Amelia than a nanny. She wasn't an easy baby and screamed through the night, racked with colic, her red angry face wet with tears.

James would never have coped on his own, but Eloise spent hours trying to soothe the fractious child. He proposed to her on Amelia's first birthday, mostly out of desperation to make sure she wouldn't get fed up and leave him on his own with his bad-tempered daughter. To his surprise and relief, Eloise agreed.

James had discovered he was the kind of man who needed a woman around. Up until he had met Marge he had no idea of how much better life could be with the right person at his side. He had come to value companionship and, it had to be said, being well looked after.

James also knew he wouldn't be able to cope with Amelia without Eloise around to help. It was tough enough having a baby, but Amelia would soon be at school, and then there would be the horrors of boys buzzing around her. He didn't have the energy to deal with all of that on his own.

He had such mixed emotions about his child. She made him feel guilty, resentful and baffled, but also inadequate and weak, and mixed in with all of that he felt an overwhelming sense of protectiveness. In order to function he needed Eloise. Thank God she had agreed to be his wife.

Eloise had actually grabbed his gruff marriage proposal with both hands. She was lonely and missed having people to look after, and both James and Amelia needed a lot of care and attention. She knew some people would make fun of her and James walking down the aisle at their age, but she didn't care.

Eloise just liked to feel useful, and in her own way she loved James, and doted on Amelia. She dismissed the child's bad temper and outbursts of anger as totally understandable, "After all she had been through as a baby."

They sold their houses and moved to the outskirts of Seattle where Eloise had worked for a few years. She didn't know many people there anymore but felt comfortable and settled. It might rain a lot but compared to Alaska it was positively balmy.

James left most of the childcare to Eloise and spent much of the time sitting on his favourite chair reading and listening to the radio. He'd managed to tune into Radio Scotland and found himself becoming overly emotional hearing the commentary of an Aberdeen v Dundee United game.

'I'm a silly sentimental old fool,' he thought to himself. 'I had a shitty childhood and I couldn't wait to get away, but right now I'd do anything to see the grey granite streets of Aberdeen even in the horizontal rain.'

As he grew older, he thought more about his homeland. He would knock back a couple of whiskies every night and grow maudlin and homesick. After being off the booze for so long, it seemed as though he were making up for lost time.

Eloise rolled her eyes when he listened to 'Flower of Scotland' and drunkenly and tunelessly roared the lyrics out with tears in his eyes, frightening Amelia and making her cry. When James tried to soothe his daughter, she would wriggle in his arms and push him away, wrinkling her nose at the smell of booze on his breath. He felt rejected by her, and sometimes even jealous of the close relationship between Eloise and Amelia.

Instead of making more of an effort with his child, he shut down and turned to the bottle for solace and company. As she grew up, Amelia had given up trying to get his attention. She knew it was hopeless and so she hardened her heart.

Eloise would tell him he was driving her away and that he needed to make more of an effort, but James was too set in his ways.

"Stop nagging me, woman. I'm doing my best but she's a difficult child to love. There's not a bit of her mother in her and she does nothing but defy me."

Eloise was near to tears, "You vowed you would look after her and love her. You promised you would do the same for me and all you do is sit on your behind and drink whisky. No wonder she won't talk to you."

James would mutter something under his breath and pour himself another drink. Eloise would give up and leave him to it. She had come into this marriage with her eyes open, but she hadn't thought he would turn into such a grumpy, bitter old man quite so soon.

The years on the fishing boats and in the oil fields had taken their toll on James. He was wracked with arthritis and in constant pain. He had also become increasingly forgetful. Eloise would come back from the shops and find him out in the street looking frightened and confused and calling her name.

"Where were you?" he would demand plaintively. "You left me alone for so long and I couldn't get into the house." She'd grab the front door key hanging from a stout strap she had fastened around his neck and tell him for the hundredth time that he could let himself in. At first, she had felt deeply sorry for him, but that soon turned into guilty exasperation.

By the time Amelia was ten years old, it was clear her father was deteriorating badly. One terrible night, Eloise realised that his mind was going when he kept calling Amelia by another name: 'Cara'. He was holding onto his daughter's hands, weeping and begging for her forgiveness.

"James, what's going on, you're frightening her," said Eloise, and she was all the more perturbed when James turned to her, his eyes suddenly lucid, and whispered he had to confess something. Eloise sent Amelia from the room.

"What on earth is the matter?" she whispered. And James finally told her he had another daughter. A daughter he had never met, and whose very existence was an accident, the result of a one-night stand.

Eloise hadn't expected this. She couldn't believe he had never told her about something so important. She clasped her hand over her mouth, her thoughts reeling. He had kept this daughter a complete secret. From her, from Marge, and now from Amelia. Her half-sister.

"I should have gone back to Orkney and tried to be her father," James was weeping. "But it's too late now."

"It's never too late, James. Why don't you try and contact her?" said Eloise, her mind running to what might be possible. She was picturing a family reunion, a happy ever after with herself in the middle accepting praise as the one to have made it all happen.

James shook his head violently.

"No. No! This has to be kept secret. No good will come of it, too much time has passed. It's better for Cara and for Amelia that they don't know."

He lapsed into a stubborn silence leaving Eloise in turmoil. Surely Amelia had a right to discover she had another family, even if her father didn't want her to find out.

Recently, Eloise found she was worrying constantly about Amelia and now she would have the added stress of feeling guilty about keeping this enormous secret. She had no idea what to do.

Amelia had grown into a strange, intense child. The rest of her classmates at school found her odd and cold, but even the bullies were too scared of her to make her life a misery. Everyone just gave her a wide berth. Perhaps stung by the isolation, she could be sneaky and snitched to the teachers on the kids who smoked cheap cigarettes under the bleachers by the football field.

She treated James with complete disinterest, but she showed a softer side with her step-mother when it suited her. It was Eloise who told Amelia the story of how her mother had died giving birth to her, turning the very real tragedy of Marge's death into a sort of turgid soap opera embellished with every retelling, complete with heavenly choirs of angels clasping Marge to their bosoms, and weeping medical staff proclaiming Amelia to be an angel.

Eloise was a decent woman, but she was the worst possible influence on a child like Amelia. She was forever telling the little girl she was far more beautiful and clever than everyone else.

With his drinking and his bad temper, James had proved to be such a disappointment to Eloise, she poured all of her affection to Amelia, who in her eyes could do no wrong. The more Amelia misbehaved, the more Eloise defended her.

When Amelia pushed the neighbours' five-year-old son off his bike, his enraged father turned up at the door after work only to be met with a furious Eloise falsely claiming his child was a menace who had started it by chucking stones at her precious step-daughter.

Earlier that day, Eloise had readily accepted Amelia's tearful explanation that it was all the little boy's fault even though deep down she knew the truth. She continued haranguing the poor man, "My Amelia would never do anything so terrible. She's a good girl and she's been brought up properly, unlike your son."

He walked away muttering that she had better stay away from his boy or there would be trouble. Eloise then darted upstairs to comfort Amelia, insisting on giving her hugs and treats and painting poor Amelia as a precious victim of other people's jealousy. So Amelia grew up neglected by her father and smothered by Eloise. All of which made for a very mixed-up girl.

Chapter Twelve

Kirkwall Airport

Evie was waiting nervously at the airport for the morning flight from Edinburgh. She had barely slept the night before, going over and over in her mind whether she had done the right thing.

Three cups of strong coffee had left her jittery, clammy and queasy. She kept looking at the arrivals board and hoping the flight would be delayed indefinitely, but the weather was fair and mild with no wind and the plane was due to land on time.

Amelia had wasted no time in taking Evie up on her offer, booking a flight for the very next week and telling Evie in an email dotted with exclamation marks about her excitement.

She would arrive in Heathrow in the wee small hours of that morning from her flight from Seattle to JFK in New York, sleep at Heathrow and take the first flight to Edinburgh and then on to Kirkwall.

Evie remembered how tired and fragile she herself had felt arriving back to Orkney. Amelia would no doubt be similarly exhausted, and probably in need of a nap. She wondered if she would recognise Amelia, if there would be some kind of family connection, before deciding she was being silly, and wishing she'd asked for a photo.

Through the glass doors, Evie saw the plane come into view and descend through a clear blue sky to touch down on the runway. A few minutes later, Evie watched the passengers climb down the steps from the plane, breathe in the sweet, salty air and hurry inside.

A young couple with a tiny newborn bairn were first through the door into the terminal, welcomed with hugs and tears from already besotted grandparents. They were followed by a group of wide-eyed young archaeologists on their way to a dig near Skara Brae, excitedly chatting about the treasures they hoped to find. A couple of twitchers with state-of-the-art binoculars and cameras asked about ferry times to North Ronaldsay and enthused about the rare birds they hoped to spot there.

As time went on, Evie thought Amelia must have missed the flight as more and more locals and visitors disembarked and poured inside to be met by friends and family. Tourists wandered off to pick up their hired cars, always astounded to find the keys were in the glove compartment and they could just drive off.

Finally, a woman who looked about her own age, slim and lithe, ran down the stairs, gazed up at the sky, took a big deep breath, spun around and strode confidently into the airport on her sky-high heels.

She let out a shriek when she saw Evie and teetered over to her, giving a hug that made Evie stiffen and tense up.

"You must be Evie. I am SO glad to meet you! I'm Amelia. I am super excited to be here, this airport is SO cute. And the sea, it's just SO beautiful. You are SO lucky to live here. I can't wait to explore!"

Evie was stunned, both by Amelia's whirlwind energy and by their physical similarity.

Aside from Amelia's long black hair, and the fact she was about three inches shorter, Evie could have been looking in a mirror. They even had the same emerald-green eyes. They were like twins. Two peas in a pod. It was uncanny.

"Oh my gosh!" exclaimed Amelia, clutching at Evie's arms and looking at her intently, before drawing her into another hug. "Look at us. There's no way we aren't related.

You look like the sister I never had! I just know we are going to be the best of friends."

All of this was said in a loud, harsh American accent that sounded as though Amelia was shouting into a gale. People waiting on their luggage couldn't help wincing but also smiled at this enthusiastic woman who was clearly beyond excited to visit their island home.

Evie eventually forced herself to say something. She stuttered, "Amelia, you've taken me by surprise."

"Ha!" Amelia replied, with a wink and a flash of her straight white teeth in a smile. You were thinking I'd be a wrinkled old grandma. I'm actually not that much older than you, Evie. My mom had me when she was forty-five and my dad was in his late fifties when I came along."

Evie tried to backtrack. "N-no, of course I didn't think that I– um– your age didn't enter my head."

"It's OK, don't worry about it! I'm forty-eight years old and I've had all the Botox a body could stand, but I draw the line at a face lift." She giggled. "I actually can't believe I'm really here. It's just so cute and you all sound as though you are singing with that adorable accent."

This was uttered in a fake baby voice and Amelia made one of those really annoying pretend pouts to show just HOW cute she felt everything was. Evie felt a jolt of irritation before telling herself not to be so judgemental.

'Now that she's actually here, I have to at least give her a chance,' she thought. 'Although she is a bit much.'

Amelia didn't draw breath and chirruped, "I have so much to ask you about everything and I just don't know where to start. Listen to me going on and on. I guess I'm just a bit nervous, Evie. You'll have to forgive me. I'm just super happy to meet you and to actually be here."

She gave Evie a beaming smile that didn't quite reach her eyes.

Evie immediately felt a bit ashamed. Of course, Amelia was nervous. It was a huge thing to come halfway round the world to try and find your family.

"Don't worry," said Evie. "I feel the same. It's bound to be a little strange at first, but you'll be very welcome."

They picked up Amelia's tiny suitcase, and she oohed and aahed over Florence which made Evie warm to her a little more.

"Why don't I drop you at the hotel and you could have a rest and then we could have a chat later? You must be tired after such a long journey."

"Oh no, Evie, I am just fine and dandy, and I don't want to waste a moment of being here! I feel really refreshed. It must be this pure clean air."

Evie had to admit that Amelia looked as though she'd just come back from three weeks in the Maldives. She was glowing. Her skin was perfect, and her biscuit-coloured jumpsuit was pristine and barely wrinkled. She was also wearing those impossible high spiky-heeled sandals that would have killed Evie's feet in five minutes flat.

Amelia continued, "I want to say right from the start, I don't want to take up too much of your time. You must be so busy with all your painting and running the gallery."

"Oh, thanks, Amelia – but that's OK."

She was interrupted by Amelia who had barely heard her reply.

"I was wondering, who's the other lady who runs it with you? The one with the most fabulous dress sense?"

"Oh, that must be Freya."

"Freya! I can't wait to meet her. And then there's the two little children you babysit for. They are just adorable."

Evie felt a tiny twinge of discomfort – how did Amelia know all that about her? As if she'd read her mind, Amelia said, "I'm sorry, I've been stalking you and your friends on Instagram. I hope you don't mind, but I am just so hungry for any information. You really do have a wonderful life here. So many friends and with such a successful business. I just want to know everything about you."

Evie wondered why this made her feel so uneasy, after all she had tried to look Amelia up on social media, too, and she was being charming and friendly. Evie didn't put much on Instagram – anything she did was to promote the gallery – but Freya, Delima, Kate and some of the others all followed her account, and she knew Freya loved posting colourful photos and sweeping landscapes of the island for everyone to see.

On the other hand, she was coming across as what Kate would witheringly call 'full of herself', but in fairness that could just be put down to an over-enthusiastic eagerness to please. Evie decided to change the subject.

"Well, if you're sure you're not tired, we can drop your bag off and then I can take you for a drive if you like and then you can come to mine for a bit of tea?"

Amelia said that all sounded absolutely wonderful.

"Alright," said Evie. "Of course, at some point you need to meet Freya, who knew Sheila and Cara, and you'll want to go to Hrossey to meet the cousins."

"Ah, yes. Tell me, do they have red hair?"

"They do," said Evie, wondering if Amelia had somehow managed to look them up too.

Amelia smiled. "Well we have something in common. I'm a carrot top too." She flicked her long black hair and added conspiratorially, "I started dying my hair years ago. I got bullied at school and called all sorts of names. Of course, I should have just ignored it all but having no mom and such an ancient old fart for a dad, I was always being beat up on."

There was silence. Evie wasn't too sure how she felt about her own grandfather being called an 'old fart' even though she didn't know him and he had never been part of her life, but that small glimpse into Amelia's childhood made her feel sorry for her. It sounded tough.

Evie replied: "I'm sorry you went through that. My dad used to say that he would rather his daughters were being bullied than them being the bullies and I always thought that was very wise."

"Forgive me, Evie, but that's a crock." She put her feet up on the dashboard and took out a packet of cigarettes.

"You don't mind if I smoke do you? Filthy habit, but I'm down to a couple a day and I'm gasping after the flight."

Evie did mind. She minded very much indeed, but she felt she couldn't say anything to this increasingly unsettling woman who looked so much like her. She murmured "Of course not" feeling like a total blancmange.

"Want one?" said Amelia.

"No, thanks, I don't smoke."

At least Amelia cracked open the window slightly. "That's OK. Now where were we? Oh yes, we were making a plan to go and see Freya and of course the cousins in Hrossay."

She bombarded Evie with questions. "Is it easy to get there? What's the island like? Do you have to get a fishing boat? Do they have wifi there? God, do they even have *electricity?*"

Evie felt a stress headache coming on. Maybe Amelia was just genuinely ignorant, but Evie's voice was a few degrees cooler as she said, "They have electricity and everything, Amelia. There's a regular ferry or a plane. There's a lovely hotel and a pub and shops. It's a beautiful island and they will make you very welcome."

Amelia made a gesture with her cigarette.

"Oh my God," she yelled. "Look at that view! Stop the car, Evie. I have to get out."

Evie pulled up sharply.

She tippy-toed over the road on her high heels, making a car on the other side swerve to avoid her. Oblivious, she turned to Evie and exclaimed. "This is just darling. Look at the quaint little village and that cathedral in the middle! It's just like Disneyland."

Evie cleared her throat. "That's actually our capital, Kirkwall, and it's quite big really. I can show you around if you like. If you need anything at all there's loads of shops."

"I'd love to get a few selfies in there. But don't worry about shopping for now, I've got everything I will need with me."

Amelia's phone buzzed. She read the text and pursed her lips.

"Actually, Evie, could you just drop me at the hotel after all? Turns out I have a few things to sort out."

She tapped at her phone before adding, "Although I would still like to come and see you tonight but could we do it after dinner?"

"Of course," said Evie, surprised at how relieved she felt that she wouldn't have to babysit Amelia. "I sent you all my numbers. Just ping me a message and I can come and get you. It's no trouble. You are only about ten minutes away, my house is just over there on the hill also looking over Scapa Flow. It's a tremendous view, don't you think?"

"Peachy," said Amelia distractedly, with a tight smile.

Evie gave a running commentary for the rest of the short journey to the hotel, pointing out landmarks like the hospital and the Scapa whisky distillery, but sensed that Amelia was no longer all that interested. Evie thought the tiredness must be kicking in after her long journey. It was a lot to take on: travelling here on her own and meeting strangers, even if they do turn out to be family.

Instead of going straight home after she'd dropped Amelia off, Evie drove on to Freya's cottage. Now that the gallery was such a success, Freya spent most days creating new jewellery, as well as encouraging new talent to come up with their own ideas.

As she went up the path, she heard Freya on the phone telling a young potter to bring in some more of her beautiful handmade green-and-blue vases. "They have the sea and the air in them, so delicate but also strong. You should be very proud of yourself, my love. See you soon then."

As always, her door was open. She saw Evie and beamed.

"That was Fraser's lass Helen on the phone. She's a shy peedie thing but so talented. She just needs a bit of encouragement. Her work is lovely."

She looked at Evie keenly. "You look a bit out of sorts. So, tell me everything – how did it go with Amelia?"

Evie shook her head. "She seems nice enough."

She wasn't sure what to say and could tell Freya was waiting, knowing there was more to come.

Evie blurted out: "She looks just like me. Apart from the fact she has dark hair and I'm a fair bit taller, we could be identical twins. Actually, because she had the most ridiculous high heels on, we were just about the same height."

Evie was on a roll now and her words tumbled out in a rush, "Also, she admitted having 'assistance', as you call it, with the Botox and all, but she looks well under forty and not the older woman I imagined. To be honest she looked brand new, even after that long journey."

Freya said slowly, "Go on."

Evie did indeed go on, "She called Kirkwall *quaint*. She thought everything was cute! She wondered how to get to Hrossey and she asked if they had wifi there as though we were all barbarians."

Freya raised her eyebrows. Evie wasn't done yet, "She was all for coming back to my house when she got a text and couldn't wait for me to drop her at the hotel and make myself scarce."

Evie's voice rose to a crescendo: ". . . And she smoked a fag in Florence." Freya told Evie to sit down, made her some hot tea and a large slice of cake and watched her munch it down. Evie's heart was pounding and her face was flushed.

"Feel better?"

"Actually, I do," said Evie through a mouthful of sumptuous Victoria sponge.

"Good. Because I'm going to say something to you. Put yourself in her shoes. She's in a strange place and you know she's not the first visitor to think we live in stone houses like Skara Brae and paint ourselves blue like Mel Gibson in *Braveheart*. It's annoying, I know, but come on, Evie. It sounds like she was a bit nervous."

Evie winced. "Yes, you're right. I'm being really judgemental. I did try to tell myself she must be a bit anxious and jet lagged. And she did say something along those lines herself."

"There you are then. How did you leave it with her?"

"She's coming to see me later tonight. She says she would rather stay up and be on Orkney time. I'm going to pick her up from the hotel after dinner. Freya do you think . . ."

Freya interrupted her.

"Don't worry, I'll come along tonight too. I can't wait to meet this intriguing woman. And Evie, don't take it upon yourself to have to entertain her. We will all help and there's loads of things to keep her occupied."

"You're right and I will make a list. What about a visit to Jack and Delima's sanctuary – I could call on them and see what day suits them best?"

Freya smiled as she watched Evie relax now she knew there was a plan and that everyone would rally round.

"Perfect idea. So, let me know what time tonight, and I'll see you there."

Chapter Thirteen
Jack and Delima's Home

Later that day, Delima's handsome husband Jack Randall was nursing a cup of strong green tea and looking out down to the shore in front of his comfortable newly restored Georgian manor house.

Two of the young trainee vets working with him were tending to a seal whose flipper was caught in a fishing net. They were slowly disentangling the poor thing, who seemed to understand they were trying to help and remained still and quiet, looking at them with her huge expressive eyes.

Since Jack and Delima had started up the animal sanctuary, they had been inundated with broken, bruised and battered animals of all kinds. From baby owls with damaged wings to otters with cuts to their noses and paws.

They'd even had a very disgruntled walrus who had strayed way off course from the frozen north. He had taken out his bad temper by mounting some of the sailing yachts in Kirkwall harbour, reducing them to little more than bits of twisted metal and kindling. Jack chuckled at the memory. Somehow, they had guided 'Wally,' as he was inevitably nicknamed, back out to sea and on his way back to far away Arctic waters. It had taken days of patience and a fleet of little boats, but Jack was so proud they had saved the splendid mammal.

A photo of a very angry-looking Wally took pride of place on the noticeboard as well as various newspaper clippings about his adventures that had given their fledgling sanctuary a real boost. Jack had spent a large chunk of his savings buying and restoring the ramshackle house on the white sandy shore near Hoxa on South Ronaldsay.

They still had enough money to live on, but he had underestimated the amount of cash it cost to save all the animals needing help, and he knew they would increasingly rely on donations to keep the place running properly.

From the outside, Jack looked like the strong one in their marriage. He was ridiculously good-looking and bore more than a passing resemblance to the Viking god Thor, but it was his tiny wife, Delima, who was the real powerhouse.

They had met when Jack went to work in Singapore. He had always wanted to have a job outdoors, on the land or by the sea, but his father said he needed a steady career, so to please him he went to university to study accountancy. He found the job soul crushing, but Jack was talented and hardworking and quickly gained promotion, ending up in the City of London working for a multi-national merchant bank.

Overworked, stressed and thoroughly fed up with all the wide boys and chancers he had to deal with on a daily basis, Jack was totally disenchanted with London high finance and decided to apply for a job overseas in Singapore. He thought if he had to work in this corporate world, he might as well do it somewhere warm, interesting and that would be a safe base to explore a fascinating part of the world.

So there he was in Singapore and what a place of wonders. He'd spent hours walking around Little India and the Arab quarter visiting temples and buying gifts of perfume and carpets for his family back home in Orkney. He didn't join in very much with the heavy drinking ex-pat scene, but finally agreed to go on a night out with some of his colleagues from the bank.

And that's where he first set eyes on Delima, who was with a group of her friends in the Ku De Tat bar atop the Marina Sands Hotel. Jack was planning an early escape and desperately trying to ignore the braying, red-faced Aussie opposite, bragging about his latest killing on the stock exchange. He glanced over at a table by the window, saw Delima and was hit by a thunderbolt.

She was slim and elegant and apart from a tiny bit of black eyeliner, her face was make-up free, but her skin glowed. Delima's hair was jet-black, shiny and cut in a perfect bob and her green silk dress was deceptively simple and fitted her to perfection. Jack thought she looked like a Singaporean Audrey Hepburn.

Everything in the bar seemed to go into slow motion and all he could hear was the thud of his heart beating. He locked eyes with the woman he wanted to spend the rest of his life with and gave her what he thought was his most charming and winning smile.

In fact, his expression was so completely gormless, Delima looked hastily away. He turned to the group of financial blowhards and asked if any of them knew the girl in the green dress, but they shrugged and told him not to waste his time.

The boastful sunburnt Aussie with the peeling nose roared there were plenty of girls who would be glad to spend the night with him. He waved his mobile phone around. "Just one click away my friend."

"I'm not interested in paying for a woman," said Jack tersely. "Not my style guys."

He called the waiter over and asked him to send a bottle of champagne to the ladies at the table opposite with his compliments.

When the bottle arrived, Delima looked over at him with a puzzled look on her face as if to say: 'Do I know you?' Her friends giggled but they didn't send it back.

Emboldened, he walked over and addressing Delima, he said: "I know you must hear this all the time, but I think you are the most beautiful woman I have ever seen in my life. I would love to get to know you better. Maybe just take you out for coffee and we could have a chat sometime."

There was more giggling from her friends and one of them said in Malay. "Who does this big-nosed hairy apeman think he is? Coming up to you like that without being invited and trying to make you go out with him. Tell him to get lost." She gestured with her hand for Jack to beat it.

But to her horror and surprise he replied in almost perfect Malay, "I am most sorry. I do have a very large nose and I am indeed hairy but that does not change the fact that your friend is beautiful and looks kind and I would very much like to take her out. I am quite new here and I hope she will take pity on me and help me to get to know Singapore better."

Delima burst out laughing. Her friend looked sheepish. Delima was intrigued, "What is your name?"

"I'm Jack Randall," he said in English and added to himself, 'And I am going to marry you and take your home to Orkney and we will have a house full of beautiful babies.'

This time his smile actually was devastatingly charming.

And that was that.

Jack thanked the Lord he had decided to go out that night and that he had learned passable Malay before moving to Singapore.

The two of them decided to get married after six months and move into a tiny and overpriced one-bedroom apartment in Duxton. Although he loathed the world of banking, Jack was raking in a fortune and Delima earned a top salary as a buyer for a fancy department store in Orchard Road.

They talked long into the night about their plans for the future, deciding to give it two more years in the rat race and save up enough money to be able to move back to Orkney. Jack hesitantly told Delima of his dream to raise a family and own a wildlife sanctuary.

Instead of being appalled she agreed to go with him and help him live his dream.

Her friends were not convinced and her sister Laya told her, "I looked it up. Orkney is freezing, you will die of the cold and it's also dark for half the year. You will have to eat disgusting deep fried food and your insides will clog up and then you will die of that, if the ice and wind doesn't get you first."

Delima sighed. "That's not true Layla and you know it. Orkney can get cold, but we will have fires in every room and the sea food is the finest you can find. Better than here even. I can make the best chilli crab and dumplings and that spicy fish curry you love when you visit."

Layla was not in any way convinced. "He will make you have giant babies with huge heads and you will die because you won't be able to push them out," she said darkly.

"I'm not going to die" said Delima tersely. Then she smiled at her sister. "And I will come back as often as I can. I will only be a day away."

Delima was trying to convince herself as well as everyone else. She loved Jack with all her heart, but it would be hard leaving her home and her family.

She embraced her sister who had begun to cry, but lifted her tiny determined chin and told herself firmly, 'I've made my decision and that's that. My life is with Jack now and we will build a good future together.'

She had a leaving party with her friends at the office and there were tears and hugs. Delima said briskly, "Now wish me luck and keep in touch. You can come and visit anytime, and I will come back here to see you all."

"It won't be the same," they grumbled.

Delima's family wept when she left and implored Jack to take care of her. He solemnly vowed that he would make sure she was happy and if she was too homesick, he would bring her back.

Finally, they were sitting on their posh seats on the plane with a glass of champagne in their hands. Jack knew he should feel elated but suddenly was overwhelmed by an enormous wave of responsibility and doubt. Delima was giving up so much for him, what if she was utterly miserable and hated Orkney?

He panicked, grabbed her hand and babbled. "We haven't taken off yet. You can still change your mind. I will understand. It's OK. I can stay in Singapore and get another job."

She looked at him with wise understanding and love and said quietly: "Hush now, Jack Randall. I am content to follow you anywhere. What's did Mary Queen of Scots say to her final husband, Lord Bothwell? 'I will follow you to the ends of the earth in my nightie' or words to that effect. Well, that's me. I love you Jack and I know we will be happy."

Back home in Orkney, Jack smiled to himself at the memory. His tea had grown cold, but he would make some fresh. Delima had introduced him to green tea, telling him it would stop him getting fat. He wasn't sure about that, but he obeyed his wife in all things and anyway he liked the taste and drank at least a big full pot every day.

He saw that the two young vets were red-faced and sweating but triumphant. The seal was free and luckily she hadn't suffered any serious cuts or wounds. They got out of her way to let her gallumph back into the water where she quickly swam off all sleek and silky.

Another animal saved. Jack gave them the thumbs up and waved for them to come back up to the house. They both deserved a beer.

He went into the kitchen to ask Delima about their plans for the day, and to spend time with their precious toddler Ola and baby boy Hari.

Delima had been extraordinary during the births of both of his children. He was humbled by her courage and sheer tenacity. Those were the most incredible moments of his life and he felt tears well up every time he thought of his children.

He heard a car turning into the drive, and saw it was the distinctive yellow Beetle that belonged to Evie. She waved as she got out.

"Right on time, Evie," he quipped. "You've missed the hard work of setting a seal free."

"Perfect timing then," Evie smiled back. "Although you know I would have been a brilliant supervisor."

Evie loved visiting the sanctuary but was too soft hearted to tackle the rescue missions, although happy to help nurse sick animals back to health.

"Come in for a drink," said Jack. "You can have one even though you're driving and we have to celebrate that seal getting its freedom back."

"I'm afraid I can't," said Evie. "I've got paintings to get on with. But look, I did have a favour to ask you. It's about a visitor to the island . . ."

Chapter Fourteen

Evie's House

When Evie got back from Jack and Delima's she spent the rest of the evening pacing about her kitchen, unable to settle. She had already ruined a very promising painting of Rackwick Bay because she couldn't leave it alone and managed to overcook the whole thing. She'd have to paint over parts of it or abandon it altogether.

She told herself not to be so nervous and on edge now that Amelia had arrived in Orkney, but there was something about this stranger that was unsettling. Evie wasn't in a fit state to do any more work, so she put down her paintbrush and went for a walk down to the shore.

It had been a long time since the night of Brodie's death and the sight of the beach no longer brought back pain and horror. Instead, the sound of the rolling waves actually gave her a sense of peace, especially since she had overcome her fear of the water. Evie sighed. So many secrets and lies.

She told herself it was better to focus on the present where everything was out in the open. She sat down on a rock and gazed out to the purplish-blue evening waters of Scapa Flow. She asked herself why she was feeling so strange around Amelia? 'Maybe it's because has also had the burden of secrets in her family. Her father is my grandfather, but none of us knew the other existed until now,' she thought.

Evie knew she would have to get up shortly and head back up the beach to her house. Freya would be arriving soon to give Amelia a proper Orkney welcome. She told herself she needed to get over her reservations, and help this American stranger find out as much as possible about her heritage. Hopefully, that would give Amelia the sense of peace and belonging that Evie herself had rediscovered.

When Evie returned, Freya was already in the kitchen unloading bags of homemade pies, scones and cakes, having let herself in as usual. She plonked a bottle of Highland Park whisky on the table.

"I thought we might need this tonight," she grinned at Evie. "Right, you go and pick up our visitor and I'll put some picky bits out."

Evie smiled, "There's enough grub there to feed an army. She's only a peedie thing."

"Aye, but she will be famished with all the travelling and experiencing our fresh air. I didn't want to risk her going hungry."

Amelia was waiting for Evie at the hotel reception. She leapt to her feet when she saw Evie, throwing her arms around her for a tight hug.

Evie gently disentangled herself and the two of them got into Florence. On the short drive back to Evie's home, Amelia sat quietly looking out of the car window at the green rolling fields and sparkling sea.

Evie was relieved by her much calmer energy.

Amelia said softly, "It really is lovely here, Evie. I can see why you wouldn't want to live anywhere else."

"Well," Evie replied, "It's the spring now and we've been lucky with the weather. Not much rain and the wind has been soft but come back in the winter and we'll talk then."

Amelia smiled. "I hope I can come back, Evie, and I really hope we can be friends. I don't have any close relatives and because we moved around a lot when I was little, I don't have any proper friends. It's something I always struggled with."

Evie felt awful. She hadn't given this poor lonely woman a chance. She knew the pain of being alone – she'd been very lucky to meet a friend like Sophia in London, who had been so kind and understanding.

Feeling guilty, she said warmly, "Well, you have found family now and you will make lots of friends here. People are very welcoming. And Freya is really looking forward to meeting you."

They turned into Evie's drive. Freya waved to them from the window and then Amelia found herself wrapped in the kind of warm embrace that makes you want to stay in that sweet smelling softness for ever.

"Let me look at you," said Freya. "My goodness you truly are the spitting image of our Evie. There's no need for DNA tests, you two look like sisters. Come and sit down and let me get you something to eat. I've made a few peedie snacks."

Amelia looked at the kitchen table groaning with all kinds of homemade goodies that would have defeated an entire rugby team after a hard-won match.

The three of them would hardly make a dent in this spread. Freya smiled at her. "Would you like to try a wee dram?"

"That would be lovely, Freya. I usually drink bourbon, but obviously I know Scottish whisky is better."

Freya nodded approvingly and poured three generous measures. Amelia asked her, "Do you have any Coca-Cola?"

Evie frowned. "I think I have some left from when Kate's girls were round. They aren't really allowed it but I got the zero-sugar stuff and I've sworn them both to secrecy."

Amelia gratefully took the can and poured it into her whisky, drowning the dram with the sweet brown stuff. Freya looked appalled.

"I think that's what's known as sacrilege, Amelia. It's actually against the law to do that to whisky here."

Amelia looked shocked, her eyes wide, staring from Freya's stern expression to her glass. She gave a hollow laugh. "You had me going there. I actually thought I might get arrested, but I guess you are just messing with me."

"I wouldn't be so sure," said Freya. She kept her voice light but she was genuinely shocked at such terrible treatment of good whisky.

"Mind if I smoke?" said Amelia, getting her cigarettes out and preparing to light up. "I can lean out the window?"

"Actually," said Freya, politely but firmly, "I do mind I'm afraid. Evie has bad asthma, and no one should smoke around her. Even if you're leaning out of the window, it will linger in the room."

Amelia looked stricken. "Evie. You should have said something when I was smoking in your cute little car. I am so very sorry."

She looked distraught and almost on the verge of tears.

"And Freya what must you think of me. Can we start over? Let me drink this up so as not to waste it and then I will have it neat, or would it be OK to add a bit of water?"

Freya nodded approvingly, "Just as God intended."

Amelia was eager to make amends. "I really can't apologise enough. Having a cigarette always calms me down but I won't ever smoke around you guys again. To be honest, I think I'm going to quit while I'm here on the island anyway. And I will never, ever again commit the crime of adding Coke to my whisky. Can you forgive me?"

She looked like a puppy pleading not to be kicked.

"Of course," said Freya warmly. "Now look, you must have so many questions for us."

Amelia took a deep breath.

"Well, like I said to Evie, I've been doing a bit of research, but it's only got me so far. My dad had two letters in his belongings from a woman called Sheila – who I guess is Evie's grandmother – and they had a daughter called Cara who was brought up on Hrossey and married a man called Duncan when she was sixteen. I then found out online that they had two daughters."

Evie nodded. "Yes, and that would be me and my older sister, Liv."

Amelia leaned forward eagerly. "I can't wait to meet her. I want to talk to as many people as I can with a connection to my father. Do you think Liv would also be up for telling me about the past?"

Evie and Freya glanced at each other. Liv's own past was littered with malicious lies, and a sad track record of trouble-making and addiction to drugs and alcohol, although recently she had tried to clean up her act.

Freya jumped in, "Of course you must meet Liv, but she's been going through a lot. Evie's helped her with rehab—". She stopped herself, the whisky had loosened her tongue. "That stays between us. In the meantime how can we both help you right now?"

"I would just like to know more about my Orkney family. I felt like I never fitted in back home in America and maybe that's because my roots are actually in Scotland and here in Orkney.

"So what can you tell me about Sheila and Cara?"

"Well," said Freya slowly. "I was born on Hrossey and of course it's a small and close-knit community, so I knew Cara

Rendall as she was then, quite well. She was a few years younger than me and was more a friend of my sister when they were in the same class at primary school."

"Your sister! Would she be willing to talk to me?"

"Ah, Amelia," said Freya sadly. "If only she could, but Anne Marie died of breast cancer a long time ago. She was a lovely woman and apart from Evie here, she was my staunchest ally."

"I'm so sorry for your loss, Freya," said Amelia, reaching out to squeeze Freya's hand gently.

"Thank you, it was a long time ago, but I still miss her. Every time I go back to Hrossey, I expect to see her there waiting to greet me off the boat. Even after all these years."

Freya shook her head and went on, "Anyway. I'm afraid Cara and I didn't get on very well. She didn't approve of me you see." It was seventy years ago but Cara's cruel stinging words calling her a freak still hurt, although just a pinprick these days compared with the deep raw ache when she was a child.

She continued on, "Like all the teenagers, Cara left the island to go to secondary school in Kirkwall, and that's where she met Evie's dad Duncan. They were just bairns of sixteen when they got married."

Freya smiled sadly, remembering the big, soft-hearted man who doted on his Cara but could never make her happy, and his bafflement when his firstborn daughter Liv turned out to be such a difficult child. But then there was his unconditional and overwhelming adoration of Evie, who he called his Teenie.

The more they talked, the more Freya warmed to Amelia, and Evie began to feel less on edge.

Amelia seemed to be so interested in Orkney, and Cara and Evie's extended family and asked them many intelligent questions. She was careful never to ask anything overly intrusive, and both Freya and Evie found themselves opening up.

There was only one awkward moment, where Amelia asked about Evie's time in London and Evie was stunned – she didn't remember telling Amelia about that.

"You mentioned you'd lived away, and that a friend from London was coming to visit," said Amelia. "Sorry, I was just putting two and two together."

"London was . . . a difficult time," said Evie. "I was glad to get back here where I belong."

Amelia smiled at her. "Say no more, Evie. I've had difficult times in my own life as well."

The three of them chatted for hours. Amelia was apologetic when she saw Freya yawning and realised it was way after midnight.

"I'm so sorry. I didn't notice the time. I've been so selfish, keeping you both up."

"I'm amazed you haven't hit the wall after all your travelling, Amelia. You are made of strong stuff," said Freya. "It's been good to talk to you about Hrossey and most of my memories are good ones. Like I said, I will get in touch with the Rendalls and you can hop up and visit them."

Amelia smiled, "You've both been so good to me. I really appreciate it. I didn't know what to expect. But you've been so very kind." She added, "There's so much to discover and I would like to know much more about Orkney. And to meet everyone else, especially Liv, of course."

Freya said, "I know the very fella to help, I will put you in touch with my dear friend Andrzej. He came here from Poland many years ago and knows more about Orkney than most of the locals. He will talk to you until your ears bleed."

She chuckled, "They do say the rescue donkeys he keeps on his land only have two front legs because he's talked the back ones off of them." Freya had made this joke many times in the past, and it always made Andrzej laugh too.

“And I dropped past the animal sanctuary today,” said Evie, keen to show Freya that she was doing her bit to welcome their new visitor, but also to distract from another mention of Liv. “They’d be so happy to show you around.”

Amelia clasped her hands and tears came to her eyes as she told Evie and Freya just how grateful she was for their kindness. Freya gave her a hug, which led to Amelia enthusing about them both for so long that Evie felt decidedly uncomfortable. She wasn’t used to such over-the-top displays of emotion.

She told herself that maybe this is how people behaved in America, but she wasn’t sure how to respond to such effusive praise. In the end, she simply patted Amelia’s arm and said she was very welcome.

Freya said she would share a cab with Amelia and drop her off at her hotel, they’d talk in the morning and sort out the trip to Hrossey.

When they had both left, Evie sat with her hands wrapped around her whisky glass. The conversation with Amelia and Freya had stirred up so many memories of the past. She hoped that Amelia would get what she needed from her visit to Orkney.

She wanted to know more about her too. She realised Amelia had asked so many questions that they hadn’t really had a chance to get to know more about her background, especially her own childhood and father.

Evie was overcome with tiredness and went to bed thinking there was plenty of time to find out more about Amelia.

Chapter Fifteen

Liv's Flat

Evie's sister Liv was still getting used to waking up without a hellish hangover and that feeling of clammy nausea with her insides jangling and her mouth like the bottom of a budgie's cage.

A year ago, she would have reached for either a joint, a half-empty can of flat lager, or even nudged the bloke beside her for a quick loveless shag. These days she got up, opened the curtains and took in the views over the high island of Hoy.

It looked so beautiful in the morning sunshine. She had never bothered to take the time to appreciate the spectacular scenery of her island home when she was a child, and from her teens up until recently she was rarely sober enough to care.

Liv looked over her spartan home in Stromness with satisfaction. She had scrubbed clean every inch of the tiny one-bedroom flat, painted the walls white and ripped out the worn, stained carpet revealing a shiny wooden floor which she had polished until her arms ached.

She took pride in keeping her place neat and tidy but had managed to erase any trace of her personality. The small bedroom was like a nun's cell with a single bed and white sheets, and there were no photos or prints on the walls to give a bit of cheer and warmth.

It was the same in the other room that doubled as a kitchen and living room. You could have eaten your dinner off the floor, and everything smelled strongly of TCP. There was an uncomfortable stiff-backed two-seater couch and a TV in the corner and that was it.

Despite all her years living in a grimy, stained pigsty of a house after she left home, Liv was her mother's daughter at heart and Cara had been manically clean and tidy. Liv remembered how her mother ended up cooking meals in the microwave and serving them to her husband and daughters on paper plates so as not to make a mess in the kitchen.

Liv had been badly affected growing up in a home where her father walked on eggshells, always frightened of making her mother angry or upset. Her dad had doted on Evie and as far as Liv was concerned had always thought the worst of his eldest daughter.

In fairness, Liv didn't help herself. She was a bully at school and vile to her sister at home. She turned into a wild child, hanging around with a crowd of druggies and petty thieves. Part of her behaviour was because she simply enjoyed being a rebel, but if she was honest, it was also an attempt to get her parents, especially her dad, to notice her; it hadn't worked.

She made herself some dry toast and watched *Four in a Bed*, scoffing at the contestants snuffling for traces of dust on the skirting boards and ripping apart the bed covers to find pubic hairs on the mattress. No one would ever find anything to complain about in Liv's flat, but then no one had ever been over her door, and she intended to keep it that way.

Freya had given her basic crockery and kitchen utensils, left in a box outside her door with a note to say she was about to give them to a jumble sale, but thought Liv could use them. Liv would never know Freya had bought everything brand new in Kirkwall and painstakingly removed all the labels. Freya was aware that proud, prickly Liv would never accept gifts, but might grudgingly use stuff that was being thrown out anyway.

Liv tried not to dwell too much about the past, but after her lies to Evie had finally been revealed when her sister had returned home, Liv finally had to face up to the consequences of her actions. Her first response when she had been found out, was to reach for a bottle of Bacardi, but something had stopped her.

She knew she was at a crossroads. If she opened the bottle, her life would continue to spiral out of control. She was facing eviction from her old place and had no savings. She was growing older and had no real friends.

After a spell in rehab paid for by Evie, Liv returned home and plucked up every ounce of courage she possessed and went to an AA meeting. She almost backed out and would have run away if a kindly man she recognised from working on the ferries hadn't opened the door and told her to come in. She remembered his name was Rab.

"We've got coffee and doughnuts," he grinned.

"Well, I'm not sure if I will be able to cope with the excitement of that," Liv drawled sarcastically, but seeing the man's smile falter she quickly added. "But it sounds alright and I do actually need some advice."

"That's why we are all here," he replied reassuringly.

She found herself sitting down and saying in a trembling voice, "My name is Liv and I'm an alcoholic, but you all already know that."

The group of nine people sitting in a circle chorused "Hello Liv". She thought to herself, 'Oh Christ, this is going to be harder than I thought.'

"Look, most of you know me already. Orkney, right? It's a small world." Rab smiled at her again.

"Don't worry, Liv. This is a safe place. Anything you tell us will remain totally private. Think of it like a confessional."

Liv thought, 'That's what I'm afraid of. I can't tell these people what I've done. I just can't.' She looked around in despair.

A washed-out, wispy young woman about half Liv's age said in a surprisingly strong voice. "You don't need to tell us anything if you don't want to. We are all different and we've all done things we are ashamed of, but there's no judgement here."

Liv found herself welling up. She impatiently wiped her tears away, but knew she had found people who understood.

Six months on and she had a job working as a waitress in one of the old-fashioned bars in Kirkwall. She was all too aware that serving booze was putting her right in the way of temptation, but Liv was never going to go for the easy option. She saw it as one more test she needed to endure and overcome.

She had come a long way already. There were no more hangers-on using her home as a doss house in exchange for booze, drugs or sex, or a mixture of all three. Those days were gone.

Her old 'friends' had been incredulous at first, scoffing that she would never be able to stay clean and would soon grow bored and go back to her old ways. At first, some of them turned up at the bar to jeer and make fun of her.

One even ordered a pint and poured it all over the floor while looking at her right in the eye the whole time. The old Liv would have grabbed him by his long greasy hair and repeatedly banged his head on the wooden counter of the bar until it burst and bled. The new Liv simply mopped up the mess without a word.

She had also started to change her appearance. Gone were the thick heavy layers of mascara and black eyeliner. She had also stopped dying her hair blue-black and had cut it herself into a sort of pixie style that suited her thin face.

Going grey actually made her look younger and abandoning her former diet of fags, drugs, booze and coffee, she filled out a bit and no longer looked like a haggard spider.

Liv actually found she enjoyed her job. She felt smugly superior to the mumbling barflys and the giggling youngsters tipsy on sticky sweet cocktails. She'd half listen to their burblings, moans and drunken ramblings, take their money and even squirrel a few extra bob into her tip box. She hadn't changed completely.

It wasn't much of a life, but Liv discovered that the company she enjoyed best of all was her own. A night at home in front of her TV was enough.

She never let her guard down or let anyone in. There was a shield of glass around Liv that no one would ever be allowed to penetrate ever again. Or at least that's what she told herself.

Chapter Sixteen

Tankerness

Evie was having lunch with Kate at The Kirk Gallery – it was one of their favourite places to go together, and it was good to get some one-on-one time with her school friend. The morning rain had lifted and now the sky was bright blue with a few fat fluffy clouds and just the right level of wind to hang out the washing.

Kate was very happy to leave her sheets drying in the breeze and have a catch up with Evie. It was a treat for them both to enjoy the tasteful surroundings of the beautiful converted church, filled with Sheila Fleet jewellery, and enjoy some of the best food on Orkney.

Evie had the famed fish soup and Kate the special pie of the day. Both knew no matter how full they were, they absolutely must have a large slice of homemade cake. The only dilemma was deciding which kind. Even while she was talking to Kate, Evie was eyeing the glorious cake table, torn between lemon drizzle and chocolate torte.

"Well go on then. What's this Amelia like?" asked Kate. "What does she want? Give us all the goss."

"She's lovely," said Evie. "Really friendly and keen to get to know everyone." She was determined to be more positive about Amelia and push aside her early misgivings.

"So tell me more? What does she look like? What's her story – is she retired now?"

"No, she's more like our age. Her dad had her really late in life. Actually, she looks a lot like me – she's a bit shorter, but she wears these giant high heels and her hair is really dark and not fair like mine."

"Well, your hair is only that gorgeous shade of blonde because Agnes dyes it for you."

"Thanks a bunch for that," said Evie in mock outrage. "Although you're right. If it wasn't for Agnes, I'd be as grey as granite."

"You would, Evie, but annoyingly you'd still look gorgeous. Anyway, never mind all the simpering stuff about her being lovely and friendly. This is me you are talking to you, so save all that for everyone else. What's really going on? I can tell she's rattled you."

Evie sighed. "Well, as I told you, she's here to find out more about her dad James and my granny Sheila and my mum, of course, but there's not that much we can tell her. Everyone who would have known my granny Sheila is dead or dottled."

"You know my mum has more bad days than good ones these days. I'll be honest with you Kate, I'm not sure I want to risk Amelia upsetting my mum by asking questions about her past and especially about her dad. My mum never even met him. I mean he left before she was born. It could be really hard for her, and just make her even more confused."

Kate nodded sympathetically.

Evie went on, "And, as you well know there's a hell of a lot of skeletons in my family closet. My mum might blurt something out that could cause all sorts of problems."

"I do understand that," said Kate. "And you are right, she doesn't need to visit your mum."

"I know. I'm sure it will be fine. It's just that she arrived so quickly after she got my email. I didn't have time to prepare myself. I didn't even have a photo of her. We didn't do a Zoom or even talk on the phone and get to know each other a bit. It's all been so fast."

Evie wondered what Amelia's life was like in the States, that she was able to just drop everything and fly straight to Scotland. It was frustrating that she knew so little about Amelia, and that how unwilling she was to share information about herself. She had told Evie she didn't have many friends or family but what about a job or even where she was living? Was she running away from something?

Evie knew all about that. Perhaps they had more in common than she thought, but she needed to find that out for herself.

Kate saw Evie's frown and tried to reassure her friend. "Maybe she was just so fixated and curious about her wild Orcadian relatives, she wanted to get over here as fast as possible.

Evie tried to sound convinced. "You're right. I suppose I just feel unsettled by it all. I hadn't really ever thought about my grandfather. He was never talked about, although I knew granny Sheila wasn't married when she had my mum. Liv told me when I was a teenager and said I should ask mum about it. As usual she was setting me up. When I did ask, I thought my mum was going to tear my head off. She was raging. It's only now I can see how hurt she was by being abandoned by him."

She sighed and thought, "I just think there's more to her coming back here than she is letting on."

Kate looked at her friend with deep affection, but she said briskly, "Stop furrowing your brow like that, if the wind changes you will end up looking like a Klingon."

"Charming," Evie said tartly.

"Look," said Kate. "I've an idea. Why don't you invite

everyone over to ours to meet this Amelia tomorrow night? We've got more room than you have, and it will give us all a chance to have a look at her and take some of the strain off you. We can also lovebomb her and find out more about her. I'm amazed Freya hasn't winkled out all of her secrets already."

Evie smiled, "Believe me, she has tried her best. Are you sure you want to go to all that trouble?"

"Positive. Edwyn is on early shift at the hospital, and he can help me throw some food together and get in some drinks. We can ask the Selkies, Freya, obviously, Patsy and Delima and Jack and the babies. Any excuse to give that new wee fatso a cuddle."

Kate grinned. She was hugely fond of baby Hari but having had two girls she was taken aback when he peed on her hair in a perfect arc while she changed his nappy. She was both simultaneously impressed and appalled. She added, "And Andrzej and Maureen, of course, if she's feeling up to it."

"Sophia is back tomorrow too," said Evie. "I forgot to tell you. She might be busy with a ton of make-up sex with Finn, but we can but ask."

Kate grinned: "Aye, she will have more than her hands full with that one."

Evie rolled her eyes. "Anyway, you're right, it would get it all out of the way at once and then I think Amelia will want to go to Hrossey and meet the cousins, and Jack and Delima have invited her to the sanctuary."

Kate replied "That's all up to her, Evie. You don't need to chaperone her around the islands. She's a grown woman."

"I know but I feel I need to make those introductions. Freya said she will come with me."

"Good, but you need to stop fretting, Evie. The only thing you should be worrying about right now is whether we share a slice of cake or have a whole one each."

"Share!" squeaked Evie, instantly diverted. "Are you mad. I'm having a massive slice of that chocolate cake and you aren't getting a crumb." They both laughed and placed their order.

In the car on the way home, Kate said to Evie, "Oh God – we completely forgot to talk about Freya's surprise party and come up with some ideas that will actually surprise her. Any suggestions?"

Evie groaned. "That was supposed to be the whole point of today, wasn't it? But we got sidetracked with Amelia."

"Well, whatever we come up with," said Kate, "we all know that Freya will have an outfit for any theme no matter how outlandish. Her wardrobe looks like the *Strictly* costume department."

Evie laughed, "I actually think she'd make that lot look dowdy."

Kate nodded in agreement, "You know she would be happy just with everyone she loves gathered together with some banging music and good whisky."

"She would," said Evie. "But I want this party to be really special. I missed a lot of chances to celebrate with Freya, and this one is a landmark."

The unsaid hung in the air between them.

Their precious Freya was turning eighty which these days wasn't exactly ancient, but there was a sense of time passing too quickly and wanting to grab every precious moment. Evie didn't want to think about what life would be like without Freya there. She was a constant, like the sun coming up every morning.

Evie vowed she was going to give Freya the best birthday ever to show her just how much she meant to all of them. And she made another promise to herself to find out more about her American visitor. Surely Amelia should be welcoming the chance to open up about her own past too. If not, then what secrets could she be hiding?

Chapter Seventeen

Orkney

Liv was taking a quick fag break from work outside the pub. She sat enjoying the sunshine and puffing furiously on her cigarette. She'd thought about quitting altogether, but instead had cut down drastically. She couldn't be expected to give up all her bad habits.

She tossed the fag end away and made her way back to the empty pub. Trade was slow in the afternoon, just a few tourists and a couple of regulars. Liv busied herself wiping down the gantry and the sticky counter.

The door flew open and Liv saw a woman stride up to the bar. She did a double take. Was that Evie with dyed black hair? She blinked and quickly realised her mistake, but this woman was the double of her sister.

The woman smiled at her. There was something about that smile, so smug, perfect and white that put Liv on edge.

"Hi there," she drawled.

"Oh Christ," thought Liv. "It gets worse. She's a fucking Yank." Liv had complete disdain for most people, but especially Americans, who she considered offensively cheerful and over-friendly.

The woman in front of her bucked that trend and demanded imperiously, "I'd like a glass of decent red wine. Is that possible around here?" Liv quickly got over her shock of the sight of her and managed to reel off the choices from the wine list.

The woman ordered a large Malbec and asked if she could smoke. "Nope. You have to go outside and as you can see it's started to rain and there's a fair breeze blowing. I'd not advise it."

"Actually, I hope you can help me. Is it . . . Liv?" Liv was immediately on her guard.

She growled warily. "How do you know my name and what the hell do you want?"

"I'm Amelia. Now don't freak out, but I know all about you. My dad was your grandfather. So, we are sort of related I suppose. It's complicated."

"What the hell are you going on about?" said Liv, completely confused. She got a lot of drunks in here talking crap but this was on another level.

"Sorry, I blurted that out. Do you have time to sit down?"

"No, I'm busy," snapped Liv. Who was this woman? What the hell was she going on about?

"Don't get all antsy. We're family. We can be civil. Your mom, Cara, was my half-sister. We both shared the same dad. He left Orkney when he got your grandmother Sheila pregnant and sent them money. He never properly told me I had a half-sister. I only discovered it after he died."

Despite herself, Liv was interested, but instead said coolly, "Well good for you. But I really couldn't care less. My mother told me her dad buggered off before she was born, so I really don't have anything to say to you."

"Well, I think it would be worth your while to hear me out," said Amelia. "I know all about you, Liv, and much more importantly I know all about your sister."

Liv remained silent. The two women stared at each other. Eventually, and much to her annoyance Liv cracked first. "OK.

What's your game? You obviously know you look just like her. Apart from the hair, of course. What the fuck do you want with me?"

Amelia replied, "I just need to know that I can rely on your help."

"My help, for what?"

Amelia took a large swig of her wine. "Look, I know I am just a stranger, but we are family Liv, and something doesn't feel right or fair to me. Can you tell me why Evie is swanning around with her own art gallery and is the sole owner of that cute cottage? And you're working here?"

She looked around the bar, her nose wrinkled in distaste.

"I'm guessing you don't own a house of your own?"

Liv replied tightly: "That's none of your fucking business. I don't know who you think you are or what your beef is with my sister, but you can fuck right off."

"Oh come on, Liv. Be smart. She's living the dream. I ask you, is that fair? Where is our share of good fortune – why does she get to have it all?"

Liv swallowed hard. She couldn't help the old feelings of resentment and rage against Evie welling up inside. And then there was Brodie. He was just a boy, but Liv had loved him and had to watch as he became besotted with Evie and barely registered her existence. She was deeply ashamed and overwhelmed with guilt after that fine young man had died on that terrible night.

"Look I just want a quiet life and no hassle. I don't know why the hell you think I would ever want to help you. I don't know you from a bar of soap and I don't know what game you are playing here."

Amelia looked at her levelly. "Oh, I think you do, Liv, and once you hear what I have to tell you, I guarantee you will be fully on board. What have you got to lose?"

Liv grunted. "The will to live for a start."

Liv was genuinely torn. This woman who looked so much like her sister had intrigued her and she wanted to hear more. But she had also worked so hard to get her act together and leave the past behind. Was it really worth raking it all up again? Eventually curiosity won.

She sighed, "Oh go on then. Say your piece. You are obviously desperate to tell me your little scheme. Then you can fuck off."

Amelia leaned in and revealed her plan.

Chapter Eighteen

Amelia's Story

1989–1996

Just before her 11th birthday, Amelia's father, James McLean, woke up in the middle of the night in the downstairs bedroom where he slept alone at their home in Seattle. He'd been suffering from dementia for several years but had grown increasingly more confused. He turned on the gas on the stove and went outside in his pyjamas.

In the morning, his wife, Eloise, had come down from her bedroom, switched on the kitchen light and caused a massive gas explosion. She died instantly. James was found dead by the side of the road later that same day. The coroner's verdict was hypothermia.

Young Amelia somehow escaped out of her bedroom window and scrabbled down the other side of the house into the backyard. She twisted her knee, broke her nose and suffered minor scratches and bruises. The police said it was a miracle she survived but now she found herself completely alone in the world.

An investigation discovered the only living relative of her parents was a distant cousin of her mother's called Ruth, who had moved to the UK when she was in her twenties. As the authorities on both sides of the Atlantic tried to track Ruth down, Amelia was placed in care.

The house was uninsured and, in the fog of his dementia, James had squandered his hard-earned savings on dodgy money-making schemes and had been a scammer's delight. There wasn't all that much left, and it was tied up in a tangle of red tape. Amidst his tattered possessions, most of which she'd thrown out, Amelia found two short letters. They were from a woman called Sheila, and they mentioned a daughter. James's daughter. She was called Cara. When she read them, she felt like she had been punched. So this is who he had been ranting about. This was his secret. That knowledge festered in her heart: she could do nothing with it yet, but it contributed to her feeling that nobody was to be trusted.

While living in the home, Amelia had to grow up fast. She learned about survival and never to trust anyone.

She also became something of an expert in lying. It started small and sneaky. She'd tell lies to get herself out of trouble or to make sure someone else took the blame. Lying became second nature and, at first, she was amazed how easy it was to get people to believe her; then it became her normal.

She knew how to lie to get attention, to weasel her way out of trouble and to end up with exactly what she wanted.

By the time her cousin Ruth had been tracked down living in a respectable terrace in Crawley, thirty miles south of London, Amelia, who had been thoroughly spoiled by her step-mother, was a deeply unpleasant young woman.

She had always been a strange child, but now at just thirteen, she was cold-blooded and flinty, motivated by money and hellbent on getting her own back on a world she believed was out to get her.

Ruth was married to Eric, a clerk in an insurance company, who was struggling with new technology and was painfully aware he would never be promoted. He had one of those faces you just don't quite remember, pale and slightly pudgy with washed-out light eyes and deep lines on his forehead and around his mouth. He had a soft belly and sunken chest and walked with an apologetic stoop.

Eric couldn't believe his luck when Ruth decided to marry him. She was thirty-four years old, small, thin, dark-haired and sharp-elbowed. She'd just been dumped by her married boss and had lost her job along with her lover. He'd found her sobbing into an Eccles cake at his favourite cafe and hesitantly asked if she was OK.

Bitter and full of resentment, she had felt soothed by gentle Eric's quiet demeanour and open admiration. He'd ended up buying her three cups of tea and a selection of baked goods and they'd bonded over her whining about her ex while he murmured sympathetically.

It didn't take Ruth long to realise Eric worshipped her blindly and would never cheat on her or leave her. He had some savings and a decent-enough job and Ruth believed she could whip him into shape and give him some much-needed backbone.

Eric was bedazzled, deeply in lust and convinced they could be happy together and cried tears of joy when she agreed to be his wife.

For the first few months, Ruth poured her energy into spending their savings on modern-but-uncomfortable furniture for their box-like two-bedroom house then painted everything magnolia. She set her heart on a peach bathroom suite and told Eric she wanted thick shag-pile carpets in every room.

He was aghast at the bills coming in but too scared to upset Ruth by telling her she would have to rein in her spending. After six months they were up to their necks in debt. Ruth was constantly telling her husband he was useless, weak and stupid. He meekly accepted all the insults she threw at him which made her even more furious.

"Why can't you stand up for yourself for once!" she would yell at him. In fact, she had seriously considering leaving him, when she got a call from child services in Seattle, Washington USA. Ruth's beady greedy eyes lit up when she discovered there was money in it if she were to become Amelia's guardian. Not nearly as much as there should have been but with child benefit and allowances, Ruth thought it would be well worth her while.

And so, Amelia arrived in the UK and found herself in the middle of a one-sided battle ground. It was a deeply unhappy marriage. Ruth constantly chipped away at Eric, belittling him with insults and the occasional slap which he meekly accepted.

After a few months, Amelia also felt the back of Ruth's hand and was clobbered on the legs and the backside more times than she wanted to remember. Her way to survive was to have as little to do with them as possible.

She put her shields up, shut out the rest of the world and spent most of her time studying in the library after school. At first, her talent for lying quickly made her popular. She spun stories about the exciting life she'd led in the States and the tragedy of both her parents dying.

The other pupils in her class thought she was impossibly glamorous with her American accent and claims to have met movie stars. She told them her parents had both been killed in a plane crash while on their way to visit friends in Hollywood and everyone gathered around her at break time enthralled.

Amelia loved the sympathy and the attention but she couldn't resist taking her flights of fantasy to absurd and easily disproved levels, and soon found herself being laughed at, a figure of ridicule.

At a sleepover she was caught going through the handbag of the mother of one of her new friends and although nothing was proved, she had acquired a bad reputation and was soon ignored and left alone.

Back at the cold, unwelcoming house, Ruth and Eric slept in separate rooms and Amelia made do with a pull-down sofa bed in the living room which she gradually took over and turned into a sort of one-roomed studio flat. No one ever came round to visit them, and Ruth or Eric stopped coming into 'Amelia's room'.

Ruth spent her time lying down in her hot stuffy bedroom, cocooned in blankets, watching TV and munching Gypsy creams, and Eric sat at the small formica table in the kitchenette reading his paper and skulking off to his small monk-like bedroom at a ridiculously early hour.

Amelia had no idea what he got up to in there and she didn't want to know. She was left to her own devices which suited her just fine. She landed herself a job as a waitress after school, was paid cash in hand and given a decent meal every night, which made a big difference, as Ruth existed on cakes and biscuits and Eric nibbled on sad sandwiches and sipped on packet soups.

Amelia didn't get many tips for her efficient-but-charmless service but the boss knew she was reliable and could be called on at short notice to do extra shifts.

She also began taking on work at a local nursing home. The money was terrible but it was rich pickings for her sticky fingers. The residents were taken in by 'such a nice young American girl' and she found it so easy to steal small sums of money and bits and pieces of jewellery. She made sure she picked on the loneliest and most confused.

She worked hard at school, passed her A-levels and applied to universities in Cardiff, Newcastle and Edinburgh. Accepted for them all, she opted for Scotland's capital as it was the furthest away. It had absolutely nothing to do with sentiment over her father's nationality; Amelia just wanted to sever all ties with her life in Crawley.

She coolly informed Ruth and Eric she was leaving and didn't need anything further from them. She saw university as another chance for reinvention. When she arrived in Edinburgh, she would choose exactly who she was going to be.

On her first day at registration, she saw a dark-haired, black-eyed boy across the hall and everything changed.

He was ridiculously handsome and Amelia felt as though an electric shock was running through her entire body. She was certain he was 'The One' and she had to get to him first before anyone else. Everyone knew cast-iron friendships and relationships were forged in those first fresher weeks, more by chance than anything else. People living in the same block of student flats, or doing the same course, or just meeting up in the pub.

Amelia just had to have this young man, despite the fact they hadn't even spoken to one another, and she didn't even know his name. She was sure he was the prize she deserved. Suddenly he glanced in her direction, and she gave him a beaming smile filled with adoration and longing, but he looked right through her as though she was made of air.

Amelia's heart was beating so fast she felt she couldn't breathe and, in a panic, found herself stumbling towards him and ended up falling flat on her face at his feet. She couldn't move for shame and embarrassment but then felt two strong arms lifting her up.

She looked into the darkest eyes she'd ever seen, and a soft Edinburgh accent asked her, "Are you OK? You took a right tumble. Here, let me help you up." She managed to whisper, "Thank you so much. I don't know what happened. I just felt faint."

He smiled at her. "I bet you haven't eaten anything today. Girls never eat enough. Why don't we get you a roll or a pie or something and some Irn Bru. That'll make you feel better."

She could only nod at him, and as she got to her feet, she deliberately stumbled against him so he would have to catch her and hold her again. "Let's sit down for a minute until you feel less wobbly. I'm Lachlan, by the way."

They sat down on a nearby bench. "I'm Amelia. Thanks for being so kind. I'm sorry to be a bother."

"Och, don't be daft. You are looking a wee bit better at least. I still think you should eat something though. It's my first day here as well, but I know where the canteen is. Fancy chasing a pie around the room? I don't imagine they are all that fresh."

Amelia laughed and goosebumps popped up on her goosebumps. He was perfect. "It's my first day too and I would love to chase a pie with you."

He chatted to her all the way to the cafe and told her he was studying architecture and had all sorts of plans and designs buzzing around in his head. She said she'd considered being an architect too but, in the end, opted for a degree in design. She said she wanted to bring order out of chaos.

He paid for them both, and told her he lived with his mum and dad in Musselburgh but wanted to get a flat with his friends as soon as possible. She replied that her parents were dead and she had been brought up by foster parents who didn't really care about her, and that she was all alone in the world.

Amelia knew exactly how to wring the pathos out of this latest version of her story. She gave him just the shocking bare details and would embellish it later. She could tell Lachlan felt sorry for her from the sad look in his eyes. She gave him a brave smile.

"I'm hoping to make some friends here in Edinburgh. Everyone says Scottish people are friendly and I really hope that's true. I've been a bit lonely to be honest."

"Well," said Lachlan, finishing up his pie. "You've met me already Amelia and I think I'm friendly." He grinned at her. "See you later. Take care of yourself."

Her stomach was full of hummingbirds. Lachlan walked out of the cafe and Amelia felt as though she could exhale properly for the first time since seeing him. She might have made a bit of a fool of herself, falling over like that, but it had been a masterstroke. They had bonded over pie, beans and chips, and she had to have him. He was hers.

She could also tell that he had money, was from a decent family and very popular. She'd seen him greeted by a big group of lads through the window of the cafe. Amelia imagined herself at the centre of a loving clan, adored and taken care of; finally living the life she was supposed to and she couldn't wait to start planning her next move.

Lachlan was a kind, open and sweet-natured boy who thought the best of everyone and was surprised and delighted to bump into Amelia again at a pub in the Grassmarket a week later, not realising she had been stalking him since they first met and this was no chance encounter.

She had compiled a detailed dossier on all of his movements and discovered he went to The Last Drop pub with a few other boys most nights around 7pm. She also found out he had joined the debating society and the rugby club and was thinking about taking up hillwalking.

She had no interest in any of these pastimes and considered them almost offensively boring, but she'd walk to the top of Ben Nevis barefoot if it meant she could spend time with Lachlan.

Amelia had to stop herself from turning up at the pub right away. She didn't want to appear too obvious, so she waited a couple of days, and made sure she was carrying a guidebook to climbing the Scottish Munros, hills over three thousand feet, all 282 of them.

Lachlan was at the crowded bar with his back to her, laughing at something his friend had said. She had a half pint of cider in her hand and deliberately backed into Lachlan spilling her drink all over her blouse and jeans.

He was full of apologies and then looked at her properly. "Amelia, right? Christ I'm sorry, I'm a clumsy idiot," he added. "Here, let me get you another drink."

"Not at all. It was my fault. I wasn't looking where I was going."

She looked up at him, "Oh, you are the guy who was so nice to me the other day. What's your name again?" (As if it wasn't carved into her heart.)

"It's Lachlan."

"Of course. I remember now." She looked around, "I was supposed to be meeting some new friends here but it's so busy I can't see them anywhere." She waved the guidebook. "We were meant to be talking about going hiking."

This was obviously a downright lie but Lachlan's eyes lit up. "I've been wanting to find a walking buddy, but you look like you're way ahead of me."

"Not really. I'm just aiming to bag all the Munros, maybe we could build up to grabbing a few together?"

He bought Amelia a cider and Babycham then another. They yelled into each other's ears over the babble of loud music and other people's raucous conversations. After a few more drinks, Lachlan walked her back to her halls of residence past the castle and up Lothian Road.

They talked easily. Amelia had done her homework and knew his interests. He was charmed that they liked the same music and movies and he felt protective of this poor orphaned girl who clearly needed looking after.

He kissed her on the cheek and said shyly, "Amelia. I'm not really looking to have a steady girlfriend but . . ." She interrupted him. She had decided it would be best to pay it cool at the start, so said, "I understand. You've just arrived here and you want to have some fun. I get that. Don't worry about it."

"No. I mean I was going to say I hadn't planned on meeting someone so soon, but I really like you, Amelia, and I want to get to know you better. Would you come out with me on Saturday? We could grab something to eat. Or just go for a walk." He paused and looked worried, "Or maybe you think it really is too soon?"

She smiled at him, putting on her most innocent-looking, sweet and naive expression. "I'd love to go out with you, Lachlan. Here's my number. Give me a call."

She ran up the stairs to her tiny room and danced around in glee. It was all falling into place. Soon they would be a couple and then she would have him all to herself. Amelia told herself she would have a completely different life from her father and step-mother and from the ghastly Eric and Ruth.

After a few weeks, Lachlan and Amelia became inseparable, and she managed to keep up her act of being the perfect girlfriend. In her mind, the only way to be completely sure of Lachlan was to give him what she believed every man wanted.

So she'd sit freezing and bored stiff at rugby games but cheer, smile and pretend to be having a great time. They'd go for long walks up Arthur's Seat and she'd prepare picnics that Lachlan would carry in his backpack complete with real glasses and a red-and-white check table cloth.

She helped him study and laughed at his friends' lame jokes. Lachlan was generous, Amelia quickly noted, picking up the tab for drinks and dinners, and when she was worried about affording a textbook, he bought her a brand-new copy.

She sometimes helped herself to money from Lachlan's wallet, especially after a drunken night out, when he'd groan and wonder how on earth he could have spent that much. But she knew that his family kept him generously provided for, so why shouldn't she have some of that cash.

She quickly realised Lachlan couldn't cope with unpleasantness of any kind, especially anyone being sad or upset. He was a people pleaser, so she only had to frown slightly or make tears come to her eyes, and he'd do whatever he could to avoid her crying.

Her chin would wobble if he said he was going out with the boys or couldn't make it to one of their dates, and he would end up cancelling and spending time with her instead. This made him more and more uncomfortable, and he was beginning to have niggling doubts about Amelia. He had caught disconcerting glimpses of the real person when her mask slipped.

There was the time she had ranted at a beggar in Princes Street for touching her hand when he asked her for spare change. He saw venom and hatred in her eyes and flinched. She had tried to make light of it saying the man had scared her, but, a few days later, he had caught her looking at one of his friends with bored disdain when he was talking excitedly about being picked for the rugby team.

Lachlan came to realise he knew very little about Amelia. She had no friends and no interest in meeting other people, whereas he wanted to enjoy the social side of university.

"You are more than enough for me, Lachlan. Why would I want to spend time with anyone else?" she would say. If he encouraged her to meet up with some of his pals' girlfriends she would look worried and ask if he was bored with her.

Then he would have to reassure her, and they would inevitably find themselves in bed together. By now they had slept together a few times and although Lachlan had enjoyed himself enormously as only a testosterone-fuelled 18-year-old boy can, he increasingly felt as though Amelia was acting out a part for him.

As she lay under or over him, writhing, panting and squealing, it felt as though she was waiting on the director of the movie in her head to shout 'cut'. He had to admit that the sex was good, although he didn't have much to compare it with. He just felt that having a girlfriend shouldn't be this difficult. It was exhausting.

He realised he was never completely at ease with her and they didn't laugh together at silly things. When he made a funny remark or attempted a joke she would look at him in complete bewilderment. It gradually dawned on him that they just weren't right for each other, and she was making him miserable.

They continued to see each other for the next few months but Lachlan was feeling increasingly trapped by Amelia. Things came to a head when she visited his family. She'd kept dropping hints about spending a weekend with them, but it was a big mistake.

Perhaps she was nervous or maybe she thought she didn't have to try too hard anymore, but for once Amelia forgot to keep up her perfect girlfriend act. Truth be told Amelia was becoming bored with the part she'd been playing and Lachlan wasn't living up to her expectations.

She offended his strictly religious parents by laughing at them saying grace, didn't eat her food, talked over his younger sister and was generally deeply unpleasant.

After they'd left, his mother called him. An expensive necklace that had belonged to his grandmother was missing. She didn't want to point fingers but wondered if it had anything to do with Amelia.

When Lachlan tentatively mentioned if maybe Amelia had taken it by mistake, she flew into a blind rage, accusing Lachlan's mother of trying to turn him against her, swearing blind that she had nothing to do with it.

He tried to calm her down, but she was hysterical, pummelling his chest with her fists and swearing and crying. Lachlan knew he had to put this relationship out of its misery and from that moment on he avoided her completely.

She left increasingly manic messages on his answerphone and even came round to his flat banging on the door demanding to be let in. The days turned into weeks and Lachlan stayed away from classes as she kept following him there. He told his lecturers he was ill and worked hard at home, trying to lose himself in his studies.

Lachlan was too embarrassed to complain about her, believing he would be laughed at for being scared of a wee bit of a lass. So he swerved his usual haunts and mostly stayed in by himself while his flatmates enjoyed Edinburgh's nightlife. When Amelia battered and kicked his door, screaming like a banshee, he hid in his room and refused to answer or got one of the other boys to say he was out.

Another couple of months went by, and the threatening texts and messages dwindled to a few a day instead of more than a dozen every hour. Amelia had finally stopped coming round and creating a scene and Lachlan thought he was in the clear, especially when he saw her draped on the arm of another boy.

He wanted to go over and tell the poor sucker to run for the hills as fast as his legs would carry him, but he couldn't risk Amelia's wrath. He was just glad to have escaped but there was one last sting from her.

She messaged him, saying she was pregnant and needed money for an abortion, demanding £1,000 or she would tell his parents. He was so afraid of the trouble she would cause and how upset his mum and dad would be that he cashed in savings from his godmother and sent her the money.

Amelia pocketed the grand and wished she'd asked for more. What she really wanted was for Lachlan to come crawling back to her so she could have the satisfaction of telling him to go and fuck himself.

In the flick of a switch, Amelia's all-consuming infatuation with Lachlan had turned to disdain. She told herself it didn't matter. There were always other victims and she had made a fair bit of easy cash from selling the necklace that Lachlan's mother had loved so much.

And that was the beginning of her downward spiral.

Chapter Nineteen

Evie's Gallery

Evie was on her way to the gallery with four small seascapes in the back of Florence. If she was honest, Evie could turn out these sorts of paintings in her sleep and they didn't give her much sense of satisfaction anymore, but the tourists loved them and they were vital for the gallery's profits. By spending a couple of weeks working on paintings that were more commercial and quickly snapped up, she could indulge herself with bigger and more complicated works that came from the depths of her soul. These days her work had taken a brighter and more positive turn, using oranges and yellows and reflecting her sense of belonging and happiness, but she had to admit that some of her best art evoked the pain of the past as she worked through her feelings of sadness and loss.

Although striking and thought-provoking, these larger paintings were a bit too intense for most people who came into the gallery just looking for a pretty souvenir. The place was quiet and one of the local art students, Una, making herself a bit of extra money, was busy dismantling some of Freya's more ambitious displays and dusting the shelves full of hand-carved wooden puffins and kittiwakes.

Stepping into the gallery and seeing her works displayed on the bright white walls always gave Evie a surge of joy. She noticed a man with his back to her at the very far corner of the room. Her heartbeat rose, and she felt herself blush.

It was Ross Isbister, the craftsman who had repaired her great grandmother's old Orkney chair, and had once clumsily asked her out. He was gazing intently at one of her massive blue-black ocean scenes. She approached him quietly. "Hello, Ross. Well, what do you think?"

He looked startled at the sight of her and had to tear himself away from being engrossed in the painting. He blinked, "It's really good, Evie. I can't stop looking at it."

She could feel that sizzle between them again. They could barely make eye contact with one another. He mumbled, "I'm not really into art. Mum has her old prints of Orkney scenes in the living room, but this is something else altogether, Evie. I'm not clever enough to figure out what it means, but it unsettled me when I first saw it and I come back in for a look whenever I can."

Evie felt her heart leap at his words. She loved that he felt connected to her paintings, and felt a rush of affection towards this quiet, thoughtful man.

She gazed fondly at him. "You don't have to be clever to appreciate a painting, Ross. If it speaks to you then that's enough. This one is supposed to make you a bit uncomfortable. I'm glad you've picked up on that."

He smiled shyly back at her. It was a grin that would have had most women, and a fair few men, melting to the floor.

Evie often thought Ross must surely have had an ancestor from the doomed Spanish Armada that tried to invade Elizabethan England back in 1588. Some of the surviving ships limped up the coast all the way to the Hebrides and even as far as Orkney. Maybe one of the stranded Spaniards fell in love with an Orcadian lass and hundreds of years later here was the result; Ross Isbister, with his perfect olive skin, jet-black hair and dark chocolate-brown eyes.

He was considered to be one of the most eligible bachelors in all of Orkney, but was cripplingly shy, and had no idea how to talk to women, so either simply ignored them or ran away. That was until Evie came back to Orkney and he repaired her chair. He had tentatively asked her out that once, but they somehow couldn't make it work, and because he feared a rebuff he hadn't asked her again.

For her part, Evie had given her heart to her first love, Brodie, when she was very young, and had it broken into a thousand pieces when he had died. Then she endured an abusive relationship with her hideous ex, a twisted blowhard who had mentally abused her, eroding her confidence and making her deeply unhappy. She stayed with him because she felt she didn't deserve to be treated with love and kindness.

Evie wished she could let her guard down with Ross, and ask him to go for that drink, but she was too badly burned by the past. She felt it would be safer and easier just to keep him as a friend, even if standing so close to him did make her feel as though her innards were melting.

To cover up her confusion, she said in a warm-but-businesslike fashion, "Come round and see it anytime. Or you could always buy it and hang it up in your workshop," she added cheekily.

"I'm tempted, Evie. But I'll tell you what, your work belongs where everyone can see it. It should be in a permanent exhibition or in a museum. No one person should be able to shut this away inside their house."

Evie felt tears well up. It was one of the loveliest things anyone had ever said to her. But she just cleared her throat and muttered, "Och, I don't know about that." She smiled at him, a silence grew between them and Ross knew it was now or never. He cleared his throat.

"Evie, I w-was wondering . . ."

He was cut off by a woman's harsh screech of excitement. Amelia came hurtling towards them, her arms outstretched.

"There you are, Evie! I hoped to find you here. I know I already messaged you, but I wanted to say thanks in person, and of course you must tell Kate how much I am looking forward to tonight to come and meet your friends." She looked at Ross and raised an eyebrow.

Evie stepped back from him. "Sorry, Amelia. Where are my manners? This is Ross Isbister."

"The 'chair man' of course. That makes you sound like you're in charge here."

She gave a high-pitched giggle. "What a pleasure to meet you, Ross. Evie has told me all about you." Ross's face turned crimson. He sputtered something about being behind with his orders and ran out the door like a man with his trousers on fire.

Amelia turned to Evie. "Was it something I said?"

"No. He's just a bit shy with strangers that's all, especially women."

"Well, I wouldn't mind getting better acquainted. He is quite the hottie. Unless that would be treading on your toes, Evie," she added hastily.

"Not at all. We're just friends."

She forced herself to add, "To be honest with you, Amelia, I have absolutely no interest whatsoever in any man right now."

"That sounds to me like someone who has had their fingers and their toes burnt," Amelia replied.

Evie said firmly, "Well, that's a story for another day." Amelia looked disappointed and Evie realised she had probably wanted to bond over one of those 'All men are bastards' conversations, but that was a road she didn't want to go down, certainly not in front of someone she barely knew, even if they did happen to be related.

Instead, she said, "How about I show you round the gallery? We obviously sell my paintings here and Freya's jewellery, of course. My friend Maureen, who you'll meet tonight, makes gorgeous shawls, hats and blankets. We've also got pottery and crafts from talented people over the islands. We like to encourage and give them a chance to sell their work. You know," she added shyly, "we were even featured in a magazine."

Amelia smiled at Evie. There was something unsettling about her tight grin that didn't reach her eyes. She glanced round. "Wow. Imagine a little place like this getting all that attention!"

Evie frowned slightly. She didn't want to be over sensitive but that sounded like a patronising dig.

"Look, I'd love to see everything, but another time perhaps," Amelia said shortly. "It all looks marvellous, and you must be so proud. Anyway, I really must run. See you tonight then."

Evie was deflated. She was incredibly proud of the gallery and crushed that Amelia didn't seem at all interested in seeing what she had achieved. She'd thought they were making progress, but it was one step forward and two steps back.

Then Evie had a thought: "She's probably gone to chase after Ross. That poor bugger won't stand a chance if she catches up with him."

She was surprised how annoyed that made her feel.

Evie might tell herself she didn't want a relationship, even with someone as kind, gentle and handsome as Ross, but she realised she definitely didn't want anyone else to have him either, and certainly not Amelia.

Chapter Twenty

Kate's House

Evie and Freya had come over to Kate's about an hour before anyone else to help with the preparations for Amelia's night. Freya had brought fat golden homemade samosas; from a recipe she'd seen on James Martin's Saturday morning TV show. Freya was obsessed with James and recorded his show to watch when she came back from her morning swim with the Selkies and after the free art classes she gave at her house for local bairns. People knew not to disturb her on a late Saturday afternoon.

Freya told Kate, "I might have made these a bit spicy, but James said not to go easy on the chilli and anyway I do like them hot."

Kate looked up at her and laughed, "We all know you are talking about James and not the samosas."

Patsy had bought cheeses from the deli and their peedie pies. There was crusty bread, plates of ham and jars of chutney. No one would starve. They helped Kate put the food on the big table in the living room.

Edwyn came in with two bags full of beer and wine, looking tired from his shift at the hospital but pleased to see his friends. He kissed Kate on the cheek while she was at the sink, and she waved him off.

Without looking round, she told him to put the samosa he had snaffled back on the plate.

"Edwyn," she said sternly. "You know those are for guests."

As usual Edwyn was baffled. "How do you do that? You must have eyes in the back of your head. It's a medical miracle."

Kate just laughed at him. "Go and wash the stink of antiseptic off yourself. You reek of the hospital. The girls are upstairs doing their homework. Give them a cuddle and make sure they aren't on that bloody iPad. I told you not to get them one for Christmas. You are such a pushover."

"Your wish is my command. She who must be obeyed," said Edwyn, running up the stairs in case she flicked her dishcloth at him. Her aim was uncanny, and he had no desire to have his backside stung again.

Maureen arrived soon after with Andrzej. She'd put on some make-up, slightly overdoing it with the rouge, not wanting to look too pale. As always Andrzej thought she looked beautiful and beamed with pride to be at her side.

To everyone's dismay she was clutching a Tupperware full of shortbread. This was bad news as Maureen was without doubt the worst baker on the island. As Patsy had succinctly put it once: "Her rock cakes could be used as bricks to build a coo byre and her tablet would leave you toothless."

Andrzej was quick to squash any misunderstanding. "Don't worry, young Rory made these for you all. He's turning into a really good baker."

"Obviously, he doesn't take after me," laughed Maureen. She had lost count of the times she wailed at Andrzej when another disaster came out of the oven. "I don't know what happens. I follow the recipe to the letter but nothing turns out the way it should."

These days she was happy to leave the cooking and baking to her boy. He was a quiet lad who adored his mother and hero-worshipped Andrzej. And it was a relief for Maureen to save her energy for the things she loved to do with both of them, and not to fret about cooking meals and baking cakes.

Maureen handed her coat to her husband, slowly took off her hat and sat down in one of Kate's comfy armchairs.

"Oh Maureen, you've had your hair done. I love the curls," said Freya.

"Well, it's nothing like my old hairstyle. It's a bit wiry, don't you think," she said worriedly.

"Patsy said I look a bit like Brian and Peter when she saw me yesterday." Kate burst out laughing.

Patsy just grinned. She adored Brian and Peter, two giant hairy Hungarian pigs who were as happy as clams rolling about in their field by the road out of Kirkwall Airport.

Tourists stopped to have their photos taken with them and there was a little 'Pig Sty' honesty shop where you could buy fridge magnets and tiny Brian and Peter piggie souvenirs.

"The cheek of her," said Andrzej. "You are a whole lot bonnier than the piggies, my love." Andrzej always stopped to give Brian and Peter an apple when he drove past and have a quick chat with them in Polish. He would tell them seriously: "I know you can't understand a word, you being Hungarian and all, but it's kind of you both to indulge me."

He looked at his beloved Maureen. "I like your hair even better this way. You look so sophisticated, like Helen Mirren."

"Oh Andrzej, you are daft," said Maureen, but she looked so pleased and happy that everyone felt the glow of their joy. Seeing them so contented made Evie think again about Ross. She kept on telling herself she didn't want a man in her life, so why did she keep on thinking about him?

She also couldn't believe how nervous she was waiting for Amelia to arrive. They all jumped as the door burst open, but instead of Amelia, it was Sophia looking windswept and dishevelled. Evie flung her arms around her friend.

"Come away in!" She noticed Sophia's eyes were red and raw, and her mascara had run down her cheeks. Her friend had been crying, which was completely out of character. Sophia was one of life's optimists, with her glass overflowing.

Evie whispered, "Are you OK?"

"I could use a drink," said Sophia, looking round at the room as her friends greeted her with smiles, delighted to have her back with them. Evie passed her a large glass of red wine.

Sophia knocked back half a glass in one large glug, all before announcing: "I've had another fight with that arsehole Finn. He's doing my head in. I decided to leave his flat before he could drag me into bed. He's not using sex to get round me like that again."

Sophia wiped her mouth with the back of her hand, exhaled loudly and then looked alarmed. "Oh Christ, the girls aren't down here are they?"

Kate rolled her eyes. "No, you are fine. They are upstairs, which is just as well, Sophia. You are as bad as Patsy."

"That's not fair, I always watch what I say around the girls," said Patsy indignantly.

"So that's why Louise called Claire a bugger after you came round to put shelves up for their books then is it?" said Kate darkly. "I hit my thumb with the hammer because the girls were making me laugh. I don't remember saying that exact word," mumbled Patsy.

Sophia had already refilled her glass. She sighed, "He's going to be the death of me. You see the thing is I can't live with him . . ."

"But you can't live without him" they all chorused together, before dissolving in giggles. Sophia looked round at the room and smiled. Her shoulders relaxed. It was good to be back amongst her friends on Orkney.

Her voice was calmer as she went on. "Exactly. It's just the same arguments over and over again." She took another big gulp of wine.

"He won't move south, and as much as I love it here, I can't just quit my job and spend my time looking at seagulls. And I do know there's actually no such bird. I got a lecture on that from Finn. He says people are lazy to call them seagulls and that there are loads of different species of gulls and they have specific names."

She looked at Evie in despair. "That's what my life has become. Arguing with Finn about effing sea birds."

But before Evie could reply, there was the sound of a taxi pulling up and then a knock on the door. "That has to be Amelia now," said Evie. "Anyone else would have just walked in. She mustn't know doors here are always open."

Sophia added, "It took me a while to get my head around it. It's so different from back home."

"Come away in," yelled Kate. When no one came through the door, Kate shrugged her shoulders and got up to answer it.

Amelia stood there with two enormous bags full of toys for the girls and half a dozen bottles of wine. "You must be Kate?" she said tentatively.

"Jeez, you've brought the whole shop with you," said Kate. "Here, let me help you with that. You didn't have to bring all this you know."

With all the skills gained as a mother of two, Kate expertly took the bags in one hand and put the booze under her arm.

"I couldn't visit empty-handed," said Amelia with a hesitant smile.

Kate looked at her properly and even though Evie had told her the two of them looked alike she was shocked by the resemblance. Amelia was smaller and thinner and her hair was jet black, but they could have been separated at birth.

"It's lovely to see you, Amelia. Come and meet everyone," said Kate. Amelia found herself welcomed into the circle of friends. Andrzej gave her a hug and three kisses on the cheek. Sophia told her she loved her shoes. Maureen said how lovely she looked and Edwyn almost spat out his fourth sausage roll at the sight of her. "It's uncanny."

"I know. We could be twins," said Evie and Amelia together. They looked at each other and laughed nervously.

Evie watched as Amelia talked to her friends. Even the hard-to-please Patsy was charmed by her bright-eyed enthusiasm and interest in their Orkney home.

Evie remembered how keen and interested Amelia had been when she'd talked to her and Freya about their lives. Yet something about how quickly she'd left the gallery the other day still rankled. Amelia could switch her enthusiasm on and off like a cheap lamp.

Evie could see Andrzej was beside himself at having someone who wanted to know all about Orkney's rich history. Amelia looked up at him with seemingly rapt attention, "I've been reading a bit about Orkney, and it is so fascinating, especially the stuff about the wars. It would be so good to talk to someone who really knows their stuff."

Andrzej almost spontaneously combusted in delight. He may have only been living in Orkney for a decade but he was fiercely proud of his adopted islands, and considered himself as much Orcadian as Polish.

He had met and married the love of his life and his construction business was thriving. He was one of the most contented people Evie had ever met, always finding hope and light, even when his Maureen was diagnosed with breast cancer.

Andrzej was just about to launch into a detailed rendering of one of his favourite stories of how Lord Kitchener, famous for pointing his finger in the World War One *Your Country Needs You* recruitment poster, was drowned off the northern coast of Orkney in 1916 when a German mine sank his ship, when Maureen gently interrupted and said, "Amelia. My Andrzej can, and indeed given half a chance he most certainly will, chunter on about this for hours. So, I think a good idea would be for you and him to spend some time, just the two of you, going for a long drive to see all the sights and hear all the stories. But only if you want to."

"I'd love to," said Amelia. "I really do want to know everything." Andrzej beamed.

"Amelia, it would be my honour to show you round and I promise not to bore you to tears because I do not want to face the wrath of my dear Maureen."

Andrzej had never actually faced Maureen's wrath, nor was he ever likely to. Partly because she was incredibly easy-going, but also because this kindest of men would never do anything to upset or hurt her. Their love for each other had grown even stronger after their wedding. Living through Maureen's cancer treatments had forged a link between them of unbreakable steel. They tried to squeeze every last drop of joy from every single day.

Maureen found herself delighted with Amelia. Andrzej loved to share his knowledge and she was soaking it up like a sponge and asking all kinds of questions. She'd given him her number and made him promise to set up a date as soon as he was free to meet up, so she could see all of the wonderful sights Orkney had to offer.

After they had all stuffed themselves with food, Amelia helped Kate clear the table and followed her into the kitchen, exclaiming, "Oh Kate, you have an Orkney chair just like the one Evie has in her kitchen."

"It's not quite the same" Kate replied. "Ross Isbister repaired Evie's chair and he is in a class of his own, but this one has been in our family for years. Edwyn's great aunty gave it to him when he was a peedie boy."

Amelia was in raptures. "I'd love to get one just like this and ship it home. It would be a proper connection with Orkney."

She went on excitedly, "Maybe Ross could make me a chair. I met him at Evie's gallery, you know. She told me he's single. I can't believe such a handsome man hasn't been snapped up years ago."

"He's single alright," said Kate. "He runs away from women so fast no one has been able to catch him. I was sure he had a thing for Evie, but she says they are just friends. It's a shame. I think they would be good for one another."

"Oh, Evie's so lovely, and they would be a sweet couple. I'm just surprised she hasn't met someone here. I'm sure she would have had plenty of offers."

"I don't think she's ready for all that. Evie had a very bad experience, which I am sure she will talk to you about in her own time. It's not my story to tell, but it has definitely put her off men for the time being, anyway."

Amelia nodded. "She did mention something about that. Maybe when we all get to know each other better?"

The two women went back into the living room. There was a kerfuffle outside and the sound of a baby crying. Jack burst into the room with Hari in a car seat bawling his lungs out, followed by Delima holding Ola's hand.

"I'm sorry we are so unforgivably late," said Jack, "but trying to get out of the house with these two is a nightmare."

"Actually," said Delima calmly. "Ola and Hari are no trouble at all. It was Jack who made us late."

She took off Ola's pink coat and deftly lifted Hari up into her arms where he instantly stopped crying and just hiccupped gently. "We were all organised and heading out the door when Jack decided we had to turn back for Hari's toy penguin, and then he couldn't find it."

Kate smiled. "I hear you. My Louise had a disgusting rubber giraffe she chewed to bits but she just wouldn't go to sleep without it. We ended up buying about half a dozen and locking them in a drawer and replacing them when they got too revolting. Edwyn used to chew their ears off so she wouldn't get suspicious."

"The thing is," said Delima, "Hari isn't all that bothered about the toy, but Jack just wants him to like penguins."

"Well, they are adorable," said Jack defensively. Delima patted him on the arm. "They certainly are, my love."

You would never guess this calm, serene woman was the mum of a toddler and a demanding new baby, with the added responsibility of the ongoing refurbishment of their old house, as well as running the animal sanctuary. On top of that, she had to manage her husband. She often said she had three children and Jack was the most demanding of them all.

She was wearing beige sweatpants and a simple cream T-shirt and managed to make this ensemble look effortlessly elegant. She didn't have a scrap of make-up on, but her skin was flawless and her hair bright and shiny, and she hadn't an ounce of baby fat.

Kate and Maureen looked at her with affection and awe, remembering how they both felt as though they had been run over by a tractor when their babies were as tiny as Hari.

Jack on the other hand had bags under his eyes that could have housed all the luggage for a Joan Collins trip to the South of France. Even his hair looked stressed, and he wore the frazzled expression of a man with sleep deprivation.

Delima said soothingly: "Hari's fine now. Nothing to worry about. He just cried because the car stopped suddenly, and he was woken up from a delicious sleep."

Jack looked at his son lying contently like a fat cherub in his mother's arms and was instantly reduced to a pile of mush. "Sorry for fussing, everyone," he said.

"Don't be daft, Jack," said Freya. "Come and meet Amelia. She will be wanting a hold of that peedie one, but not until I've had my turn."

Delima gave Hari to Freya. He made a tiny bat squeak and happily settled into her arms.

She turned to Amelia. "Gosh, you are Evie's double right enough. How are you settling in?"

"Well, everyone has been so kind to me and so welcoming. It's all been a bit of a whirlwind, and I've a lot to take in, but I am so glad that I came over, even though it is so different to what I'm used to."

"It was the same for me," said Delima. "I came here to live when I met Jack in Singapore and we got married. We run an animal sanctuary by the shore over the barriers near Hoxa. Evie mentioned you would like to come and see us."

Amelia smiled. "That sounds amazing. I would love to."

"Jack has always wanted to work with animals and wanted to settle back home in Orkney, but he ended up in the Far East in merchant banking, which is just as well, or we might never have met. Life is strange like that. Anyway, tell us all about yourself. Where exactly is home and what do you do for work?"

Evie's ears pricked up, wanting to see how Amelia would respond to the kind of direct questions she'd been dying to ask. Amelia looked slightly uncomfortable but said, "I'm sort of between jobs at the moment, which is why I have the chance to be over here now and to find out more about my family."

Delima was about to ask more when Kate came in with a huge plate of food for Jack. Evie silently cursed the timing.

"There's plenty left so fill your boots. Delima, what can I get you?"

"Ooh, the same for me, thanks. That all looks delicious."

No one could understand how Delima managed to eat like a sumo wrestler and not gain an ounce.

Kate returned with another giant plate and Delima and Jack chomped happily while Freya sang old nursery rhymes to Hari. Evie hoped Delima would continue to ask Amelia questions, but the moment seemed to have passed.

Amelia chimed in, changing the subject, "I was in Freya and Evie's gallery today," she said. "It's such an amazing space and the paintings and works of art are to die for."

She went on, "Freya, your jewellery is just wonderful and Maureen, those throws and blankets should be sold in Saks Fifth Avenue in New York."

Freya and Maureen weren't good at receiving such sugary compliments, but they thanked Amelia, who now turned to Evie.

"I couldn't help noticing that Kate has an Orkney chair like yours. I would so love to own one. Do you think your Ross Isbister would make me a chair, Evie?"

Evie couldn't help being irritated. "Well, he's not *my* Ross, Amelia. I told you we are just pals, but he is the best on the island."

Jack agreed and through a mouthful of homemade ham-and-egg pie mumbled: "He is your man for sure, but he's really busy, Amelia, so you might have to wait a while, but you can order it shipped back to your home."

Delima said, "He sends his chairs all over the world so it would be no problem for him to ship it to the States, or wherever it is you stay. Where was it again?"

Amelia chose to ignore her probing. "Oh I'm not in any hurry at all. Actually, I don't need to go home for another month or two."

Evie's heart sank. Another month or two? That wasn't what Amelia said in her email.

She thought this was more of a flying visit. Looking round the room at her friends, she was obviously the only one unhappy at the news.

Freya beamed, and with her usual spirit of generosity said, "Well, if you are staying here that long you can't possibly bide in a hotel. I've got a spare room. You can stay with me." Then she added, "Of course you can come and go as you please and treat the place like your own."

"Oh Freya," said Amelia. "That's way too kind of you. I don't want to be a burden."

"Don't be daft. I'll enjoy the company and as long as you don't mind my grumpy cat then the offer is there."

"I don't know what to say," said Amelia blushing with pleasure.

Evie was dismayed. She loved popping in to see Freya, it was like her second home but it wouldn't be the same with Amelia there.

Freya clapped her hands. "That's settled then. Pack up your things tomorrow morning and Evie can come and collect you and bring you to me."

She added, "I'm going to hand this wee man back to his daddy to change his bum and when he comes back all clean and sweet smelling you can have a hold of him, Amelia."

Evie, who adored Hari, had just been about to ask for a cuddle, but she kept quiet. Should she be feeling a bit guilty for not offering her own spare room to Amelia? The thought of having this strange woman in her house would have been like a dark cloud hanging over the place. She thought, 'She really is bringing out the worst in me, but just look at her, turning on the charm for everyone and they are all falling for it. Even Freya. Is it just me?' She shook her head and tried to smile and join in the conversation.

Kate and Sophia made pots of tea and coffee, and everyone chatted until Andrzej said it was past his bedtime and he'd need to steal Maureen away so he could go home. He had been watching his wife like a hawk and could see that she was drooping from tiredness.

Andrzej could have continued drinking and talking into the wee small hours, but he rationed himself to a couple of zero-alcohol cans of Guinness (which he deemed the least worst of all the booze-free drinks) and feigned being tired so as not to let Maureen think of herself as spoiling his fun. Of course, everyone saw through him, including Maureen, but that didn't matter.

Soon after they left, a sleepy Ola and baby Hari were strapped into their car seats and Delima drove her big man child and her tiny children home. Jack had only had one beer and a nip of whisky but was gently snoring before she had even pulled out of Kate's road.

Sophia asked Evie if she could stay at her cottage tonight. She was in no mood to go back to Finn's, especially after five large glasses of Rioja. It would just end up in another argument.

Evie was so relieved. Having Sophia over was the perfect excuse for not asking Amelia to stay, and she also needed some time alone with her friend. "Sure thing. Let me call a cab for us both. You know I always have a spare toothbrush and a nightie."

Back at Evie's cottage, the two women sat on the sofa with a large whisky in their hands. Sophia had become tearful in the taxi, and now that they were safely back, the floodgates had opened. Sophia wept as she poured her heart out to her best friend.

"I feel as though I am stuck in *Groundhog Day*. We have the same argument over and over again. I love him, Evie. I've never felt this way about anyone, and I know he loves me too, but I don't want to live like this, snatching a few days together a couple of times a month."

She went on, "I want the kind of relationship my parents have. I want to say goodnight to him, and to wake up with him. I want to share all the silly little things like running out of bog roll or fancying a night in with a takeaway watching *Better Call Saul* all over again. I can't keep doing all the running. He needs to meet me halfway. It's just not working."

Evie gave her a hug. "I'm so sorry, Sophia. I wish I had the answer. You know how happy I would be if you moved up here, but I don't want you to have regrets and be miserable. It has to be the right decision for both of you, not just for him."

Sophia wiped her eyes with a soggy tissue.

"I've gone over and over it in my head, but if he won't even come to London for a visit and isn't willing to make any compromises then how can he say he really loves me? I know his work is important, but I thought I was too."

Evie sighed impatiently. "I know but you can't be the one making all the sacrifices. Of course you both adore each other, and the sex is spectacular as you have told me on many occasions."

"The sex really is utterly glorious," said Sophia. "But is that enough? Is Finn really and truly in love with me or is it just pure lust?"

Sophia blew her nose, gave a watery smile and told Evie that they'd done nothing but talk about her own troubles and it was Evie's turn now.

It was a sign of their strong friendship. Sophia was never just on transmit, she wanted to receive Evie's news, and had noticed how unsettled she seemed by Amelia.

"Take my mind off Finn and tell me all about this long-lost relative from the US. What she's like and how are you coping with it all?"

"Oh, I'm fine," said Evie lightly, but Sophia knew her too well to let her get away with that.

"Come on now. Amelia seems to have gotten under your skin. I saw the way you looked at her tonight."

Evie hesitated. She wasn't proud of the twinge of jealousy she felt when Amelia was cuddling a contented Hari and when Freya had asked Amelia to stay with her, but she simply couldn't help it. She loved popping in to see Freya for a chat or a coffee and update her on the gallery. It was her sanctuary and now she'd have to share it with a woman she barely knew, and it made her feel resentful.

"I don't know," Evie admitted. "I don't know much about her. I've tried to ask her about her life and her background and about her father, but she just brushes every question aside or changes the subject."

"Mm," said Sophia. "She was certainly friendly enough tonight, though."

"She was. I'll give you that, but she didn't give away a thing about herself," said Evie. "It makes me think she has a secret to hide. Am I just being daft?"

But as she glanced back at Sophia, she saw how exhausted her friend looked after her long journey north and her arguments with Finn.

"Time to get you to bed, Sophia. You look done in and you need a good sleep. Things will look better in the morning."

After tucking her friend up in the spare bedroom with a hot-water bottle in her comfy bed, even though it was the middle of spring, she vowed to do something to help Sophia. She couldn't help trying to fix things. After all, if she hadn't told Andrzej that Maureen adored him, the two of them might never have admitted their love for each other and had that wonderful wedding and such a happy life together.

Evie had told Freya not to interfere, but maybe that was a mistake. They could both try and help Sophia and Finn find some way to stay together.

Chapter Twenty-One

Liv's Flat

Liv was spending most of her waking hours thinking about the offer Amelia had made. She'd actually run into her sister at the bookshop in Orkney, a rare occasion as Liv rarely went shopping in the High Street.

Liv was buying a copy of *The Orcadian* and a notebook to record her thoughts. Rab from her AA meetings had told her it was a lifesaver. He wrote in his journal every day and said it kept him sane.

Evie looked effortlessly elegant in a mustard-coloured checked shawl over a caramel jumpsuit. She'd just had her hair done and was laughing at something the shop owner had said. She looked classy, happy and golden. Liv was pea green with envy.

She tried to make a quick getaway, but Evie had spotted her and called her name, asked how she was doing with a big smile and approached her for a hug. Liv mumbled that she was fine and went as stiff as a board as her sister awkwardly embraced her.

Evie always made her feel grubby. She realised her fingernails were chewed down to the quick and she had a hole in her black tights.

"Come by and see me anytime, Liv. You know you are always welcome, and Freya would love to see you. And I'd really like to show you around the gallery and tell you all about how it's doing."

Part of Liv ached to accept the invitation, but she hardened her heart. Evie had inherited the family house under her father's will and turned it into a beautiful home complete with her own art studio and Liv still felt cheated.

She was the eldest. The house should have been hers or at least she should have been given a half share. And she still hated the fact she owed Evie money for that stint in rehab. There it was again. The feeling of being cheated of her father's love and all because of Evie. The feeling of not being good enough.

She turned on her heel and almost ran out of the shop in her eagerness to get away from her kind-hearted and infuriatingly decent sister.

In the days and weeks after she returned from rehab, Liv had often thought about visiting Evie and trying to make amends, but something always stopped her. She could hear the voice of her calm, reasonable therapist saying that one of the ways to recovery was to apologise to those you had hurt or wounded and make peace with them whenever possible.

Liv knew her behaviour towards her young sister was unfair, right from the moment her parents brought her home from the hospital. Liv had loathed her, and the more Evie trotted after her on her tiny little toddler legs and held up her plump arms for a cuddle, the more Liv shoved her away.

Evie was the golden child, adored by her father and Liv felt rejected and neglected by him. She had come to realise that her damaged mother could never truly love anyone, and she used Liv as a weapon to beat her husband, always making excuses for Liv's bad behaviour and then giving her money to try and buy her affection.

Growing up, she pretended she didn't care that Duncan was so besotted with Evie, who he called his Teenie, but it broke Liv's heart and made her hard as nails, at least on the outside.

He had called Liv a monster, so she had vowed to behave like one, but inside her heart was breaking.

Liv knew she owed so much to Evie and her friends who had tried to help her, but just couldn't bring herself to say sorry to her sister. There was too much bitterness and resentment. She flatly rejected Evie's kind offer to come with her to rehab to help her settle in, and to support her at the AA meetings.

Liv curtly told her that she'd rather do it on her own but had at least managed to mumble her thanks, and when she had come back, had taken the trouble to travel to Inganess beach to watch her sister and all the Selkies swimming in the sea from afar.

She had been tempted to walk down to the shore and speak to Evie, but she'd experienced a flashback to the trauma of Brodie's drowning and instead waved solemnly from the top of the hill, turned away and walked home alone.

Since then, she had made a point of avoiding Evie, not all that easy in a small place, but they moved in very different circles and Liv made sure their paths never crossed.

Sometimes she would see Freya bustling up and down the high street, greeting everyone with a cheery wave and taking hours to get from one end of the town to the other because she kept stopping to admire babies, ask after mutual friends or just exchange some gossip and a cheery chat.

Liv had shut herself out from that world and her life was low key. There was work, her AA meetings and then time at home on her own. She thought she was doing fine until Amelia dumped a big massive turd of a dilemma in her lap and brought back all those feelings of jealousy and being second best.

Liv knew she was at a crossroads and couldn't decide which path to take. On the one hand she was getting her life back together, and holding down a steady, albeit poorly paid, job.

But then, despite everything that had happened and how her sister had come to her rescue, there was her ingrained resentment of Evie and this was a chance to get her own back.

She was well aware that Evie had not only helped her to get into rehab but also to rent this flat. On top of that, her sister had stuck by her promise not to tell anyone what had really happened the night Brodie had died, but if Liv was honest, she hated feeling beholden to her.

Liv knew if she agreed to help Amelia – this strange malevolent woman who looked so much like her sister – it could lead to disaster not just for Evie but also for herself. Right now, Liv was clean. She had no desire to drink or take drugs, but if this plan backfired there was a chance she would relapse and sink once more into that black hole of despair and her life would spiral out of control again.

Amelia was very persuasive, and Liv was all too aware she was being played like a violin; but there was this persistent little voice inside her head that would not quieten down and kept telling her that this new life she was leading was dull and boring and a bit of excitement and getting her own back wouldn't necessarily be such a bad thing.

There was a lot to weigh up and time was running out. Amelia wouldn't wait for an answer much longer. Liv sat outside her flat chain-smoking cigarette after cigarette, before making up her mind.

Chapter Twenty-Two

Hrossey

Like all of the Orkney islands, Hrossey had its own unique charm. No matter where you happened to be you could hear the sea, the sandy beaches were white and soft as caster sugar, and the air smelt of salt and green grass.

In the summer it was like a chilly Maldives, but the winters were long and harsh, especially for youngsters who missed playing outside in the sunshine and became as restless and bad tempered as cooped up honey badgers.

Freya and Amelia had planned the trip on the evening she moved in. Amelia couldn't believe her luck. It was even more comfortable and welcoming than Evie's beautiful cottage and it smelt of fresh bread and sweet herbs.

Freya had shown her to her bright spare room, the bed festooned with cushions and shelves groaning with beloved and well-thumbed books. It was the very place Evie had sought refuge when she first came back home, broken in spirit and needing to heal. And here, thought Freya, was another young woman who looked as though she had experienced a tough life and held dark secrets close to her heart.

Freya had seen that Amelia's smile didn't always reach her eyes and she was trying a peedie bit too hard to fit in. It was understandable she wanted to make a good impression, but something wasn't quite right. Freya told herself there would be time for Amelia to grow to trust her enough to share her story and she thought it could well be a very sad one.

'Aye,' thought Freya. 'That one is carrying a heavy load.'

Her heart ached that the poor lass had never known her own mother, and from the little she had gleaned about Amelia's dad James, she couldn't imagine he would be a contender for father of the year. Freya decided she would wait until Amelia was good and ready to unburden herself.

When Amelia had unpacked, which hadn't taken very long, Freya poured them both a large glass of Scapa whisky. She sat on her comfy chair, plumped up with fat cushions, and her feet on the footstool Ross had made her for her seventy-fifth birthday, almost five years ago.

Amelia was curled up on the sofa being eyed up by Bette Davis. The sleek black cat was licking her paws and making up her mind whether to nestle herself in Freya's lap or attack this usurper and use her as a scratching post. Freya asked when Amelia might fancy a visit to Hrossey. "We can either get the ferry, which is a couple of hours, but it's a lovely sail if the weather is right or jump on the plane which will take about fifteen minutes."

"What do you think is best, Freya?"

"This time of the year I would go for the ferry. It's a bonnie trip and will give you a chance to get a feel of the place."

"Sounds perfect."

"And I'll check when Evie might be free."

Amelia was quiet a moment, sipping her whisky before she answered.

"Would it be too much to ask if we could go alone? Just the two of us. I know how busy Evie is and I don't want to take her away from her work. You've both been so kind, and I don't want to be a bother."

Freya smiled. That could actually work out. Freya had been worried Amelia would take up too much of Evie's time. Of course, she would never let on to Amelia so she merely said, "Certainly, if that's what you want. You're right, Evie is up to her eyes in work and she's not always great on the ferry. She won't mind at all and it will give us a chance to really get to know each other, especially as we are going to be housemates."

A couple of days later, the two women were sitting together outside on the ferry enjoying the wind and the sun on their faces. Approaching Hrossey they were accompanied by a school of dolphins, frolicking, leaping and showing off to some very bored-looking seals on the rocks by the ferry terminal.

Freya chuckled at their antics. She adored dolphins and always thought it was a good sign when they followed the ferry. "Looks like we have another welcoming committee," said Freya. She waved enthusiastically at the dozen or so people lined up on the pier.

"Oh this is just lovely," said Amelia. "I didn't expect everyone to come and meet us."

"Well," said Freya. "You coming to visit is a big deal. They want to make sure you get a good welcome. Be prepared to eat until you burst because they will have prepared a feast."

Amelia and Freya were engulfed in the embrace of a gaggle of red-headed men, women and children who all looked alike and all spoke at once. Somehow, they were bundled into the back of an old Land Rover, and drove in a convoy past the shops, museum and hotel to the very top of the island where a clutch of white farmhouses looked across to the bay to the small island of Papay.

Cousin Drew, who was married to Inga, yelled over his shoulder at Amelia, "Do you see the windsock over there? That's where we are heading. We live just beyond."

Amelia nodded. "There's a tiny little plane there."

"Aye," he said. "That's the plane that flies across to Papay." He added proudly: "It's the shortest scheduled flight in the world. Depending on the wind you can do it in under a minute."

Freya sat quietly in the front seat taking in the familiar scenery. She loved the island where she grew up. She might have made her home on the Orkney mainland, but this was where her heart was.

She thought, 'I will tell them to bring my ashes back here to be scattered to the winds so I can be part of Hrossey forever.' Freya gave herself a shake. What was she doing thinking of death and funerals on such a bonnie day?

She leaned over to ask Drew, "How are you all? How's Inga and the bairns? I can't believe you are a granda, and peedie Daisy is five years old already and at school."

"We are all fine, Freya. It's good to see you. What a shame we won't see you on your birthday."

"Away and behave yourself. I know fine well everyone has booked the ferry across and you will be coming to my surprise party," Freya laughed.

Drew chuckled. "I told them you would know all about it. Inga owes me a fiver."

He turned round to Amelia again, "Inga's my wife and she was up at the crack of dawn baking all day yesterday, Amelia, so I hope you've brought your appetite."

Amelia was shown into the 'big' room kept for visitors and special occasions. The furniture was polished until it shone and there was a mantelpiece full of framed photos of red-cheeked, flame-haired children and the all-important graduation photograph of their eldest son, Angus.

A glass cabinet in the corner held an impressive collection of crystal and fruit bowls that were never actually used. The overheated room was full of women with fat babies on their knees, men laughing and a gaggle of shrieking bairns running around the best big table.

All the teenagers were away at school on the mainland or there would have been no room to swing any of the bad-tempered cats that fought each other on the rug in front of the fire. Amelia was introduced to everyone and looked rather startled at the noise level and the bewildering number of names.

"You've met my husband, Drew. I'm Inga and this is Elspeth, Yvonne, Lara, Kayla and their husbands big John, big Angus, big Rab and peedie William."

Amelia was given handshake after handshake and looked more and more confused as members of the clan queued up to greet her.

"Don't worry," said Drew kindly. "It's not a quiz. We don't expect you to remember everyone right away."

"We should have had name badges, mammy," chirruped his granddaughter, Daisy. "Like we made at school. I could have drawn the names on them."

"That would have been a lovely idea my pet," said Inga. "Although there's only five of you in the whole school so I'm not sure you really needed those name badges, even though you did a fine job. Your handwriting is beautiful."

She gave Daisy an affectionate kiss on top of her head and then looked at Amelia. "So, what do you want to know about us then?"

Before Amelia could answer, Inga went on, "It's such a shame granny Sheila has passed. She would have been able to give you such a lot of information."

Drew chimed in, "There's a few of the older ones here who remember her coming back from Orkney pregnant with Cara, but I'm sorry we don't have all that much information about her. Cara left here when she was in her teens and didn't visit much after that, except to get married to that fine man Duncan. That was a good day but after the accident here the family rarely visited."

"What happened?" asked Amelia. The older ones looked down at their feet, but Inga eventually burst out, "Well, everyone says they don't really know exactly what happened, although I have my suspicions. The bairns were all playing in the sea when a big wave pulled peedie Evie right under. Her dad, Duncan, was convinced that her sister, Liv, had deliberately tried to drown her, and he wasn't the only one."

"Hush Inga, we don't know that for sure. I still say Duncan overreacted and Cara swore blind it was all blown out of proportion. She was fuming with Duncan."

"Well, I know what I saw," said Inga, her mouth in a firm line. "Anyway, they left right away and we hardly saw them for years. It really upset aunty Sheila. She doted on her granddaughters. It was awfully sad."

"And then of course Cara went round the bend," said Drew.

"For goodness's sake, Amelia doesn't need to know all that," said Inga.

"Actually, I want to know everything. That's why I'm here and please don't worry, all families have their dramas. Ours certainly did."

She paused nervously, and looked around, before continuing. "Look at how my dad took off. He might have sent money, but he was never a father to Cara. That must have been so tough for her."

Amelia went on sadly, "My mom died giving birth to me, and I know my dad did his best, but he was so old, and I am sure I was a right handful."

"Evie told us about your mammy. I'm sorry, Amelia," said Inga. "That must have been so hard for you."

"Thank you," said Amelia with a sad sigh, "I didn't know her, so I didn't miss her. I mean I missed having a mom, but my dad rarely talked about her and by the time I was old enough to ask questions he had gotten rid of all her clothes and personal stuff. He just didn't think to keep them for me. He did hang on to her wedding ring, and I have a few photos of her from just after they got married, but not much else. I think that's why I wanted to come here and try to find out a little bit more about Cara. She and Evie and Liv are the only family I have."

"Well, you have us too, Amelia," said Drew.

"That's so sweet of you and it means such a lot to me." Amelia gave a dazzling smile, her eyes shining with tears.

Freya could feel her own eyes growing misty. The visit was going so well she decided to make the most of her time here and take a walk to the nearby churchyard, where her parents and sister were buried.

"I will be right back but I need to walk off some of that delicious spread"

"Don't be too long, I'm putting the kettle on again. There's so much cake left," said Inga.

When Freya had left, Inga turned to Amelia and said, "We thought we would see Evie today with you. It's been a while since she was here. She likes to come and catch up with the other painters and she sells some of their work in her gallery."

"I did ask her. But, well . . ." Amelia pretended to hesitate.

"Go on," said Elspeth.

"She actually said she'd rather not come if I didn't mind. I think she was worried I would find it all too quiet and maybe even a bit boring. At least I think that's what she said."

Inga's eyebrows disappeared into her shiny red fringe.

"She did? That's not like Evie."

Amelia said hastily, "Oh, I'm sure she didn't mean it like that. It's just that she said she hated the ferry crossing and the plane also made her feel sick. I'm certain she loves it once she is here seeing you all, but she did say she was going to cut back her visits and get the artists to bring their work to her at the gallery to save her the inconvenience."

Inga frowned. "I thought she'd got better with the sea sickness. She's not mentioned to me that she found it such a chore to come here."

Amelia went on, "I mean I don't understand it myself. It's such a beautiful place and you are all so lovely and friendly. It's been a joy to meet you."

Amelia dabbed her eyes with a hanky, which instantly resulted in an outpouring of coos and soft words from the women and looks of approval from the men.

Freya came back into the kitchen to see Amelia going through old family albums with Inga and the others. She looked up and told Freya that she'd had the most wonderful time and learned such a lot about Sheila and Cara and the extended family. Freya smiled at her fondly but said they had better go if they were going to catch the last ferry.

Amelia had gifts of sugary tablet, homemade cakes, and sandwiches thick with Hrossey butter and cheese pressed upon her for the journey. She was hugged hard and told to come back soon.

Everyone piled back into the cars to take them to the ferry terminal and waved them off. Inga was not best pleased at what Amelia had said about Evie.

She huffed, "I knew that Evie thought she was better than all of us," she grumbled. "Haven't I said that to you all before? She ups and leaves for London for twenty years, then swans back and expects to be welcomed back with open arms."

Drew sighed. "From what Amelia said, I don't think Evie will be coming back anytime soon."

Inga was on a roll. "I don't think she told us the half of it. You could see she was embarrassed to have let it slip that Evie thinks we are all dull backward bumpkins."

"Don't take it to heart, Inga. She's family and we told Sheila we would look out for her. We need to stick together."

Inga sighed and kissed him: "You are a big soft lump, Drew. Well, for your sake I will be perfectly pleasant the next time she shows her face here, if she ever does."

Coming back that night as the sun set and the sea turned to purple ink, Amelia and Freya sat quietly on deck. Each woman alone with her thoughts. Going back home to Hrossey always stirred up both good and bad memories for Freya. She loved the island of her birth, but it was also where she'd gone through some of the toughest times of her life.

She reflected on how lucky she had been to have a family who supported her and a community who simply accepted her as Freya. They were all dead and buried now. On her visit to the gravestones of her parents and sister Anne Marie, she told them she was doing just fine and they weren't to worry about her, and that soon she would be eighty years old and how unbelievable it all was.

Freya especially missed her sister who was kind and open-hearted and defended her from cruel bullies. She looked at Amelia, unaware that she'd managed to upset the Hrossey clan with her sly untruths about Evie.

"I hope you feel as though today was worthwhile, my pet. They are a good bunch but I was afraid they wouldn't have much to tell you about Sheila or Cara."

Amelia was quick to reassure Freya, "They were lovely, and it was just good to be where Sheila was born and raised and where Cara grew up. I learned a lot. Thank you so much for coming with me."

Amelia's busy brain was thinking about the way she had unsettled everyone with her lies about Evie, and all she had learned from them, especially about Evie's relationship with Liv.

There was even more bad blood there than she had realised, and that would come in very useful later if Liv were to falter. She had plenty of ammunition to persuade Liv to see things her way.

Chapter Twenty-Three

Freya's House

Freya hadn't been feeling well. Since the trip to Hrossey she'd suffered from a bad cold that had settled on her chest. It was as though all the energy had seeped out of her body. It was frustrating for someone always on the go, but Freya was also frightened at feeling so helpless. Her mind was strong, but her body was letting her down.

Edwyn had looked in on her and said she had to rest: "I mean it, Freya. You have to remember you aren't as young as you used to be. I don't want this to turn into pneumonia and have to admit you to the Balfour."

Freya promised she would stay in bed for a few days. To be honest she didn't think she would have the strength to get up. "You need looking after. I'll get Kate to bring over some of her chicken soup." He added half to himself, "It's worked out well that Amelia is here. You might need help to get to the loo."

Freya looked scandalised. "She can help me to the toilet door, but I'm not having anyone wipe my backside. Not even you, Edwyn. I couldn't bear it."

Her bottom lip trembled and she was near tears. "Well, let's see how we go," he said gently. "I will get Kate to come round with your prescription when she brings the soup, but I'm banning any more visitors for today, otherwise you will be inundated and won't get a minute's peace. You need to sleep and get better."

Amelia was hovering outside the bedroom door. "Is she OK? Does she need anything?"

Edwyn tried to be reassuring, but seeing Freya laid up and looking so pale had worried him. "She'll be fine. She's as stubborn as a mule so your job for the next few days is to make sure she gets proper rest and isn't bothered by lots of people. They will all want to see how she's doing, and she will tire herself out talking to them and fretting about them being fed and watered."

"Of course. I will make sure she's taken care of. You can count on me," said Amelia. Edwyn smiled at the woman who looked so much like his friend Evie. "Thanks, Amelia. I know I will be leaving her in good hands."

Evie swerved into Freya's driveway in Florence. She'd received a text from Kate about Freya being poorly, which was the first she'd heard about it. She leapt out of the car and ran to the door, pushing it open.

Amelia stepped into the hallway, her arms folded.

"Ever heard of knocking?" she said mildly, eyebrows raised.

"We don't do that here. Where's Freya?"

"She's sleeping."

Evie went to go past Amelia, who moved subtly to block her path.

"I'm sorry, Evie. But Edwyn has left strict instructions that Freya must rest, and not be bothered by anyone."

"I'm sure Edwyn didn't mean me, Amelia. I just want to look in and make sure she's OK."

"That's what they've all been saying, Evie. Look, I'm so sorry but I don't want to upset Edwyn. He has trusted me to look after Freya and make sure she gets better. He said no exceptions."

Evie stared at Amelia, who met her gaze. Her face was perfectly poised and calm and she wasn't backing down.

"If you don't mind, I think maybe it's best if you leave?" said Amelia. "I'll message you with any updates, but I don't want Freya waking up to all this noise in the hallway and trying to get up. I'll let you know when it's OK to visit."

Evie left seething. 'If anyone should be looking after Freya, it should have been me. How dare Edwyn ask Amelia? She barely knows Freya.' Evie was so annoyed she called Edwyn at work, which always irritated him unless it was Kate needing something urgent.

The two of them snapped at one another, with Edwyn saying angrily that Amelia was staying in the same house as Freya, so it made more sense for her to take care of her and that she was doing a fine job. He added that anyway Evie was always busy with her painting and couldn't be relied upon.

Evie furiously told him that he still should have asked her first and she should be allowed to visit Freya and not barred from her presence because of his stupid orders.

Edwyn was about to say that of course she wasn't banned from visiting and could pop in and see Freya anytime, but Evie had already hung up on him. She texted Amelia to ask for any updates; Amelia simply replied tersely that there was no change.

Evie wondered how it was possible for her to be effectively shut out of Freya's life by Amelia, who refused to back down and clearly enjoyed getting one over on her.

After a few days Freya started to rally. Amelia brought her coffee in bed and a tray with fresh fruit and thick buttered toast, then told her she was going out for a bit of shopping.

"I want to get my hair done and I need to get something to wear for your surprise party that of course you know all about."

She looked down at Freya, who was managing to nibble a bit of toast. "Are you sure you feel well enough for the 'surprise'? I could tell them to postpone it, you know."

"Away with you. Not a bit of it", said Freya, her voice still hoarse. "I've got a fabulous orange and yellow kaftan I've been saving for a special occasion. It is all trimmed with massive sequins and makes a noise when I walk so it will be even better when I'm dancing. I will be like a living tambourine."

Amelia thought it sounded hideous, but said ingratiatingly, "You will look absolutely beautiful, especially with those scarlet velvet slippers and lots and lots of chunky bracelet and necklaces."

Freya smiled happily. She planned on wearing as much bling as she possibly could.

She wanted to dazzling for her party and was determined to be back on her feet in time for her big night.

Amelia told her, "I will be away most of the day and I'll bring you back something silly. I've made you up a chicken salad sandwich with that mayonnaise you like; it's in the fridge. Call my mobile if you need anything," she said, disappearing out the door.

Amelia's cheery demeanour vanished as she drove Freya's car into town. She had a plan. First up was a visit to Agnes at the hair salon. Sitting on the chair Amelia told her, "Agnes, I need you to give me a makeover. You did Evie's hair so beautifully that I want exactly the same."

Agnes lifted up a strand of hair and tutted, "Well, it's not going to be easy going from your black hair to blonde. It might take a while. And more than one session. Are you sure that's the way you want to go? And I know everyone says this to you, but you look so alike already – this is going to make it tough for us to tell you and Evie apart."

Amelia gave her a worried look. "Oh, do you think Evie will be upset? I wouldn't want to do anything to offend her."

"Don't you worry, I'm sure she will be flattered," said Agnes with a smile. "She's the most easy-going person I know".

Looking closer at Amelia's hair she said, "Well, look at that. Your roots are strawberry blonde. What made you dye your hair so dark?"

"I hated my red hair when I was growing up. I got bullied at school and I just wanted to fit in. As soon as I could, I changed the colour. I've been dyeing it black for years."

"Hmmm. I can see that. It's not in the best of condition and you've dyed your eyebrows too. I can lighten them for you, because they might look a bit strange when your hair is blonde."

"I never thought of that. That would be wonderful."

"I will need to strip off all this black colour. Let me get you some magazines while I work my magic."

As Amelia flicked through the glossy pages, the two women chatted happily. Agnes told her, "I've always wanted to visit America. We were going to go to Disneyland years ago when the kids were young, but that awful attack on the twin towers made me too scared to fly over there. We usually just go to Spain or the Canary Islands now. Cheap and cheerful and I come back as red as a fog lamp."

They spent a happy half hour talking about holidays and then got on to the royal family and the time passed swiftly by. Agnes had given Amelia a deep-conditioning oil treatment, and her hair was now a sort of bizarre salmon pink which they both thought suited her very well, but the plan was to have her hair blonde just like Evie's.

"I can cut and style your hair and give it a blow-dry now, and you can come back tomorrow for me to finish up with the colour. Any thoughts on the cut?"

"Can you make sure you cut it just like Evie's. I think her hair looks so incredible."

Agnes laughed happily. "Although I say so myself, so do I. In fact, she's due to come in for an appointment soon. I might just give her a ring."

Amelia said, "Oh I'm sure she said something about going to the hairdressers on the mainland just before Freya's party. She said she felt her hair needed a proper cut and colour."

Agnes paused with the hairdryer in her hand. "I don't think I heard you right there, this thing makes such a racket. Did Evie say she wanted a 'proper' cut and colour?"

"I'm sure she didn't mean it like that," said Amelia hastily. "I probably picked her up wrong, but I did see her looking up hairdressers in Aberdeen on her iPad."

Agnes bit her lip and looked crestfallen. She was distracted enough to put the dryer so close to Amelia's head she almost burned her scalp. Amelia yelped in pain and Agnes was hugely apologetic.

She was also hurt and upset and told herself that, after all, Evie had spent lots of time in London and maybe thought Agnes wasn't trendy or good enough now that Evie was appearing in magazines and ran such a successful business.

The truth was that Evie had been far too busy to visit Agnes, though she was about to make an appointment in time for the party. However, when she phoned up later that day to book herself in, she was told rather curtly that there was nothing available.

Meanwhile, Amelia had continued down Kirkwall high street, popping into several shops and exclaiming over the clothes and accessories. She found herself outside Hume Sweet Hume where Evie had once tried on a green dress in the window and then wore it on the way home, feeling all sophisticated and daring.

Amelia was going through the rails when the assistant went over to speak to her. "Goodness, I thought that was Evie for a minute there with a daring new hair colour. You must be Amelia. News travels fast here and Kate was in earlier telling me all about you coming over from America. I'm Fiona. Can I help you with anything?"

Amelia gave her a dazzling smile.

"I need something for a very special party."

"I'm guessing that will be Freya's surprise eightieth birthday party? We've had a fair few of her friends in here buying new dresses. Does Freya really not know all about it?"

"What do you think?" Amelia said with a giggle. "Course she does but she's going to pretend that it's a huge shock. I've left her planning her outfit."

Amelia looked around. "This really is a lovely shop. You have so many interesting and unusual things. I don't understand why Evie told me to go online for Freya's party because she could never find anything to wear in Orkney."

Fiona couldn't believe what she was hearing. This didn't sound like Evie.

Amelia continued, "And then I found her throwing out that gorgeous green dress she got from here. I had to rescue it from the jumble sale bag. I said to her, 'If you don't want it, I will have it.'" She gave a tinkling laugh.

Fiona looked stricken. "Are you sure? Evie is one of our best customers. She pops in a lot, and she told me she loved that green dress and would still be wearing it when she was an old woman."

Amelia said in a rush, "Oh, I must have got it wrong then. I'm sure it's all a misunderstanding." She continued flicking through the clothes rails.

"Can I try on this blue silk top with the matching trousers? It's gorgeous and will be perfect for the party. I have just the right shoes, but I might need your help with a bag."

"Of course," said Fiona, but she was frowning, and Amelia could see she had successfully planted doubts in her mind about Evie.

'So far, so good,' she thought. 'And this shop really is a treasure trove. I am absolutely treating myself to this fabulous outfit, and that handbag is a must.'

Back at Freya's, Amelia showed off her new hair and her purchases. Freya loved the pink look and heartily approved of the whisky-flavoured tablet Amelia had bought her as a present, immediately scoffing the whole lot.

She wasn't so sure about the new blue outfit, which she considered to be very much on the plain side. "Maybe if you jazzed it up with some silk scarves and massive earrings and a really colourful belt it might be dressy enough for my party. You can borrow some stuff from me if you like."

Amelia gave her a broad smile. "You are so kind Freya, and you always look spectacular. I don't see how anyone would ever think your outfits are too much."

Freya looked at her. "Well, I hope they wouldn't. I like to be colourful. It makes me happy." Throwing her arms in the air, she added with a laugh, "It's my signature look."

"Of course it is, and no one would want you any other way. That's why I can't get my head round it," said Amelia.

"Can't get your head around what?" asked Freya.

"Oh it's nothing. Just that when we were talking about the party, Evie said she hoped you would tone it down a bit, that's all. She said something about us all needing sunglasses on the night."

Freya's face fell. Amelia said hastily, "But of course she was just joking."

Whether it was because she was recovering from her illness and feeling a bit wobbly, Freya felt herself becoming really upset. She'd also been wondering why Evie hadn't visited her.

She looked up at Amelia and said quietly, "I don't think Evie would ever say that to anyone about me. I know she wouldn't."

Amelia decided she had gone too far. She had been right to think Freya was going to be the most difficult nut to crack. She'd have to be more subtle. "Of course, she wouldn't. I must have picked her up all wrong. I'm so sorry, Freya. I should never have mentioned it. She adores you. We all do."

She went on, "Let me pour you a drink and we can watch that daft show we love. You know the one where the couples get married despite the fact they've never even met each other."

"Actually Amelia, I'm feeling a peedie bit tired. I think I will take to my bed."

Lying in bed, Freya tried to work out what was going on. She had grown very fond of Amelia and didn't think she was trying to cause trouble, but why say anything like that in the first place? Would Evie really have spoken so unkindly about her? It was unimaginable. She had to admit that sometimes she did go a bit overboard with her clothes and her jewellery, but it was her suit of armour, and it made her feel pretty. What if they all think the same? That I'm just a ridiculous sad old woman. Someone they feel sorry for and put up with?

She had a restless night, but in the bright morning light, felt much better. She told herself she was being daft. Amelia had said it was just a joke after all. She heard her in the kitchen making breakfast.

"She's a good lass really," Freya told herself. "I need to behave myself. Christ, I'm going to be eighty soon. I need to be a bit more thick skinned."

She gave herself a shake and called out. "I'm getting up for breakfast this morning, Amelia. I feel much better."

"Oh, I'm so glad. I've been worrying that I upset you by putting my foot in it about Evie. I shouldn't have said anything. Honestly, I need to learn to think before I open my mouth and let my belly rumble."

"Forget it. Just a misunderstanding, like you said."

Amelia looked relieved. Freya grabbed her mug of coffee and took a long sip. "Perfect. Just the way I like it," she smiled at Amelia.

"Now I've got a back log of work to be getting on with, so right after breakfast I'm going to get started. Evie says we need more of those silver earrings that look like peedie shells and I have a heap of stones to paint."

"I wish I could help you," said Amelia, "but I'm hopeless at anything arty and I need to get back to see Agnes at the salon. Are you certain it's alright for me to take your car? I'll make sure I fill her right up to the top."

"Away with you," said Freya. "That poor car sits there in the drive bored out of its tiny mind. Hardly anyone drives it these days. It was good of you to get yourself insured online. I had no idea you could do that for short spells." She chuckled, "The interweb is an amazing thing altogether."

'You have no idea,' thought Amelia. Out loud she said, "Well, I will bring back some shopping, we are nearly out of butter and cheese. I'm away to get this pink washed out and when I come back, I will be a new woman."

At the salon, Agnes outdid herself and Amelia's hair turned out to be just like Evie's, shiny and thick and streaked with different shades of blonde. The transformation was uncanny. Amelia looked in the mirror and even she gasped. It could have been Evie's face staring right back at her.

"Thanks, Agnes. This would have cost me an absolute fortune in a salon back home. Are you sure that's all it costs?" she gushed.

"You get mate's rates, Amelia. And maybe when Evie sees how good you look, she might not be so snippy about my skills as a hairdresser."

"I told you I'm sure that was a misunderstanding."

Agnes thought she really was such a kind-hearted woman, sticking up for that snobbish Evie. She gave her a beaming smile and a massive hug.

As Amelia walked out of the door, she told herself, 'This is going to be a piece of cake.' She almost purred with satisfaction.

Chapter Twenty-Four

Orkney

Amelia came out of the hairdressers and into a beautiful sunny afternoon; heavy clouds fat with rain had threatened to scud in from the west but had held off for now.

She went to the deli to buy essentials for Freya. Fresh crusty bread, butter and cheese, ground coffee and full-fat milk, and was waiting to pay at the counter. Someone tapped her on the shoulder.

"Hello, Evie." It had taken Ross five minutes of walking up and down the street in front of the shop before he had the nerve to approach the woman he thought was Evie.

When Amelia turned round and smiled, he found himself completely on the back foot. "Sorry to disappoint you, Ross, it's Amelia. We met at Evie's gallery. Remember?"

He stuttered his apologies.

"You look so like her, especially with the hair and everything, and that's just the kind of outfit she would wear." But not those daft shoes he thought. They are totally impractical for cobbled streets and walking through fields.

Amelia put on a sad face. She knew just how to play this one. "It's really nice of you to say that. I just admire her so much and I think she's so beautiful and I suppose I want to be just like her. But I don't think she likes me. I feel so pathetic." Amelia managed to squeeze out a tear that trickled down her cheek.

Ross had no idea how to cope with a crying, emotional woman and frantically looked round for help, eventually saying desperately, "Here, let me get your shopping and I can carry it for you."

"You are so kind," said Amelia. Ross was busy paying for her groceries so didn't see her triumphant smile. "Why don't you let me take you for a drink? I don't really have any friends here and it would be lovely to get to know you."

Ross couldn't think of an excuse and found himself agreeing but only if he paid. In the trendy bar, Ross bought her a glass of red wine and a pint of orange juice for himself which he gulped nervously.

"I don't drink much," he said, "To be honest, I'm snowed under with orders. I just came into the toon to get my mum's favourite sweeties. She's virtually bedridden now, but she loves her peedie pokes of Soor Plooms and Clove Rock."

Amelia had no idea what he was on about but she smiled at him and said softly, "I really admire that you take care of your parents, Ross. It must be tough on you."

"Och, no. It's fine. They are no trouble at all. And I get a lot of help from friends and neighbours. We've got cracking carers who come in every morning. The auld yins want to stay in their own house and that's not too much to ask after they spent so many years bringing me up and teaching me the ropes."

He went on, "My dad was a brilliant craftsman until the arthritis struck him down, but he taught me all he knew. I learned from the very best there is." Ross was taken aback. This was about the longest conversation he'd had with a woman that he could remember, apart from Evie, of course. Usually when a girl chatted him up in a pub, he looked for the nearest exit.

He never opened up like this or talked about his parents, but he felt himself relax with this woman who reminded him so much of Evie.

Amelia gazed at him, her bright green eyes full of admiration. "I have seen your work, Ross, and it's so beautiful. I'd love to own one of your chairs. Maybe when you aren't too busy you could show me round your workshop and I could choose the designs that I like best."

He smiled at her. "Of course. It's a date." He blushed and blurted, "Well, not a date. But you know what I mean." He took a large slurp of orange juice to hide his confusion.

"Course I do," she laughed teasingly. "Anyway, I am sure you are already spoken for."

Ross blushed. "I'm not actually. To tell you the truth, I've never really had a proper girlfriend. I was always too busy working and I'm not good with women. I never know what to say to them."

"Well, you know how to talk to me," said Amelia. "I've really enjoyed our conversation."

Ross smiled again, his cheeks blazing, and looked down at his feet. "You know, I thought there was something between you and Evie, before she put me straight," smiled Amelia.

He frowned, "I haven't seen her much recently. Well, not properly. We seem to always be missing one another."

"Like ships in the night?"

"Exactly."

Amelia sighed. "Well, there might be a reason for that, Ross."

"Really? What?"

"I hear she has a new man in her life. Someone from her past. I don't really know much about it as she hasn't said anything to me, but I did overhear her on the phone talking to someone and well . . ."

"Go on," said Ross.

"And they were making plans to meet up."

"I see," said Ross.

"So maybe that's why she's been avoiding you?"

"Now you mention it, she may well have been giving me the bum's rush and I didn't realise, which would make sense if she had someone else on the go."

"I'm sorry, Ross. I hope I haven't upset you. But I thought you ought to know."

"It's fine. We were never together. I never even managed to get her to go on a date. I just somehow thought . . . but clearly, I had my wires crossed all along . . ." He trailed off.

Amelia realised she had done enough fibbing about Evie and said briskly. "Thanks for the drink, Ross. I'd better get back to Freya. I've never known anyone who goes through so much dairy produce. I swear she sits and eats handfuls of butter straight from the dish."

Ross said, "Let me give you a lift. That was a big glass of wine and it's more or less on the way, and I can look in on Freya. I know she's not been well."

Amelia beamed at him. She could always pick up Freya's car later.

"That would be really lovely. Thank you."

When Ross and Amelia come through the door, Freya looked up from working on her jewellery and thought for a moment he was with Evie. It was only when she heard Amelia's American accent and saw her properly in the light that she realised her mistake.

Amelia was positively bouncing with delight. "Look, Freya. I bumped into Ross in the deli and he bought me a drink. I feel very naughty having red wine in the middle of the day. He drove me back, but I will go and pick up your car later.

He also paid for our shopping, which was so kind. I'll just put things away in the fridge."

Amelia disappeared into the kitchen.

"Can you believe how much she looks like Evie?" said Ross, shaking his head.

"Yes. It's uncanny" said Freya, wondering how often she'd have to have this conversation.

Ross lent in and whispered, "Amelia is a lovely woman. I'm thinking of asking her out. Do you think she would say yes?"

"Ross. Every woman on this island, married or single, dead or alive, would go out with you. Of course, she will say yes, but are you sure? I thought you and Evie had something going on."

"Nah," said Ross. "She isn't interested in me. She's made that very clear."

Freya wasn't convinced. "Are you sure? You never actually asked her properly did you?"

"I did. That time I delivered the chair to her. I distinctly remember asking her to come out for a drink with me. Anyway, that ship has sailed," said Ross. "She's got someone else on the go."

Freya looked puzzled. Evie hadn't said anything to her about meeting another man. She felt hurt. Normally, she and Evie shared everything, but then Evie hadn't even visited when she'd been ill. So maybe she did have someone else. She was just about to ask Ross for more details when Amelia came in with a pot of tea, three mugs and a plate piled high with homemade biscuits.

"Not for me, Amelia love," said Ross. "I need to get back to the grindstone. But if you aren't doing anything tomorrow night, do you fancy a drink?"

"I'm not. Doing anything, I mean. And I do. Fancy a drink, that is."

"Where and when?"

"Same place as today? Seven o'clock?"

"It's a date," she said, instantly beaming at him.

"See you tomorrow then," said Ross, grinning shyly.

"Bye, Freya." With an awkward wave, he turned and left.

"Well," said Freya when Ross had roared off in his car. "That was something I never expected to see with my own two eyes. Ross agreeing to go on an actual date. Who would have thought it?"

She looked at Amelia seriously, "Be careful with him, Amelia. He's not a man to give his heart lightly." Freya remembered saying almost the exact same thing to Evie around this time almost two years ago when Ross had hesitantly asked her out.

She heard Amelia sigh and say, "I reckon I'm the one who will have to be careful. I think he might just be the most wonderful man in the world. He's so kind. Fancy buying our shopping and then taking me for a drink to cheer me up, and giving me a lift home, and now we are going on a real date. I can't believe it."

Freya looked at Amelia and saw the excitement in her eyes. Perhaps she and Ross could make a go of it. She remembered what he had told her and asked, "Has Evie said anything to you about meeting a new man?"

"Not a thing," said Amelia. "But I still don't know her very well. I am sure if there was someone she would have told you, Freya. She tells you everything."

Amelia added, "Anyway, where did you get that idea?"

"It was just something Ross said."

She shook her head, "He might have got it wrong. Nobody can keep a thing like that quiet for long here, everyone would know in a minute if she was serious about someone."

Then Freya thought to herself, 'I hope she hasn't met some clown online and got herself into another mess. She stayed with that vile ex Jeremy for years and he nearly sucked all the life and happiness out of her. And I know how much of an oyster she is at keeping secrets. She kept the most important one of all from me for over twenty years, but I thought those days were behind us and she trusted me. Surely, she would tell me if she had met someone else?'

Amelia said reassuringly: "If she is seeing a guy, I am sure she will tell you when she's ready."

She looked hopefully at Freya. "But right now, I really need your help. What am I going to wear for my date with Ross? I obviously don't want to be too overdressed and like I've made a huge effort, but then I don't want to look scruffy either."

The two of them spent a happy hour chatting about outfits and jewellery, and how to get that difficult 'I haven't tried a bit' look that takes hours of effort.

Chapter Twenty-Five

Evie's House

Evie had been up since daybreak working on the portrait of Freya that was to be her special eightieth birthday gift. She hoped Freya would hang it in her sunny front room beside the one she had painted of her more than twenty years ago.

Evie was painting from memory and a couple of favourite photos as she wanted this to be a genuine surprise for Freya, but as always when she painted someone's portrait, the hands were giving her endless trouble and driving her crazy. She was feeling the pressure as this had to be perfect for Freya.

She stepped back and took a good long look at her work so far. Evie was happy with the eyes that glowed with kindness and wisdom, and she had swathed Freya in bright purple like an empress. She had toyed with the idea of a crown and a cloak of ermine but decided Freya didn't need those trappings to look like royalty.

Evie was tired and in need of a break and was surprised to see it was already 2pm. She was meeting the others later to plan the final details for Freya's party so didn't have as much time as she would have liked.

She put down her brush and went into the kitchen to make herself a coffee, when she heard a car drive up and Amelia calling her name.

"I hope I'm not disturbing you, Evie, but I just wanted to pop in and see if you needed anything in town. I'm getting dinner in for Freya."

Evie almost dropped her mug at the sight of a newly blonde Amelia. She quickly shut the door on her painting, she didn't want anyone seeing her unfinished work, least of all Amelia. She was still annoyed at not standing up to her and insisting on seeing Freya when she was ill, and they hadn't really spoken since.

"Your hair . . ." Evie said faintly.

"Oh, you haven't seen my new hair style. Do you like it? I asked for the same as you and I think Agnes has done a great job."

Evie was taken aback. There was something vaguely creepy about Amelia's transformation. Imitation was supposed to be a form of flattery, but Evie just felt uneasy.

"It's very nice," she said quietly.

"Are you sure? I don't want you to think I'm being a copycat, but I just love your hair. Do you think it's a bit too much that it makes us look so alike? I can change it."

That was exactly what Evie was thinking but instead she heard herself say unconvincingly, "No, it's fine. It was just a bit of a shock. But it looks good on you."

Amelia nodded. "Well, that's a relief. I'd love a coffee if there's one going and it's not too much trouble."

'Why does she always make me feel so uncomfortable and on the back foot?' Evie thought. Then said out loud, "Course not. I was just about to offer."

"I smell fresh paint. What are you working on? Can I take a look?"

"Oh, I'd prefer you didn't . . ."

But Amelia was already through the kitchen door and into the sunny front room which Evie used as her studio and stood admiring the portrait. Wincing, Evie followed. She felt so exposed. She hated people seeing her work before it was ready. But Amelia had her hands clasped over her mouth theatrically.

"Oh Evie, it's amazing. You've really caught Freya's likeness. I'm expecting her to talk to me."

Evie wished she could believe Amelia was being sincere, but to her ears the praise came across as false and patronising. She managed to say, "I'm reasonably happy with it but I'm having trouble with her hands. I need to get a move on if I am to finish it before her birthday. Don't let on though as she really doesn't know about it. I want something to be a surprise on her big day."

"I think it's perfect already and I won't say a word. I promise. You are so clever. It must be incredible to be so talented." Amelia was laying it on thick and Evie found herself feeling uncomfortable again. "But look, I'm also here to run something past you. Ross Isbister has asked me out and I just wanted to make sure that you are alright with that."

Evie was about to reply when Amelia added hastily, "You see, Freya thought the two of you had something going on and obviously there's no way in the world I would want to step on your toes. One word from you and I will just back right off."

Evie didn't know what to say. She supposed it was decent of Amelia to ask if she was OK with it, but truth be told, once again this strange woman had unsettled her.

Evie swallowed hard and uttered faintly, "Don't be silly, Amelia. Ross and I are just friends, that's all. I have no claim on him or him on me."

"So, I have your blessing then?"

Evie winced. It was a date, not an engagement. She also sensed Amelia was enjoying herself. "You don't need my approval to go out with Ross," Evie said evenly. "You are both single."

Amelia giggled and went on, "You know it was so funny. I was in the deli and he thought I was you for a minute. He was so embarrassed he asked me for a drink and then you know how it is. One thing led to another, and he wants to see me tomorrow night."

Amelia hugged herself, "Between you and me, I am so excited but also a bit nervous. He really is the most delicious man I have ever met. You could drown in those brown eyes. And I don't mean to be crude but he has the very best butt."

Evie thought, 'She's right. The first time I met Ross I thought his bum was like a perfectly ripe peach and wondered what it would be like to sink my teeth into it.' She stopped herself from going any further down that particular road.

Instead, she said, "Yes, a lot of women seem to think he is handsome, but he doesn't do it for me, I'm afraid. And he's a workaholic. You know he still lives with his parents."

Actually, Evie admired how Ross looked after his mum and dad and she also completely related to how absorbed he was in his work. He created beautiful pieces and spent hours making sure they were perfect. She knew exactly how that felt. It was the same when she disappeared into one of her paintings.

She had a fleeting vision of Ross making one of his beautiful chairs in the corner of this very room while she worked on a nude portrait of him. She shook her head to get rid of such thoughts.

She heard Amelia say, "Well, I happen to think it's really swell that he still lives at home. It shows what a nice man he is." She added, "You know I can't tell you how glad I am you don't fancy him. I wouldn't have had a chance if you were interested."

She drained her mug of coffee. "Now, I need to go and get the shopping. Freya's got the offer of a lobster and we are having her famous Cullen Skink tonight."

Evie watched her go out the door full of joy about her date with Ross and looking forward to enjoying one of Evie's favourite meals cooked by Freya.

She was surprised at how crushed she felt that Ross had asked Amelia out. She told herself that she didn't want him as anything other than a friend, but she really wasn't happy he was going out on a proper date with Amelia.

Ross Isbister didn't go out on dates. True, he had asked her out for a drink once, but he never followed up on that properly, and he always looked as though he would rather be anywhere else when she ran into him. She had thought for a brief moment at the gallery that he was going to ask her out again, but she must have been mistaken.

'Well, he's transferred his affections pretty bloody fast for a man who apparently had a crush on me. That was obviously a load of old bollocks,' she thought to herself bitterly.

And another thing that really was hard to bear: Freya always asked her over when she nabbed a lobster. It was their 'thing', but Amelia had taken that away from her too.

Chapter Twenty-Six

Maureen's House

Evie turned up to Maureen's house in Florence looking forward to seeing everyone. She'd been putting in long hours working on paintings for the gallery as well as the surprise portrait for Freya, and her social life had suffered – there were unanswered messages piling up on her phone. The party was just three weeks away now, so they had lots to get sorted today.

Kate and Edwyn were already there. Their girls were happily chatting to young Rory and colouring in on the big kitchen table. Delima and Jack had driven over with Ola and baby Hari.

Evie was welcomed in and sat down beside Delima who handed Hari over to her. He laughed and gurgled contentedly on her knee. Evie couldn't resist kissing the top of his head and inhaling the scent of freshly washed newly baked baby. She adored him so much, she was even happy to risk being peed on, or worse, when his nappy needed changing.

Patsy was helping Andrzej put out snacks and hand out drinks when Amelia arrived. Evie felt like she couldn't escape from her.

"I hope you don't mind me joining in but Maureen did say it would be OK," said Amelia, slinking round the door. They all gasped at her new hair and said how much she resembled Evie. Maureen smiled at her, "You are more than welcome but what did you tell Freya? I hope she doesn't know we are all meeting up to plan her party."

Amelia replied, "I told her I was going over to Evie's for a catch up and she seemed to go along with it, but to be honest I reckon she knows exactly what we are up to. She's already sussed out that there's going to be a party so why don't we just stop with the pretence and let her join in the planning?"

Patsy was about to stuff her face with a giant samosa when she turned to Amelia and said with the utmost seriousness and sincerity: "But that wouldn't do at all, Amelia. We have to keep up the facade. She knows that we know she knows, but she doesn't really want to know what we know. You know?"

Amelia not surprisingly looked utterly befuddled.

"Right," said Kate, clapping her hands. "Let's get started. We've a lot to get through." She began to run through her long list.

"We've obviously got the venue and the caterers sorted for lots of food and booze.

"We decided on also having extra big bowls of dolly mixtures and Maltesers on all the tables for everyone to snack on, as well as pickled onion Monster Munch." She looked over at Jack. "You have all that under control?"

Jack nodded, "All bought and in our kitchen. I might have overdone it, though."

"Not possible," Kate replied shortly, and continued. "We are all going to deck the hall in pink streamers and with giant balloons spelling out Freya's name and her age, of course. Patsy, tell me that's all done?"

"Affirmative. I have the helium and I will blow them up on the day."

"Great," Kate said, checking it off her list. "Evie sourced that candy floss machine and, of course, we've got the bouncy castle."

"Did The Minions tableware arrive?" said Delima worriedly. "I know you ordered it, Kate, but it will be a disaster if it doesn't get here in time."

"Don't worry, it's all here safely and we've also got a six and a half foot tall Minion costume that your Jack will wear when he brings in the cake."

Delima and Jack nodded as though this was the most normal thing in the world.

Amelia had sat quietly at first, clearly growing more and more confused. Eventually, she burst out, "I'm sorry everyone, but this *is* a party for an eighty-year-old woman you are talking about?"

They all looked at her.

"Yes," they chorused. Kate added "And your point is?"

Amelia looked flummoxed. "I mean, it just seems a little . . . silly and childish. Would she not prefer something more classy, like, I don't know, an afternoon tea or a sitdown meal or something?"

Kate patiently explained on everyone's behalf, "Amelia, just think of this as being a party for a hyperactive toddler and you will get the drift. We are throwing everything at this event. Freya adores Minions. So Minions she will have."

Delima added: "I caught her teaching Hari how to say, banana, in the style of a Minion. You know it's going to be his first word. Not 'mama' or 'dada', but 'ba-na-na'".

Patsy said to Amelia: "Not sure you have *The Vicar of Dibley* in the US of A, but if you've seen it, just think of Alice's wedding when she had Teletubbies as bridesmaids and multiply that by a million and that's kind of what we are going for."

"I'm just not sure it's very Freya," began Amelia, and then she caught the disapproving gazes, and said hastily: "But you know her far better than me, of course."

Delima nodded curtly and went on, "So Jack will be bringing in the cake? And are we all absolutely sure it will be big enough?"

"It's going to be gigantic," said Kate. She added, "As we all agreed, it will be decorated with the faces of Take That around the bottom layer and then with figurines of Hugh Jackman and Ryan Reynolds on the very top as Wolverine and Deadpool."

"Just make sure that it's all of Take That," said Edwyn seriously. "We don't want a repeat of her seventieth birthday when Jason Orange was left out."

Everyone paused and lowered their eyes remembering Freya's disappointment. They had vowed never to make that mistake again.

Kate said, "Big thanks to Patsy for getting Whisky Kiss sorted for the ceilidh. They will be on until midnight and then we have special permission to have a disco until 3am."

"Won't Freya be exhausted by then?" Amelia asked. Evie clenched her jaw and inwardly rolled her eyes – everything Amelia said just proved she didn't know the first thing about Freya.

"Are you kidding me?" said Jack. She's always the last to leave any party and she will wear us all out. Just make sure young Rory plays plenty of songs by The Clash and The Spice Girls and we'll be fine."

"Freya has eclectic taste in music," said Patsy dryly. Kate nodded. "She certainly has, and all of us want this night to be just perfect."

Delima added, "Every one of us here is grateful to Freya. She made me feel so welcome when I first came here from Singapore. She made a point of coming to visit me often, and I remember pouring my heart out to her. I felt so homesick and lonely but she asked me to become one of her Selkies and that's when I met all of you."

She beamed at them and went on, "Do you know my mother in Singapore video calls her once a week just for a chat? Freya phoned to reassure her I was settling in, but now they are on WhatsApp talking for hours."

Kate said, "She was the first one I told when I was pregnant with Louise. Even before Edwyn. She was so kind to me when I wasn't sure he really wanted to marry me and encouraged me to be patient because she knew for a fact Edwyn would eventually propose. I'm sure she gave him a kick up the arse, even though they both deny it."

Edwyn looked sheepish. Freya had indeed read him the riot act and told him to get down on one knee before a prize like Kate slipped through his fingers.

Maureen spoke up: "She's been my friend for as long as I can remember. It was Freya I told about the cancer as soon as I was diagnosed and she was so kind and understanding." She added, "When I was really sick from the chemo, Freya would come over, give the place a clean and stick a washing on. She'd leave a basket of bread and a Tupperware full of homemade soup or stew to save Andrzej cooking for himself after a hard day at work. I'd be upstairs sleeping and when I came down it was as though someone had waved a magic wand and the fairies had visited."

She smiled at Andrzej. "You all know what a help my Rory and Andrzej are in the house, but men never really do housework properly, do they?" She patted Andrzej's hand.

"I know you do your best love, but Freya sees all of the bruck and muck."

Patsy agreed, "She's a diamond. An absolute diamond and I don't think I would be here without her."

That was all they would get out of the taciturn Patsy, but it was enough to know that Freya had stepped in and helped when she was at her lowest ebb.

Amelia said, "She really is a very special woman. I've only been here a short time but already I can't imagine my life without her in it."

Kate grinned at her. "And that's why we're glad you are staying for a bit longer, so you can be part of the celebrations. This is one party you don't want to miss."

"Well, I have nothing to go back home for right now. I am so looking forward to it, and I want to thank you all for making me feel so welcome."

They all smiled at her fondly. Evie felt that creeping sense of unease again. Amelia couldn't stay indefinitely, could she?

Chapter Twenty-Seven

Evie's House

The next morning, Evie rang Kate to talk about Amelia. "I just think it's weird. She got her hair done just like me and she's even wearing the same sorts of clothes."

Kate replied, "Think of it as a compliment. She obviously idolises you and she's desperate to fit in here. I think you should cut her some slack."

"Do you think that's all there is to it?" said Evie, desperate to believe her friend.

"Yes. What else would it be? I know how sensitive you can be sometimes, but I do think you are overreacting a peedie bit. There's no harm in the girl."

"I know. You're right. I'm sure you are right. Did I tell you that Ross Isbister has asked her out on a date tonight?"

"Seriously? That's a turn-up for the books. I never thought I'd see the day," said Kate. "Wait a minute, is that why you are out of sorts, Evie Muir? It's nothing to do with Amelia being a copycat and it's actually all about Ross?"

"Absolutely not," said Evie indignantly. "He can ask whoever he likes out. I'm not bothered at all."

Kate was unconvinced but instead she said, "It's a big adjustment for both of you. She's family, but you don't know each other at all. I think she is just trying too hard. Give it time."

Kate hung up and looked around the room with exasperation. She had frantically tidied up when Amelia had come over to meet everyone, but the house was back to the chaos that comes with an untidy husband and two small children.

Kate decided there was no point in trying to sort everything because it would just be a guddle again in no time. The dogs, Eric and Ernie, looked at her hopefully.

"Come on then, let's go for a morning walk and clear away the cobwebs. Those two little monkeys can clear up their toys when they get back from school and it will do them no harm to wear un-ironed uniforms tomorrow. I don't feel like making the tea so we can get fish suppers from the chippie instead."

The dogs barked for joy as they headed out the door. Kate was surprised by how restless she felt. She loved being a mother, but since the girls had both gone to primary school she had a bit more time on her hands. She wasn't artistic like Evie, but she did feel as though she had unfinished business when it came to having a career.

She'd never used her law degree, getting pregnant with Louise soon after she graduated, and then having Claire shortly after meant she never had the chance. With Edwyn working such long hours in the hospital it wasn't possible for her to take on full-time work.

She bundled the dogs into the back of the messy, muddy car and they settled happily in the back seat knowing this would be a proper hike. Kate drove all the way to the Kitchener Monument. She decided to do the full circuit which would tire out even Eric and Ernie, two boisterous border terriers, named after the famous Morecombe and Wise comedy legends, even though they were both girls.

It was a tradition started by Evie's dad, Duncan, who lived in a house of women but pretended his dogs were boys. "I know it doesn't make any sense," said Kate where Edwyn had brought them home as cute little black-faced puppies, "but I want to do it for Duncan."

As with everything, Edwyn bowed to the wisdom of his wife. He considered himself the luckiest man in the world.

He was married to his best friend. The sex was still good for both of them and although his job at the hospital was often exhausting and demanding, he loved being a doctor. Best of all, he had two funny, bright and beautiful daughters.

Everything seemed just as it always was to Edwyn. He hadn't noticed that Kate had grown quieter these past few months, but she knew they would soon need to have a serious conversation.

She marched the dogs up to the monument and started a brisk walk along the cliff tops. She was soon breathless and even the dogs were panting. As always when she was up here, she looked out at the views of the sea and down to Hoy where she could just about make out the Old Man, the famous sea stack pointing proudly skywards.

Andrzej had told her the other day that climbers were back on the Old Man and how a particularly daring, if foolhardy, acrobat had once strung a tightrope from the cliffs to the stack and wobbled across. "They must all be off their heads," she murmured. Like everyone on the islands, she treated the cliffs with deep respect and had taught the girls to be careful when they went on puffin watch.

"Right, you two," she said to the dogs. "We've a way to go before we get back to the car and it looks like it might rain." Kate was right. She was caught in a downpour and soaked to the skin. She gave the dogs a hot shower and a bone each to chew on, while she had a bath before collecting the girls from school.

She put her daughters on tidy duty, making it into a game, while their cat, Joan Crawford, looked down on them from her shelf with haughty indifference. The girls had given up trying to wrap Joan in cuddles after being spat and hissed at, and Edwyn still bore the scars from when he had to take her to the vet and she had almost clawed him to the bone.

They had repeatedly wondered who would triumph in the feud between their bad-tempered Joan Crawford and Freya's grumpy Bette Davis. It was too close to call and they all vowed never to leave them both in the same room alone together. The whole family eyed Joan warily, especially the dogs, who gave her a wide berth.

Kate thought, "This is my life, being intimidated by a cat and at the beck and call of the kids and dogs. It really is about time I did something for myself."

Edwyn came home after another shift where he'd stayed on late to reassure a woman who was beside herself about her husband having a heart attack. He'd patiently explained that if he took care of himself, took his pills, cut down on the beer and the pies and did a bit of exercise, he would live to a grand old age.

Edwyn came home to a warm, messy house and a piping hot fish supper in the oven.

Kate and the girls had eaten, had their bath and were happily giggling in front of *Sponge Bob Square Pants*. To him, this was the perfect scene of domestic contentment.

When they finally went to bed after Edwyn had read them far more stories than Kate ever did, she told him: "We need to talk."

"Oh Christ," said Edwyn. "What have I done?"

She sighed at him, "You eejit, you haven't done anything. Well, not that I know of anyway." She looked at him through narrowed eyes and asked, "Have you done anything?"

Edwyn replied hastily: "Absolutely not. I just thought because you had your serious voice on that I was in trouble for something."

"Behave yourself," replied Kate. "I just want to talk to you about the future. Well, my future anyway.

"You know I love you and the girls, and the dogs and even Joan Crawford, although God knows why."

Edwyn nodded, suddenly worried. "Where's this heading, love?"

Kate met his gaze. "I need something for me. I'm just feeling as though life is passing me by. Look at Freya and Evie. They have the gallery and their art. Delima has Ola and baby Hari, but she also does all the fundraising and admin at the sanctuary. Patsy has her work as a joiner with Andrzej, and then there's Agnes with the hair salon. Even though Maureen has been poorly, she still makes those beautiful blankets and hats and here I am just a housewife and a dog walker." Her voice began to wobble as she finished speaking.

"Oh come here," said Edwyn, drawing her into his arms. "You are so much more than that. I couldn't do my job if it wasn't for you holding everything together at home and the girls are still so young and need you to look after them."

"I know, but soon they will be at high school and then away to university or living on their own and I will be left behind. I want more than that, Edwyn. I don't just want to be your support act. I really want to use my law degree to help people and make a difference and if I'm honest the money would come in handy too."

Edwyn looked at her with affection. "If that's what you want to do then of course I'm right behind you. I can ask for my hours to get cut if that would help."

"No, I don't want you to do that, at least not yet. I know how much you love your job."

She looked at him seriously. "I've thought about this a lot and I'm going to take a refresher course online. It will take longer, but I think I can make it work. I might have to get my mum to babysit a bit more often and you might be getting more teas from the chippie, but I want to give it a go."

Edwyn nodded. "Of course. I'll support you all the way."

"Thank you," whispered Kate.

"You don't have to thank me," said Edwyn. "We're a team." Then he grinned, "I can just see you in court in a black gown with black stockings underneath and spikey high heels."

Kate smiled and swatted at him playfully. "You are such an idiot, but if the girls are fast asleep, I might read you your rights while I decide on your punishment."

"Will there be handcuffs?" asked Edwyn hopefully.

"You are such a fool. Get your arse over here."

"Yes, ma'am."

Chapter Twenty-Eight

Liv's Flat

Amelia was on her way to meet Liv at her flat when her phone pinged with another text. She read it carefully and smiled. Everything was going to plan. She'd charmed all of Evie's friends, had a date with Ross that night and now just needed Liv to complete the last piece of the jigsaw.

Liv answered the door and blinked hard as she saw the newly blonde version of Amelia, who said in a bored voice, "I know I look like your sister yadda yadda. Whatever."

Amelia stepped into the cleanest, whitest and emptiest living room she had ever seen. She said incredulously "Do you actually live here or rent it out as an operating theatre?"

Liv shrugged. "I like things simple and uncomplicated. I've had enough chaos in my life," she replied tersely.

"Well, this is certainly basic. It looks like a jail cell. A few cushions and a couple of plants around the place wouldn't kill you." She laughed, "All you need is a toilet in the corner and a poster of Rita Hayworth on the wall and you've got the full *Shawshank Redemption*."

Liv had been trying to keep her temper, but this was just plain rude. "This is how I like to live," she said icily. "If you don't like it, you know where the door is."

Amelia gave a harsh laugh. "That's a nice way to talk to the person who is going to turn your life around for the better and give you the chance to finally get back at your sister."

Liv sighed wearily. "Look, I told you I've already got things back on track. I'm doing OK and Evie isn't even on my radar."

"Oh keep telling yourself that and one day you might believe it, but I don't buy it for one second," said Amelia. "You know how she's running that business? She's used the money from your dad and from that fat fool Freya to set herself up."

Liv felt her skin prickle.

"Surely that business should be yours too?" Amelia carried on. "It's the money from your dad that's made it possible. And, all the time, she's talking about giving back to the community, supporting local artists . . . blah blah blah. All so she can look good and be Lady Bountiful."

Amelia went in for the kill, "And you still owe her money, right?"

"How do you know about that?" Liv said, sharply.

Amelia shrugged. "Your sister likes to gossip, especially when you are the subject. All this talk of how she saved you. Sending you to rehab. To me it just looks like she likes to control you, Liv."

Liv responded, "That's none of your business. You obviously have your own issues with Evie. What the hell has she done to rattle your cage?"

Amelia ignored her, "And that time you nearly tried to drown her when you were kids . . . no one has forgotten about that. And – what else? Something about when a local lad died . . .?"

The colour drained from Liv's face, "Who the fuck told you that?"

Amelia smirked, "Let's just say Evie's not as trustworthy about keeping your secrets as you would like to think."

Liv's mind was racing and she thought, 'I finally believed I was safe and that no one would ever know what happened.

I've worked so hard to put the past behind me and move on, and now this. And if Evie has blabbed to this hard-faced cow, then who else has she told?'

Liv had always been 'the problem child' in the family, making Evie the golden girl. This had only festered as they grew older, with neither of their parents able to provide the love, stability or fairness both their daughters needed. Liv spent far too much of her time thinking of ways to get back at her little sister.

Back in 2004, after Evie and her first boyfriend, Brodie, had quarrelled at a bar in Stromness, Liv had seized her chance. She got Brodie blind drunk and spent the night with him in a hotel room. She claimed they had slept together, and she was pregnant with his child: telling these spiteful lies during a fearsome confrontation with Evie and Brodie on the beach.

Evie had hurled a bracelet he'd given her as a gift into the freezing water; Brodie had waded in to try and find it and had drowned. Liv lied that the tragedy caused her to miscarry, and Evie fled Orkney in horror, believing she was responsible for a double tragedy: Brodie's death and the loss of her sister's baby.

It was only after their father's death, twenty years later, that the truth finally emerged. That Brodie had never slept with Liv. That there had never been a baby. That Liv had planned to ruin their relationship with her lies.

Amelia watched as Liv tried to regain her composure. Her breathing had increased and her eyes were darting around the room.

"Not got much to say for yourself, have you, Liv?" Amelia drawled.

Liv glared at her with deep loathing.

Until coming back home from rehab, Liv wouldn't have given a flying fuck about what anyone thought of her, but it was all different now. She had built a life for herself and made friends with the people in her AA group.

They were understanding and forgiving and had all made mistakes in their lives, but Liv was terrified they would turn their backs on her as soon as they found out what she'd done.

Her stomach churned, she couldn't bear the thought of them looking at her with contempt and pity, especially Rab. She knew for certain she wouldn't survive if his friendship and respect were lost.

Amelia looked at her much in the same way a snake would look at a fat baby chipmunk. This was going even better than she hoped. Liv was obviously falling for her story and running scared.

She laughed to herself and thought, 'As if Evie would tell me anything. But I have my own ways of digging up scandal and my source is impeccable.'

She said aloud, "You know, your sister really seemed to enjoy telling me all your dirty little secrets. She reckons you broke your father's heart and made your mother so unhappy she lost her mind."

Liv burst out, "That's a lie. My dad was a spineless sack of jelly, and my mother was always crazy. I had nothing to do with him dying or her going off her head. That bitch Evie. I can't believe she told you about Brodie."

Liv was shocked at the level of betrayal she felt. With a lot of therapy and many long talks with Rab, Liv had begun to overcome her feelings of jealousy and resentment towards Evie and had almost decided to tentatively establish contact with her sister, who had said her door was always open.

She thought bitterly, 'Evie has no intention of wiping the slate clean. She's just been biding her time and now she wants to ruin my life. I believed her when she said no one would ever talk about what happened, and now she has told this weirdo the whole story, but maybe she actually can help. It might not be a total waste of time to find out what she has to say.'

She looked at Amelia and affected a drawl, "OK, I'm listening. What's your cunning plan?"

When Amelia had outlined what she wanted Liv to do, she didn't wait for a reply but abruptly got up to leave. At the door she turned round, "Don't take too long to make up your mind. And don't even think about warning Evie, because I have many other ways to make her life hell that don't involve you. Remember, all I have to do is call your good pal Rab and all the others in your AA group and tell them all about your past. That's all it would take to bring you down. It's your choice."

Liv sat alone in her cell-like room, mulling over Amelia's plan and wondering if she could go through with it.

Evie would be ruined and left with nothing. Liv would be in the clear with money in the bank.

In her dark days as an addict, Liv had frittered away the money her parents had given her, as well as the modest sum left over when Granny Sheila's cottage on Hrossey was sold.

Liv was now existing from one pay cheque to another and Evie was living in the family home, which Liv always thought should have been hers, by rights, as the eldest child.

As far as Liv was concerned, looking in from the outside, Evie had effortlessly built a successful business and was popular and well-liked. Once again, the golden child had triumphed, leaving Liv looking like a pathetic failure.

'It's not fair. It's never been fair. All the odds have always been stacked against me.' Liv sat in the growing dark going over and over in her mind what Amelia was planning.

'It could work and I would be protected. No one would believe Evie. Even if she shouted the truth from the rooftops, but can I really live with myself if I go along with it? And what the hell has Evie done to this Amelia woman to make her so hellbent on revenge. She wouldn't tell me but it must be something epic.'

The one person she wanted to confide in was Rab, but she knew that was impossible, and she also knew she was in for a restless and sleepless night. Amelia had said she would be in touch.

Liv knew what she had to do.

Chapter Twenty-Nine

Kirkwall

When Amelia walked into the bar Ross was already there looking handsome in a pair of jeans and a freshly washed and ironed sky-blue shirt. He'd had a shower, combed his hair and shaved, and he smelled of soap.

He smiled at her, his eyes crinkling up, showing perfect white teeth and that adorable dimple. 'It really is ludicrous how handsome this man is,' she thought. 'I find it very hard to believe he hasn't had a steady girlfriend or even a revolving door of casual women in his life.'

He got up and gave her an awkward peck on the cheek. Not knowing that Amelia would expect two kisses, they had a bit of a clumsy dance around each other.

"I got you a red wine. Is that OK?" said Ross. He looked embarrassed. "I'm an eejit. You might want something else. I can take it back, no bother."

Amelia smiled at him. "Not at all. Red wine is perfect. I'm glad you remembered. Let's go over there on a comfier seat."

They sat down and there was an awkward pause. Amelia tried to get the conversation going, "What do you think of my outfit? I was going to keep it for Freya's party but I thought I'd wear something new tonight."

'Oh bugger,' thought Ross. 'I should have told her how beautiful she looks right away.' Aloud, he said: "I'm sorry. You look very nice."

"Thank you. So do you." She raised her glass. "Cheers."

Ross took a nervous gulp of his pint and Amelia realised she would have to do all of the heavy lifting if they weren't to sit in an increasingly uncomfortable silence. She leaned forward and feigned fascination, "So Ross, tell me all about making Orkney chairs. I'm so intrigued. When did you start and how long does it take to make one?"

"You don't need to humour me, Amelia. We both know you would be bored stiff if I rambled on and on about my chair-making skills."

Amelia grinned and held up her hands palms up, as if she expected Ross to handcuff and arrest her.

"You caught me bang to rights. I thought it just might get you talking. I can sense you're a bit nervous." She smiled at him encouragingly. "I don't bite you know. Well, at least not on the first date."

He laughed and they could both feel a bit of the tension melting away.

"I'm sorry, Amelia. I'm just not very good at this. Never have been."

She looked at him, "It's not an exam, Ross. Just two people getting to know each other a bit better, that's all. I thought you said you found it easy to talk to me?"

"But we weren't out on a date then. We were just chatting. We hadn't got all dressed up and everything."

Despite herself, she was finding him increasingly adorable. Well, she may as well enjoy herself a little too. "Ross, you are wearing jeans and a shirt not a fancy tuxedo."

"I know, but these are my good jeans and I happened to have ironed this shirt."

Amelia smiled at him. "I'm honoured." She reached over and touched his hand.

"Right," she said firmly. "Here's what we'll do.

"Why don't we just pretend that this evening we happened to bump into each other and decided we were both hungry and fancied a bite to eat? No date. No pressure. Is it a deal?"

"It's a deal" he said, and let out a long sigh of relief.

"Actually," he added, "I'm suddenly really hungry. This place does a fine plate of steak and chips. Might be a bit too much for a peedie thing like you."

Amelia laughed, "No way. I could eat a whale sandwich. I'm starving."

With the pressure off Ross believing he had to be witty and entertaining, he relaxed and found he was enjoying being in Amelia's company. They chatted happily about music they liked and films they loved.

They both loathed rom-coms and were obsessed by the original *Blade Runner* with Harrison Ford and Rutger Hauer (the director's cut, obviously) and confessed to shedding a tear at *Dumbo*. The two of them had howled with laughter at the end of *Some Like It Hot* and declared *Singin' In The Rain* to be the greatest film of all time. Ross said emphatically that he didn't think he could be friends with someone who didn't love all those films. Amelia said that it was just as well they were in her top ten then.

They discovered they had a lot more in common. They both couldn't abide sweetcorn and were driven crazy by people smoking while they were trying to eat.

"Imagine this steak being ruined by somebody blowing out their fag breath on it," said Ross, shuddering. "That's what it was like in the old days. You'd come home reeking of stale smoke."

"What's your view on people who use leaf blowers, especially on a Sunday morning?" said Amelia.

"Anyone using one of those machines in any circumstances should be boiled in oil," said Ross gravely. "Agreed" said Amelia with a grin.

Amelia scoffed her steak dinner and finished off the chips Ross couldn't manage.

She ordered apple pie with cream *and* ice cream, followed by a plate of Orkney cheeses and oatcakes.

Ross was impressed. "I don't know where you've put all that food but I do like a woman with a healthy appetite."

"I'm very glad you like me, Ross" she said lightly, and added more seriously, "I'm having a really nice time tonight on our non-date."

He blushed. They continued to chat about other places Amelia needed to visit in Orkney and she told him all about her trip to Hrossey and how kind Freya and everyone had been to her.

Evie's name hadn't been mentioned until Amelia said, "Evie has been kind too, but as I told you, I get the sense she doesn't altogether approve of me. I might have gone too far getting my hair done like her, but I think she looks so beautiful, and I just wanted to fit in and feel like part of her family. Is that really dumb of me?"

"Not at all. I think you look lovely and I'm sure she doesn't mind really, why would she?"

"You're right. I'm sure I'm worrying about nothing. I just thought I might have put my foot in it, especially when I asked her about her sister."

Ross frowned. "That Liv is a piece of work. Although apparently, she's been working to turn over a new leaf, but you can make your own mind up when you meet her."

Amelia replied, "I've heard they don't get on, but I feel as though I should get to know her as we are related."

"Of course, you'll want to see her but just be aware she's not like most of the people here in Orkney. She's trying her best and that's all I want to say."

Ross had no idea that Amelia had already made contact with Liv and she was a key part of the whole plan. She widened her eyes. "Ross, you're making it sound as if she's dangerous! What exactly has she done?" But he shook his head and said he'd rather talk about more pleasant things.

Amelia wasn't getting any gossip from the decent and loyal Ross, so instead she asked him about what he thought she should buy Freya as a thank you present for letting her stay.

"She won't take any money, Ross. Obviously, I offered, but she was so offended I haven't brought up the subject again."

"Freya is easy pleased, said Ross. "Just looking after you and seeing you having a good time is all the thanks she needs, but if you really want to get her a present, they do special bottles of Orkney whisky and local gin. You know she loves a wee tipple."

"I had noticed, but she looks well on it," said Amelia with a grin. "That's a really good idea, thank you. Actually, do you fancy one for the road?"

The two of them looked up and realised the bar was empty. They hadn't been aware of it getting so quiet. It was past midnight and time to let the staff get home.

"I seem to keep everyone here in Orkney up late," said Amelia.

"Time goes fast when you are having a great time," said Ross, surprising himself. He added, "I've had a brilliant night, but I better be getting you home to Freya. I bet she will be waiting up for you."

Ross paid for the bill, left a generous tip to the waitress and ordered Amelia a cab, which he prepaid. She gave him a hug and they kissed each other on the cheek. Getting it just right this time with no awkwardness.

"We need to do this again," said Ross, blushing.

"Anytime," she replied.

When she got back, Amelia took off her high heels and tip-toed into her room only to hear Freya call out: "Well, how was it? Tell me everything."

She popped her head round the door of Freya's bedroom. "Oh Freya, it was lovely. No undignified scuffles at the end of the night, just a hug and a kiss on the cheek, but he is a very special man."

"That he is," said Freya.

"Please tell me you've not been waiting up for me to get back in?"

"I could pretend I was re-reading my very worn copy of *Greenvoe* but I knew I wouldn't get to sleep until you were back. I was the same when Evie stayed here although she seldom went over the door."

"Well, I'm home safe and sound and I'd better get to bed. I'm so tired. You get to sleep."

"Good night, my love. See you in the morning and you can tell me all the details. I want to know absolutely everything."

Chapter Thirty

Freya's House

Waking up early the next day with the morning sun shining, and the weather set to hold up, Freya declared it was the perfect day for a swim with the Selkies. She messaged everyone on their WhatsApp group and told them to meet at the usual time: 10am at Inganess Beach.

Everyone was up for it, even Maureen felt well enough to join in after checking with Edwyn that it was OK. He replied that not only was it a great idea, but he'd be happy to write a prescription for her to have a dip in the sea as often as possible.

He told her: "If it makes you feel better inside and out then I'm all for it. Just take it easy, but it will be good for you to get out into the sunshine and be with the girls. Kate is here chomping at the bit to get going. She'll see you later."

Freya had asked Amelia if she could swim and did she want to come, but Amelia said she didn't want to intrude and anyway she hadn't packed a swimming costume. She didn't think she would need one in Orkney.

"Well, you obviously can't borrow one of mine," said Freya. "It would be like a circus tent on you."

Amelia thought she'd managed to dodge a bullet, but Freya told her, "Let me message Evie. She'll have one to fit you. She can bring it over and take us both to the beach in Florence for a peedie change." She added, "I'm away to get ready. It's best to go with your cossie on already so you can just strip off and dive straight in. I'll give you one of my big towels so that when you get out of the water you can get changed underneath it."

Amelia was horrified, "Aren't there changing rooms and showers?"

"Afraid not. You will just have to rough it, my girl." She grinned at the look on Amelia's face.

"Don't be such a fearty. We are all in the same boat and nobody cares if they see a bit of bum or a boob. Just bring clean knickers so your bits are nice and dry afterwards." She added encouragingly, "Then we can sit on the sand and have some coffee and cake. That's the bit I like the best."

"Won't it be awfully cold?" said Amelia nervously.

"It absolutely will, but you'll be all tingly and you'll feel so alive that you won't even notice, especially when you have a mug of my special coffee laced with whisky."

She winked at her. "And if you get in the water, you'll have something to tell Ross Isbister on your second date, won't you?"

They had both spent a happy hour sitting in their dressing gowns going over details of the night before. Freya declared it to be a huge success and told Amelia she'd have to invest in some new underwear as they would be sleeping together soon, and it was best to be prepared.

Amelia shrieked with laughter but thought to herself that sex with Ross would be an added bonus and Evie would be livid. She hadn't fooled Amelia one bit by pretending not to care that Ross had asked her out. The hurt in her eyes was plain to see.

Freya stood up and took the coffee cups into the kitchen, "Right, get yourself ready, Evie will be here soon and we need to make the most of this fine weather.

*

Down at the wide, open beach with the sun shining on the waves and the seagulls squawking, Evie tried to shake off her bad mood. Seeing Amelia always seemed to put her back up and Freya hadn't helped by happily chatting about her date with Ross all the way here.

Evie also wasn't altogether proud of the fact that she packed her most unflattering and oldest swimming costume for Amelia, and was taking comfort from the fact she looked glum and apprehensive.

"Don't feel you have to come in, Amelia. It's fine if you want to stay on the shore," said Evie.

"Nonsense," said Freya. "She wants the whole Orkney experience and it's a lovely chance to see all the girls again. She's well up for it, aren't you?"

Amelia gave a watery smile. "Of course, Freya. You are right. I'm just a bit worried about being freezing, that's all. Can't icy water kill you?"

"Only in Antarctica. Come on now. Let's go. We don't want to keep the others waiting."

Kate, Delima, Patsy and Maureen were already stripping off. Jack had brought them all in his car. He was considered an honorary Selkie and the only man in the group, but this morning he was looking after Ola and Hari and not getting in the water himself. He felt very proud of the fact he had helped by carrying the picnic basket to the car after Delima had spent hours filling it with goodies, after washing, changing and feeding the children.

Jack was sitting on a deck chair while Ola made sandcastles and Hari lay on a tartan blanket kicking his legs and being impossibly cute. Amelia lingered on the shore, reluctant to head in.

She watched as Freya ran into the sea and did a surprisingly elegant dive into the waves. Kate and Patsy were strong swimmers, but Evie was close behind them. With the help of her friends she had become as happy and confident in the water as a little mermaid.

As always, Delima seemed oblivious to the cold. She looked like a teenager in her tiny bikini and there was only the merest trace of fine silver lines on her tummy to show she'd given birth to two big babies, one just five months ago.

She grabbed Amelia's hand and told her not to be scared and that they would run in together. Amelia screeched as a chilly wave hit her right in the stomach and splashed up on to her face. "I don't want the water to sting my eyes," she yelped.

"You get used to it, don't worry," said Delima. "Get your shoulders under and swim towards the shipwreck. Look, Kate and Evie are there already. I'll be right here with you."

The sea was bracing, and the cold made Amelia gasp at first, but Delima was right, after the first shiver she was feeling much better. The water was so clear she could see the white sand underneath and a few little fish swimming around her ankles.

She soon reached the shipwreck, spluttering when a wave almost reached the top of her head. She was greeted with whoops and cheers from Freya and Patsy. Evie managed a tight smile and Delima gave her a wet hug. Maureen was close behind. She was taking her time, doing an elegant slow crawl.

"Well done, Amelia," she said, catching up to them all bobbing beside the wreck.

"How are you feeling?"

Amelia laughed. "I feel a bit out of breath but it's not as cold as I thought it would be."

Freya beamed. She loved to see people enjoy a swim. She said to Amelia, "I can see most of your hair is still dry. Fancy being a real Selkie and going right under? Come on, we will do it together."

They all held hands, counted three, two, one and ducked below the waves, coming back up shrieking and laughing.

"I think that's enough for a first time," said Freya. "Let's take a slow swim back to the shore and dry off."

After getting out of the water, everyone did complicated manoeuvres under towels to get their wet cozies off and dry underwear and clothes back on.

Jack took Ola and Hari to look for shells and when he came back, the picnic was all laid out, cakes and sandwiches thick with butter and cheese, and the Selkies were pouring out hot coffee and hot chocolate from their flasks, laced with their favourite tipple.

Freya raised her mug. "A toast," she cried. "To our brand new Selkie, Amelia. We are all proud of her for being such a good sport and joining us today."

"To Amelia", they all chorused. Amelia almost felt a twinge of shame that she was deluding these women, and for what she was about to do, but she managed to shrug it off and instead said as sincerely as she could, "Thank you all so much. I can't believe how much fun that was. You were right. I feel so alive."

"Well now," said Maureen, "Is that just down to the swimming? We're all dying to ask. How was your date with Ross last night?"

Kate added, "We're desperate to know – is he good with his hands?"

"Well, he makes beautiful chairs," said Freya.

Patsy let out a roar of laughter, "Did he make a move? What was it like? I bet he's got a cracking boaby on him."

Amelia looked puzzled.

Kate dryly explained, "She means his, you know, his manhood, but boaby sounds better. It's friendlier."

"Exactly," said Patsy. "'Prick' sounds jaggy and painful."

Amelia gasped in surprise. These women were earthy and outrageous. "I didn't actually see his, em, boaby. It was only the first date."

Maureen nodded approvingly: "Quite right. You need to get to know a man properly before you give them a look at your flower."

Kate and Patsy guffawed. "Your flower. That's a good one," said Kate.

"Well, it's a lot better than fanny," said Maureen. "I had a great aunt Fanny and she was a horrible dried-up bitter old woman. I've always felt odd when people called their noonies that."

Freya changed the subject, "That's enough you lot. Amelia will be thinking you only have one thing on your minds. It's early days with her and Ross and you know how shy he is. Come on, eat up. There's not a pick on any of you girls. I've seen more fat on a lean slice of ham."

They all tucked in. Jack brought Ola and Hari back and the little girl held out her arms to Amelia, who dried her feet and tickled her tummy.

Evie hadn't said a word when they were talking about Ross, but she was taken aback by how much she minded the thought of him and Amelia having sex. Her throat felt so tightly clenched she could barely get food down, and now she had to watch as little Ola transferred her affections. Evie knew she was being petty but she always thought she had a special bond with Ola.

She'd known her since she was less than a day old, rushing up to the hospital and crying with Jack over how perfect she was, while Delima looked at them with a mixture of fondness and bafflement.

They had exclaimed over her tiny fingers and toes and marvelled at her fat little legs and arms and perfect skin, gravely declaring her to be both the most intelligent and beautiful baby in the whole world.

Evie hadn't ever given much thought to being a mum. She'd never grown up around babies, and when they visited their cousins in Hrossey, her mother declared them to be 'fat, disgusting little red goblins'.

But when baby Ola was born, Evie actually felt her arms aching to hold her. She was always the first port of call on the odd time Jack and Delima needed a babysitter although they usually took both children everywhere with them. She watched Amelia building more sandcastles with the little girl and felt as though this woman who had come into her life such a short time ago was slowly taking her place in everyone's affections.

Evie began to understand how her eight-year-old sister Liv must have felt when she came along and grabbed a hold of their dad's heart.

'Liv was left out in the cold', she thought. 'I never knew just how painful it must have been for her. I don't remember us doing things together as a family very often. She was always sulking in her room or arguing with my mum and dad. When I compare what I have to the life Liv has led, and how she is living now, I do feel bad. I really must check up on her and find out how she's doing. I know she won't get in touch with me, so I need to make the effort. Surely, it's been long enough now for all the resentment between us to be forgiven, if not forgotten.'

She looked over at Amelia, who was smiling and playing with Ola. She's settled in so fast, Evie thought. Everyone loves her after such a short time, even Ross. And look at me, still full of insecurities. Maybe they didn't even really want her hanging around with them anymore. Amelia was so much more fun.

Evie made a huge effort to stop these negative thoughts. 'If everyone else liked Amelia so much, I must be the problem. I just need to make more of an effort.'

Evie called over to where Amelia and Ola were burying Jack in sand. "You really have got a peedie pal there. She will have you run ragged. I've never known a bairn with her energy."

"She's a lamb," said Amelia. She looked over at Delima and smiled at Jack. "You are both so lucky to have such a cute little girl and such a gorgeous baby boy." They beamed.

"We think so," said Jack. Ola banged her plastic pail with her spade and shouted "Aa-mee-ah".

"Did you hear that? She said my name. You clever, clever girl." Amelia lifted her up and gave her a hug.

Jack said proudly, "Well, she is very advanced for her age. We do notice she's way ahead of other toddlers."

"Away with you," said Delima. "She's a perfectly normal little girl. She just loves her aunty Amelia, don't you, my pet?"

She added: "Right, let's take her home now before she gets grumpy and spoils the illusion of being the perfect angel, and Hari needs his nap, too. Amelia, you'll have to come and visit us at the sanctuary. You've not been by yet. It would be good to see you and the baby seals would love to say hello too."

They all started packing up, chattering happily and making plans to meet up again next week, and there were plenty of whispers about Freya's party, that she pretended not to hear.

Evie dropped Freya and Amelia off, refusing an offer of more coffee and cake, saying she had a painting to finish. She sat in her kitchen in the Orkney chair lovingly restored by Ross and found herself near tears. She had been with her friends today but had felt like an outsider. It was a lonely place to be, and all because of Amelia.

Her phone rang, a welcome distraction from her sad thoughts. It was Sophia, her voice hoarse from crying.

"Evie, can I come and stay with you? We've had another bust-up."

Chapter Thirty-One

Evie's House

Evie only had time to put the kettle on before a red-eyed Sophia appeared on her doorstep and started crying as Evie wrapped her in a hug. She bundled Sophia inside and onto the sofa in the kitchen, gave her a cup of hot sweet tea and asked what was going on.

"It's the same old story," said Sophia. "We just end up arguing about everything. We are going round and round in circles." She wiped her eyes with a sodden tissue.

"You and I have had this conversation so many times, Evie. I can't keep doing all the heavy lifting. You know that he won't even visit London. My family still haven't met him. It's ridiculous."

Her parents and brothers were so important to Sophia, and Evie remembered how she had been welcomed into their warm embrace while living in London. It was one of the few times she remembered being happy there.

"I have never understood why he can't meet you halfway. It's not fair. He's being completely selfish."

Sophia sighed. "I know, and I feel like it's becoming too much of an effort to make this work," she said, flatly. "It shouldn't be this hard. I'm at the end of my rope."

"Is it worth going to see him today?" asked Evie. "And try and talk to him?"

Sophia shook her head impatiently. "Why is it always me doing the running? All I did was ask him about Christmas, and his plans. And then it turns into a massive argument."

She checked her phone, "He hasn't even tried to call me. Not that I would answer him and you know what, I am not going to spend all day waiting for him to get in touch."

She turned off her phone and shoved it under a cushion.

Sophia and Evie spent the day together. They talked about Finn and then about Amelia and discussed Freya's upcoming birthday party. Evie showed Sophia the work in progress of her painting of Freya, and Sophia looked at it long and hard and told Evie it was beautiful but the hands weren't quite right.

Evie looked at her friend with affection. "You're probably the only person honest enough to tell me that and, of course, I know I haven't cracked it when it comes to her hands. They are too big, aren't they?"

"Yep, they look like pink bananas but you will fix it and the rest of it is gorgeous. Freya will love it."

They talked until well past midnight and both women felt better. Sophia's calm advice had helped Evie's anxiousness about Amelia, and Evie had convinced Sophia that Finn would call her before she had to go back to London and they would work things out.

But the next morning, when Sophia turned her phone back on, there was nothing from him, and Evie saw the bitter disappointment in her friend's face.

"Does he know you are getting the last flight back south?" asked Evie.

Sophia nodded. "It's always the same one."

"There's still time," said Evie, but when she dropped Sophia off at the airport, there still had been nothing from Finn, and there was no romantic gesture at the departure gate. He was nowhere to be seen. Sophia tried not to cry as she boarded the plane and told Evie maybe it was all for the best and she'd be in touch.

Driving back home in Florence, Evie did a lot of thinking. She was furious with Finn, and Sophia was well within her rights to give up on him altogether. And yet, when they were together you could see they truly loved each other, it was much more than terrific sex, but he was going to have to change his attitude, or he would lose Sophia for ever.

Evie decided to take action and when she got home, went online to get as much information and ammunition as possible. A few days later, she called Freya to say she had invited Finn over to her place that evening and could she come over too? She had a plan and needed Freya's help.

Freya readily agreed. She was very fond of Sophia and thought that although Finn was utterly charming, he needed a boot up the arse, just like Edwyn all those years ago when he was dithering about asking Kate to marry him.

"I can't believe that clown Finn would let such a terrific woman slip through his fingers. He needs a right talking to and we are the very women to do it," Freya told Evie.

Finn was feeling sorry for himself when Evie called. He'd been desperately upset that he'd quarrelled again with Sophia and ruined another of their precious weekends. When she had stormed off and decided to stay with Evie, he had stubbornly refused to get in touch, waiting for Sophia to make the first move.

He knew he should have gone to the airport with an enormous bunch of flowers and thrown himself at her mercy with a fulsome apology, but instead he went for a long walk, telling himself she should be the one to say sorry for starting an argument with him and then going off in the huff.

He heard the little plane take off and saw it head south, taking the woman he adored back to London, maybe for ever. He cursed himself for being an eejit and immediately texted her to say he was a clown and he was sorry and waited for a reply. But there had been no response from Sophia.

That was three days ago. They never went this long without keeping in touch. It looked like he had completely blown it. He didn't know what to do and was glad to receive Evie's call to ask him round for a drink with her and Freya.

He thought that maybe they could help him. Evie had known Sophia for years and Freya was the wisest woman he had ever met, but deep down he thought it was too late, and it was all his fault.

Finn split his time between his messy flat in Stromness, which Sophia referred to as 'the love nest', and a no-frills bothy on Hoy where he spent happy hours monitoring sea eagles and chatting with fellow twitchers and amateur birders.

He thought he'd been happy in the past, having a succession of flings with female tourists, bowled over by his Irish accent and prowess in bed. Sometimes they would have vigorous sex outdoors on the soft grass or on the beach if the weather was fine and he built a fire. Finn had learned an awful lot from one particular German girl who had done several things to him that he thought would be considered illegal back home in Ireland.

He'd never wanted to settle down and maintained the very idea of weddings, babies and mortgages would bring him out in hives. And then along came Sophia and his heart was no longer his own. He loved her so very much, and if he was honest that was part of the problem.

The depth of his love frightened him. He was terrified of being hurt and broken by his feelings for her, which is why he had been so pig-headed about visiting her in London. He knew he was pushing her away, but he couldn't stop himself.

He headed to Evie's with a bottle of whisky, still not having heard from the woman he adored and feeling as though there was no hope. He was given a huge hug from Freya, who then gave him a slap on the hand as though he was four years old.

"You absolute bloody idiot. Why are you still here? You should be on a plane down to see Sophia, full of apologies and an engagement ring in your pocket."

She snatched the bottle of whisky from his shocked grasp and told him to sit down. Finn did as he was told.

A drink was thrust into his hand and both Freya and Evie drew up their chairs to look him in the eye. "You are both scaring me more than a bit," he said, cowering into the back of his chair.

"Good," said Freya. "You should be scared. You are in danger of throwing away the best thing that has ever happened to you. That poor girl deserves better. I'm so cross with you, Finn, I'd dearly like to kick some sense into you."

Finn looked really worried now. He felt sure Freya could kick like a mule and do him a fair bit of damage. Evie said soothingly, "It's not going to come to that. We just want to help you."

Freya grumbled, "We want to help him alright. We want to knock some bloody sense into him." Finn was totally on the back foot with this 'good cop, bad cop' act, and he wailed: "I just need you both to help me. I don't want to lose her but I don't know what to do. I can't imagine a world without Sophia, but she will never come here to live, and do you honestly see me in a suit and tie working in London?"

"For the love of God," said Freya, "would you listen to yourself. No one wears suits and ties anymore. Most people down south are working from home and when they go out they wear shorts and football tops."

Freya knew that wasn't exactly true, but she had no intention of letting Finn off the hook. She went on, "You are just being pig-headed. All Sophia wants is for you to go down and visit her for Christ's sake. She thinks so much of you that she wants you to meet her family. I can't think why you are being so stubborn."

Finn looked tortured, "I know I'm not being fair, but I am just worried when she sees me down there, she will compare me with all those sophisticated fellas and I'll be found wanting. I won't be polished enough and she'll think I'm a culchie."

Evie and Freya looked at him with exasperated affection. "Do you honestly think a woman like Sophia would ever be as shallow as to worry about fancy clothes and affected manners?" said Freya.

He sighed. "I know. I am being ridiculous but apart from Sophia there is nothing there that interests me, and I feel safe here. I'm part of a community. I'd be a square peg in a round hole down south."

Evie said, "You know, Finn, I don't think you have thought this through. I've been doing a bit of research on your behalf, and I had no idea that there's so much wildlife to see down there, and such interesting projects going on."

He looked at her doubtfully. "Like what?"

"Well," said Evie artlessly, "Did you happen to know that they have reintroduced wild beavers in Essex?" Freya snorted and almost choked on her whisky.

Finn said, "What's so funny about that? I love beavers. It sounds brilliant."

Freya looked at him innocently and said, "Nothing. There's absolutely nothing funny at all about wild beavers rampaging though Essex, no doubt on the look out for hard wood to gnaw on."

Evie began to splutter with laughter, which set Freya off again. "Oh I get it. Honestly. What age are you two?" said Finn, exasperated. He added primly, "I have actually read a wee bit about it, and it sounds like interesting stuff. It might be good to see what's going on for myself."

Evie hadn't expected him to fold quite so fast. He was obviously just looking for an excuse to climb down from his self-appointed high horse. She added, "Even if it meant having to go to That London?"

"Well," he replied, "I do feel bad that Sophia is always the one having to do the commuting. She's been really good about it, but it costs her a fortune and she's always exhausted when she first gets here."

Evie thought she might as well push her luck. "Why don't you check a few other projects when you are south? There's all those red kites that have been reintroduced. They are as common as sparrows there now."

Finn interrupted her. "Actually, sparrows are quite rare now. It's a terrible shame."

Evie rolled her eyes. "There you are then, go and see the endangered cockney sparrows while you still can. You can spend some time with Sophia at her place, and you know it might not be as bad as you think."

Finn smiled at them and looked relieved. "I see exactly what you both did there. You've tucked me up like a kipper. You are right, though. Thanks both of you. I'll call Sophia right now."

When he left, Freya and Evie looked at each other in triumph and guffawed again. Freya wiped her eyes.

"Oh Evie, that was a stroke of genius, getting Finn to go south by dangling the prospect of beavers in front of him. It's too much."

"I don't care what it takes to keep them together. He just has to meet her halfway and everything will work out fine."

Chapter Thirty-Two

Freya's House

The next morning, Freya was congratulating herself on helping Finn and Sophia get back on track and happily talking to Amelia about her plans for another date with Ross, weighing up whether it was better to go out for a meal again, or should she cook him something.

"I can always make myself scarce," suggested Freya. "If you want the place to yourself. Evie or Kate would have me for a sleepover, or I could stay with Maureen."

"No way," said Amelia hastily. "I don't want to turn you out of your own home. Anyway, he might get the wrong idea and think I'm trying to seduce him by inviting him here, especially if I'm on my own."

"Aren't you, though? Trying to seduce him, I mean?" said Freya with a wicked smile.

Amelia laughed, "You are terrible. He's gorgeous and I really fancy him, but I think we might have something special together and I don't want to rush things. It's only the second date after all."

She frowned and looked at Freya. "Do you think I am being utterly ridiculous?"

Freya smiled reassuringly. "Not at all. But to be honest I'm not sure that boy will ever make the first move. You might have to jump on him like a ninja."

"I can do that," said Amelia with a giggle, "but maybe not quite yet."

"Let me make us some coffee," said Amelia, "and we can have some of your chocolate shortbread that I've become addicted to."

Amelia got up to go to the kitchen and saw Evie's car pull up into the drive. Florence screeched to a halt, and Evie raced out of the car and burst into the room, out of breath and looking distraught.

"Freya, are you alright?" said Evie.

"I'm fine. Whatever is the matter? What's happened?" said Freya, bewildered.

"You haven't seen it then?"

"Seen what? Evie, you aren't making any sense."

"I hate to be the one to tell you but there's been some disgusting posts about you on Twitter, or X or whatever the hell it's called these days. I wouldn't have given it a second thought but it's getting a lot of attention and has already been retweeted hundreds of times. It must be some kind of bot, not just a vile troll."

"I have absolutely no idea what you are going on about," said a baffled Freya. "I didn't understand a word of that last bit, but it's obviously got you all upset. Sit down and take a deep breath and tell me what's going on."

Evie was becoming tearful. "Oh Freya, it's horrible lies about you on social media and it's being seen by loads of people."

Freya replied, "You know I don't take any notice of all that nonsense. I've just about got my head round Instagram but I'm not going anywhere near the other mad stuff." Freya had once been on Facebook but had hastily given it up after Rory had dismissively told her it was for 'old people'. She'd never bothered with Twitter.

Seeing Evie so het up, Amelia asked worriedly: "Exactly what sort of lies are they telling about my Freya?"

Evie was too distraught to take umbrage at Amelia claiming Freya as her own.

"About her past," she said tersely.

Freya said quietly, "What about my past?"

"About Magnus."

"Ah, I see," said Freya with a heavy sigh. "But that's never been a secret, Evie. You all know that. I've never hidden anything in my life. I admit I rarely think of it these days. It all seems so very long ago. It was another life."

"Who is Magnus?" asked Amelia. "Was he an old boyfriend?"

Freya signed. "I was Magnus, my love. But Magnus has been effectively 'dead' for almost sixty-five years. Why would anyone bring it up now?"

The penny dropped. "So you were actually born a boy," said Amelia, adding hastily, "not that it matters one bit."

Freya rubbed her hand over her face, the weariness settling. "I truly thought that part of my life was over forever." She turned to Evie. "I know you mean well by warning me, but there's no need to be so dramatic. Surely no one cares. I suppose there will be people here in Orkney who didn't know, but why ever would they bother?"

Evie said in despair, "That's the trouble. It's blowing up already, Freya."

She took out her phone and brought up the tweet, handing it over to Freya, who put on her glasses and read aloud:

> *There's a vile predator on Orkney who has been hiding in plain sight for years, living a lie, posing as a female and with access to our youngsters.*

Freya looked at Evie sharply, "Why on earth do you assume they are talking about me?" Silently, Evie scrolled up to another post from the same source. Freya started to read it out but gave a strangled sob and couldn't continue.

You know her as Freya but she's living a lie. We need to take action and get the police involved to protect our vulnerable young girls and boys.

Freya couldn't take it in. "What on earth do they mean? I don't understand." She looked completely bewildered. "They want to protect youngsters from *me*? But that's crazy?"

Freya looked at Evie in horror and gasped, "Where is this coming from? Who is doing this?"

Evie said, "I'm so sorry, Freya. I think they mean you have access to kids at your free art classes and they are trying to make people think the children are in danger. It's utterly vile."

Freya whispered, "I wish you hadn't shown me that. I really would rather not have known." A single tear rolled down her cheek. Evie was crushed and felt terrible. Maybe she had been too hasty in coming straight to Freya, but she had wanted to prepare her for the worst.

Amelia was looking at her own phone. She said, "These messages were posted early this morning and already they've had hundreds of likes and just look at these replies."

Amelia continued scrolling and shook her head, "Jesus Christ, some people are vile."

Freya said, "Please don't look and don't tell me what they are saying. I can't bear it. And is this really someone I might know? You really think it might be someone with a child who comes to the art class? I mean I just can't think who would do such a cruel horrible thing . . ."

"We don't know who it is," said Evie, "It could be anyone. These people hide behind screens. They are ants with megaphones."

Amelia turned to Evie, "I can't believe this is happening. Surely we can sue? Or at least get the posts taken down and whoever is in charge can issue a retraction and apology."

"It's not that simple," said Evie grimly, "I can look into it but these big tech companies don't give a shit about tracking down these trolls."

"Still," said Amelia "it's worth a try. We don't want this getting out of hand. Or getting into the papers – you know how they like to pick up stories like this. Just look how upset you have made her."

Freya was ashen. "What do you mean? The papers wouldn't be interested in me would they?"

Both Amelia and Evie were silent. They knew all too well how stories like this could get out of hand. More and more newspapers and online sites relied on clickbait stories to get readers' attention.

"I need to lie down," Freya whispered. "I have a splitting headache and I don't feel well." Evie was distraught, her dearest friend looked so defeated.

"Let me call Edwyn or I can get you some tea."

"No, thank you. I just want to be left alone. Just leave me be." She went into her room and shut the door. They could hear her sobbing.

"This is terrible," said Evie. "Who on earth would be so disgusting as to do this to Freya, and why would they post such cruel lies?"

"Beats me," said Amelia, pouring herself a cup of coffee. "But it seems like there's nothing we can do."

Evie frowned, "I should sit with her and make sure she's alright."

Amelia said quickly, "But you heard her, Evie. She wants to be left on her own." She added, "Don't you worry, I will look after her. You gave her a horrible shock. I think you could have been a bit less blunt, if I'm honest."

Evie looked stricken, and Amelia added, "I think Freya was also disappointed you said you couldn't do anything to help."

She then half-heartedly tried to reassure Evie. "I guess it's not really your fault. Here's hoping no one will take it seriously and it will be forgotten about in a couple of days."

Evie said grimly: "I hope you are right."

Chapter Thirty-Three

Liv's Flat

Liv hadn't heard anything more from Amelia aside from a text to say everything was on track. In the meantime, her life continued in a routine that she found strangely comforting.

She'd been promoted to assistant manager at the bar, not quite as good as it sounded as they had an almost weekly turnover of staff, and she hadn't been given any more money in her pay packet. It was on a trial basis for a month and if things worked out, she might get a bit of a pay rise.

She kept a low-profile, still preferring to stay in at night, mostly sleeping or just watching a bit of TV. The only time she went out was to her AA meetings which to her surprise she really enjoyed. She felt a deepening bond with these damaged people who were trying their best to turn their lives around.

The kindly Rab had become her sponsor and he told her to call him anytime she felt she might fall off the wagon or just needed a chat. She hadn't got in touch with him yet, but found it comforting that there would be someone there to talk to if it all become too much.

She had just finished her usual spartan breakfast of toast with a scrape of butter and a cup of strong tea when her phone pinged.

Hey – I would really like to see you. I'll pop round this afternoon if I don't hear back from you. Evie x

Liv tutted. It was a cleverly worded message that needed a response, even if it was just to be told to get stuffed. Liv knew if she didn't reply, Evie would be as good as her word and turn up at her door.

After Amelia had falsely told her Evie had shared her darkest secrets about Brodie, she felt a simmering anger towards her younger sister and a deep sense of betrayal. 'She promised me she wouldn't say a word. I should never have been so stupid as to trust her. I should just tell her to bugger off, but maybe I need to look her in the eyes and hear her trying to wriggle out of it.'

Liv sent a short response:

Suit yourself.

A few hours later, Evie was at her sister's door. She decided to knock rather than just walk in. Liv scowled at her. "What do you want?" she said stonily. "If it's the money I owe you for rehab, I told you I would send it to you as soon as I could."

"Liv, you know fine well I said at the time I don't want your money. We all chipped in anyway, not just me. Kate and Edwyn helped and Freya obviously, and Andrzej and Maureen too. We just wanted you to get a fresh start."

Liv affected boredom: "Well what *do* you want then?"

"Just to see you and to make sure you were doing OK."

"Checking up on me you mean."

"No. Nothing like that. Look, I brought you a present. It's the view of the Yesnaby cliffs in the sunshine. I thought it might brighten the place up a bit."

Liv made no move to take the gift Evie had spent such a long time creating. She'd used bright blues and golden yellows to make the painting as cheerful as possible. It was glorious. Even Liv had to acknowledge that.

"I prefer my place to be minimalist, but you can leave it over there if you like."

Evie placed the painting carefully on the floor across from the sofa. "Is it OK if I sit down?"

"Please yourself."

Evie winced. She'd expected the sofa to have a bit of give but it was like sitting on a rock.

Liv didn't sit. "I've actually got plans this afternoon. So if you have something to say I don't have long."

"I just wanted a chat, that's all. We haven't spoken properly at all and I wanted to make sure you were alright."

"I'm doing just fine," Liv said tersely.

"I'm glad to hear it. I know you've got a job and been going to AA meetings. That's really great."

Liv replied icily, "That's none of your business, but yes, I am getting by. But I'm not your problem, Evie, and I don't need you to fix me. I'd rather you just left me alone and I will pay that money back. I don't want to owe you anything."

Evie knew when she was beaten. Now was not the time to tell Liv that she had given her a share in the gallery. She got up and left, but not before turning to her sister and saying, "It's Freya's birthday soon and we are having a party for her. I know she would like you to be there and I would too. I'll text you the details. Despite everything, we are family. And I will be here if you ever need me. Don't ever forget that. I am on your side."

Liv burst out, "Oh come on, Evie. Drop the act. You promised me you wouldn't say a word about what happened to Brodie that night, but Amelia told me you couldn't wait to spill the whole story to her."

Evie was so outraged she couldn't speak for a few minutes. Eventually, she said breathlessly, "That's a damned lie. I haven't said a single word to Amelia about you. She's making it all up."

Evie had gone bright red with anger and was stumbling over her words, which as far as Liv was concerned made her look guilty as sin. She said coldly: "Shut the door on your way out and just leave me in peace."

After Evie left, Liv sat on her hard couch mulling over her recent visits from two women who might look alike but had absolutely nothing in common. Which one of them was lying to her?

She knew Amelia's type and considered her to be something of a kindred spirit, but that made her afraid of her. Amelia had threatened to destroy her sister and if Liv refused to help, she would bring her down too. This wasn't an empty threat. Liv knew for sure that Amelia would go through with it.

But despite her fractured relationship with Evie, she knew her sister to be a decent woman. Was it really credible she would tell Amelia all of Liv's secrets? Who was telling the truth? It felt as though neither of them could be trusted. What the hell was she going to do?

Meanwhile, a fuming Evie vowed to have it out with Amelia. She had caught her out in a bare-faced lie. She would never dream of talking about the terrible night to anyone outside of her close circle of friends, and especially not to Amelia of all people.

'That sneaky two-faced weasel. I knew she's up to something. I will bide my time until I get her on her own and then thrash things out. I won't say anything to Freya and the others until I have all the evidence and information. I need to prove that she is a liar and we can send her packing.'

Evie desperately needed some time on her own to think about what to do next.

Chapter Thirty-Four

Kate's House

Preparations were well underway for Freya's big birthday party the following week, and the next day everyone gathered round at Kate's house. They were all horrified at the online trolling Freya had received. She hadn't left the house since, and Amelia had said she didn't want any visitors.

Kate had said the best thing to do was carry on with the party plans and show Freya how much she was loved. Amelia told them all she hadn't wanted to leave Freya on her own, saying "We really do need a big shop and I also have to collect some jewellery supplies for her as I think it would be good for her to get back to work, and we know how much she loves creating her earrings and bracelets."

"That's so kind of you," said Maureen. "You've been an absolute treasure. Thanks for looking after Freya."

Kate smiled at Amelia. "You get off now. It will take you all afternoon to get up to Birsay and over to Harray for Freya. We've got things under control here."

When Amelia had left, Kate said, "She really has been such a great help, especially as Evie seems to have done a disappearing act."

"I thought she would have been here today," said Kate. "But never mind. There's a lot to get through so we'd better get started."

They had been hard at work ordering the decorations and amassing as much pink and silver as they could get their hands on. The Minion plates and glasses were all boxed up and everyone assured each other the yellow tablecloths were bright enough.

Delima had ordered fresh flowers for the centre of each table and was decorating the vases with stickers of Kylie Minogue in her 'Can't Get You Out of My Head' outfit, which was Freya's favourite. Kate was packing little bags of silver and pink stars that would be scattered over all the tables, trying not to think about how long it was going to take to clear it all up.

The Minion cake and costume were safely in her kitchen alongside eight giant candles, one for each decade, otherwise, Kate had joked, eighty candles would have had the fire brigade on standby.

Jack had tried the Minion outfit on at home and made Ola giggle but terrified the life out of poor baby Hari, who had yelled his head off at the sight of his dad engulfed by a bright yellow monster. Delima had to make a few alterations to make the costume fit but declared it to be a triumph.

"I'd only do this for Freya," Jack grumbled. "It's boiling hot and I look like a right eejit."

They had ordered jumbo bags of sweeties and helium balloons and Happy Birthday banners. "Christ," said Patsy, "It's going to look like a bunch of unicorns have thrown up in this hall. Have we gone over the top?"

Kate looked up from threading multi-coloured fairy lights through pink feather boas that were to be draped over chairs, and said, "This is Freya we are talking about. She will love it. And she needs cheering up. She's been through such a lot."

They all fell silent. Poor Freya had actually told Kate and Edwyn to cancel the party.

They'd talked her out of that, but it was shocking to see her so distraught.

Andrzej said he would go round and visit her to make sure she was OK. She had said she didn't feel up to seeing anyone, but he couldn't bear the thought of her being alone. He was furious about the online abuse and told Maureen that all he wanted was just five minutes in a room with the person who had started all the rumours. It took a lot to rile the big man, but any upset caused to the people he loved turned him from an amiable teddy into a ferocious grizzly bear.

Andrzej was appalled to see Freya sitting in her darkened kitchen with all the curtains drawn, wearing an old grey dressing gown. He didn't even think she would have possessed such an ugly garment. She had a defeated look in her eyes that he had never seen before.

Andrzej sat down beside her, took her hand, and said, "Don't let these bad creatures dim your light, Freya. They are not worth it."

She'd glanced up at him briefly. Her expression was so hurt and she looked shrunken and defeated. "I know that, Andrzej. It's just been such an awful shock. I genuinely haven't thought about my life as Magnus for so long. No one ever mentions it anymore and I really believed I was accepted. I just feel as if everyone will look at me differently now, when I go out or into town and I couldn't bear it."

"But you are accepted, Freya. No one has paid any attention to these stupid lies." He saw Freya's chin wobble and went on, "I know you don't feel like it now but this will blow over and these sad, sick people will find another target for their spite. Anyway, don't you have an art class this afternoon for the kids? You should be getting yourself out of these drab rags and into something bright and beautiful and more like the Freya we all know and love."

"No one will come this afternoon. They won't ever come again," said Freya with a sob.

"Come on, lass, you know that's not true," Andrzej said. "Look. I can help you set things up. Please, promise me – you'll at least try?"

"It's the thought that amongst the parents, there might be someone who thinks these horrible things about me," whispered Freya.

Andrzej shook his head. "We don't know that, Freya. It might just be some vile idiot on the internet making trouble."

Freya really didn't think anyone would turn up for her Saturday class, but she would have to make the effort now she had promised Andrzej. She got herself washed and changed and they both put out the paints, paper and jam jars of water on her big scrubbed pine table.

Andrzej asked if she wanted him to stay, but she told him she needed to do this alone. Freya took a deep breath, squared her shoulders and focused her gaze, like Ripley in the movie *Aliens*, just before she took on the monster.

Freya was a big fan of that film. She often asked herself what Ellen Ripley would do when confronted with a problem.

"She'd tell them all to go to hell!" Freya said out loud. She told herself she wasn't going to be cowed by the kinds of bullies she'd had to deal with when she was a much younger woman. 'At least back then, the feckers would be rude and vile to your face and you'd have a chance to tell them to bugger off. These days they hide behind their phones,' she thought.

Looking out of her window later that afternoon, Freya saw dozens of young girls and boys with their parents, waiting in the front garden. The children clutched handmade cards and little bunches of flowers for her. They didn't make a fuss. They just filed into her sunny room and sat at the table or on the floor, quickly becoming engrossed in painting bold prints of their tiny hands and covering everything with glitter.

Their mums and dads waved at Freya and said they would pick their kids up in a couple of hours, as usual. Their trust in her was unspoken but it was deep and powerful. Freya managed not to break down in tears, but her heart was full of gratitude. She loved these people.

Chapter Thirty-Five

Yesnaby Cliffs

Evie realised guiltily she hadn't seen Freya since she had told her about those awful online posts a few days ago. She'd been reeling from what Liv had told her and worrying over how to confront Amelia.

She had gone for a long walk along the cliffs at Yesnaby to try and clear her head, and back home continued to work on her painting of Freya, but knew if she kept going there was a danger she would make Freya look sad and diminished. Evie realised she needed to go round and make sure Freya was OK, and she would have to have it out with Amelia.

Arriving at Freya's, she let herself in as usual and was about to say a cheery hello when she felt punched in the stomach by the scene in front of her. Amelia was sitting with Hari on her knee while Freya was reading Ola a story. Kate and Maureen were chatting and knitting while Ross was sitting quietly, looking at Amelia with adoring eyes.

Evie hated to admit it, but Amelia looked gorgeous. The sun streaming in caught her newly dyed golden hair, so she appeared almost angelic. Evie knew Amelia was trying to look like her, but hadn't really appreciated *just* how much, right down to the silver jewellery gifted to her by Freya. Evie felt cold hard rage. This woman had effectively cuckooed Evie out of her life.

She thought, 'That should be me cuddling baby Hari with Ross gazing at me with love in his eyes. How could I not have seen this coming? She's wormed her way into all of our lives in such a short time, and she obviously wants to take my place, and they are all going along with it. It's as if I don't exist anymore.'

Evie felt queasy and angry. 'None of these people can really be my friend,' she thought. 'Look how easily they have welcomed this usurper. They don't care about me at all.'

She heard her voice, high-pitched and querulous, say far too loudly: "I thought you would be in need of some company, Freya, but I see you are all having a lovely time without me." She knew she sounded petty and jealous but she couldn't help herself.

Freya looked up from the story book and said mildly, "Evie, it's good to see you. Come and join us."

"Oh, I wouldn't want to impose."

Kate glared at her. "Stop acting like a clown and come and sit down. I was going to make Maureen a coffee. Do you want one?"

"No, I don't. Why didn't you all tell me you were meeting up here? And did none of you think to invite me?"

Evie knew she sounded like a petulant child, she knew her cheeks were bright red and her voice was wobbling, but she was past caring.

Freya said in the same measured tone, "It was all very last minute. I'm feeling a lot chirpier. The art class was crowded and look at all the cards and flowers the peedie bairns brought."

Evie was too furious to look at the heartfelt presents or to reply. She was trembling with rage and self-pity.

Freya went on, "Delima was in Kirkwall shopping with the bairns, when she got an emergency call from Jack that she was needed at the sanctuary. She asked if she could drop them here with me, and then I asked Amelia to see if anyone wanted to come over for the afternoon."

She smiled at Amelia, "Funnily enough, everyone was together, doing something secretive involving cake decorations."

Amelia said nervously, "I did try to call, Evie, and I left you a text message."

"You know I don't answer my mobile when I am in the middle of a painting," Evie snapped at her. "And strangely, I didn't get your message. But then I bet you didn't actually send it did you? And none of the rest of you thought to invite me."

"Evie, that's enough," said Freya. "I don't know what's got into you. Please stop this. It's not like you."

They were all looking at Evie, aghast. Even little Ola seemed upset. Maureen said quietly, "Evie, we would never deliberately exclude you from anything. None of us would do that to you."

Evie realised she was making a fool of herself but her emotions were out of control. She looked at Amelia, sitting at the heart of the group in what was Evie's usual chair, holding the baby she adored, and bathed in the love and admiration of her favourite people. 'Oh God, I'm so jealous of her. This is ridiculous and I am being absurd.'

Evie was just about to blurt out an apology to everyone for her behaviour, when she saw a sly look of triumph come over Amelia's face and she blew her top. She yelled at Amelia, "Don't you dare smirk at me. You planned this all along. You've been telling lies about me to Liv, and now—"

Freya interrupted and said firmly, "Evie. If you can't behave yourself and control your temper, I'm going to have to ask you to leave."

Evie responded angrily, "You seriously want *me* to leave, when it's her you should be kicking out?"

Amelia started to cry and got up sobbing, "I don't want to be the cause of any arguments between you. I'm so sorry you feel like this, Evie. If I have done anything to upset you then please forgive me. The last thing I want to do is cause problems. I will leave right away."

Kate went over to her. "Don't be silly, Amelia. You haven't done anything wrong. You don't need to go anywhere." She turned to look at Evie. "I don't know what's going on in your head. You've been rude and objectionable and bloody odd to Amelia ever since she got here, when all she's done is to be kind and help Freya, and the rest of us. Where have *you* been? You need to take a long hard look at yourself."

Freya interrupted quietly but firmly, "I really think you should apologise to Amelia before this all gets any worse."

Evie was furious. "Apologise to that two-faced sneak? No chance. You ask her what she said to Liv. And just look at her. She has copied my hair, my clothes and she's slithered her way into our lives. She's a snake and you can't trust her."

Amelia was shaking her head. Freya stood up, trembling, but her voice was strong and cut Evie to the bone.

"That's enough, Evie. If you can't be civil, I don't want you in this house."

"Oh, I wouldn't stay here a minute longer," said Evie. "Don't worry, I'm going. I know when I'm not wanted. I will leave you all to it."

Evie wanted to tell them all she was sorry for being angry and lashing out, that Amelia brought out the worst in her and really had told Liv those lies. She found her throat was so choked up with unshed tears, she simply couldn't get the words out.

Amelia was still sobbing and being hugged tightly by Kate, who looked at Evie in bewilderment.

She turned on her heel and stormed out, slamming the door so hard the windows rattled. Amelia had planned this whole thing all along. She didn't fool her. She knew exactly who Amelia was. Getting behind the wheel of her beloved Florence she could barely see out of the windscreen for her tears. Angrily brushing them aside she headed home.

'Oh Christ,' she exclaimed. She'd played right into Amelia's hands. Amelia wanted her to rant and rave at everyone and she'd have made it easy for her to be portrayed as the victim of big bad Evie. Amelia had turned them all against her.

Back at Freya's, everyone was trying to comfort a distraught Amelia, who was tearfully telling them it was all her fault, and she was so sorry for upsetting Evie and causing a scene.

Kate said grimly, "You didn't cause anything, Amelia. Evie was way out of order. I don't know what's gotten into her lately." She added, "Agnes is really upset with her. Apparently, Evie wasn't happy with how she did her hair, so she went to a salon in Aberdeen."

Maureen was desperately upset at Evie for causing such a scene. She managed to whisper, "When I was in Hume from Hume, Fiona's sister said she was very sad to hear that Evie didn't like any of the dresses that she bought from there, even that bonnie green one that I know she loves. At least I think that's what she said. You know how these stories grow arms and legs."

"Yes," said Freya uncertainly. "But there's usually a kernel of truth in them. Amelia, didn't you say Evie thought my style was a bit too flamboyant?"

"Oh Freya, I'm sure she didn't mean it. I told you I must have picked her up wrong. She'd never say anything so hurtful about you."

"I'm worried about her," said Freya. "She's acting out of character. She's saying all sorts of mean things and that display we all just witnessed was not the Evie I know." She sighed heavily. "I know she's been through a lot in life, but I feel like I don't know her anymore.

Kate nodded in agreement. "She has been completely different since Amelia arrived."

Amelia burst out, "See. Evie was fine until I arrived. I knew it was a mistake coming here. I've caused all this turmoil. I should have stayed at home in Seattle. I wish I'd ignored those letters from Shelia I found all those years ago. I'm so sorry everyone. You've been so kind, and I've ruined everything."

They all started talking at once to reassure Amelia that none of this was her fault. Amelia sniffled, "I know she was very cross when I got my hair done like hers, but she is just so beautiful, and I thought as we looked quite similar it would suit me too." She started to cry again.

Freya patted her hand. "There now love, don't be upset and you don't want to be crying on peedie Hari or you will start him off too. And anyway, that's not how we wet the baby's head in this part of the world."

Ross spoke up. "I think we could all do with a drink, Freya. Let me sort it." He got up and made his way into the kitchen.

Freya smiled in approval. "That boy doesn't say much but when he does, it's always very sensible indeed. I for one would like a wee dram to calm my nerves."

Chapter Thirty-Six

Evie's House

As soon as she arrived home, Evie disappeared into a bottle of red wine. She was so angry with herself for doing Amelia's dirty work with that out-of-character display of anger and jealousy. She also realised, with a sharp pang of regret, she'd managed to fall out with the people who mattered most to her. It was such a mess, and she had no idea how to fix things.

Evie polished off the bottle far too quickly and then opened another. As she hadn't eaten all day, she was soon blind drunk, feeling maudlin, weepy and sorry for herself. She sat slumped in her beautiful Orkney chair. Tears of self-pity rolled down her cheeks as she muttered to herself, "Oh Christ, I am so blootered. They all hate me and I've ruined everything and it's all that Amelia's fault. She's turned everyone against me. I should never have answered her email."

Evie vaguely remembered dragging herself to bed and going through the 'whirlies' as the room spun round before she crashed out. She woke up the next morning with a blinding headache and feeling sick to her stomach.

She squinted into the bright early sunshine beaming in through the window, and felt her heart sink as she remembered the events of the night before. She groaned and her cheeks burned with shame, but there was also cold rage in her heart against Amelia, who had spread her tentacles into every part of Evie's life.

'What am I going to do about her?' she thought in despair. 'What the hell is she up to? It's creepy and scary and I can't believe they are all on her side. How has she been able to turn them against me? Even Freya.'

She couldn't forget Freya's look of bitter disappointment as she told Evie to leave and go home. That really had been the final punch in the stomach. Evie couldn't bear to think of Freya being angry and upset with her. She was always her staunchest supporter and ally.

She hauled herself up and out of bed with a loud moan and headed downstairs.

There was only one thing that would take her mind off her monstrous hangover and all of her woes. Evie had to paint. She went into her studio, took off the sheet covering her painting of Freya, and gasped in horror.

The portrait she had slaved over for months had been ruined, with red and purple paint violently smeared thickly all over the canvas. Great globs of angry colour had vandalised the paining. It was completely beyond repair.

Evie couldn't take it in. This was to have been Freya's precious birthday present. She had poured her heart and soul into the portrait and now it was utterly destroyed. She knew right away that somehow Amelia was responsible.

No one else would be so vindictive and she'd seen the painting the other day when she came to crow over the fact Ross had asked her out, pretending all the while she was there to ask for Evie's permission. It must have been her.

The paintbrush and paints were scattered all over the floor, leaving trails of what looked like blood on the wood. Then Evie looked down at her hands. They were smeared red and purple, and when she ran upstairs to wash it off, she saw splotches of the same colours smearing the sheets.

Up until then, she had been certain Amelia had ruined the painting, but now it looked like she had blacked out and done it herself. After all, she had been completely drunk and beside herself with self-disgust, but even in that state, could she really have destroyed the painting of Freya?

She felt clammy and her stomach started to spasm, and she barely made it to the toilet before throwing up until there was nothing left but bile. Feeling shaky and trembling, she curled up into a ball on the cold stone floor of the bathroom and sobbed her heart out.

Chapter Thirty-Seven

Freya's house a week later

While Evie fretted and felt her world was collapsing around her, Freya was looking out of the window and counting her blessings on the day before her big birthday. Despite all the upset with Evie the week before, Freya was trying to focus on the positive. It had always been her way of coping with bad times in the past.

It was such a bright sunny morning and Orkney was putting on a real show. Soft light rain falling overnight had given everything a sheen; and when the sun broke through there was a vivid rainbow lighting up the sky. It was as though the whole island was getting ready to celebrate with Freya and wishing her happy birthday. The emerald-green fields, azure skies and silver seas had never looked more beautiful.

Freya had woken up to the arrival of Paul the postman, who was delivering an armful of carefully wrapped presents and a sackful of cards. "There will be more tomorrow on your actual birthday, Freya, but I thought I would get these to you now," he said cheerfully.

Freya thought Paul looked just like a snowman. He was remarkably pale, but so chubby that his body was almost completely spherical. He seemed to have no neck, just a perfectly round face with coal-black currant eyes, and he was completely bald. The snowman look was complete with a floppy hat and a scarf. Freya honestly wouldn't have been surprised if she had seen him 'walking in the air' above Kirkwall Cathedral.

They'd had a cup of tea together and a chat about Paul's bunions. He was a martyr to his feet and last month Freya had given him a large bottle of homemade lotion to dab on them. He thanked her over and over again and said it had made all the difference. Wishing her many happy returns, he left with his pockets and cheeks bulging with homemade biscuits.

Freya decided she'd watch an old Bette Davis movie, probably *Now, Voyager*, although she had watched it so often, she knew all the dialogue. She had her bath, painted her nails, attended to a few rogue hairs on her chin with her trusty tweezers, and gave her feet a going over in the foot spa Patsy had bought her for Christmas. It had been put in the cupboard under the sink and was being used for the first time. She popped on a bright-green avocado face mask and settled down for a much-needed chunk of 'me time'.

Amelia had gone over to see Ross for a Friday-night date and planned to stay with him overnight. She would be back the next day in time to get ready for the 'surprise' party. This was going to be *the* night for them both. To be honest, Freya was enjoying having her house to herself for a few hours.

Amelia was no trouble, but sometimes Freya just wanted to have a bit of time on her own, with beans on toast on a tray for her tea in front of *A Place In The Sun*. With a guest you always had to make a bit of an effort, and even someone as sociable and gregarious as Freya needed a break.

On the upside, she knew when Amelia got home, she would get a full rundown of the evening's events. She was surprised at how quickly Amelia and Ross had become a couple. Things had moved fast and they seemed besotted with one another. It had taken

Ross a long time to find love, but he had seemingly fallen hard.

'Perhaps we might be hearing wedding bells,' thought Freya. 'And then Amelia would stay in Orkney and build a life here.'

Freya tutted, 'I'm getting ahead of myself again. I really need to just leave them be so they can find out whether they are meant to be together. It wasn't all that long ago I was making plans for Ross and Evie. I had high hopes of those two.'

Freya sighed. She had expected Evie to come over the morning after her outburst and apologise. They would have both had a good cry and put it all behind them. But there was no sign of her, and it wasn't like her to sulk.

Freya had reached for her phone right away to call Evie but there was no answer. She tried many times. She didn't want to leave a message as she always got flustered and talked for too long. So eventually, her chubby fingers painstakingly drafted a text.

Hello Evie. I don't want us to fall out. Amelia says she forgives you and so do I. The party wouldn't be the same without you. Hope you can come tomorrow night.

Evie was so desperately embarrassed and ashamed of herself she couldn't bring herself to answer Freya's call. She knew the longer she left all the bad feeling to fester, the harder it would be to mend. She read the text, and felt relief that Freya still wanted her at the party, but she was livid at Amelia. 'She can stick her forgiveness up her arse, but I'm just not sure I can face everyone, even on Freya's big night.'

Her phone rang again. This time it was Sophia, probably the only person Evie felt she could talk to, so she decided to answer.

Sophia sounded utterly distraught, as though she was trying to stop herself breaking down. "Thank God you picked up, Evie. I honestly don't know where to begin. I can't do this anymore. I'm telling Finn it's all over. He hasn't been in touch, and he obviously doesn't care enough about me to make this work. I'm still coming up for the party, though. Can I stay with you? I'm heading to the airport in a couple of hours. Could you pick me up?"

Sophia was so downhearted Evie felt she couldn't burden her with her own troubles. She would wait until they were together, sitting in the kitchen and sharing a bottle of wine. She told her that of course she could stay and she'd be there to pick her up in Florence. They could talk more tonight.

Evie was bitterly disappointed that Finn hadn't immediately made things right after the talking-to he was given by herself and Freya. For the next half hour, Evie busied herself sorting out the spare room for Sophia's arrival.

"Men are such clowns," she muttered to herself, as she changed the duvet and left clean towels on the bed. "All Finn had to do was tell Sophia he was sorry, and then look at Ross mooning all over that two-faced Amelia. I expected better of him. I thought he was way too good for her, but now I'm not so sure. I would have expected him to realise she's a complete phoney."

Evie had talked about Amelia going out with Ross in one of her many WhatsApp calls with Sophia. She also confessed to her friend that she felt as if she was in the movie *Single White Female*, where a deranged Jennifer Jason Leigh creepily copied the looks and life of Bridget Fonda.

They had laughed about it, but Evie knew Amelia had now crossed a line. The trouble was Amelia had fooled everyone else and it felt as though she was the only one who could see what Amelia was really like. She needed to see Sophia in person for a proper catch up, and she needed her friend's reassurance she wasn't overreacting and losing her mind.

She jumped as her phone pinged with a message from Sophia. Evie expected it to say her plane was delayed but instead it read:

> *You will never believe it. Finn has just walked through my door. He is babbling all sorts of nonsense and keeps apologising and saying he wants to go and see Essex beavers. I don't know what you and Freya said to him, but it has done the trick.*
>
> *He's in the shower right now and I think I will be tied up for the foreseeable future if you get my drift. Sorry I won't make the flight today. I hate letting you down. But I will let you know how it all goes and we will both get the first plane up tomorrow.*

Evie was deeply disappointed not to see her friend, but at the same time, relieved that Finn had taken action after all, and made the long trek down to London to make things right with the woman he loved.

Chapter Thirty-Eight

Orkney, two weeks earlier

Liv received a curt text from Amelia telling her that it was all systems go and they had a solicitor's appointment at 2pm on Kirkwall high street. Liv sighed heavily.

For the first time in months, she found herself desperate for a drink. A freezing-cold can of lager, almost painful to swallow, burning her throat on the way down, or a bottle of big-bodied red wine, full of fruity oblivion.

She spent the morning trying to distract herself, cleaning every corner of the already clinically pristine flat, and pacing up and down her tiny living room until she had to leave to meet Amelia at the solicitors as planned.

Liv gasped when she saw Amelia. The resemblance to Evie was uncanny, and Amelia had played it up even more by perfectly replicating Evie's distinctive elegant casual style.

They agreed that Liv would do all the talking as Amelia's American accent was too much of a giveaway.

Liv told the receptionist bluntly, "We both have an appointment with Mrs McIver. I'm Liv Muir and this is my sister, Evie."

"Just take a seat in the waiting room. Mrs McIver's with a client but she's just finishing up and won't be long."

The receptionist, Mirren, a plump fair-haired woman with a most impressive bosom, which she kept hidden under baggy brown Fair Isle jumpers, sneaked another look at Liv, who clearly didn't remember who she was.

Mirren had been a few years ahead of Liv at school, but she recalled her as a troublemaker and a bully. Mirren had been one of the many kids who was forced to hand over their pocket money to Liv and her gang.

Mirren had to admit that Liv had cleaned up her act. She no longer looked like a ravenous crow. She'd put on a bit of weight, her hair was going grey, and she looked less bitter and angry, but Mirren still wouldn't like to get on her bad side.

She vaguely remembered Evie as a bookish child who had run away to London but had returned recently and opened up the new art gallery. She remembered reading about her in a glossy magazine. She looked amazing. The combination of green eyes and blonde hair was striking. And that cashmere camel coat over a brown sweater and trousers looked so elegant.

Evie looked rich and successful while Mirren was suddenly all too aware her knickers didn't match her bra and her shoes needed a clean. She went back to a game of solitaire on her computer and waited for Mrs McIver's current client to leave.

Amelia had specifically chosen to see Joan McIver. The solicitor had arrived from Edinburgh a few months ago with her husband, Aden, and two small children. They'd sold their town-house in Bruntsfield and bought a large crumbling mansion just outside Birsay, in the north of mainland Orkney, and were busy turning it back from a hotel into a family home. It was her husband's passion project and he spent every hour of the day on site.

In the meantime, they were living in one of the small cottages on the grounds. She was overworked, stressed and worried about how much cash had to be thrown at the house which had turned into a money pit.

On the plus side, she had never seen Aden so happy and the kids were thriving with a lovely young nanny from the village of Dounby. They had already picked up her sing-song accent and said peedie instead of little.

Aden had just emailed to say that Andrzej, the builder who was giving him help and advice, had found damp under the kitchen; it would cost a fortune to put it right, and maybe they should take out another loan. He was hopeless with money. She quickly emailed back: Do Not Do Anything Until I Get Home Tonight.

Joan tried to stop herself feeling distracted, gave herself a shake and asked Mirren to send in the next client. She looked again at her notes about Evie Muir; the business was thriving, and Evie owned her own property outright without a mortgage.

She looked up as the two women came into her office. She thought, 'Well, the resemblance might be slight but you can tell these two are related. Evie is clearly the younger sister – she looks bright and intelligent. The older looks like she's had a hard life.'

Joan asked them both to take a seat and gave them her best professional smile. Liv came straight to the point.

"As you know from what I told you over the phone, Evie wants me to take over the gallery business so she can devote herself to her painting. She doesn't want all the hassle. I assume that's straightforward enough?"

Amelia nodded enthusiastically and gestured to her throat.

Liv explained, "My sister had a bad touch of laryngitis, and the doctor told her to rest her voice completely. To be honest, it's giving us all a bit of a break. So can we get this all done and dusted?"

Joan replied smoothly, "Well, Miss Muir, or can I call you Liv? Thanks to Evie starting the process a few months ago, it's really just a case of paperwork today."

Liv and Amelia looked at her, utterly astonished. Oblivious to their reaction, Joan continued, "Yes, I can see here that Evie first got in touch about sharing the business back in January, so we've been able to put the necessary steps in place. I have everything prepared. I just need to see ID from both of you. Just belt and braces you understand."

Still in shock at the unexpected news, Liv handed over two passports. Joan gave them a cursory glance and nodded her approval, before pushing over the paperwork for both women to sign. Liv held her breath as Amelia forged Evie's signature.

Joan said briskly, "Well, there we are. You're all set, and it should be official in a couple of weeks. Good luck to both of you, and if there's anything else you need, don't hesitate to get in touch."

Amelia gave her a dazzling smile and they both got up to leave.

Once outside in the street and round the corner, Amelia hugged herself and cackled with glee.

Liv glowered at her. "Stop drawing attention to yourself for fuck's sake."

"Oh lighten up," said Amelia. "You have to admit it was just so, so easy. I can't believe Evie made it even smoother for us but still has no idea of what's coming. She's so wrapped up in losing her friends and falling out with Freya, the business will be the last thing on her mind right now. It's delicious don't you think? Once the paperwork goes through, you'll be able to access the business account and take out all the money. For yourself and for me, of course . . ."

Liv's mind was in a whirl. Her sister was giving her a share of the business anyway. Amelia's plan was never needed.

She needed to think. She hissed at Amelia, "We need to get her passport back to the house before she misses it. Give it here."

It was Liv who had taken her sister's passport, going round to Evie's house when she knew she was away on one of her regular visits to their mother in her care home. She'd let herself in and quickly found the passport in her sister's desk drawer in a folder marked 'personal'.

Coming back to the family home was tough on Liv, especially as Evie had made it look so welcoming and beautiful, turning the old rarely used front parlour into a studio and refurbishing the kitchen into a cosy haven had been a stroke of genius.

She barely recognised the cold, empty shell where she had spent so many unhappy years with her highly strung mother, and a father who couldn't hide his preference for his daughter Evie, his precious Teenie, over Liv, who he found impossible to deal with. Liv couldn't wait to escape from the sad, unhappy house she had left as a teenager.

Amelia gave her a malevolent grin. "I'll hold on to this passport, thanks. I'll find a way to return it, don't worry."

Liv didn't reply and just stared stonily ahead, thinking about what had just happened. She turned to go.

Amelia elbowed her sharply in the ribs, "Oh come on, Liv. Look, I couldn't have done it without you. Fancy cracking open a bottle of champagne with me to celebrate?" She grimaced, "If there actually is such a thing as decent bubbly in this hellhole of a place."

"For fuck's sake, Amelia, I'm an alcoholic and there's enough vintage champagne drunk on these islands every weekend to float a fishing fleet. Don't be so fucking condescending. Now why don't you fuck off and leave me alone," Liv replied crossly.

"No need to be so tetchy. I will indeed leave you to celebrate however you wish. Maybe a cup of peppermint tea? Try not to have too much fun. Laters."

Liv watched her disappear down the high street, no doubt on her way to the nearest wine bar. Amelia was singing to herself as she flounced away. She thought, 'This is all working out even better than I thought. Soon Evie Muir will have nothing.'

The thought of leaving Evie desolate and broken was intoxicating. She laughed out loud, drawing smiles from people passing by, who thought she must be celebrating something really special.

Amelia had to bide her time, and a week later, sneaked back to Evie's house in the wee small hours, on the same night of Evie's outburst, when she made such a fool of herself in front of all her friends.

Amelia had actually prowled past the house a few times since the visit to the solicitor with Liv, but hadn't had an opportunity to put the passport back unnoticed.

This night she sneaked a look through the window and saw Evie passed out in the kitchen, snoring loudly due to the amount of booze she had thrown down her neck.

Amelia couldn't believe her luck. Not only had she been able to creep in the front door and put the passport back, she'd also had the euphoric satisfaction of destroying the portrait of that idiot Freya, then daubing Evie's hands with the paint so she'd think she did it herself in a drunken rage.

It was just all too fabulous, and Amelia congratulated herself on a job well done.

Chapter Thirty-Nine

London

In London, Finn and Sophia had enjoyed a whole day of make-up sex. They drank a bottle of cava and had pizza delivered to eat in bed to keep their strength up. In between orgasms they talked properly about the future.

Finn looked at this bright and beautiful woman and knew he couldn't imagine his world without her in it. He'd spent most of his life having cheerful-but-casual sex with a variety of women, mostly tourists who went back home from Orkney with happy memories of making love to a silver-tongued Irishman with no strings attached. Finn could hardly remember any of their faces. It had meant nothing to him, although he always wanted them to have as much fun as he did.

He couldn't help himself flirting with every woman who had a pulse. For every knockback he received, there were more than enough who fell for his chat-up lines. And then Sophia had come along.

She was nothing like any of the other women he had encountered. Obviously, she was intelligent and extremely sexy and good-looking, but she was also kind and strong and loyal. Sophia was the full package and for the first time ever Finn wanted to settle down and have a clutch of babies.

It was time for him to grow up and stop being so self-centred. He loved his work, but he loved Sophia even more.

Sophia forced him to get up and hit Regent Street before the shops shut. She wanted to buy him something smart for Freya's party.

Finn gulped but seeing the determination in Sophia's eyes he knew there was no point in arguing, so he suffered the ordeal of going shopping for smart new trousers and a jacket. Sophia thought it made him look like James Bond, and Finn preened in front of the mirror, saying it wasn't all that bad to dress up now and again. They had both fully intended to make Freya's birthday party.

With their flights booked and their outfits bought, the two of them headed to terminal 2 at Heathrow the next day, only to discover they couldn't check in to their early morning flight to Dundee and then on to Kirkwall. A computer outage meant every single plane was grounded.

Check-in staff were being harangued by incensed passengers who were missing business meetings, weddings and, like Sophia and Finn, special events like birthday parties. Sophia was stressed and devastated but said to Finn, "I've never understood people getting so cross with staff who are trying their best. It's not their fault that the technology is so shit and keeps breaking down."

"Agreed," said Finn. "Flying really is fucking stressful though."

She smiled at him, "Tell me about it. I've been doing the commute for over a year now and feel as if I have spent more time at airports than with you in Orkney."

He looked shamefaced. "I'm so sorry, love. I didn't appreciate it. The cost and the hassle and everything. I should have realised and not been so selfish."

Sophia said, "It's OK. I'm glad we have straightened everything out."

Finn frowned, "But what are we going to do. The party is tonight. We have left it far too late to drive up and get the ferry. I think we might be stuffed."

Sophia sighed. "I think you're right. We just won't make it. It's a real shame. I hate to let Freya down and I am really worried about Evie. She hasn't been herself recently."

Finn frowned, "What do you mean?"

"Amelia's arrival has really unsettled her. You know she's been copying Evie's looks, right down to her hair style. I know Evie is uneasy about it all. I hoped to have a really long hard look at this woman and find out exactly what's going on."

She bit her lip. "I've been so wrapped up in what's going on with us that I haven't been as good a friend to Evie as I should have been."

Finn gave her a hug, "She's tougher than you think. I was terrified of her when she gave me a right bollocking about you, and how I had to make more of an effort. She will handle this Amelia."

"I hope you're right", said Sophia. "I will just feel better when I see her in person." She looked up at the board again, showing nothing but cancelled flights.

"Let's wait a while in case things change, but it's not looking good. I will give Evie a call and let her know."

In the end they had to go back home after hours of waiting at the airport, as by late afternoon it was clear they would definitely be missing Freya's big event. There was a tearful phone call to Freya, who told them not to fret and that she'd see them soon and how glad she was they had mended their quarrel and they were to have lots of lovely sex.

Sophia tried to call Evie but had to leave a voice message when she failed to pick up. They stayed up late into the wee small hours, taking Freya's advice and making delicious gentle love. They toasted Freya with a bottle of bubbly and Finn told Sophia something that would change their lives forever.

Chapter Forty

Kate's house, two hours before the party

Kate had already received a text from Sophia saying she and Finn wouldn't make it, but she almost hit the roof when she got a call from Delima, just before she was leaving the house to make all the final preparations, saying they couldn't come either.

A huge school of pilot whales had breached on the shore on the island of Sanday and it was all-hands-on-deck if they were going to save any of the poor creatures. Kate managed to swallow her disappointment and tell Delima that she understood completely.

"What about the babies? Do you want us to bring them with the girls?"

Delima replied regretfully, "They really are too young for us not to be with them. Just like their father, they get tetchy if their routine is disturbed. Normally, I would ask you or Evie to come over to be with them, but obviously not on the night of Freya's party. Caroline, one of the volunteers at the sanctuary, is a bit gormless, but she's done some babysitting for us before and the kids know her, so she has stepped in."

She hesitated, "Kate, I haven't heard from Evie since all that upset last week. I keep reaching for the phone to call her and then I realise I don't know what to say."

Kate sighed, "Well, if it helps at all she hasn't been in touch with us either. To be honest, I'm fuming with her. She was totally out of order shouting the odds and upsetting us all like that."

Delima tutted, "It's all just so sad. I hate it when friends fall out and this really isn't like Evie. Although she has been acting so weird lately." She heard Jack shouting that the boat was ready to set off for Sanday.

"I need to go, Kate. I'm sorry to let Freya down, but this really is a disaster. We are going to do our best, but no one has seen anything like it, and I am so scared we won't be able to save any of the whales."

"Don't worry, Freya will understand. It can't be helped. Keep in touch and let me know what's happening. Good luck."

Delima hung up and rushed off to where Jack was waiting impatiently to set off.

"*Fuck!*" yelled Kate, when she slammed the phone down. "There will be no one at the bloody party at this rate."

Her daughter Louise looked at her sternly, "Mammy, that is a very bad word. You should go to your room and think about what you just said."

"Sorry darling. That was very naughty of mammy, but Uncle Jack won't be around to be a giant Minion for aunty Freya's party and mammy doesn't know what the feck to do."

"'Feck' is still a bad word you know," said Louise, in her best grown-up voice. Kate sighed and then called Maureen, who immediately offered Andrzej's services. Kate told her, "Well, get here quick so you can alter the costume. No offence Maureen, but Andrzej has a bit more girth than Jack."

Maureen laughed, "None taken. I love that there's a lot of Andrzej to go round. He's my big giant hot-water bottle."

"Well, just make sure you can stop hugging him in time for him to get his cuddly arse down here."

Kate hurried down to the hall in Kirkwall where Freya's party was being held and frenetic last-minute preparations were underway.

Kate surveyed the scene like a general. "Thank the Lord we did so much of this yesterday, or we would have been buggered. We don't have Sophia or Finn or Delima or Jack, Evie is still AWOL and I swear Patsy has already scoffed most of the Munchies."

Luckily, young Rory had arrived to set up. He was so excited about the responsibility of being DJ for the night. He asked Kate uncertainly, "Are you sure Freya likes The Clash, Madness, Wham and The Cure as well as all these cheesy boy bands?"

"Absolutely," said Kate firmly. "Just keep the hits coming and, for the love of God, don't forget a bit of Kylie or we will never hear the end of it."

The hall started to fill up with the early birds keen to see Freya's reaction to her 'surprise', to wish her well, eat and drink their fill and dance the night away.

Chapter Forty-One

Evie's House

Evie sat at home fretting. She had hoped to go to the party with Sophia and Finn, which would have made everything a whole lot easier. She couldn't believe all the flights had been cancelled on today of all days. Even with the text from Freya asking her to come to the celebrations, she was worried it would be awkward, and she didn't even have a present to give her.

She'd planned to have Andrzej wrap up the painting and bring it to the hall in his van, and she could have unveiled her work there while everyone sang happy birthday.

'It's all been spoiled by Amelia. She might not have vandalised the painting but has managed to cause a rift between me and Freya.' Evie stood up. 'She will be gloating if I don't turn up. I'm not going to give her the satisfaction.' She ran upstairs to put on some make-up and slipped on her favourite black dress. It was her suit of armour and always made her feel more confident.

It definitely took all of Evie's courage to step into the hall, but everyone was too busy enjoying themselves to do more than nod coolly in her direction. Freya was already up dancing in the middle of the floor to 'Love Cats' and Evie waved hesitantly in her direction and hoped she'd been spotted.

She backed into a corner, nursing a large glass of white wine, trying not to cry and wishing she could just run away. Evie felt as though she didn't belong anymore in the very place that had given her sanctuary. It was nerve-jangling and she could feel a growing anxiety.

Everyone was trying hard to appear perfectly pleasant on the surface so as not to upset Freya's big night, but they were treating Evie as though she were a stranger. Orkney was a small place and news travelled fast. Thanks to Amelia, they all knew about Evie storming out of Freya's last weekend.

When Evie had tried to tentatively say hello to people she knew, they simply looked through her, but Amelia, on the other hand, was being treated like a princess.

"I'm surprised they didn't carry her in here on a sedan chair. She's getting even more attention than Freya," Evie muttered to herself.

It was all hugely upsetting and Evie found herself gulping her glass of white wine and grabbing another from a sweet-faced waitress, even though she had sworn never to drink again after getting so drunk on that awful night when she convinced herself she'd destroyed Freya's painting.

Evie didn't feel like eating anything, even though the buffet looked delicious and there were bowls of sweets and snacks everywhere. She had no idea what to do next. She felt as though everything was spiralling out of control.

Amelia was like some kind of wicked puppet master, and everyone was dancing to her tune. She had fooled them all and Evie didn't know how to fight back.

She started to feel uncomfortably hot and clammy, and her stomach flipped over as the woman who had been dominating her thoughts for weeks approached, bearing two overfull glasses of wine. With a cold smile, Amelia handed Evie a glass and drawled, "Have a drink with me and then we can step outside and clear the air?"

Evie hesitated. Her instinct was to tell Amelia to go to hell, but she didn't trust Amelia as far as she could throw her and wanted to know what was going on in that conniving mind of hers. She took a large gulp of her glass of wine.

As they headed for the exit Amelia told her, "Don't worry. This won't take long."

Evie felt a chill of apprehension. Amelia's face was tight and frozen, but her cheeks were bright red. She grabbed Evie by the elbow, spilling some of her wine, and huckled her out of the door and into the night.

Evie gasped with the cold. The stars were out and there was a bright full moon, and it was so still and clear there was already frost on the pavement. It was freezing in the way that made your throat and your chest hurt when you breathed in.

Amelia looked at her with ice in her gaze.

"Was it a night like this when Brodie died?"

Evie's mouth dropped.

"What? Why on earth would you ask me that? What does that have to do with you?"

"Little Miss Perfect Evie Muir," said Amelia coldly.

Evie felt a growing sense of dread.

"What the hell is going on, Amelia?"

Amelia leaned in so close Evie could smell the wine on her breath. She hissed, "You walked out on your friends and family for over twenty years and then you swan back into their lives and they all forgive and forget. Your poor father leaves you the family home even though you have an older sister. Then with his money and Freya's help you are set up in a successful business. It has all just fallen into your lap."

Evie was outraged and burst out, "You have no idea how much I suffered, or what I've been through. And how hard I've worked."

Amelia gave a shrill shriek. "Oh boo hoo. You act like you are so above us all, but I know the truth about you and I got all the information I needed from your mother, when I visited her. How Liv was second best, her jealousy of you and her love for Brodie and what she did that night. Everything."

"You visited my mother? What are you talking about?" said Evie, utterly confused.

Amelia smiled malevolently, "Oh, we are good friends now. She's a right chatterbox if you get her on the right day. She told me all your secrets. I know everything about you."

Evie was beginning to feel lightheaded and nauseous. She heard herself say, as if far away, "You are talking utter nonsense. My mother is ill and she lives in a care home. You couldn't possibly have visited her. Anyway, you live in Seattle and you told me you had never been to the UK before."

Amelia looked at her with utter contempt. "You know nothing about me. Of course, I didn't come here from Seattle. I live in London, have done for years, I got a flight to Glasgow and then up here to Orkney."

Evie was stunned. She couldn't take this in. She shook her head and thought, 'That explains why she looked as fresh as new milk when she arrived at Kirkwall airport. She'd simply had two short hops in a plane that took just a couple of hours.'

To Amelia, she said, "Why would you lie to me? To everyone? You said you wanted to find out about your family?"

Amelia looked at her with scorn. "You honestly don't know?" Her voice was cold and low as she continued, "It's because although you are just my father's bastard granddaughter, you have everything I ever wanted."

She went on in the same icy tone, "My mother died giving birth to me and when I was just ten years old my father's mind went completely. He used to harp back to his past in Scotland all the time. It was pathetic."

Evie could only stare at her. Her tongue felt too big for her mouth and she was struggling to respond.

Amelia continued, "Do you know, he'd talk about Sheila, your disgusting old grandmother who couldn't keep her legs together. He would actually call me by your mother's name. Can you imagine that? He called me 'Cara'. The child he had never met and he thought more about her than he did about me."

Amelia hesitated, remembering her father grasping her hand, sobbing and thanking her over and over again for coming to see him. He'd call her Cara and beg for forgiveness.

She spat, "The stupid old fucker never loved me. Not really. He pretended to care but I know that every time he looked at me, he blamed me for the death of my mother."

Evie felt increasingly numb. "I need to go back inside," she said faintly. "I need to let everyone know that you are a liar and I think you are dangerous."

Amelia blocked her way. "Don't even think about it, no one wants you in there."

She gave another high-pitched giggle. "Do you know the best thing, Evie? You don't know just how much worse it's going to get. You are about to lose everything."

Chapter Forty-Two

Freya's Party

Back at the party, no one had any idea of the drama unfolding outside. Freya and Ross were dancing to 'Rock the Casbah', with Ross proving he had some pretty decent moves.

"I love The Clash," he roared at Freya. "And this song is a right belter."

Freya had feigned delighted surprise when she walked into the room to see everyone clapping and cheering for her 'surprise', and she was having a blast. Everywhere she looked she saw people she loved, eating and drinking and laughing. All her favourite food and snacks were on display, and she felt so blessed. If only she could make things right with Evie, everything would be perfect.

She'd seen her away at the back of the hall and fully intended to say hello and arrange to talk properly after the celebrations, but so many people had crowded around to wish her happy birthday and take photos, and then the ceilidh band took over and started playing traditional Scottish dance tunes and they were all whirling and burling.

When she looked over to where Evie had been standing, she'd disappeared.

"Bugger," said Freya. "I must ask Kate to go and try and find her."

She caught Kate's eye, and beckoned her over, asking her to find out where Evie was. Kate nodded and said she'd look for her.

Outside, Amelia was trembling with the elation of taunting Evie. She heard the music briefly get louder as the door opened, and Kate came out.

Thinking quickly, Amelia shoved Evie, who wobbled and fell backwards. To keep her balance, she reached out for Amelia, grabbing her coat. Knowing she had a witness, Amelia fell to the ground as though she had been shoved hard and started screaming in agony as Kate rushed toward them.

Amelia had hurled herself onto the pavement so violently, her cheek was scraped and bloodied. When she saw Kate she clutched her ankle and began sobbing hysterically and reached out to her, "Please help me. Don't let her hurt me anymore."

Kate was appalled and didn't know whether to comfort Amelia or confront Evie. While she hesitated, Evie took a step towards them both. Feeling as though her head was full of cotton wool, Evie heard her voice slurring, "This is not what it looks like."

Amelia began screaming again in faux terror, grabbing at Kate and begging for her protection. "Evie, what the hell is going on? What have you done? Amelia is terrified."

"I can't stand," howled Amelia. "My ankle – I think it might be broken. And my head, I've hit it hard, I think I might have passed out for a second."

Evie sounded robotic as she said, "She did it to herself. It wasn't me. She shoved me first and then she threw herself to the ground. She's making it all up. She's dangerous. We need to call the police."

Kate looked from Evie to Amelia. She didn't know what to do. She was sure she had seen Evie violently push Amelia, who now lay in agony on the ground in front of her, and Evie sounded like a zombie.

Amelia grabbed at her hand. "Please, please Kate. Don't call the police, she doesn't know what she is doing, but she will be the one in trouble and I really don't want that. Just keep her away from me."

Kate was torn. She glared at Evie. "Promise me you won't do anything stupid. Maybe we can sort this out ourselves without involving the law, but it's obvious Amelia has been assaulted."

Evie felt as though she was in a waking nightmare. Nothing made sense. "You can't possibly be on her side. She's playing some sort of sick game. It's a trap and you have all fallen for it."

Kate was usually so cool headed in a crisis, but she felt herself panicking, and was so relieved when Edwyn came out of the hall towards them. He had been looking for Kate to tell her they were about to cut the cake, not wanting her to miss out, and was told she had gone outside.

"Kate, what's going on? Amelia, you're hurt. Let me help you." He instantly became the cool, calm medic and took complete charge.

Amelia was still weeping and wailing, pretending to be terrified out of her wits. He tried to soothe her. "It's all right, calm down, love, and let me look at your face. He made an expert assessment: "OK. You've a bad graze to your cheek and it's still bleeding, but looks a hell of a lot worse than it really is. We can clean you up easily. You will be fine."

"It's her ankle too," said Kate in a trembling voice. "And she thinks she may have hit her head and even passed out."

"Can you stand?" Edwyn asked.

"I can try," Amelia answered, her voice a tiny whisper. She made a huge show of attempting to get to her feet, before gasping in agony and slumping to the ground again. "I'm so sorry, I feel dizzy and the pain is terrible."

Edwyn kept talking to her gently. "You've had an accident and a shock, but you are alright, but if you passed out even for a second you could have a concussion. I will call a cab and take you to the hospital and get you checked out, just to be sure. I've had a few beers or I would drive you myself."

He turned to his wife. "Can you get Amelia's coat?" He looked at Evie, who was standing silent and pale like an alabaster statue. "Evie, what's the matter with you? Call a cab while I help Amelia."

He looked at her again. "Are you OK? What exactly happened here? Did Amelia have a fall?"

"Yes. I fell," said Amelia quickly. "I just stumbled over my own two feet. I think I might have had too much to drink or maybe I just lost my balance on my stupid high heels."

"Well, they are lethal," said Edwyn kindly. "Maybe stick to flat shoes or trainers for a while." He gave her his most understanding and reassuring smile and then looked over at Evie with irritation.

"Evie, I told you to call a cab." She didn't reply and still didn't move.

He sighed impatiently, "Never mind, I will do it myself." He called the local taxi firm, who said they were minutes away. There was no point in going back inside and causing a scene. He took off his jacket and put it over Amelia's shoulders. She was shivering and crying.

Kate still hadn't gone inside and Evie hadn't moved either. Edwyn was on the verge of losing his temper. "Don't bother about her coat. The cab will be here soon. And don't make a fuss, we don't want to spoil Freya's big night. If anyone asks, Amelia has had a fall and I'm taking her to the hospital as a precaution. I'll see you back at home, Kate."

He got into the taxi with Amelia and they set off to the Balfour. Kate looked at Evie in horror, shaking her head.

"You attacked that poor girl! And she just covered it up to save you. I should have said something to Edwyn but she obviously wants to protect you. God knows why. I just can't believe what you've done. What is wrong with you?"

Evie didn't reply. She just stared at Kate, unable to speak. Kate's voice rose, "You've been acting weird ever since she came here. You've behaved appallingly to your friends, you've upset us all and now you've turned violent. I don't know you anymore. Maybe I never did."

Evie felt like she was underwater. Everything seemed distorted and muffled. She took a gulp of fresh, clean air and managed to slur to Kate, "You don't understand. She's the one who shoved me first and she's had this all planned out. She hates me and she's out to destroy me. I don't understand why or what I've done."

Kate turned to walk away. "I'm going inside to wish my dear friend Freya a happy birthday. I'm going to watch her cut her cake and I'm going to sing and applaud and, for her sake, I will try somehow to pretend all of this didn't happen. Then I'm going home to my husband."

She went on, "But what I really want to do is report you to the police, but that's Amelia's call. I've never seen anyone so terrified and traumatised."

Evie couldn't believe what she was hearing and mumbled, "Jesus Christ, Kate. I didn't think you were so completely thick, she's played you like a fiddle."

Kate gave a shaky sigh. "Just go away home and leave us all alone. You've caused enough pain and havoc in all of our lives for far too long. Why don't you do us all a favour and disappear again?"

Evie was left alone, utterly bereft. She stumbled to the bench and held on to stop the world from spinning. Maybe it would be better if she did just leave again, Evie thought. She'd caused so much suffering to the people she loved. It might be better if she just walked away.

Chapter Forty-Three

The Party, 3am

The party was finally winding down and, as predicted, Freya was the last woman standing. Some of the revellers were snoring with their heads on the table and half-melted Maltesers in their hair. Others had long gone into the night, after wishing Freya eighty more years of happiness.

Ross and Patsy were having 'one for the road'. It was actually their fifth for the road, but no one was counting. Patsy looked around. "I haven't seen Evie and Amelia for ages and Kate and Edwyn disappeared too."

"Wimps," said Ross.

"A bunch of one-pot screamers," said Patsy. "They will be at home in their beds or lying drunk somewhere."

"Amelia told me she was going to sort things out with Evie tonight. They will be on their second bottle of red somewhere, I hope," said Ross.

Freya waddled over with a smile. "Anyone else fancy a last dance?"

Patsy groaned. "I had to take off my high heels hours ago. The soles of my feet were burning. I was dancing to Kylie's 'Padam' in my bare feet and Andrzej stood on my big toe. It's still throbbing."

Ross smiled charmingly and bowed his head in Freya's direction. "I will do a trip of the light fantastic with you, birthday girl, but it will have to be the last for I am a man barely alive."

Freya gave a chuckle. "You aren't the only one, the piper has passed out so maybe we should all think about going home."

Patsy picked up her phone. "I'll call us a cab. We can drop you off." Ross smiled at her. "Thanks Patsy, but I think I'll walk home. It's not far, but I could do with clearing my head. Make sure her majesty gets to bed safely. She's very precious."

He took Freya's hand and gave it a kiss. "I hope you had an unforgettable birthday."

Freya sighed happily. "I really did. I wish I'd been able to have a word with Evie, though. I will make sure I see her in the morning."

She smiled up at Ross. "And if I were forty years younger, I'd show you a thing or two young man."

They all laughed and hugged each other.

Chapter Forty-Four

Orkney

Ross was walking home, enjoying the stars and the silence, when he saw what looked like a scarecrow slumped by the side of the road not far from his house. As he got closer, he was horrified to see it was Evie.

She was staring straight ahead, eyes wide open and muttering to herself.

"Evie?" he said. "Evie, love?" He shook her gently, but she just stared at him looking catatonic. Her hands were ice-cold when he touched them. "Hush now, lass. You are freezing. Let me get you into the warm."

He picked her up and carried her to his house, placed her carefully on the sofa and covered her up with a soft woollen blanket. He didn't know what to do. She seemed drunk but there was something in her glassy stare and the weakness of her limbs that just didn't sit right with him. He wasn't sure whether to call an ambulance but didn't want to embarrass Evie. He resolved to stay up and watch her for the next few hours, as she fell into a fretful sleep.

He held her hand and lay down on the floor beside the sofa. Looking at her now, so vulnerable and fragile he realised that, despite everything, he still cared for her deeply. There had to be a good explanation for her recent behaviour. He wasn't good at analysing his feelings but not for the first time, he wished he had told Evie long ago how he really felt.

He realised with sudden clarity that Amelia was just a distraction, and he was attracted to her because of her resemblance to Evie and, if he was honest, the sex was very good. But he had made a mistake and would need to tell her.

Freya had been dropped off at her house and was sitting with Bette Davis on her lap and a glass of Scapa in her hands. It had been a lovely party. She was sad that Jack and Delima and their kids hadn't been able to come but she understood completely. The news of the poor whales struggling to survive and the desperation of those trying to help was dominating the news. And although disappointed that Sophia and Finn hadn't made it home, she was happy they were back together.

She chuckled remembering Andrzej dressed as a very large Minion bursting at the seams. She felt so lucky they had all made such an effort with the food and the decorations. The only niggle was Evie.

Freya frowned and thought to herself, 'I need to make things right between us. I will have a long chat with Evie in the morning and hopefully we can move on. I hope she will be in a better mood, but at least she didn't make a scene at the party.'

Freya smiled again to herself, 'Amelia was the life and soul. I think she enjoyed the dancing more than I did and she picked up those Scottish dance moves so fast. Mind you, that bonnie fella from Whisky Kiss made it easy for us all, counting out the steps so well.'

She yawned and said, "Right, Bette. Us old biddies need to go to bed. Everything will sort itself out in the morning."

Just as Freya stood up and Bette Davis jumped to the floor, her phone rang and Edwyn's name appeared on the screen. Freya pressed answer with a sense of dread . . .

Chapter Forty-Five

The Balfour Hospital

In the wee small hours, Edwyn left Amelia at the hospital. She'd been kept in for observation and he headed back to his own house. When he arrived back home, Kate was sitting at the kitchen table and jumped up as he came in the door.

She gave him a hug and said, "You look done in. I'll make us some tea. Is Amelia really going to be alright? I can't believe Evie would do such a thing. I keep telling myself it was all just a mistake."

Edwyn sat down and sighed, "Amelia told me all about it in the hospital. I had to drag it out of her, though. She doesn't want Evie to get into trouble. It's such a mess, Kate. I had to call Freya and tell her Amelia had an 'accident'. What a way to end her night."

He rubbed his hand wearily over his tired eyes. "Evie wasn't answering her phone either and didn't go home last night. I got Andrzej to swing by to check and there was nobody at her house."

He gulped down his tea. "Thanks, love." He looked at her. "I know you were up all night waiting for me, but you should try and get some sleep." He got up from the table and stretched. "I'm going to have a shower and freshen up. I promised Freya I would drive Amelia back from the hospital in the morning. I know she will be fretting."

*

A few hours later, Edwyn drove out of the hospital with Amelia in the front seat wincing every time the car turned a corner. Unsurprisingly, she had been given the all-clear by the medics and her ankle wasn't even bruised, but she still had an air of martyred suffering about her, that had Edwyn completely fooled.

When they arrived, Freya enveloped Amelia in a massive hug and clucking over her, sat her in the best chair, covered her in a blanket and plied her with hot sweet tea and cake.

"You poor thing. What on earth happened? Edwyn didn't really tell me anything other than you'd fallen and hurt yourself. I've been so worried."

Amelia looked at her wanly. "It was my own silly fault. I went outside for a bit of fresh air . . ."

"You mean a ciggie?" said Freya, but she was smiling.

"Well yes, exactly. And I just fell over."

"It's those high heels of yours, my girl. They are an accident waiting to happen."

"I know," said Amelia. "And lo and behold the accident happened. I just toppled over and the next thing I knew, Kate and Edwyn were taking care of me."

"Thank goodness they were there," said Freya, smiling at Edwyn.

"I know," said Amelia, she gave what she hoped was a brave smile and said "I'm all fine now. So don't worry about me."

Freya sighed, "Well, I'm going to look after you."

Edwyn looked at Freya with concern, "And who will look after you? Have you actually had any sleep at all?"

"I'm perfectly fine, thank you," said Freya. She added, "I've been up for hours. I didn't want to waste the day and I've had plenty of sleep and you know I never get hangovers."

Edwyn looked at her fondly. She really was a force of nature and appeared so much younger than her years, but the fact had to be faced that she was now eighty years old. Edwyn thought to himself that this wasn't the time to tell her to slow down. It took a lot to get Freya cross but telling her to take care because of her age was the one thing that would guarantee the rough end of her tongue. Anyway, they had bigger problems to deal with right now.

Edwyn asked Freya, "You haven't heard from Evie, I suppose?"

Freya replied, "No, I haven't. I had hoped she went home with you. I thought you all left at the same time but, of course, you and Kate were looking after Amelia when she fell."

She looked confused, "So where was Evie then?"

Amelia said quickly, "We didn't see her, but she didn't look very happy at the party."

Freya sighed. "You know, it's all very odd. Evie has been behaving so strangely. I feel as though I hardly know her. I keep telling myself that she has been through such a lot, but I thought we had all managed to make her feel safe and secure."

Perhaps it was because of the lack of sleep or worry over Amelia's accident but Freya was on the verge of tears and Freya never ever cried. She went on, "I thought Evie was so happy with her painting and with the gallery. I know it's not been easy but she did seem as though she felt at home here again."

Freya looked stricken, "I must have missed something. I should have noticed she wasn't herself, maybe I pushed her too hard into staying here on Orkney with me. I've been selfish."

Edwyn raised his hand: "Freya, stop right there. You have got nothing to blame yourself for. You have been so good to Evie. Don't forget she left this island for twenty years without telling us why. I know she kept in touch with you when it suited her but the rest of us had no idea what had happened to her."

Freya said quietly, "I'm so sorry I didn't tell you where she was, but she made me solemnly promise. I was worried that you would try to find her, and she'd disappear again and I would lose her completely."

"Oh Freya," said Edwyn. "You don't need to apologise to me. Evie put you in an impossible situation. You shouldn't feel in the least bit guilty. You've lavished love and affection on that girl and she has thrown it back in your face."

He went on determinedly, "Amelia, I think we need to tell Freya the truth about what happened last night. I know you are trying to protect Evie but I think she needs to know . . ."

Chapter Forty-Six

Ross's House

Evie woke up with no idea where she was, and with her head pounding and the room spinning. She was terrified and let out a stifled scream. She heard a groan from the floor and was relieved to see it was only Ross, black hair standing on end, eyes half-shut, clothes crumpled and still looking impossibly handsome.

"What happened? What am I doing in your house?" she yelped.

"Don't you remember? I found you by the side of the road last night, well early this morning to be exact. I carried you back here, but I couldn't make it up the stairs, so I put you on the couch. I was worried you'd throw up and choke to death, so I sat up with you."

"I don't remember a thing," Evie said, rubbing her eyes. Ross went and fetched her a glass of water. She gulped it down.

"Some hangover," said Ross. "Do we need to call out the big guns and get you an Irn Bru and a roll and sausage?"

He suddenly looked serious. "I was really worried about you, Evie. I thought about calling an ambulance and maybe I should have. You were totally out of it."

Evie shook her head. "I know I was drinking, but this doesn't feel like a hangover. I can usually remember what went on, but this feels different. It feels like I have been drugged."

Ross frowned, "Do you think someone spiked your drink? Who would be shitty enough to do that? Last night was a party for Freya and it was with all of our friends. Both of us knew every single person who was there."

Evie looked at him uncertainly. "You're right, that doesn't makes sense. I had a couple of big glasses of wine, that is until . . ."

She stopped, sat bolt upright and winced in pain. "Oh my God. We need to warn everyone about Amelia."

Ross held her gently by the shoulders, "Calm down, love. You aren't making a lot of sense. What has Amelia got to do with all of this?"

Evie was babbling in panic. "You don't understand. She's dangerous."

Ross said sternly. "Evie Muir. You are talking nonsense. Now what the hell is really going on and why are you acting so weird?"

Evie looked at him, distraught. "Your precious Amelia, that's what. And I'm not the one that's weird. She is off her head. I'm scared she will really hurt someone. She threatened me and she said she had visited my mother in the care home without telling me and she doesn't live in the States. She came up here from London and she's the one who must have spiked my drink, and she's been telling terrible lies about me to Liv. She wants to destroy me . . ."

Evie couldn't go on. She was shaking and sobbing. Ross sat beside her, held her firmly and said, "Take a deep breath and take your time. Tell me everything."

Chapter Forty-Seven

Ross's House

When Ross had heard Evie's story, he cursed himself for being such a fool and falling for Amelia's lies. There was only one thing to be done. He had to take her to Freya's and they would confront Amelia.

He told Evie firmly, "I'm taking you home so you can get showered and changed. I have some calls to make and then we are going to get all this sorted out."

Evie shook her head. "I don't think I can face her and Freya won't believe me anyway. Amelia has fooled her, just like she fooled all of us."

He looked at her beautiful green eyes, brimming with tears, and once again berated himself for being such an idiot. Why didn't he have the courage to ask Evie out properly when he had the chance?

"I'm so, so sorry, Evie. I've let you down badly. Well, we all have. I can't believe I was seduced by that manipulative piece of work. What must you think of me."

"Oh Ross. She's cunning. She seemed so interested in learning about her family in Orkney and it was all a lot of rubbish."

She wiped tears from her eyes. He would have kissed her then, but she sensed his intention and pulled away, saying, "I must look terrible. I need to charge up my phone. It's completely dead. Take me home to get cleaned up and have a strong coffee and a couple of paracetamols and I will be ready to face the enemy."

She managed a wobbly smile. "I will also have that Irn Bru and roll and square sausage if it's still going, as long as you put on tons of HP sauce."

"Evie Muir. You know it has to be tomato sauce on a square sausage. Anything else is just barbaric."

He gave her a hug and said, "We will get through this, you know. It's going to be alright."

She looked up at him and said simply "As long as you are with me then I know I will be fine."

This time he did kiss her, deeply. They were both shaking as they clung to each other.

"Tell me you felt that?" he said. She simply nodded and smiled up at him. He told her gently. "It's always been you for me, Evie. Ever since you came home. You can never think of leaving me again."

Evie was near to tears. That kiss had stirred up so many emotions. She felt wobbly and confused, but much safer and far less scared. She said, "We have wasted so much time, Ross."

He stood up, took her hand and said, "Let's deal with Amelia first, and then we can get on with the rest of our lives."

He took Evie back to her house. It didn't take long for her to get ready. Once she was out of the shower, she checked her phone, now charged enough to have received a clutch of missed calls and messages from Liv.

I'm at yours – where are you?

Evie – where are you? I need to speak to you.

Text me – I'm worried.

This was so unlike Liv. Evie messaged her back.

I'm sorry. My phone was dead. I'm back at the house now but I have to go to Freya's.

On the short drive to Freya's, Evie asked Ross: "What will we say? Do you think Freya will believe us?"

Ross squeezed her hand. "Freya is the wisest woman we know. She will be able to suss out who is telling the truth."

Evie wasn't so sure. Amelia had alienated her from her friends and who knows what other lies she had been spreading.

Kate was at her front door when they arrived. She was furious.

Without even looking at Evie, she said to Ross, "I don't want her in Freya's house. We all know what she tried to do to Amelia last night."

Ross sighed. "Well, don't you think we should at least give Evie a chance to explain herself? That can't be too much to ask? I know Freya would want to hear what she has to say."

Kate reluctantly moved aside and ushered them both in. She stood with her arms folded, "This is against my better judgement. It had better be good."

Edwyn was sitting beside Amelia checking the graze on her face. Freya was sitting on her comfy colourful sofa, but she looked haunted and nothing like the laughing woman at her birthday party just last night.

Amelia's version of events had been so upsetting, particularly as she had seemed so unwilling to put any of the blame on Evie. It made her story all the more shocking and believable.

Edwyn glared at Evie and said coldly. "The last time I saw you, you had just attacked Amelia. She's been in hospital and luckily she's OK, but that's no thanks to you. Explain yourself, if you can."

"Actually," said Amelia. "I really don't think she should be here at all." She clutched Edwyn's arm and made her voice tremble with fake fear. "I'm scared of what she might do to me if she gets angry again."

Edwyn stood up. "Amelia's right. Ross, I am surprised at you for bringing her here. Evie, you need to leave right now, you can see how much you frighten Amelia."

Ross interrupted him. "Just hang on a minute. None of you know the full story."

"But I do," came a quiet voice from the doorway. It was Liv. She looked nervous but determined. There was a man behind her, even bigger than Andrzej, in faded jeans and a worn-out black biker jacket. He was grey and grizzled, and his belly had gone a bit soft, but he wasn't someone you would mess with.

He squeezed Liv's shoulder for reassurance as she looked over to Evie. She held her sister's gaze and asked, "Are you OK?"

Evie was astounded. Her sister had never once asked if she was alright. If she spoke to her at all it was to be defensive and dismissive, but Liv looked genuinely concerned.

Kate spluttered, "What is Liv doing here? Who's that with you?"

Liv scowled at her. "You might want to listen to what I have to say. This is Rab. He's a . . . friend."

Amelia said smoothly, and as though they were complete strangers, "You must be Evie's sister. I've heard so much about you," almost as though she was at a posh dinner party.

Liv ignored her, "Whatever Evie has to tell you about Amelia, it's the truth. She's been in constant touch with me since she arrived here. She's tried to bribe me and she's also threatened me."

Liv was breathing heavily, clearly anxious, but determined to say her piece. As she tried to continue, Amelia cut in, "You know that's a downright lie. I have never set eyes on you until tonight."

Liv glared at her in contempt and went on, "She came to the pub where I work to see me, almost as soon as she landed here. She told me she had a scam to get her hands on Evie's gallery and to alienate her from her friends. She wanted me to help her."

Amelia laughed shrilly, "What is all this nonsense? What are you talking about, Liv?"

Liv's voice shook a little, "You know exactly what happened. You told me to steal my sister's passport and then we went to that new solicitor in Kirkwall."

Liv swallowed hard and pushed herself on, "You pretended to be Evie. You already had your hair dyed blonde and wore the same kind of clothes, and you chose a solicitor who was new to the island and who wouldn't know our family history. You forged my sister's signature so I'd be able to access the business bank account and withdraw all the money leaving Evie and the gallery in ruins. All the gallery's artists and makers would be out of pocket too – Evie would have had to leave Orkney for good."

Amelia looked at Freya and Edwyn and Kate and said calmly to Liv, "Why on earth should these good people believe you? Anyone can see you and your sister have cooked up this ridiculous nonsense against me."

"You know I'm telling the truth," said Liv.

Amelia sighed: "Let's get this straight. *You* stole your sister's passport and *you* made the appointment with the solicitor. It has nothing to do with me. And it's not my fault if you are now having a change of heart and want to lay the blame on someone else, but it's not going to work."

Amelia sounded so reasonable and rational that Freya, Edwyn and Kate didn't know what to think. But then Liv smiled.

And Rab pulled out a bundle of paperwork from his jacket pocket. He handed it to Liv, who said, "I went back to the solicitor and got all of this immediately after I said goodbye to you. You were so full of yourself and had no idea that I was never part of your scheme."

Liv allowed herself to look triumphant. "I took copies of the paperwork from the solicitor – we'll be able to prove that this signature isn't Evie's. Evie still has the money. I didn't touch a penny and I never would have. I just went along with you to see how far you would go."

Ross chipped in. "You've been spreading lies about Evie all over the islands, stirring up bad blood with her friends. And I wouldn't be surprised if it was you who was behind those dreadful online attacks on Freya."

Liv joined in, "But Edwyn, Kate and especially Freya were the toughest ones for you to crack, weren't they? You realised you would have to do something really over the top to convince them Evie was not to be trusted, and so you made it look as though she attacked you."

Liv looked at Amelia with a mixture of loathing and pity. "You really are a pathetic and nasty piece of work."

Edwyn looked appalled. "That surely can't be true. No one in their right mind would do such a thing."

"Agreed," said Liv. "But she's clearly not in her right mind. She's eaten up with jealousy and spite and hate."

Freya had gone very quiet. She looked grey and old and tired. She turned to Amelia and gave a heavy sigh from the depths of her soul. She couldn't bear all of these lies and accusations. She held her head in her hands and started to weep. Evie went to comfort her.

"Don't shed any tears for her, Freya. She isn't worth it."

Ross said grimly, "I think we should phone the police."

"Go ahead," said Amelia, looking completely calm and composed. "What do you reckon the coppers will charge me with?"

Rab had been silent up until this point, but now he stepped forwards, his voice deep and strong: "Maybe I can answer that one. So Liv came to me, in a right state, and finally told me everything that had been going on."

Pointing at Amelia, he continued, "How this one was trying to manipulate her. I told her to tell you all the truth right away but she was worried you wouldn't believe her. We had a long talk and Liv convinced me that, by pretending to go along with Amelia's scam, she would have the evidence she needed to convince you all."

He looked around the room. "I reckon she had done that alright." He looked at Liv, squeezed her hand and whispered, "I'm so proud of you and I told you it would be OK."

Rab continued. "With someone like Amelia there's usually a history of bad deeds so I did a bit of digging. The biker community look out for each other so I put out feelers on social media, and it turns out a friend of mine from Shetland knows a bloke down south who was scammed by someone using the self-same tactics – wheedling her way into someone's life then taking it over bit by bit – and fitting Amelia's description."

He looked straight at Amelia. "She's done this before and I'm not surprised that she's wanted by the police in England."

The room fell silent. Before Amelia could reply, Freya made a guttural noise and collapsed. Edwyn rushed to help her and everyone crowded around.

"Kate, call an ambulance!" he said tersely . . . "She looks like she's having a stroke. Tell them it's urgent. We need to get her to hospital right away."

Amelia took advantage of everyone's attention being on Freya and slipped out of the back door.

Chapter Forty-Eight

The Balfour Hospital

When news of Freya's stroke got out, the hospital was inundated with worried callers and people turning up to find out how she was doing.

A harassed receptionist said to Edwyn, "I'm going to have to put up bulletins on the front door like they do with the royals." She looked at him tearfully. "How is she doing really, Edwyn? We are all worried about her. Was it the excitement of the party?"

He tried to smile at her reassuringly, although inside he felt his nerves were shredded. Edwyn was used to working long hours with scant sleep, but the past few days had been intense.

"I'm not sure, but she's Freya and she's a fighter. We are all hopeful." He'd had to tell Ross to keep Evie at Freya's house. She was almost hysterical with fear for Freya and rage at Amelia. Ross had managed to calm her down and told her they could do more good trying to find Amelia, and she had to let the professionals take care of Freya now.

Edwyn promised he would keep them updated on her condition. As a doctor, he had never felt more helpless in all his life. He couldn't even begin to think about what would happen if Freya didn't pull through. He took off his glasses and rubbed his tired eyes. Looking up, he saw Maureen and Andrzej approaching the front desk, worried and anxious.

Andrzej gave Edwyn a bear hug and Maureen was trying not to cry. She asked him in a trembling voice, "What's happening? What can we do to help?"

Edwyn sighed, "She's still in intensive care, and we won't know how badly the stroke has affected her for a while, but her heart is strong and we got her here really quickly."

Maureen asked him, "Could I sit with her? Just in case she wakes up. I don't want her to be all confused and upset when she comes round."

Edwyn replied, "Well, she is getting the best care from our nursing staff." He saw Maureen's chin wobble and her shoulders slump and added quickly, "But I think that's a good idea Maureen, and I have to fill Andrzej in on what's been going on."

Chapter Forty-Nine

Hoxa

Now that her plan had gone horribly wrong, Amelia knew she had to find somewhere to hide. By now, she should have forced Liv into releasing all the funds from Evie's gallery and she'd have been on the first plane out of this godforsaken place, leaving chaos in her wake.

Amelia was fuming. She had underestimated Liv, and now she needed to get away from Orkney before her past crimes caught up with her. Running away from Freya's, she crossed over fields to the back road into Kirkwall and ordered a cab that dropped her off close to Jack and Delima's house in Hoxa. She knew they hadn't turned up at the party, and vaguely remembered they were away on some half-arsed animal rescue mission, so wouldn't be at home, and hopefully wouldn't have heard anything about what had happened.

She needed to buy some time and work out an escape plan. The door was answered by a young English girl. She looked wild-eyed and harassed and peered at Amelia, saying fretfully, "Can I help you?"

Amelia gave her most dazzling smile and made a stab at an Orkney accent. "I'm a friend of Jack and Delima's." The girl looked relieved. "I thought you looked familiar. It's Evie, isn't it?"

Seeing an opportunity to jump on her confusion, Amelia lied smoothly. "That's right. I don't think we've met properly, though."

"I'm Caroline, one of the new volunteers at the sanctuary. You've probably heard they are all away on Sanday, trying to save the whales that breached there." Amelia had no idea what she was going on about and cared even less, but was relieved to hear that, as she had suspected, Jack and Delima were far away.

The young girl looked stricken. "It's just so awful. We don't know whether we can do anything but everyone is trying so hard."

Amelia played along, giving an exaggerated frown of concern. "Oh I know, it's just such a tragedy. They mentioned you were here taking care of the children, and I thought I'd pop by and check you were OK."

Caroline rolled her eyes, "Well of course I wanted to go with them to help, but someone had to look after the animals in the sanctuary, and those two of course, but they are a right handful. I'm at my wits' end."

"Oh you poor thing" said Amelia, with a sympathetic pout. "Why don't I look after them for you, at least for a little while, and you can get a break or catch up with the animals?"

Caroline looked at her hopefully, "Do you mean it? I really do need to pop down to the sanctuary. The baby seals need feeding and monitoring, and there's so much work I need to do there." She rattled on, "I was just trying to get the kids ready to come down with me but it's like herding cats. I've put them both in their cots but they keep yelling at me. Then the phone kept ringing downstairs and I couldn't answer because they won't do a thing I tell them, and I must have changed Hari's nappy a hundred times." She made a gagging noise. "It's so gross."

"Well, give them to me then. They love their aunty Evie." Caroline blushed and said uncomfortably, "Do you mind if I just check with Delima? I don't want to get into trouble. She can be quite scary."

Amelia grinned tightly. "Well, now, haven't they chosen the right person to help them out. I think it's admirable to be so very conscientious. Do give Delima a call. Meanwhile, I will pop upstairs and give Ola and Hari a cuddle."

Caroline rang Delima's mobile. "What's up?" she answered tersely.

"Your friend Evie has just come round and says she wants to look after Ola and Hari. Is that OK? Only I've got so much to do at the sanctuary."

"Of course it is," said Delima impatiently. Despite Evie's recent strange behaviour and that bizarre row with everyone, Delima knew how much she loved the kids.

"Look, Caroline, it's pretty bad here so I need to go. Tell Evie thanks and she might have to stay overnight. She won't mind. She's done it before for us."

Amelia, successfully pretending to be Evie, waved a relieved Caroline off and told her she'd make Ola and Hari their tea later, and put them to bed, and was happy to stay the night, so there was no need for her to come back.

Caroline almost ran down to the sanctuary by the shoreline, vowing never ever to have children. She had no idea they were such hard work. Give her baby seals and otters any day.

Chapter Fifty

Sanday

Delima put her phone away. She was cold and anxious. They were losing the battle to save the whales and the weather was threatening to take a turn for the worse. She was so relieved Evie was there. Caroline was a nice girl, but she was a bit useless, and Delima had been worried about leaving the children with her for more than a few hours.

She was about to shout over to Jack that Ola and Hari were in safe hands, but he was in the middle of an interview with Norman Macleod from STV's *North Tonight*. The story had gone viral all over the world, which was a double-edged sword. It meant more people were aware of what was going on and wanted to help, but Jack was tripping over all sorts of well-meaning media and volunteers who were getting in the way.

Delima looked at the beautiful creatures slowly suffocating on the beach and felt like weeping again. It was more than likely one of the whales had become sick and the others had rallied round and tried to help, finding themselves trapped in shallow water. They would be lucky to save any of them but they had to keep on trying.

Delima consoled herself that at least she didn't have to worry about her precious babies back at home as Evie would be taking good care of them.

*

Amelia settled herself in Delima and Jack's cosy kitchen. It was deliberately designed to look old-fashioned, but everything, including the huge lilac Aga, was brand new. There was underfloor heating and the massive wooden table had been artistically distressed.

Although it was spotless, the kitchen was also the proper heart of the house, with comfy mismatched chairs around the table, colourful pottery on the windowsills and posters of Singapore on the walls.

The massive fridge had snaps of all the rescued seals and otters stuck to the door, and the room smelled of fresh bread and home-cooked meals. The spice rack covered an entire wall and there were recipe books stacked up on every shelf. It was usually a place of comfort and solace, but with Amelia squatting there like a malevolent toad, the atmosphere had turned rank with menace.

She had already snapped at Ola for being noisy and made the little girl cry. Baby Hari was lying on the floor in a dirty nappy and grizzling fretfully, but Amelia wasn't going to be changing him any time soon no matter how much he whined.

She had to consider her options. The last plane and ferry off the islands were long gone, so she decided to stay here in the warmth overnight then somehow get back to the mainland in the morning.

Before fleeing Freya's house, Amelia had grabbed her handbag with her passport, credit cards and keys to her London flat. The rest of her stuff could be left behind, she just needed to put as much distance as possible between herself and Orkney.

Her plan to ruin Evie might have backfired, but she had managed to create havoc and cause enormous upset and, for

Amelia, that was all part of the fun. She told herself, 'If that old bag Freya dies, I know Evie will blame herself. It's something, I suppose, and anyway I'm not finished with her yet.'

Back at Freya's, Evie and Ross were waiting for news. Liv had crawled back into her shell and retreated into the kitchen with Rab, trying not to stare too hard at the open bottle of whisky by the sink.

A visibly upset Kate had apologised to Evie over and over again, and had gone back to her mother's to pick up the girls and take them home. Evie made yet another call to the hospital and was told there was no change in Freya's condition.

She also left Maureen a message making her swear to call her the instant Freya showed any signs of waking up. Ross had been keeping busy, calling round all the hotels and boarding houses. He didn't think Amelia would be daft enough to check into any of them, but he needed something to do. They were all going quietly round the bend.

So it was heartening to receive a phone call from Andrzej, who'd been ringing round his pals in the taxi trade and discovered a woman matching Amelia's description had been dropped off in a cab near Hoxa.

"A lead at last," he told Ross. He added, "She got out near Jack and Delima's house. I have a strong feeling she's hiding out there now. I can go and check it out."

Ross replied, "Are you sure? There won't be anyone at Jack's. They're all on Sanday right now, trying to save those poor beached whales."

Evie looked up, "The babies will be there. Delima will have left them with that new girl, Caroline, because everyone else was at Freya's party.

Andrzej nodded. "And that's exactly why that snake Amelia would go there. I will take the van and head down right away."

Ross replied, "Makes sense. But you're not going alone. Evie and I will come too and meet you there. We're closer. I'll call Jack to let him know what's been happening."

Evie told him: "I'll call the landline at the house and check." She kept on trying the number but there was no answer.

When Ross called Jack he could barely hear his voice over the roar of the sea, the heartbreaking cries of the dying whales and the frantic noise of the rescuers. The line was cutting in and out, and Ross wasn't sure how much Jack was taking in.

He tried to explain about Amelia, but the signal failed and he was talking to himself. It was getting dark. Ross put the phone down and turned to Evie. "We need to head off to meet up with Andrzej."

On Sanday, it was getting difficult to see in the gloom. People had brought their cars to the edge of the beach and put on their full beams and there were kids with powerful torches; even fires were lit to try and help the rescuers. It was a race against time.

Jack was almost asleep on his feet. He had hardly seen Delima all day, but they were both sitting on a rock drinking hot sweet coffee when her phone rang. She was going to ignore it but saw it was Evie.

"Hi, Evie. Thanks for calling. Are the kids alright? I hope they have been behaving for you."

Evie was totally confused. "Sorry? What do you mean? I haven't seen them." It took a lot to make Delima lose her cool, but she'd sat bolt upright and her voice rose to a shriek.

"Aren't you with my babies? Caroline called me. You turned up at our door an hour ago and said you would look after them and stay overnight?"

There was silence, then Evie managed to say, "Delima. I know this will sound mad to you, but I think Amelia must have turned up saying she was me and Caroline believed her. I'm so sorry but I think it's more than likely Amelia is with the children."

Delima relaxed. "Oh well, that's all right then. The kids love Amelia. You had me so worried for a minute. But wait a minute, why would she pretend to be you? That really is mad."

"Delima," said Evie urgently. "Has Jack not told you what's been going on with her?"

"No, we've hardly seen each other. He's with me now but we haven't had a chance to catch up. What's happening? Is everyone alright?"

"I'm sorry, Delima, but I think you need to talk to Jack. I just wanted to let you know they're heading to your place. Andrzej is already on his way, so don't worry. The kids will be fine."

Delima was confused and feeling panicky. "I don't understand. Evie, what's going on?"

"I need to go. Jack will explain."

"No, stay on the line. Don't hang up, please," Delima turned to her husband.

"Jack, what's happening over there? I thought Evie was looking after Ola and Hari. But I've got her on the phone now. She's been at Freya's and they are on their way to our house."

Jack frowned and replied, "That doesn't make any sense. I didn't know anything about Evie or Amelia babysitting. You didn't tell me."

"I meant to, but you were so busy and this is the first time we've been able to talk all day."

Jack swallowed hard, "Ross called me earlier but it was a bad line and I couldn't really hear what he was saying, and with everything going on here, I didn't give it enough attention."

"Evie, are you still there?" Delima was beside herself. "Please tell me what's been happening before I go crazy." Evie quickly brought her up to speed.

Delima couldn't believe what she was hearing.

"Oh my God, Evie. Are you alright?"

"Aye, I'm fine, but Freya . . ." Evie's voice broke. "It's bad. The shock of it all brought on a stroke and she's in hospital. I really need to go and check on Ola and Hari. I will call you as soon as I can."

Delima whispered, "Don't let her hurt my kids, Evie." And hung up. Jack had never seen his wife so shaken and that made him full of dread.

She glared at him. "Jack, that hideous woman has fooled us all, she's caused Freya to be taken to hospital and now she is with our babies," said Delima, her voice trembling. "If anything happens to them, I will never forgive myself or you. We need to get back home right now."

Jack felt sick. His mind had been so focused on the rescue, he simply hadn't understood the seriousness of what Ross had been trying to tell him. He'd barely listened and now Ola and Hari might be in danger. How could he have been such an idiot?

He tried to stay positive but the thought of his children being in any sort of danger made him want to kneel in the sand and scream.

"We are stuck here, Delima. Even if they could spare us the fastest boat on the island, the others will get there long before we could. What are we going to do?"

He started pacing up and down, running his hands through his hair. Delima ignored him.

She was on her phone calling the landline at their house, then the sanctuary, and finally Caroline's mobile, but there was no answer. Amelia ignored the persistent ringing in the house; meanwhile, Caroline was happily washing a baby seal, humming a Harry Styles tune. She couldn't hear her phone. Delima turned to Jack in despair.

"There's no answer at the house and I can't get hold of Caroline. Anything could have happened." She could feel her panic rising but then remembered something.

She grabbed Jack's arm and asked him urgently, "Didn't some of those Norwegian news guys arrive here by helicopter? The one the hospital uses sometimes?"

She didn't wait for a reply but ran towards the big house by the shore which the kind owners had allowed to be used as a rescue headquarters. A fierce mother on a mission.

Chapter Fifty-One

Jack and Delima's House

Andrzej was already in his van and on the way to Jack and Delima's; Ross and Evie would get there around the same time. They'd decided Liv and Rab would stay at Freya's in case there was any news.

Before Evie left, Liv mumbled to her, "Be careful, won't you." Evie caught her sister's eye for a moment. She had never heard Liv say anything kind to her like that. She nodded: "I promise."

They drove as fast as possible to Hoxa and parked up outside Jack and Delima's house, noticing the lights were blazing downstairs. Andrzej pulled up behind their car, and the three of them let themselves in and went through to the kitchen, where Amelia was sitting in front of a roaring fire.

She had a tearful Hari in her lap and Ola was in her playpen. The little girl looked as though she had cried herself to sleep and was hiccupping plaintively, while clutching one of Maureen's homemade blankets.

"Well, look who it is," Amelia drawled. "I suppose you expect me to come with you quietly and not make a fuss."

Evie said firmly, "I think that would be best, Amelia."

"But I happen to be very comfortable here and I have no intention of going anywhere. But where are my manners, do sit down."

The three of them stayed standing, wondering who would make the first move. Eventually, Evie broke the silence. "Why did you come after me now? Why wait so long to find out about your past?"

Amelia replied, "It was really all your fault, Evie. Your ego got the better of you. I saw a nauseating article all about your success and your fabulous life in Orkney. That's how I was able to finally track you down. When it mentioned your mother's name was Cara, I just knew it was the same person my stupid father was always going on about. And there you were. Living a perfect life with your happy family and friends."

Evie shook her head in disbelief. Amelia had twisted reality into a warped fantasy. She had no idea of the kind of life Evie had led.

Amelia laughed scornfully at her, "Your senile old mother helped. I was able to track her down and she told me all sorts of things about you. Of course, it just confirmed what I already knew. And I fooled you and that ridiculous bunch of freaks you call your friends. You do realise that it wasn't very hard to make them think the worst of you and the best of me."

Amelia frowned and went on, "Although it wasn't easy having to hear Kate's boring plans to go back to university and to try and look interested in whatever drivel Freya was yapping on about. Posting those fake comments online about Freya helped though; I've never seen someone so upset. I knew she would even start questioning her beloved Evie when she felt so vulnerable and low."

She gave Ross what she thought was a sultry look. "Although the sex with you wasn't all that bad. A bit vanilla, but I could have worked on that."

Ross looked at her in disgust as she turned to Andrzej. "Oh, and listening to you droning on and on about Orkney history.

I thought I was going to scream. I never want to hear another word about this ghastly place."

"Jesus Christ, Amelia," said Ross. "You've caused such a lot of pain and for what?"

Amelia looked surprised and glowered at Evie. "Why don't you ask her? She knows."

"What are you talking about?" Evie shouted, enraged. "I didn't even know you existed. I only found out about you when you got in touch with me. I wish I'd never replied to your email."

Amelia was becoming more and more agitated: "My father talked about your mother all the time. If he hadn't got sick, I know he would have come back here to find her. He would have met you too, his perfect granddaughter and he would have forgotten all about me."

Evie said witheringly, "I never knew your father and he was never even talked about when I was growing up. You have built a fantasy in your head and blamed my mother and me for all your mistakes and troubles. It's ridiculous. You are completely delusional."

Ross and Andrzej shared a look. Evie was making Amelia angry and she still had a hold of baby Hari. There was no telling what she might do.

"That's enough, Evie," said Ross. "Come on now, Amelia. Give me little Hari so I can stop him crying. Ola needs a cuddle too." He smiled at her in a way he hoped was reassuring, "Then we can all sit down calmly and have a cup of tea and talk this through. It's way past their bedtime. What do you say?"

Amelia hesitated and looked as though she was thinking about giving up and doing what Ross had said, until she saw Andrzej take out his phone.

"Who are you calling?" Amelia said sharply.

In fact, Andrzej was checking to see if he had a message from Maureen about Freya, and was about to text her to call the police, now they knew where Amelia was, but before he could press send, Amelia stood up with baby Hari in her arms.

"Don't come near me. Throw me your keys, Andrzej. I need to get away. I am going to take this brat and if you follow me in the car, I will throw him out. Believe me, at the speed I will be going, he won't survive."

The three of them were appalled and Evie pleaded, "Amelia, please don't hurt Hari. We'll let you go. Just hand him over."

"I haven't called the police," Andrzej said, desperately. "Look, check my phone, there are no calls. Amelia, like Evie says, we will let you go, but you can't take him. Everything will be OK. You can have my keys and take the van and disappear." He put his keys on the floor and kicked them across to where Amelia was standing.

"Why should I believe you?" sneered Amelia. "I'm not stupid. The second you have Hari back, you'll come after me."

The child began to wail, "Be quiet, you little bastard," hissed Amelia, her face twisted and furious. She held Hari in front of her. "Shut up!" she shouted loudly into his face. Hari was terrified and started roaring at the top of his lungs.

Evie was in despair at seeing him so upset. This woman was dangerous and unstable. She could not be allowed to take Hari.

Amelia crouched down in order to pick up the keys, holding Hari awkwardly with one arm. The baby tried to escape from her grasp and Ross made a split-second decision to lunge at Amelia, taking her by surprise. He managed to pull Hari out of her grasp, thrusting him towards Evie and safety.

Amelia kicked out at Ross, knocking him off balance, and he fell to the ground. In the melee, she grabbed the keys from the floor and raced out of the room.

"After her!" shouted Andrzej, and Ross scrambled up from the floor. All three of them raced out and into the night air.

Amelia was ahead but not by much. Andrzej had left the door open, she ran into the van, fumbled with the keys and turned on the engine.

"She's getting away," panted Evie, clutching Hari to her. But she hadn't reckoned on Ross, who sprinted to catch up with the van, almost managing to grab the door handle. To Evie's horror, Amelia swerved viciously, crashing into Ross and sending him flying through the air.

Chapter Fifty-Two

Jack and Delima's House

Evie felt as though everything happened in slow motion after that. She was still holding on tight to little Hari and stood rooted to the spot. She saw Andrzej rush forward. Ross was lying on the ground, a heap of twisted limbs, blood seeping from his head. She looked at his face. It was chalk white and he wasn't moving.

Andrzej felt his neck. "There's a faint pulse," he said. "But I'm afraid to move him. I don't know how badly injured he is. I'm calling for help."

Evie stumbled over to him. Little Hari was clinging to her and sobbing quietly. "Ross," she said, desperately. "Ross, please stay with me."

Suddenly, the sky was filled with light and a deep rumbling. They were blinded for a moment by a helicopter flying overhead. As it came into land, the downdraft whipped Evie's hair across her face and blew Ross's jacket across his body, making him look as though he was trying to get up.

Andrzej was frantically waving his arms to let the pilot know where they were. As soon as the propellers stopped moving, Delima leapt from the chopper and tried to take in the scene before her.

"What's happened?" she gasped, her face the colour of spoiled milk. "Where's Ola? What's happened to Ross?" She took Hari from Evie and held him as though she would never let go.

"Ola's safe," Evie said, her eyes wild. "She's inside. But Ross, Amelia was driving the van and she hit him deliberately. I think she might have killed him."

Iain, the pilot, was right behind Delima. Working for the hospital, he'd seen some terrible accidents, especially on the offshore rigs, and he was cool-headed in a crisis. He quickly appraised Ross.

"I'm going to call the hospital again, we need to get him help right away. It will be quicker in the chopper, but we need the paramedics to help me move him." He ran to get a stretcher from the helicopter.

With Hari clinging to her chest, Delima ran inside to check on Ola. Evie kept talking to Ross, although she wasn't sure he could hear her. She felt Andrzej's reassuring hand on her shoulder. "Listen to the sirens, lass. The paramedics are almost here." Evie felt as though she was in a nightmare.

"Why hasn't he come round?" she sobbed. "There's so much blood."

"He's taken a bad blow to the head," said Iain. "You just keep talking to him. It's the best we can do for now."

After what felt like an eternity, two paramedics came running up beside them. To Evie they looked just like the men who had tried to save Brodie over twenty years before. They speedily and efficiently transferred Ross into the helicopter. His lips looked blue and the dressing they'd put on his head was soaked with blood.

There was room in the helicopter for Evie and Andrzej told her he would drive to the hospital and meet her there. It was a race against time.

Chapter Fifty-Three

The Balfour Hospital

As soon as they landed, Ross was urgently wheeled away into theatre. He still hadn't regained consciousness and his head injury was more severe than the paramedics had initially thought.

Evie was being checked out while an anxious police officer hovered at her elbow, desperate to take her statement about Amelia. The young sergeant managed to piece some of it together before doctors told him Evie was in no state to answer any more questions.

Edwyn burst into the room where Evie was being looked after. She started to cry when she saw him, "Oh Edwyn, she attacked Ross. It's all my fault. I made her angry. And those poor little babies." She began to wail in distress.

Edwyn hugged her and said, "She's a psychopath. I should have seen it. We were all taken in by her. It's not your fault. Try not to worry about Ross. They are doing everything they can to help him. The kids will be fine. They are with Delima and I've sent a doctor to see them at home. It will be easier for all of them."

Evie looked at him in fear. "Where's Amelia?" she whispered.

"Everyone is out looking for her and they will find her. Don't you worry. I will go and try and find out what's going on."

"And Freya?" gulped Evie. "Is she any better?"

Edwyn hesitated. This was always one of the toughest parts of his job. The hard truth was Freya wasn't getting any better. Edwyn had been checking up on her when the call had come in about Ross. Maureen was sitting by Freya's bed, knitting a bright orange scarf and bravely chatting away, but it was clear her friend was in a bad way.

"We've not seen as much change as we expected," Edwyn said gently. "But that's no reason to give up hope."

Evie went very pale. Ross and Freya, both in hospital. Could she really be facing the loss of the two people she loved most in all the world?

"Normally, we would be relying on Freya to get us through this. She'd be here reassuring us all. It's like we have lost our anchor," whispered Evie.

Edwyn put his arm around Evie's shoulder. "Try not to worry too much. It's early days and Freya is strong and stubborn. I'm going to ask Maureen to come and sit with you for a bit."

"Thanks," Evie said weakly. Then a thought occurred to her. "Edwyn, could you ring Liv? She needs to know what's happened. I just don't have the strength to talk to her right now."

"Of course, I will," said Edwyn.

Chapter Fifty-Four

Hoxa

Amelia was driving away from the house in a panic. She still had her money and passport in the bag around her waist but she was trapped. In the rearview mirror, she saw the helicopter landing and heard the ambulance sirens blaring. She knew she had to get as far away from the scene of her crimes as possible.

She muttered to herself, "That idiot, Ross. Why had he decided to try and act the hero?" She blocked out the loud thud of the van hitting his body and the sight of him bleeding on the road. Under cover of darkness, she'd find a place to hide out while she thought of a plan.

Liv and Rab had waited at Freya's, hunkering down on her sofa, until Liv told him to go home and get some shuteye in his own bed. Unable to sleep herself, Liv kept checking her phone, but there were no messages.

"Forgotten about me again," she told herself. "They couldn't even be bothered to tell me what happened after I told them the truth about that bitch Amelia." She sighed, "Always the same old story. I'm the one at the back of the queue that no one cares about."

Feeling sorry for herself, she went to the kitchen to make herself a pot of tea when the phone rang. It was Edwyn. "Liv,

I know it's really late and I'm so sorry no one contacted you yet. It's been an absolute nightmare. Evie asked me to call. It's desperate." Edwyn quickly filled her in on what had happened.

"The police are out searching for Amelia now." He went on urgently, "Did she say anything to you about her plans? Or was there someone else on the island she knew? Or somewhere she could hide?"

Liv told him, "I don't think so. She lived with Freya all the time she was here, and I really only saw her a few times, but you know how sly and sleekit she is. She'll have found a hole to hide in." Liv swallowed hard and asked, "How is Evie?"

"Not great. She might appreciate a call or a message. Or you could come to the hospital to be with her." Liv laughed scornfully. "I'm the last person she would want to see."

"Don't be so sure. You were the one who helped the most in showing us all what Amelia was really like. We owe you a great debt."

Liv wasn't used to praise. She coughed uncomfortably, said goodbye and hung up, putting her head in her hands. "What a clusterfuck this all is," she groaned. Then she remembered something.

Amelia had been to visit Liv and knew about her AA meetings. The community centre where they held the meetings was always left open. It was only a twenty-minute drive from the sanctuary and would be the perfect place to hide.

Liv reached for her phone to call the police and let them know and then hesitated. What if she had got it completely wrong? She'd had so many run-ins with the law in the past. They all had a low enough opinion of her when she was taking drugs and boozing. She couldn't bear to risk their scorn and be accused of wasting police time, and it was only a hunch, after all.

'I'll check it out for myself,' she thought. 'Then I can give the police a call if it turns out Amelia is there.'

It was a cold night and Liv trudged in the darkness up to the back door of the centre. There was no sign of the van but if she was here, Amelia would have probably abandoned it somewhere and walked the rest of the way.

Liv peered in through the window, into the tiny kitchenette. It was dark inside, but then she spotted a light moving. She was right. It was Amelia, walking up and down, looking at her phone screen.

Liv's heart was pounding so loudly all she could hear was the blood rushing in her ears. She realised, too late, that she should have brought Rab with her, but for the same reason she didn't call the police, she hadn't wanted to appear ridiculous in front of him if it turned out she was wrong.

She crouched down and pulled out her phone, calling the police with the details, speaking softly. She hung up and stayed still, but then she heard the groaning squeal of the front door opening.

"Well, well," said Amelia menacingly. "Look who's here." Much to her dismay, Liv found herself looking at Amelia with a deep sense of dread. Past experience around criminals and lowlifes had taught her you must never ever show your fear. So she breathed in hard and said in her strongest voice: "I knew you would be here. It's all over. Get your sorry arse back inside. Now."

Amelia cackled, "Are you going to make me? Take a look at yourself. You look like a scarecrow. I could snap you in half like a rotten twig." Then she hissed, "Why don't you do us both a favour and just fuck off."

Hoping to take Liv by surprise, she made a run for it but Liv was too quick for her. She grabbed Amelia and slammed her to the ground. "I thought I told you to get back inside," Liv shouted, dragging a writhing, spitting Amelia over the open doorway and into the kitchen.

There was only one way in and out. Liv slammed the door shut and stood with her back to it, facing Amelia, who glowered belligerently at her. "Oh, Liv. What a complete asshole you are. This could have been so good for both of us. You just wouldn't listen to me."

Liv knew the police were on their way. She just had to keep Amelia talking. "Well, I'm hearing you now. Why don't you tell me what this really has all been about?"

For a flicker of an eye, Amelia looked vulnerable. "Do you really want to know?"

"I'd like to try and understand how we got here," said Liv.

Amelia stared at her, and then she began to talk . . .

Chapter Fifty-Five
Amelia's Story

1996–2026

Amelia had thought Lachlan was the one but when he rejected her, she realised he wasn't worth the trouble. He didn't deserve her and she'd never allow herself to be so vulnerable ever again. Amelia also hadn't appreciated just how hard she would have to work in order to get her degree, and it was too much effort when there were so many idiots in the world she could shake down for money.

Her ultimate goal was to marry someone filthy rich, take them for everything in the divorce and be set up for life. So she dropped out of university after the first year and moved back south to London. Eric had died of cancer a few months earlier, which made no impression on Amelia, but she sensed an opportunity. He had left the house to Ruth, who was now wracked with ill-health and virtually bedridden.

Amelia managed to cajole her into selling up and splitting the proceeds with false promises they'd buy a nice little bungalow and she'd become Ruth's full-time carer. As soon as she had the money, Ruth was abandoned and Amelia didn't give her another thought.

The money kept her afloat for a few years and she used some of it on an expensive nose job and designer clothes. It was soon frittered away, so she had to find a job, ending up in a juice bar in an expensive gym where she honed her body for free on the state-of-the-art equipment. There was no shortage of men to be used as meal tickets.

Amelia held her new nose, had loveless sex with them and was rewarded with expensive gifts. Older clients seemed to enjoy taking her out for posh dinners and some even gave her an allowance. Initially, she'd flatter their egos and pretend to enjoy their fumblings in bed, but all of these arrangements ended abruptly when Amelia would inevitably let her sweet-and-sexy mask slip.

She never managed to hook a permanent sugar daddy and, thirty years later, she was living a small life in a tiny, rented flat, telling herself resentfully that she deserved so much more. She was also still working in a gym, but this one was in a seedy backstreet with dodgy deals being done and illegal steroids swallowed like sweeties. It smelt of rubber, rancid sweat and despair.

For the past decade, Amelia had been using online dating under a fake profile as a way of scamming mostly older men out of as much money as possible. She was currently embroiled in a fake relationship with an elderly man who was on his own since his wife had died a year ago.

She spent hours online, reeling him in until he trusted her completely. She'd gone in for the kill a few days ago, pleading she needed help to get temporarily out of a financial jam, assuring him her funds were tied up and she would pay him back as soon as possible.

He'd already transferred £5,000 to her bank account and she was sure she could squeeze him for a hell of a lot more. But today she'd received a message on their chat thread from his oldest son, who worked in IT, and, like his two younger sisters, didn't pay the poor old soul much attention unless money was involved.

The five grand leaving his father's online bank account had rung alarm bells and he'd phoned his father to find out what was going on. Now, he wanted to meet up with Amelia and she was scared he'd discover her scam.

The old man was just the latest in a long line of other faceless, nameless stooges she had conned out of their cash. She'd been getting away with it for years but the money she made slipped through her fingers and she had little to show for it.

Amelia went to work, frantically trying to think of a plan to escape justice. After her shift and a tough workout, she headed for the showers, when one of the regulars, an affable dullard with biceps bigger than his waist, called her over.

He was squinting at a copy of a magazine that he'd found in the tiny reception area. He let out an enormous guffaw and roared: "Hey, Amelia, come take a look at this. You've got a lookalike. Right here in this magazine. You could be twins if she wasn't a blondie."

She snatched the magazine from his meaty grasp. There in front of her was a photo of a woman who really did resemble Amelia, especially now she had her nose fixed and her body was so lean. She scanned the article, feeling a chill in her stomach that turned into pure cold rage.

It was a feature on a female painter who'd launched her own art gallery showcasing other artists' work in Orkney and also just so happened to be incredibly beautiful, ethereal and photogenic. The biggest image of all, taking up an entire page, was of a beaming Evie Muir. It mentioned that Evie was the daughter of parents Duncan and Cara who had lived in Orkney. Amelia knew those names instantly from her father's scraps of letters.

Amelia had never had any desire to track down Cara. At first, she worried Cara would want a share of her father's money, but now that was all gone what was the point? She didn't want a weepy reunion with some old woman who lived in the arse end of nowhere and might want something from her. So she shut that part of her life down and hadn't thought about her for years.

But now this. It couldn't possibly be coincidence. This woman had to be her father's granddaughter. The fact the two of them looked so alike and Evie Muir's mother was called Cara meant that her half-sister had given birth to a beautiful successful golden child.

Evie was dressed in an expensive cashmere cream jumper and matching wide-trousered leggings with a simple lilac and pink plaid scarf. She wore a pair of silver and amethyst earrings. Her blonde highlights glinted in her thick, wavy hair and she had a fresh-faced 'no make-up' glow that few can carry off, making her emerald eyes look enormous and full of life. It was an image of sheer understated class.

She was photographed sitting in what looked like her own kitchen, on a comfortable wooden chair, smiling confidently, every inch the successful creative businesswoman who had made it to the top. The article gushed about her talent and generosity in nurturing young talent and giving back to her community.

As she took it all in, the colour drained from Amelia's face. She couldn't believe what she was seeing. If she was right, then this Evie was her sort-of niece. The child her dad, James, had cried over in his dotage had produced this successful, confident woman, while she had bounced from a care home to the dysfunctional Ruth and Eric, and the rackety life of small-time conwoman.

Amelia gripped the magazine so firmly her knuckles went bone-white and her sharp nails cut into her palms. She was vaguely aware of someone yelling "Hey, you look as though you have seen a ghost. Are you OK?" She ignored him and walked out of the gym and up to her flat, where she paced up and down like a caged panther.

She was seething. Evie Muir was living the life she should have had, and she should be made to pay.

She paused, her busy brain whirring, and told herself that maybe it was a good time to pack up and leave here. Her scams were about to be discovered and her past might catch up with her.

Maybe a trip up to Orkney was what she needed. There would be fresh pickings there, especially as the magazine made out Evie was so successful, and maybe there was the possibility of even more rich relatives.

Amelia called Evie's gallery, pretending to be an old American school friend of Evie's mother, who had moved abroad many years ago but wanted to get in touch. She was told by a well-meaning and eager-to-please young girl that Cara was in a care home on the mainland. She wasn't sure which but could take a message and get Evie to call her back and give her all the details.

Amelia told her not to worry and please don't bother her daughter. She spent a whole morning calling round the nursing homes in Sutherland, claiming she had an order to send flowers to Mrs Cara Muir but wanted to confirm the postcode, and eventually tracked her down.

A week later, she was there in person. A blond wig, green contact lenses and a new outfit made her look just like Evie, at least enough to get past the weekend receptionist. She managed to quickly find Cara, sitting alone in her sunny room. The confused old woman smiled at her visitor and asked her to sit down.

Amelia took a long, hard look at her faded half-sister. She was tiny with a cloud of grey hair, a wistful smile and a faraway look in her eyes, but she looked clean and well cared for. Amelia scoffed. So this sad old woman was the little girl her father had cried over. It was absurd. She felt no sisterly bond or emotional pull towards Cara, she was just another addled-brained scrawny pensioner. Amelia had found Cara on one of her good days and she was eager to talk.

From the old woman's confused ramblings, Amelia learned all about Evie's past, about Brodie's death, Freya's childhood and also that there was another sister named Liv, who was a bad lot. If Evie could afford the fees for this place then she was obviously raking in the cash. Amelia sensed an opportunity.

A scheme was forming in her mind. She'd received another message from the stupid old man's son in London, saying he knew she had ripped off his dad and was going to contact the police, so it was certainly a good time to head off.

Chapter Fifty-Six

Hoxa

Back in the present, Amelia gave an exaggerated bow. "That's my sad, sad story and here we are," said Amelia. "I could have made a fair bit of cash until you decided to wreck my plans. You really are a sucker, Liv. I thought we were kindred spirits."

She looked at Liv, her eyes narrowed. "But perhaps it's not too late for you to be helpful. You could help me escape, you know. I'd pay you. I've still got enough in the bank. If you just let me go and say I wasn't here."

Liv stared at this woman who thought she was so clever, but wasn't even a particularly successful con artist. Liv decided to play for time, telling herself that surely the police would be here soon.

Liv said, "How do I know I can trust you? You lied about everything before."

Amelia shrugged. "Well, I guess we're both as desperate as each other. We really are very alike."

In the distance, Liv thought she heard the sound of a car approaching. It must surely be the police. The sound came closer. Amelia glared at Liv, tensed her body and desperately tried to shove her out of the way. She had underestimated her half-niece.

"You need to face up to what you've done," panted Liv, grabbing Amelia and shoving her face down on the floor. Liv might be skinny but she was wiry and strong and managed to force Amelia's arms behind her back.

"And you couldn't be more wrong," said Liv clearly. "I Am Nothing Like You."

Amelia struggled and shrieked but Liv held on.

Chapter Fifty-Seven

The Italian Chapel, one month later

Evie carefully pushed Freya into the Italian Chapel, being careful not to jolt her in the wheelchair. Her right side had been badly affected by the stroke. Her mouth was slightly twisted and she might never walk again, but thankfully there was no brain damage and her speech was coming back.

Freya had insisted on coming today and had asked Evie to dress her in her brightest clothes and with the most colourful blanket over her knees. As she recovered in the hospital, she'd had a long and tearful conversation with Evie by her bedside. Freya apologised to her over and over again. "I'm so sorry, Evie. I let you down badly."

Evie held her hand and wiped away her tears. "You don't need to say sorry to me. It's just that you don't see the badness in other people and that's a good thing."

Freya could not be comforted, "But that terrible woman turned me against you. And I allowed her to do that. I should have seen through her."

Evie tried to reassure her, "She manipulated everyone. Not just you." Freya looked stricken. "I got it all so wrong." She started to cry again.

"Now look," said Evie. "You mustn't upset yourself. Edwyn will kill me. You need your rest. Obviously when they let you out of here, I'm going to move in and look after you until you get better."

Freya's bottom lip trembled, "Do you really think I will ever get better?"

"I'm certain of it," said Evie, with more conviction than she really felt, but Edwyn had told her that they needed to keep Freya's spirits up.

Freya said vehemently, "I need you to take me to the service, Evie. I need to be there for Ross." Evie knew there was no point in arguing with Freya when she had made her mind up. The weeks since Ross was attacked had gone by in a blur and there had been so much to do in the days after Amelia was arrested.

Evie, Liv, Delima, Edwyn and Kate had given lengthy statements to the police. Evie had spent most of the rest of her time between Ross's bedside and Freya's. The others would spend hours going over the events of the last few months.

Edwyn summed up the feelings of most of the people in Orkney when he told them, "I cannot believe that one woman could cause so much suffering."

Delima nodded, "And to be so fixated on Evie. She was obsessed and Evie hadn't done anything wrong. She didn't even know Amelia existed."

Liv said quietly, "Maybe that was the trouble. By the time Amelia was old enough to have a real understanding of her father and his past, he had gone doolally and forgot who she was or mixed her up with his other daughter." She shrugged. "The more we find out about Amelia, the more I feel sorry for her."

Edwyn shook his head. "Well, make sure you don't say that in front of Maureen. She told me she wants five minutes alone in a room with Amelia to get justice for Ross." The four of them fell silent remembering what their friends were going through. Edwyn continued, "We'll have to wait a while. The police have her in custody until the trial, and that'll be months away."

Sophia had flown up from London right away and suggested they do something special for Ross. She immediately thought of the Italian Chapel. On the day of the service, there were too many people to fit inside the tiny chapel, famously built during the Second World War by Italian prisoners, far from home, but needing comfort and hope.

They created something beautiful from a pair of old Nissan Huts and over the years this had been a joyful place as brides and grooms exchanged vows, bonnie babies were christened and long lives remembered and celebrated. Approval for the service had been granted immediately.

The women had all cried together, remembering the joyous plans for Andrzej and Maureen's wedding only two years before. Sophia had ordered flowers for Ross and a beautiful, printed order of service. Everyone was utterly shocked to the core by what had happened to him – and to Freya.

A black cloud hung over the island. In a place where everyone was connected it felt as though they had all been targeted. As the service began, everyone stood up, apart from Freya, who wasn't strong enough to rise from her wheelchair at the back of the chapel. She was crying quietly.

Evie held on to the wheelchair, her knuckles turning white. She felt so much sorrow as well as deep anger. She hadn't even managed to lose herself in her art and couldn't imagine picking up a brush any time soon. All she would want to paint was canvasses full of blackness and blood.

Kate took Edwyn's hand and Sophia hugged Finn. Delima handed Hari to Jack. He was fast asleep and little Ola was sitting perfectly still beside her mother. Rory sat down beside his mum, Maureen, and Andrzej, whom he looked upon as a father. He handed the older man a handkerchief to dry his tears.

The minister spoke of the power of love and how good always triumphs over evil. As the beautiful voices of the choir soared, Evie looked up at the carefully painted ceiling of the chapel and found tears were running down her cheeks.

"I almost lost him," she thought. "That splendid, wonderful man is lying in a coma fighting for his life and we are here together, hoping and praying for his recovery."

Sophia had told them that getting everyone together to show their love for Ross would give them all strength and hope, especially his elderly parents, who looked so grief-stricken and bewildered.

She said to a sceptical Evie, "I know you aren't religious, but that doesn't matter. I honestly think it will help to have everyone together, praying for Ross."

Evie had lashed out at her friend. "It's like you're having a funeral while he is still breathing. It won't make any difference and it's just self-indulgent and mawkish." She had instantly regretted her outburst, but she was utterly exhausted, raw with grief and terrified Ross would never recover. She was also worried sick about Freya, who looked so frail and diminished.

But now, seeing the way everyone was wrapping Ross's mum and dad in so much kindness and love, Evie had to admit that Sophia was right. Coming together was deeply powerful and, for the first time, she felt a glimmer of hope that maybe he just might pull through.

At the end of the service, she pushed Freya down the path in her wheelchair, through crowds of people shaking her hand and wishing her well. They gave Evie their love and tentatively asked her to pass on their good wishes to Ross.

Freya smiled at them all, but Evie could see she was exhausted. "Let's get you to the hospital. Look, the ambulance is here to take you back. I'll come with you."

"No, Evie," said Freya. Her voice was still faint but she was firm. "Have some time away from the hospital, worrying about me and Ross. You've been living like a hermit. You need to stay and talk with your friends. It's important."

She waved at Evie as she was carefully placed in the ambulance and taken back to her hospital bed. Evie did as she was told and mingled with the crowds outside the tiny chapel. Gradually people melted away and she was on her own.

She walked down to the shore, sank to her knees and gave a loud grief-stricken wail like a wounded animal. She heard footsteps behind her. "Evie. I am so, so sorry. You must be shattered."

Evie turned round to see Liv, who had a genuine look of sadness and concern on her face. Liv went to help her up and Evie collapsed into her sister's arms and sobbed until she thought her heart would shatter into a million pieces.

She managed to wail pitifully, "Oh Liv. I am pure poison. I bring death and pain wherever I go. First Brodie and now Ross. If he dies too, it will be all my fault."

Liv gripped her by the shoulders. "I'm not having that," she said firmly but kindly. "Brodie died because I was a jealous bitch and he dived into freezing water with a bad heart. It had nothing to do with you."

Evie continued to cry. Liv cupped her sister's face with both hands and looked at her intently. It was as though she was trying to pour her own strength into Evie.

"Ross is lying in a hospital bed because that Amelia was pure evil. Again, it wasn't your fault." Evie gave her a watery smile. She wiped her face with the back of her hand.

"We've never talked like this."

Liv gave a wry grin, "Can you tell I've been in therapy?"

Evie's tears began welling up again. "Oh Liv, it could all have been so different."

"It will be from now on," said Liv. "I don't expect us to become proper sisters overnight, but if you give me a chance, I would like to help you through this. That's if you want me to."

Evie hugged her sister tightly and thought that this was the only good thing to come out of the whole sorry mess.

"You know, Liv. I never thanked you properly for all that you did. You made sure Amelia didn't get away with it."

Liv replied, "Well, we still have some ordeals ahead. We need to get Ross and Freya better, and there's the trial for a start. It's not going to be easy, but we will be stronger if we face it together."

Chapter Fifty-Eight

The Balfour Hospital

The day after the service, Evie was back sitting beside Ross in his hospital bed, her voice hoarse from constantly talking to him and reading his favourite childhood books, which she had found on a shelf in his room at his parents' house.

She hasn't expected to be reading *Tom Sawyer* to a grown man, but she'd do anything to bring him back. After each chapter she would beg him to open his eyes. But he lay like a marble statue, the only signs of life being the machines he was hooked up to that made his chest rise and fall.

He hadn't made any improvement, but crucially he wasn't any worse and Edwyn assured her that was a good sign. She checked in on Freya, who continued to defy the doctors and was constantly asking when she could go home. It wouldn't be long now.

When she wasn't at the hospital, Evie spent time with Ross's parents, trying to reassure them and remain positive. She felt closer to Ross sitting with them in the family home and hearing stories about his childhood. His mum proudly showed her lots of photographs of him as a boy and a young man, and Evie grew to love him even more.

She put down the book, held his hand and bent down to whisper goodbye when she felt a tiny movement in his fingers.

Her voice shaking, she said loudly, "Ross if you can hear me, squeeze my hand."

Nothing happened.

"Come on, my love. I know you can hear me. Just hold my hand tightly. You can do it." She felt a tiny twitch of movement and tried not to overreact. It could just be her imagination. She wanted Ross to wake up so badly that maybe she was fooling herself.

She felt a stronger grip on her hand and looked up at Ross's face and saw his eyes flicker. She gasped. "Oh my God, he's coming back to me."

She pressed the emergency buzzer and a doctor came rushing in. He took one look at Ross and grinned. "This is what we hoped for. He's finally coming round."

Evie hugged the startled medic and started to cry tears of pure joy.

Ross was taken off the ventilator as he was now able to breath on his own, and he continued to improve.

His throat was raw and he could only speak in a rasping voice, but it sounded like music to Evie. He couldn't remember much about that terrible night, but Evie gently told him not to worry. She could fill him in on all of the sad and sorry details when he was stronger.

He looked thinner and older, bruised and battered, but he gazed at Evie and said: "One thing I do remember is you being here. I could hear your voice reading me stories I hadn't heard since I was a peedie lad in short pants. It really helped."

Evie smiled through her tears. "I wasn't sure you could hear me at all. I kept asking you to wake up. It must have been very annoying."

He chuckled and then groaned. It hurt to laugh. "No, my precious Evie, you pulled me back. I heard your voice and knew I had to come home to you."

He took her hand in his. Ross hesitated. What Amelia had done had affected him profoundly. He felt so stupid to have been conned by her and then almost killed by her. He finally managed to speak, his voice thick with emotion and regret, "What if she had hurt you instead of me? What if she had hurt the kids? I can't stop thinking about it. I've gone over and over it in my mind and it's eating away at me."

He looked at Evie with such love in his eyes that she wasn't prepared for what he said next. "I'm not good for you, Evie. I am damaged in more ways than just the injury to my head and my broken arms and leg."

He swallowed hard. "I'm scared. I can't sleep without a pill and I just want to hide away and never see anyone ever again. They must all think I'm a right useless lump."

Evie's heart was breaking for him, but pretending to be stern she said, "Ross Isbister. I never thought I would see the day when you would feel so sorry for yourself. Shame on you. We held a service for you at the Italian Chapel, hoping you would pull through. Sophia organised it all and so many people turned up they had to stand outside. It brought us all together and it helped. You woke up the very next day. Maybe it was a coincidence, but I like to think it was the power of love."

Ross looked haunted and ashamed. Evie's voice softened. "I know you have been through a horrific trauma, and you'll need time and proper help to get through it, but never forget that so many people love you and can't wait for you to be up and about so they can tell you themselves."

"Och, Evie, we are Orcadians. We don't go in for all that smarmy stuff. If they buy me a pint that will be enough."

He managed a wobbly grin and then his expression changed. He said hoarsely, "Seriously though. You are too good for me. I don't deserve you."

Evie shrugged and picked up the tattered old copy of *Tom Sawyer*. "Face it, Ross. Your days of being single are long gone. Whether you like it or not, we are together, and as soon as you are out of here, we will be announcing that to our friends and family."

Ross opened his mouth to speak again but Evie shushed him. "Just accept your fate. You are stuck with me. Now, where was I? Oh yes, Tom and Huckleberry Finn are hunting for buried treasure. I almost know this whole book off by heart."

"Maybe one day you will read it to our children," said Ross, which had Evie smothering him in kisses.

Chapter Fifty-Nine

Inganess Beach, a year later

It was a glorious spring day, and the Selkies were out in force at the beach, enjoying the sunshine and getting ready for their usual dook. Freya had been helped from the car and was sitting on a pile of cushions, swathed in blankets and looking almost back to her old self.

She'd never dance again like she had before the stroke, but she had discarded her despised zimmer frame and was slowly learning to shuffle around the house with a stick. She was determined to be able to walk up the aisle to take her seat at the front pew for Sophia and Finn's wedding. She'd spent many happy hours with Evie planning her outfit, which would be taking her love of colour and silks, satins and bling to a whole new level.

She looked over at Evie. There were new lines on her face and dark circles under her eyes, but she was still a beautiful woman, and she and Ross were in a good place. They had found a quiet contentment in each other's company and there was a deep understanding between them.

Evie spent a lot more time at his house, keeping an eye on his parents and making sure Ross wasn't overdoing things. He'd gradually gone back to work and joked he was about two years behind in orders for his famous Orkney chairs. All of his customers said they were happy to wait. He was busy in his workshop patiently crafting a peedie chair for Ola, and had put hours of love and work into making it perfect for the tiny toddler who wound uncle Ross around her little finger.

Evie and Ross didn't have a torrid romance full of lust and passion. It was peaceful and restful. They had been through so much together and it had made them strong as steel. They weren't the sort of people to declare their undying love to one another. They just knew that they were two halves that made a whole.

She had left Ross happily at work, telling him she would see him this afternoon. Knowing she had Ross to go back to, Evie truly felt she had finally come home.

Beside her on the beach, Delima was making sandcastles with Ola and Hari the toddler was once again being handed around like a fat parcel. Neither of the children remembered the dark events of last year. Delima and Jack were the ones who had nightmares and for months wouldn't let them out of their sight.

Jack still blamed himself for putting his children in danger, but Delima had forgiven him and they were back on an even keel. Amelia's trial date still hadn't been set – she'd pleaded not guilty to attempted manslaughter, and it was set to be a huge case in Scotland.

Jack had become a bit of a media sensation himself after the attempted rescue of the pilot whales, and he found himself in demand as a wildlife expert. Saving a handful of them was nothing short of a miracle. TV companies knocked on his door with all sorts of offers and ideas. Jack's Viking good looks and his way of explaining complex issues so clearly and passionately made him perfect for documentaries, but he turned them down. He didn't want to leave the island or his family.

Delima, acting as his agent ("Well, we might as well keep the ten per cent in the family," she said reasonably) had cannily negotiated a deal for him whereby he broadcast live from their sanctuary into the BBC's acclaimed Spring, Autumn and Winterwatch programmes. He was in the middle of writing a book and put clips on social media that regularly went viral, especially when he was wearing nothing but shorts.

This had seen donations soar, with all the money ploughed back into helping animals and improving and enlarging the sanctuary.

Kate was telling Patsy about her online law course. It was hard work, but Kate was loving every minute and she'd never looked happier. She helped out at Joan McIver's practice two afternoons a week and Joan had said she'd take her on full time in a heartbeat when she felt ready.

Maureen was bringing Evie and Sophia up to date about the plans she and Andrzej had to foster older children who needed a bit of stability. "It's all Andrzej's idea, of course," she said happily. "He's really excited about it. He wants to teach them all about Orkney history and he's thinking of sponsoring the boys and girls who are interested to get an apprenticeship and a chance of a proper trade."

Maureen continued to be cancer-free and in remission. She was growing stronger every day and continued to live in the moment, relishing life's small pleasures. Both Andrzej and Maureen were thrilled when Rory announced he wanted to join Andrzej's building business after he left school, and asked if he could start as an apprentice joiner under Patsy's watchful eye.

Maureen told them proudly: "Did you see the new sign Andrzej has put up over the workshop? It says 'Kowalski & Son'. Patsy made it for him specially, and I've never seen Andrzej so happy. He's even made the sign the screensaver on his phone. It used to be a picture of me in my wedding dress." Maureen laughed and wiped her eyes. They all smiled at her with huge affection.

Sophia stood up. "Everyone. I have an announcement. You all know that I'm getting married."

Patsy drawled, "You might have mentioned it once or twice."

Sophia smiled. She really couldn't stop talking about the wedding; Evie had seen more shades of ivory napkins than she thought were possible and the discussion on wedding favours had gone on for weeks.

Sophia beamed at them all. "Anyway, that's not the only thing to look forward to." She took a deep breath, beamed, and told them: "I'm pregnant. We're having a baby."

Everyone congratulated her at once and Sophia was wrapped in hugs and warm wishes. Evie looked at her friend with shining eyes, "This is the best news ever. How wonderful. A brand-new life coming into the world."

"What did Finn say when you told him?" asked Freya.

"Well," said Sophia. "He cried. Obviously. Then he told me to sit down and swaddled me in one of Maureen's blankets. And he was up all night pacing the floor and making lists. One minute he's fretting about me eating soft cheese and then he's making plans to take the baby to Antarctica to see penguins. He goes from petrified to euphoric in a heartbeat."

Kate laughed. "Welcome to the wacky world of parenthood where you have the most important job in the world, but no one gives you any instructions and yet somehow you muddle through."

Delima agreed, "Yep, that about sums it up."

Sophia suddenly looked uncertain and blurted out: "I have more news and I'm not sure how you are all going to take it, but Finn has agreed to move down south permanently with me."

They all gasped. This was huge. Maybe an even bigger deal than the forthcoming bairn. "We're looking at houses outside of London and he's managed to get himself a transfer from the RSPB – he'll be monitoring red kites in Berkshire and he will, of course, be volunteering to be on beaver watch in Essex."

Freya smiled ruefully and turned to Evie, "So our plan worked, after all. Maybe a bit more successfully than we thought." Sophia smiled. "Yes, he told me you two had put him on the hunt for beaver. Funnily enough he is very excited about it."

Evie giggled but then looked sad, "But you will come back and see us?"

"All the time. We aren't moving right away. I can still commute for a while yet, and I've got maternity leave, so I'll bring the baby here as soon as possible. She needs to get the fresh, clean Orkney air in her lungs.

"*She*?" said Freya. "Is it going to be a peedie girl?"

Sophia smiled broadly and nodded. "Yep. We are going to have a girl. And Freya, if you don't mind, we would both like to name her after you."

For once Freya was speechless. She blinked back tears and couldn't utter a word, but her heart was full.

Sophia held her hands. "Obviously, you will be her honorary grandmother and I cannot think of a finer woman as a role model for my baby."

Freya managed to find her voice. "Oh Sophia. You have no idea what that means to me. You've made me so happy. Are you really sure?"

"Certain," said Sophia. "You know how much we all love you."

"Imagine," said Delima. "We will have a baby Freya here next year. She'll be a friend for Ola and Hari. And one day she will be a Selkie, alongside her mum and all of her aunties and her namesake, of course."

"If I'm spared," said Freya, laughing.

"You will outlive us all," said Delima.

Freya sighed happily. "This is turning into the best day. But we are missing someone."

"I'm here," said a soft voice behind her.

"Liv!" said Sophia, giving her a hug. "I've just been telling them my big news."

Sophia turned to everyone. "Liv already guessed. You all know she is working up at the hospital and she saw me going in for my scan. I had to tell her." She smiled at Liv. "Thank you for keeping my secret."

"It wasn't easy," said Liv. "I was bursting to tell you all, especially Evie." Liv kissed Freya on the cheek. "Sorry I'm late but I got some good news while I was on the way out the door. A call from the hospital. I've been accepted to train properly as a health visitor. I thought I would be far too old, but they apparently want women of maturity."

Everyone congratulated Liv. Evie hugged her close, "I'm so proud of you. You've worked so hard. Rab must be thrilled." Liv and Rab had been going out with each other officially since Amelia's arrest and were looking at buying a small house and moving in together. "He's really pleased, and with the money he's making working with Andrzej we can afford a peedie mortgage, even though we are both ancient old relics."

Freya pretended to be affronted. "That's enough of that. You two are young things compared to me." She clapped her hands. "Right, you lot. Leave the babies with me and off you go into the water. I will have the picnic ready, and the coffee laced with booze. Although not for you Sophia obviously, but I can have yours, so it doesn't go to waste."

"So kind and thoughtful, Freya," said Sophia with a laugh. They all stripped off down to their swimsuits and, shrieking, raced into the water. As always the salty coldness took their breath away but they were soon swimming like silky seals.

Freya watched them from the beach. She'd been badly affected by Amelia's vindictive lies, her attack on Ross and her own terrible scare after suffering a stroke.

She shuddered at the memory, but it had made her realise how precious life was. 'It's a cliche,' she thought to herself, 'but you really do have to seize the day. I may be almost 81 years old but I still have an awful lot of living still to do.'

She smiled, thinking of the new baby who would bear her name. It was moments like this that made life worth living. She watched Liv and Evie going down to the water's edge hand in hand. 'And who would ever have thought that those two would become proper sisters?'

They had all looked on in hope as Evie and Liv grew closer and helped each other to heal this past year. The sisters had spent many hours together, talking through their difficult childhood and the trauma of the tragic death of Brodie all those years ago. As they had grown to trust each other, Liv had even gone with Evie to see their mother in the care home.

Even though Cara had no idea who she was, Liv was glad she had visited. It was good to see her restless mother content at last. She was in a twilight world, but it was one where she could finally be happy.

Being with Ross and bonding with Liv had made it easier for Evie to cope, but it was her paintings that had truly saved her. She had been creating some complex, profound work, light years away from her seascapes, and had attracted the attention of major dealers as far away as New York and Tokyo.

She had attempted to repaint the portrait of Freya that Amelia had destroyed, and although it was still too raw, she knew she would be able to return to it soon and do her friend justice.

And one day she vowed to paint Brodie before his essence faded from her memory completely. There was only so much she could do from a photograph. For now, she had her Ross and her work, as well as her friends and her sister.

A new life coming into the world was the best possible way to stay hopeful about the future and baby Freya would be a blessing for all of them. Evie would always carry a burden of sorrow, but there was still so much to look forward to.

She stood by the shore hand-in-hand with her sister. Liv had come a long way too. She had a good man by her side, a new job she adored and she felt loved.

Evie smiled, "I think we're both going to be alright, you know."

Liv grinned back at her. "I know we are."

Liv looked at her in admiration. It had taken a long time but she had grown to love her little sister.

"Come on then, Teenie, let's jump in together."

Acknowledgements

My thanks go to:

Carly Cook for her invaluable help, support and encouragement.

Sophie Wilson for her editorial eye.

Everyone at Orion who helped bring the book to life, with particular thanks to Head of Audio, Paul Stark.

A huge thanks to Orkney for joy, beauty, friendship and inspiration.

And final and most important thanks to my readers, for their loyalty and encouragement.

Credits

Lorraine Kelly and Orion Fiction would like to thank everyone at Orion who worked on the publication of *The Island Secret*.

Editor
Charlotte Mursell

Copy-editor
Jade Craddock

Proofreader
Kate Shearman

Editorial Management
Niyati Naudiyal
Jane Hughes
Charlie Panayiotou
Lucy Bilton
Patrice Nelson

Audio
Paul Stark
Louise Richardson
Georgina Cutler-Ross

Contracts
Rachel Monte
Ellie Bowker
Phoebe Miller

Design
Charlotte Abrams-Simpson
Jessica Hart
Nick Shah
Deborah Francois
Helen Ewing

Photo Shoots & Image Research
Natalie Dawkins

Finance
Nick Gibson
Jasdip Nandra
Sue Baker
Tom Costello

Inventory
Jo Jacobs
Erika Andrejuskinaite

Production
Ruth Sharvell
Katie Horrocks

Marketing
Holly Wilson
Lucy Cameron

Publicity
Thomas Hill

Sales
Dave Murphy
Victoria Laws
Esther Waters
Group Sales teams across Digital, Field, International and Non-Trade

Operations
Group Sales Operations team

Rights
Rebecca Folland
Tara Hiatt
Ruth Case-Green
Maddie Stephenson
Ruth Blakemore
Marie Matuschka

RAISING READERS

Books Build Bright Futures

Dear Reader,

We'd love your attention for one more page to tell you about the crisis in children's reading, and what we can all do.

Studies have shown that reading for fun is the **single biggest predictor of a child's future life chances** – more than family circumstance, parents' educational background or income. It improves academic results, mental health, wealth, communication skills, ambition and happiness.[1]

The number of children reading for fun is in rapid decline. Young people have a lot of competition for their time. In 2024, 1 in 10 children and young people in the UK aged 5 to 18 did not own a single book at home.[2]

Hachette works extensively with schools, libraries and literacy charities, but here are some ways we can all raise more readers:

- Reading to children for just 10 minutes a day makes a difference
- Don't give up if children aren't regular readers – there will be books for them!
- Visit bookshops and libraries to get recommendations
- Encourage them to listen to audiobooks
- Support school libraries
- Give books as gifts

There's a lot more information about how to encourage children to read on our website: **www.RaisingReaders.co.uk**

Thank you for reading.

hachette UK

[1] OECD, '21st-Century Readers: Developing Literacy Skills in a Digital World', 2021, https://www.oecd.org/en/publications/21st-century-readers_a83d84cb-en.html

[2] National Literacy Trust, 'Book Ownership in 2024', November 2024, https://literacytrust.org.uk/research-services/research-reports/book-ownership-in-2024